Dedication

This book (and the whole series) is dedicated to the gamers, the story-tellers, the people who find themselves in exploring the worlds of imagination.

Contents

The Resonance Cycle, a LITRPG series, Book 1

Introduction

Welcome to the Resonance Cycle. This series is a love letter to my youth; a time when I read every book in the Fantasy section of the store and played Dungeons and Dragons religiously. I decided to use the LitRPG framework for the series for a lot of reasons, the primary one being that I enjoy writing a lot like I DM tabletop adventures. Thank you for reading, and I hope you enjoy the twisting adventures ahead.

P.S. If you like the book, we highly recommend picking up the Audible version (Whispersync enabled!) While we love the audiobook format in general, we believe that the production values our narrator and audio engineer has put into this series are outstanding. We also love chatting with fans and collaborators alike on Discord at https://discord.gg/GXn8csy2gg.

Chapter 1: Random Selection

Ty's computer was possessed, and he didn't want his grandmother to know. It started just a few seconds ago. Both of his monitors glitched *way* out, with swirls of color and fractals bleeding through a flurry of movement from his desktop icons. For a second, he thought he was being hacked, but then his screens flickered, and the speakers started popping and hissing. Leaning forward, Ty thought he could hear a strange voice murmuring just below the noise.

Definitely possessed, he decided.

One monitor went dark, and the other began displaying a series of images, all side by side. They were the covers of audiobooks. *The Chronicles of Thomas Covenant* came first. Then, *The Guardians, Magic Kingdom for Sale,* and finally *Heroes Die.* The tableau froze in place before that monitor turned off, too.

"What the actual fuck?" Ty murmured, standing. The barrage of images had happened too quickly for him to process, and his first thought was to unplug his PC. A wind blew through his bedroom, riffling the collage of post-it notes decorating the closest wall.

The power in his room went out. Drenched in darkness, Ty fumbled for his phone only to discover it didn't work either. His grandmother yelled in a warbling rasp, "Ty! Ty, I think the power is out. I was in the middle of one of my shows!"

Ty opened his mouth to reply when a mote of flickering fire blossomed in the air directly in front of his computer screens. The flame wavered briefly before expanding into a wall of warm, glowing text.

"You have been randomly selected to fight for your world. Prove yourself and your loved ones may survive the Resonance. In precisely six months, a portal will open for three minutes. Study the prophecy closely if you wish to survive. This is your only advice or warning. The portal will appear wherever you are located. No other sentient being may go through it with you. This offer will not come again."

Ty read the words twice before they shrank back into the fire and zipped towards his face. Screaming reflexively, he tried to dodge. The spark veered in flight, hitting his forehead. Warmth spread from the spot, radiating down until his whole body felt tingly. Ty felt a flickering, as if someone had turned the lights *in him* off and on, then he blinked. The power was back. His computer looked like nothing had happened. One monitor had the same browser, tabs carefully organized for work or gaming at the top. On the other was the collage of images.

Looking over at his notes, he saw his lists were still in order and intact. Exhaling with relief, he said, "Grandma, I think-," about to say, *"I've been visited by another world."*. He couldn't finish the sentence. Pressure radiated from the point of the flame's impact, locking his jaws together hard enough that his teeth clipped his tongue. It took him a moment to parse what had happened. Every time he tried to say anything about the fire or wind, his mouth wouldn't work. Eventually, he had an idea.

He tried texting a description of what happened. The familiar pressure rose, and his fingers went numb. No matter how hard he tried, he couldn't make the muscles respond until he put the phone back down.

"It's going to be like that, eh?" he said, musingly, looking back at his computer.

Setting his phone down on his desk, Ty took a seat. Searching his computer, he found the books in the image file and quickly skimmed their summaries, along with their Wikipedia entries. As he did, he made notes on a pad he kept nearby. A quick rundown of keywords helped him collect his thoughts. Once he'd finished his lists, he reviewed the summary of events.

He'd been visited by an otherworldly presence; one he couldn't talk or text about. That meant it had some sort of awareness of his intent or actions. Experimentally, he considered some other indirect method of sharing the event, like sharing his notes with another person. Another stab of discomfort made him wince, and his vision blurred.

On the one hand, the discomfort worsened with each of his attempts to find a work-around. On the other, their presence gave him the proof he needed. What he'd just experienced was real. Not only was it real, he wouldn't be able to share the experience with anyone. Not that anyone would believe him, anyway.

A sharp knock interrupted Ty's introspection, followed by a shrill yell. "Honey! My shows are back on! I just wanted you to know." His grandmother's hearing aid must have been acting up again.

"Okay grandma, I'm glad!" Ty replied, raising his voice for her to hear.

Ty loved his grandmother as much as anyone he knew. She was also the only person he interacted with in real life whenever he could help it. People were messy. They did things, made choices he didn't understand. Unless he could compartmentalize and control the interaction, he didn't like to have it. That was why virtual gaming and remote work were so important.

It wasn't that he disliked people. In theory, he thought people were fascinating. It was the practice that challenged him.

Once he heard her shuffling back down the hallway, Ty returned to his gaming chair. Slumping in place, he brainstormed. Bringing the books back up, he knew they had to be the clue, the cornerstone of what he needed to understand. He'd inherited physical copies of most of those books from his late father, though he'd picked up a passion for the genres on his own later in life and repurchased them as audiobooks.

Looking down at his list, he drew his finger across the words "Portal Fantasy." Based on context clues, he felt confident in assuming he'd be in the same situation. Judging by the phrasing in the fire and the last book, he guessed he wouldn't be alone after his arrival.

He added a few additional notes. That *Thomas Covenant* was in the selection worried Ty more than anything else. That book was soul-crushingly grimdark, with huge consequences for every choice the protagonist made. On the plus side, unlike any of those books, he had six months to plan. Also, he had absolute and irrefutable proof the situation was real. *Unless*, he conceded, *I have a tumor.*

Yeah, but what tumor would prevent me from texting? He resisted the urge to search the internet for explanations; once he started down that rabbit hole, there'd be no going back.

Thinking of the fire that hit his forehead gave him pause. What if someone had invaded his thoughts? Was he being led into a trap, or manipulated in some cosmic game?

Assuming the warning is true, I have a chance to save some people. That's all it offered. It might be best to just bet that I am being manipulated. If we assume the Game Master is hostile from the start, maybe we can force an advantage.

Lacking better information or context, he shelved the concern. Ty was good at focusing when he had a clearly defined challenge, and while this was neither clear nor defined, he had to work with what he'd been given.

He wrote on the pad, 'Six months—use the advantage?'

The sound of Grandma's television ratcheting up made Ty pause. Should he stay to take care of her? She was old and increasingly frail. If he went to another world, there was no way of knowing what would happen to her. She had a pension from the military, but what about transportation and safety?

Your loved ones may survive. The image flickered in his mind's eye, utterly inescapable. Blaire was his only family. That didn't mean he didn't care about other people. His friends were all virtual, but that didn't make them any less important. If his going could save lives, didn't that mean he *had* to go? Grandma Blaire and Grandpa Billy had raised him to value the right choice, to evaluate every decision carefully.

He knew what Billy would say, if he were still alive and able to discuss what was happening. *When the call comes, it's up to you to decide the sort of man you're going to be.* Billy had been full of metaphors and sayings. He'd have wanted Ty to go.

His finger slid up to the word "Dangerous."

In each of the example books, the protagonists ultimately came to realize the harsh reality of the other world. There was death, loss, and extreme physical trauma. Ty wasn't equipped to handle any of those well. He didn't have any illusions about himself: he was a loner, a man who preferred the isolation and solitude of a life spent online. Violence, although exciting in theory, hadn't ever been a part of his life.

Ty saw the risks, weighed them carefully, writing out pros and cons for an hour before reaching his conclusion. He would go. This adventure would be different. He'd make it different. Unlike the people in the books, Ty was a planner. He'd make lists, research every possibility.

He would *own* his fate.

Glancing at the clock, Ty saw it was nearing ten. It was time for him to clock-in to his remote job. The work wasn't difficult, just occasionally tedious. Instead of his usual routine of chatting or listening to a book, he spent the rest of the night focused on one thing: surviving what came next.

Chapter 2: Planning

Time Until Portal Opening: 5 months, 29 days

The image with all the audiobook covers was called *GOTProphecy.uww*. Ty discovered it halfway through his shift when he tried inspecting the file. The file behaved bizarrely; he could open and close it, but he couldn't copy, delete, or email it. There was no metadata, and the type of file wasn't recognized by any of his research. If nothing else had convinced him that what he was experiencing was real, that was it.

Bleary-eyed and sleepy, he stood and looked over at his wall to review his progress. His old notes were gone, replaced with a branching, fractal-like tree of new ones. Thanks to hours of Google searches, he'd methodically diagramed a plan.

The top of the tree listed all his assumptions. He'd made a *lot* of those. One of his first was that he'd be going to a fantasy world, and that there'd be combat. His next was that the wording of the warning was precise for a reason; once the portal opened, he'd be able to use tools from Earth to assist him on the other side. With those ideas in mind, he'd built a gamified version of what he needed to do. The next few months would have to be packed with as much combat training and physical exercise as he could manage, along with whatever applicable non-combat skills he could learn.

Daunted, but satisfied with his progress, Ty took three steps and collapsed on his thin mattress. Dreams found him the moment his eyes closed.

He was hovering over a vast, jagged mountain range. Snow-capped peaks jutted into the air, where swirls of snow danced across the ridges. Walking along one lip of stone, moving effortlessly, was an ebony woman with large, inquisitive eyes. She wore a silk gown that hugged her curvaceous body, the thin material rippling in the constant breeze. The cold did not touch her. Coming to a stop at a point along the mountain, the woman tilted her head to the sky. Her chiseled features were exquisitely beautiful, almost painful to look at even to Ty's unconscious mind.

"It is time," the woman called. Her shadow rose behind her, solidifying into a perfect duplicate of its owner. It flew into the air, hovering ten feet above the woman, before a ring of golden runes appeared nearby. Light flashed among the runes, revealing distant stars. The shadow flitted through the opening, and the runes vanished.

"Let them have their Resonance. Their ending has already been written." The woman's lips curled in a vulpine smile.

A moment later, Ty was hovering in space. Stars swirled, pooling clusters of color into a whirling galaxy shape. Hovering in the center of the light was a jagged-edged tear. Oily, winged shapes ripped free of the fissure, clawing from some distant universe and into his. A vast, wet mass pushed through the opening, forcing it wider to accommodate its bulk. Thousands of glowing red eyes covered the thing, each staring past him at a world with two moons.

Nausea gripped him. His stomach clenched, and his heart ached.

One eye twitched in his direction and the weight of the universe folded in on him, pushing Ty free of the dream.

Ty woke, the dreams as clear as memories, his breath coming in pants. He lay there, fighting terror, for most of an hour. Nothing he'd seen made sense. It could have been prophecy, warning, or a distant vision of what was happening in another world for all he knew. It didn't *feel* like the fiery visitation, but that didn't mean much.

Maybe it's a warning. Maybe I was just shown what I'll be up against? If that was true, it meant that he needed to adjust his plans. One key piece of gamer knowledge he'd learned over the years was to adapt according to the campaign he was in. If the game was a one-off, a quick little power trip or exploration scenario, he'd pick his gear and character build to optimize for a couple sessions. There was no need for anything long-term. In an epic campaign, long-term strategy was the key to success.

Ty rolled out of bed and walked to his pile of notes, adding observations and adjustments to them. He scratched out "Power level ASAP" and replaced it with "Be different."

After he'd tweaked and reviewed his outline, he got dressed and left his room. The rent-controlled apartment he shared with his grandmother was small, and it was generous to call the steps to the living room a hallway. His grandmother was asleep in her rocking chair just a few feet from the television, a blanket tucked just beneath her chin. She looked older and thinner than he'd like, but there was still stubborn strength in the line of her jaw. Despite her age, Ty knew she could still be a force to be reckoned with. The woman had raised him into early adulthood, and he knew all too well what she was capable of.

"Stop staring at me," Grandma Blaire croaked out, popping one dark eye open to glare at him. "What's up? Are you hungry? Eggs again?"

Sometimes Ty wondered whether his grandmother took notes from crotchety old people on the shows she watched.

"Cheese eggs would be good," Ty admitted. "Also, do you have any of the old gaming books stored anywhere?" Growing up, he hadn't had many friends. When he'd developed an interest in tabletop roleplaying games, his grandmother had taken on reading the books and becoming his first Game Master. This was before he'd found online gaming. None of the books in the image had been gaming books per se, but all of them included gaming-adjacent elements and he needed to be thorough.

Maybe that ten-foot pole would come in useful in the other world.

Popping her other eye open, Blaire worked her way to her feet and folded her blanket. Both Grandma Blaire and Grandpa Billy had been in the military, and Blaire still maintained some of those habits. Not that either of them had passed that knowledge down to Ty. The only trait he'd inherited from either of them was his obsessive need to control a situation as much as he could.

Grandpa Billy's motto had been, "Be prepared or be fucked by those who are." Ty had taken the saying to heart.

"Of course I have them. Why? Are you thinking of getting back into gaming with friends? If so, I support it. You really need to get out more. Make real friends, not just sit and stare at the computer all day. Hell, maybe you'll meet a girl." Blaire walked to the closet, where they stored the games. Her thin arms shook slightly as she picked out a stack of worn manuals. She carried them to the dining table and set them down with a thud.

Ty hesitated. Seeing how frail she'd become reminded him of his doubts the night before. Could he really leave Blaire behind, potentially forever?

Guilt rose, but he forced it aside. One of his assumptions was that he'd either receive some way to preserve Blaire's life, or that he'd ultimately return to Earth and be better equipped to help her through whatever came next. If he let doubt or fear rule his every thought, he'd get nothing done.

Don't complicate things. Keep it simple: prepare, train, focus on the big plan. Assume the worst, hope for the best.

"Grandma, I'm thinking of enlisting. But first I need to get myself together. I want to take some classes and learn to shoot. I may need some help getting what I need together. Will you loan me some money, if I need it for equipment or a gym membership or something?"

Blaire stood in place, glaring at him. "What does enlisting have to do with your old gaming books?" She seemed about to say more, then hesitated. One hand lingering on the books, she assessed him with a critical gaze. Ty was tall, just over six feet, and wasn't dramatically out of shape. He wasn't *in* shape either. It wasn't like he'd maintained a gym membership for the last few years, nor did he like to leave the house. If Blaire hadn't been the one overseeing their simple meals, no doubt Ty would have been in trouble. He loved chocolate.

"Enlisting?" Blaire asked, chewing on the word. "I guess it makes sense. Your mom and dad weren't big on the military, you know. But the military might be a way for you to get out and build some sort of future. Assuming you don't get dead."

Ty just let Blaire vent; interrupting when she was on a rant often led to dire consequences.

Glancing down to the books, then across the room to a small bookshelf, she said, "You know what Billy and your dad would say, right? They'd tell you to think hard about what you're going to do. They'd remind you of the importance of being a good person." After his father's death and his mother's long absence, Blaire and Grandpa Billy had become everything to Ty. They'd done their best to handle his strange behaviors, even trying to teach him to be the best person he could be.

"I know," Ty said.

Rapping her knuckles against the top book, Blaire said, "You know the military isn't going to make you into a character from your books. You're not going to become some sort of ninja-assassin, or soul-drinking badass. This is real life. You'll need to be disciplined, follow orders, and make hard decisions. Are you sure this is something you want?"

"Yeah, I think so." He didn't have a choice, not if he wanted to be the man his grandparents had tried to raise him to be.

Blaire wasn't religious, but both she and Billy had been deeply spiritual. Billy had taught Ty the basics of meditation and even given him a book on "Right Living." On nights when Blaire wasn't acting as his personal dungeon master or discussing fantasy books with him, Billy had made it a point to take time to engage in discussions about ethics and moral behavior.

Neither had said so, but Ty figured they were both worried he might act out one day. He didn't see things the way other people did sometimes. That was part of why his mother left.

Reflecting on the situation, Ty abruptly wondered what the other random people would see as their inspiration for visiting the other world? He doubted they were all just like him. Would someone with a different background be told to watch *Narnia*, *Star Dust*, or *Silent Hill*? Maybe with some *Conan* or *Rambo* mixed in?

Blaire agreed to lend Ty money for his preparation. She didn't have much. Her combined retirement with Grandpa's was enough to keep them going and put Ty back into college if he wanted, and not much more.

He thanked her, helped her make her amazing cheesy eggs, then retreated to his room. It was time to begin the next phase.

He took stock.

Ty didn't bring much to the table, other than being relatively young and not unhealthy. Compared to the characters in the books listed in the fire, he had an advantage because he knew what was coming. Only the main character in *Heroes Die* had been well-adapted and ready for his adventures. That book was odd, though. That it was included suggested several things. First, the protagonist in that book had gone back and forth between worlds based on a schedule. Second, there'd been a decidedly sci-fi and apocalyptic feel to the world. He wasn't sure how to make those facts fit with the traditional portal fantasy setup, so he ignored them.

Plan for the worst, hope for the best.

Between predatory loans and a small grant from Blaire, he believed he could scrape together around eighty-thousand dollars over the course of a few days. It felt like a lot of money, and not enough all at once.

Walking the tiny circuit of his open floor, Ty went through the plans he'd developed the night before.

There was no telling what the rules, limitations, or layout of the other world would be. He may or may not have access to fresh food or water. There might not be any local resources at all. He'd need to bring his own supplies and know how to find more if the worst came down to it. That meant hunting and fishing were a priority.

Combat was going to happen. Other than basic survival, his top priority was getting himself ready for actual life or death situations. Whether it was monsters, aliens, locals, or other players, he'd eventually have to fight.

"The question is, will this be all player-versus-environment or player-versus-player?" He asked out loud, seeing how either idea made him feel.

He didn't relish the idea of killing. Not that the notion itself bothered him; he knew, intellectually, that animals died for food and hunting as sport was a good thing. He also figured if monsters were real and attacking him, he'd have no qualms about defending himself. On the other hand, there was something inherently messy about the notion of taking a life. Thinking of killing other people, either locals or other players, made him uneasy, so he ignored that train of thought all together.

Plan for the worst, hope for the best.

Ty started a new list, making two columns. In the first column, he wrote all the things he knew he had to do. He had to get in shape; manage his time, and so on. In the second column, he listed the classes he needed to take. A lot went into that column, complete with every type of martial arts instruction he'd found in the area.

Thankfully, he and Grandma lived in one of the most metropolitan cities in the country. He'd found instructors for most of what he'd needed within a forty-five-minute drive. There was a fencing and historic martial arts group just south of the city, and one of the most popular fighting gyms in the world was just a few miles down the road.

Sitting at his computer, Ty began mapping out his ideal plan onto a spread-sheet. He listed each skill he wanted and cross-referenced it with locations, times of availability, user ratings, cost, and drive time. Treating the sheet like he would a gaming campaign, he plotted ways to maximize his uptime, minimize his downtime, and use every penny effectively. He even researched optimal nutrition and recovery times, just to be sure he was giving his body every opportunity to recover and adapt.

Once he had the list together, each line color-coded based on desirability, he began calling and emailing each of the locations, starting with the top picks and working his way down.

By noon, he had an optimized schedule, along with driving routes, mapped out. He'd even allowed himself a solid ten hours of sleep a night, once he quit his day job. Quitting was a requirement, he knew, if he was going to manage enough time to accomplish *anything* meaningful. The final total for all the training and the associated equipment was just twenty-four thousand dollars. That included multiple one-on-one training sessions with world-class professionals. Compared to his salary, it was a lot of money. Given the predicted value, it was a bargain.

Ty first called his job to quit. It was an uncomfortable conversation, considering that he wasn't giving them two-weeks' notice. He used the rest of the day to get his money in order. The shady loan companies were happy to send him the money, along with paperwork agreeing to twenty-five percent, compound interest. The rest of the day was spent filling out applications and driving to places in-person when they didn't have an online signup option.

He didn't enjoy leaving the apartment. His car was old and borderline dangerous to drive. The last time he'd been able to afford fresh brakes was nearly three years ago, shortly after he'd inherited it from his father. Worse yet, there were *people* outside. Behind computers, with the concrete clarity of text, people were so much easier to talk to and understand. In the real world, there was subtext, pretext, and agendas, none of which made any sense.

If there'd been any other way to go about his plan, he'd have done everything from the comfort of his home. The plan was everything, though. He had to execute.

As he went through the day, Ty wondered about the circumstances he'd find himself in on the other side of the portal. He'd assumed that the other world would be full of magic and other fantasy elements, but what about the variables? How would travel from one world to the other work? If he gained magical powers in one, would they function to the other? Would any of the equipment he planned to buy work in a magical world? If he brought guns, would physics apply normally? Would loot from the fantasy world transfer to back to Earth? If so, would it function?

During one of his stops, Ty sat in his car and jotted down his thoughts, listing the keywords of each carefully. He decided that, like with his training, his best bet was to assume the worst. If he planned on things breaking, on not being able to bring the loot back, and so on, then he could only be pleasantly surprised if they did.

I might die on the other side, Ty thought, twisting the idea in his mind. Oddly, the concept wasn't as terrifying as it probably should have been. People? Scary. Situations he couldn't plan for or control? Terrifying. What was death, but the ultimate outcome *everyone* had to plan for?

If he didn't return, his primary concern was leaving Blaire behind without support, and potentially saddled with covering his bills. He considered getting a life insurance policy. Would one cover him vanishing months after he got it, though? *Probably not.* He also didn't want to ask her if she had one on him. Knowing her, she probably did.

Let's face it, she takes care of me more than I do of her. I need to focus on the objectives in front of me and worry less about things I can't control.

If Ty had one superpower, it was his ability to compartmentalize. Sometimes he felt like his mind was a vault, a place he could consciously arrange and sort. Once he decided something, he just put everything else, every distraction, away. He did that now, taking every concern about his absence and shuffling them into a corner at the back of his mind. His focus renewed, he put his notes away and continued to the next stop on his list.

Once he got home that evening, Ty set about making a list of the equipment he'd be bringing with him. Since the portal would be open for three minutes, and it would open wherever he was, he took the wording to mean he could game the system. Over the next weeks, depending on his training, he would make a list of items that he could afford that were legal, and that could reasonably fit on a trailer or some sort of wagon.

The idea of driving a wagon full of modern goods into a fantasy world made Ty smile. Feeling accomplished, he went to sleep with a sense of satisfaction. Everything was coming together. He had a plan, and he'd pulled the trigger on executing it. All he had to do was hang on for six months.

Chapter 3: Hanging On

Time Until Portal Opening: 0 Months, 3 weeks, 2 days

Ty woke as he had for almost every day of the last five months: sore. Based on his estimates, he'd hoped to dedicate at least seven hundred meaningful hours of training before the portal opened. Injuries, a cold, holidays, and doctor visits for grandma had taken a chunk out of that number.

Rolling out of bed, he groaned as he padded to the wall. The note-fractal was streamlined these days, left only with the things he had yet to accomplish or was close to completing. A pile of discarded paper sat at the edge of his computer desk, complete with lists of skills he'd been unable to pick up quickly enough. Spear fishing was not as easy as he'd hoped. After his morning review, he turned to look at the mirror that he'd hung on the back of his bedroom door.

He had begun his training soft, with bad posture and no experience with anything physically taxing. Now, he looked a lot more like any other athletic college student his age. Part of him felt disappointed he hadn't changed more, maybe taken on the appearance of a fitness influencer or something. Still, he had a confidence and facility with his body now that he imagined most people his age would respect.

On a positive note, the skills he'd gained overshadowed his lack of physical transformation.

After reviewing his schedule for the day, he sat in front of his computer and re-read sections from the books mentioned in the prophecy. He'd found himself returning to *Thomas Covenant* time and time again, drawn inexplicably to the brutality of the mythical world, and of the mistakes the 'hero' had made. It was that fascination that drove many of his plans for what would come next.

There were objective truths in the world. There *was* a way to choose right over wrong, good over evil. Once he knew what he was dealing with, Ty was determined to play whatever game this was by his rules, no matter what.

He dressed, gathered his equipment, and left his room.

"You should take more time off, kiddo," Blaire announced as he walked in. He'd slept late, nearly until noon, and she was busy making lunch. Ty could smell chicken sizzling on the pan and saw several plates of fruit and vegetables already laid out. Despite the meals he prepared for himself, Grandma had insisted on doing what she could to support him.

Over the past months, Blaire had begun treating Ty differently. For years, she'd taken an overt, almost protective, interest in anything he did. Now she was supportive of 'whatever fun insanity' he was up to and left him alone.

Oddly, Ty felt closer to his grandmother lately than he had since Billy passed.

"No can do," he replied, swinging his golf bag down and resting it against a wall before taking a seat at the dining table. Their kitchen was part of the living room, less in an open-floor-plan kind of way and more of a very-limited-space kind of way. If they didn't live in apartments near downtown, someone might have mistaken their home for a single-wide trailer. Ty's kitchen seat was barely six feet away from the stove and microscopic dishwasher.

"You know," Ty said thoughtfully, "if you didn't cook the way you do, I doubt I'd have been anywhere near the shape I am now." He patted his stomach to reinforce the words. His gut was almost gone, something Blaire had remarked on regularly.

Blaire snorted. "If you'd spent literally any of your life outside for more than school, you'd be collecting girls, not swords right now."

"Are you still pissed that I took up HEMA?" he asked. The historical martial arts group specialized in recreating actual combat techniques from the past. Joining them had been the simplest way for him to learn sword fighting realistically, without taking up fencing.

No one fenced in fantasy books.

Dipping her spatula into the sizzling pan, Blaire made a practiced motion and flipped one breast onto a plate. She paused long enough to pass it to him before replying. "Fuck yes I am. Chasing people around with swords might help with your cardio, but otherwise it isn't going to do shit in the real military. The gun stuff, sure. I approve of basically everything you've said you're doing. But swords and dress up? It just feels frivolous."

Ty shrugged her complaints off and tucked into the food. She wasn't wrong, and he was tired of the argument. He'd explained more than once that HEMA and sword fighting helped with his martial arts. Like she'd said, there was the cardio aspect, but there was also the balance and diversity it brought to his skill set. Hell, one of the best things it did was teach him how to take a hit. Blaire wasn't about to accept that logic.

To Blaire's point, he had no clue which skills or equipment he'd invested in would legitimately show value in the other world. He'd had to rank his options, price them, and make educated guesses. What he *did* know was that the books in the prophecy had given him an advantage he was not about to squander. How would Thomas Covenant have fared if he'd gone into the other world optimistically, with genuine enthusiasm and appreciation for the world, as well as a high-powered, long-range rifle?

He had no plans to kill anyone who wasn't a monster. If another "player" attacked him, well, he'd see.

"What's today?" Blaire asked as she slid into the seat across from him with her plate.

Eyeing his grandmother, Ty stood up and got filtered water for them both. The little red light on the filter blinked when he turned it on. Since he'd taken his loans out and put literally everything into the training and preparation, some necessities around the house had fallen through the cracks.

"The range, then gym and Krav Maga," he answered. "Jim says I'll qualify for my brown belt soon. Another two or three months and he thinks I'd qualify for black." Ty had made progress in a lot of areas; he was at least capable of foraging for nuts and berries now, and he knew how to skin and prepare his own food.

He also knew how to shoot a variety of guns and use a bow. But the areas he'd excelled at had shocked him. When it came to knives, swords, and Krav Maga, Ty was exceptional.

Despite who he thought he was until now, Ty had discovered that he *craved* the intensity of intimate violence.

"I'm proud of you," Blaire said, forking up a bite of food. The announcement, made so evenly, almost offhandedly, shook him. Blaire wasn't one to give compliments or show warmth, not in that way.

Part of him couldn't help but wonder how their relationship might have been different if Ty had been more traditional. *Or,* he added, *what if I'd been shit at everything instead? Would she still be proud of me if I were a failure?*

"I appreciate it, Grandma," he replied.

"Now, what are we going to do with all these packages?" she said later, after they'd finished their meal. Hooking a thumb, she indicated the veritable mountain of Amazon boxes lining a wall of the living room.

"They will all be out in a few days, I promise. I rented a storage space for the next couple of weeks, which should be all I need it for. After that, I'm going on that trip I told you about. You'll have the house all to yourself until I'm back." Ty had fabricated the story of going on a hiking trip before he enlisted. In theory, most of the packages held survival goods. The reality was a bit more diverse than that. High-quality survival gear was expensive, and he'd wanted to travel as lightly as he could. If Blaire had opened boxes, most of what she would have found would have supported his story.

The rest, however...

Blaire sniffed, looking vaguely skeptical. He was fairly sure that she at least suspected he was planning to just go walkabout and not return. There was as much evidence of that as joining the military. It wasn't far from the truth, either. Depending on how everything played out, he just might be gone forever.

Whenever he thought about being gone and leaving Blaire alone, Ty reminded himself of his notes, his carefully constructed lists, and his plan. Those were the key to his success. It would make his adventure different from the others.

Flashing Blaire a reassuring smile, Ty stood and leaned over the kitchen table to kiss her cheek. She reached up and patted his shoulder, wishing him well on his way out.

* * *

The gun club was the second-furthest place he had to go in his training circuit. Just outside of the city, near an industrial complex, the range was little more than a storefront with two shooting arenas. One arena was a near two-thousand-meter range. The other was a close-combat simulation environment for law enforcement and movie star-type training. Ty had picked the place because a movie star he liked had used it to train for a movie.

A small yellow neon sign with the flickering words 'Iron Sights' greeted Ty as he pulled up. With no other signage and without the near-constant gunfire, people driving by might have assumed it was a random pawn shop in the middle of nowhere. When he'd researched the place, he'd found it didn't even have a website. Sliding out of his beat-up Honda Civic, he collected his hard-walled golf bag and made his way inside.

"Hey Ty!" Bradley called out. The elderly black man was one of the owners and had helped him choose his guns back when he'd first signed up. He'd also given him a few free lessons as soon as he'd paid his dues to the club. Without his help, he doubted he'd be as proficient as he was. Nor would he have guns that sounded as cool as "Saint Victor."

Ty considered Bradley one of his first real-life friends, one he'd added to the "Friends to Save" list he'd started a few weeks ago.

He waved at Bradley and gestured to the locked gate at the back. "I'm going for six hundred today, Mr. Bradley. Think I'll make it?"

Buzzing Ty through the gate, Bradley squinched his eyes and shook his head. "Doubt it. You're getting pretty reliable at five, but six might be pushing it. Wishin' yas luck though."

Rifles and handguns hadn't come as naturally as some of his other skills, but Ty knew that he'd be relying on both substantially in whatever happened next. This was assuming something on the other side didn't simply disable his guns. That was always a factor to consider.

Weaving past the locked gate and into the secure preparation zone beyond, Ty carefully extracted his rifles from the golf bag. He'd purchased two Tikka T3xes with .308 rounds to keep matters simple. He figured having two of the same weapon meant that in the event of a catastrophic failure or a loss, the equipment from one would work on the other.

With compatible laser sights and other accessories, both together had cost him nearly six-thousand dollars–over a tenth of his remaining funds. He knew they'd be worth it. The weapons had incredible stopping power and were easily accurate over eight hundred yards, depending on the user's skill. Sadly, Ty could barely hit a little over half that distance reliably.

Ty pulled a checklist out of a back pocket and set it beside his bench. It comforted him, despite having it memorized by heart. The list was simple, covering basic safety and maintenance, and had been a cornerstone of Mr. Bradley's tutelage.

A few minutes later, he put the now-crumpled list away and went out to the range.

He did well during practice, hitting the fist-sized pie plate at six hundred meters several times. Of course, both he and the target were still, but it was progress. One way or the other, he felt confident he was about as capable with a rifle as he was going to get, unless he could pit himself against real, moving targets. No doubt on the other world he'd find plenty of those.

"You still doing that bow shooting, too?" Mr. Bradley asked an hour later, after Ty had cleaned up.

Ty shook his head. "Here and there, but I'm not really passionate about it. Bow shooting might be more practical, from an ammunition perspective, but there's just no beating around effectiveness when you've got guns available." Mr. Bradley had an assistant who taught bow hunting. Ty had taken his survival classes from her, on top of the archery lessons. Unfortunately, in the list of skills he had gone for, archery had proven a complete dud. The best he could say about it was he knew how to fire the arrow and not scrape the inside of his forearm.

"Ain't no skin off your back. 'S not like you'll be shootin' bows and arrows in the military anyway," Mr. Bradley said.

Ty had told Mr. Bradley the same story he'd sold his grandmother. He was preparing to enlist and wanted to do his absolute best. Maybe the reason he'd gotten better shooting guns over archery was because as soon as word about his eminent enlistment got out, other people besides Mr. Bradley had taken it upon themselves to help him learn the basics.

One of the other shooters, a middle-aged woman wearing an unzipped camouflage jacket and a bright pink shirt with the words, "Pink Lovin', Shootin' Mom" on the chest walked up from between two of the aisles and leaned against the store counter. "How much longer before you go in, Ty?"

"I'll be here another three weeks, if everything goes as planned," Ty said. He felt a little embarrassed he didn't remember her name. There were a good number of women in the club, more than he might have expected, and she'd even given him some pointers once or twice.

Pink Mom hadn't even batted an eye at Ty's initial awkwardness. If he talked to her again, he decided that he'd seriously consider getting her real name, so he could add her to the "friends to save" list.

Leaning against the counter, Pink Mom turned to Mr. Bradley with a look Ty recognized as the "about to gossip for hours" phase of the social interaction. One thing Ty had learned was that gun people were way more social than he had expected, given that practice was a largely solo endeavor. Holding a hand up, he gave them both a weak smile. "Gotta go. Next practice is in thirty-five minutes, and I need to get clear through town. I'll see y'all tomorrow."

Nodding, as if to acknowledge Ty's haste, the two kept talking anyway.

Mr. Bradley and Pink Mom let Ty go a solid five minutes faster than he'd expected. Once he got back into his car, he sighed and pulled the visor down. He had copies of his schedule everywhere, and seeing the one tucked away in his car helped him regain his focus.

There were a surprising number of people on Ty's "Friends to Save" list now. It was one thing to care about real people; it was another entirely to enjoy small talk. What even was the point? If it didn't get someone to an objective, why do it at all?

"People are strange," he muttered, half smiling as he raised the visor.

* * *

A little over two hours later, after completing his functional weight training routine, Ty made his way through the gym into the connected dojo. The Ultimate Sports Arena was aptly named and almost one-of-a-kind. It was one of the few schools in the country that had a full gym, with fitness classes, and a robust fight training school all-in-one. Years ago, before it had expanded to include the additional bells and whistles of the gym, a group of successful fighters had come together to form a sort of "training federation." Their Elite Brotherhood Fighting Organization had grown into a top school for up-and-coming fighters. Ty trained MMA, Krav Maga, and Sambo with members of that team, paying top dollar for the opportunity to do so.

The dojo area was smaller compared to the sprawling gym and had two enclosed boxing rings with padded floors. This wasn't a place for mass kata practice or large group exercises, although they had an adjacent room specifically for grappling and tumbling. They had built the Sports Arena for highly practical, real-world training, not show work.

Dressed in his white combat uniform with a simple blue belt, Ty walked past a few trainees sparring with target pads. Some onlookers acknowledged him with nods or waves. One girl, a short blonde named Jessica, even smiled at him slightly as he passed. Her smiles were a recent development, one that made him feel vaguely uneasy. He'd learned a lot in the past few months. Casual conversation with women was not one of those things.

A big bald man with a shockingly bright smile approached when he stopped in front of the second boxing ring. "What are we working on today?" Jim asked, dark eyes dancing with anticipation.

Jim was a Middle Eastern man of middle age and was an expert in half a dozen fighting styles, chief amongst which was Krav Maga. Ty had seen Jim disable five opponents in a matter of seconds in a tournament demonstration once. He'd read online that Jim had real-world fighting experience, which was one reason Ty had joined the gym. According to some unsubstantiated rumors, Jim had killed in those altercations.

After training extensively with him, with multiple one-on-one sessions, Ty could confidently say Jim was the real deal. He was also one of the few people who seemed to understand Ty. Once he'd learned about Ty's need for lists, he'd set time aside and broken down every step of the training for him, going so far as to email him a list of moves to watch and learn, with step-by-step guides and a project plan to achieve his goals.

Without Jim's oversight, Ty wouldn't be where he was today. He was on the "Friends to Save" list.

"I need more practice against a bunch of people," Ty said, returning Jim's smile honestly. "I'm feeling really good one on one, but there's just something about three or four that worries me."

Without hesitation, Jim raised his voice. "Sarah, Henry, Issac, and Leslie, get in the ring. I want you to beat the tar out of Ty for me." Two pairs of sparring partners stopped what they were doing and made their way toward the ring.

"Be my guest," Jim waved to indicate Ty should head in.

Ty dropped his bag on a bench and padded up before stepping into the ring. Standard padding for the dojo required full coverage for head, hands, chest, and thighs. After a few punishing lessons, Ty had added foot pads like the rest of Jim's students. Foot stomps, along with several unconventional moves, were enthusiastically encouraged during spars, and those *hurt*. Positioning himself at the center of the four, with maybe three feet of reach between each of them, Ty shook out his hands and assumed an open, relaxed stance.

From just outside of the ropes, Jim waited for Ty to finish before announcing, "Begin."

Time didn't *quite* slow, but it kind of also *did*. As soon as Jim said the word, Ty felt bubbles rush up his spine and an inexplicable joy shoot through every nerve of his body. He felt that thrill almost every time he sparred under Jim's tutelage. It was probably why Krav Maga had become his favorite fighting style.

Ty sped forward and to his left. Sarah's arm came up, fist clenched, to block his expected attack. He jerked, lightning fast, hammering his forearm into Sarah's wrist and knocking her arm to the side using his superior strength. His hand slid down the opening he'd created, and he captured her throat as he continued to step around her feet. In half a second, he'd clotheslined her to the floor and moved away from his other three opponents.

Issac and Henry were both larger than Ty, with visible muscle straining at their uniforms, and both were incredibly fast. Each stepped forward to flank him, throwing punches as Leslie prepared to rush in on any gaps.

Bobbing, Ty attempted to block the flurry of attacks with his forearms, elbows, and head. Many of the brutal punches landed, with only the padding on their fists keeping the pummeling from taking him out of the fight. He grinned through the pain. Through practice and training, he'd discovered a uniquely meditative joy in fighting, even when he lost.

Ty twisted to one side and bent half over, slamming one of his elbows into Issac's thigh. The man grunted in pain and fell. The maneuver left Ty open, and Henry aimed a stomp at Ty's left foot. Ty slid to the side in the last instant, but the maneuver left him off balance. Leslie took advantage of the opening and surged forward, pushing his chest with both hands.

He fell.

Ty had not become as adept at other martial arts styles as the straight-forward Krav Maga, but he'd learned how to take a fall well enough. He rolled, turning his momentum so that he was within reach of Henry's leg. He grabbed Henry's ankle and kicked up into the man's stomach. The surprise maneuver lifted Henry into the air a few inches and left him gasping for breath.

Leslie followed Ty's descent, perfectly timing a stomp to his chest. Exhaling, he took the heavy blow on his sternum. Winded, he fumbled until he found her foot. Grinning excitedly, he twisted roughly. She protected her joint, twisting with the motion and falling to the ground next to him.

"Done," Jim announced once everyone was down.

The match had lasted about thirty seconds.

Jumping to his feet, Ty extended a hand to Leslie, and she took it affably. He respected her a lot. She, and most of the other students who came during the day, were serious fighters. The day crew was big on attending actual, legitimate tournament fights. Leslie had invited him to go with them more than once. Unfortunately, his schedule didn't allow for it.

In another world, perhaps...

"That was good," Jim said, proceeding to point out the mistakes Ty and his sparring partners had made in quick, simple terms. There was no discussion of who won. Ty had taken a beating during the match, with his arms, chest, and face feeling it. He'd also delivered devastating attacks to his opponents, not that any of them were seriously wounded. These people were among the top fighters in the dojo and knew how to pull a punch and take a hit. In the real world, it would have been about who got back up and how fast, not about points or perceived winners and losers.

In another world, with real stakes, Ty knew he would have lost.

"Again?" Ty asked as soon as Jim was done with his critique. As expected, his sparring partners were willing. These people, like him, paid for the extended hours and attention Jim gave. All of them hoped to have careers in the sport, or something adjacent to it, once they completed their training. To a one, none of them ever turned down the opportunity to spar unless there was a medical reason.

By the end of the session, Ty was covered with bruises and soaked in sweat. Staggering on a leg that felt like it needed a solid two days of rest before he did anything with it, he limped over to a seat and fell into place. To his credit, most of those he'd sparred with looked only a little better than he felt. Not that he'd done all that damage himself; between his bouts, the rest of the class stayed busy, too.

"Ty, can I ask you something?" Jim said, moving to sit next to Ty on the bench as he removed his protective gear.

"Sure."

"Where do you want to go with this?" He waved at the general area of the dojo. "You're easily in the top five percent of my students. You have the focus. The discipline. You've met or exceeded every goal I've given you. Give it another two years, tops, and you'll be teaching classes with me. A person like you doesn't do this so seriously without a bigger plan. You've said a few times you don't plan to fight for money. What's motivating you?"

Ty thought of how to answer Jim's question. In some ways, his unexpected skill with Krav Maga complicated things. If events went as expected, he'd be relying on his guns more than his fists. Why punch a monster in the face when he could shoot it?

To be fair, he was more than adequate with a gun and even with knives and swords. With his fists, he was on another level entirely. As an infighter, things just *clicked*. People became pieces on a game board, and the steps to defeat them were maneuvers on a list. All social constructs, every self-imposed limitation he'd ever known, evaporated when he fought. Sometimes, especially lately, he was a little scared at just how much he yearned for the thrill of a good match. It was that very draw that was a problem. He couldn't afford to default to his hands when the time came.

"We'll see in a few weeks," he said at last, flashing Jim what he hoped was an enigmatic smile. "I'll be taking a break and will try to figure out what's next when the time comes."

"Ah, yes. You mentioned that before. You still plan to enlist after?"

Ty shrugged out of his chest protection and tucked it back into his bag. "That's the plan," he said, feeling vaguely guilty about lying to Jim. "I'll see you on the -" He almost said "other side," but his tongue froze. As time passed, nearly *anything* remotely related to his trip through the portal triggered full muscle spasms. A beat later, he managed, "Way back." It sounded lame, even to him, and it probably didn't make sense. It was also all he had.

"You going to test for brown in a couple of weeks, right?"

Ty shook his head. "I'll be here to train a few more times, then out. I don't have time to do much besides prep at this point. The test can wait until I return." He wanted to take the test, wanted more than anything to prove himself. The reality was he needed to transition from constant training to staging his gear. According to the warning, the portal would be open for three minutes and he meant to make them count.

Jim nodded, gave him a friendly pat on the shoulder, and said his goodbyes. It was nearly time for him to get home. Watching him go, Ty felt a sharp pang of loss. Over the past months, he had become a different person in many ways. His list of people he considered friends was longer than he'd dared consider.

"Hey, Ty," Jessica called, walking over. She'd dressed for the evening, wearing jeans and a simple t-shirt that hugged her fit physique.

Ty glanced down, instinctively uncomfortable with eye contact outside of the sparring arena. "Hi, Jessica. What's up?"

"I was wondering if you'd like to come hang out with a few of us? We're doing a late dinner, and I'd love to discuss some of those new moves Jim has been training you on." She paused, waiting for Ty to glance at her face, then continued with a beaming smile, "C'mon. I'll bribe you with coffee."

"Coffee?" Ty asked, gesturing at the dark sky through the dojo window.

Jessica laughed. It was a pleasant, warm sound, throatier than Ty would have expected. "Or whatever it is you drink, silly."

His heart picking up speed, he struggled to respond. One of his gamer friends had asked if Ty had a crush on any of his new sparring partners. He didn't *think* he had a crush on anyone. How would he know?

They want to hang out with me? There had to be a reason, an agenda. What else could there be?

"Uh, I can't," Ty said lamely. "I've got a list, you see. And a tight schedule."

Arching a brow, Jessica said, "I just lost a bet. Leslie said you wouldn't come. I said you would." Leaning in, Jessica poked his chest. She had short, practical nails. "I'll let you off the hook tonight, as long as you promise to make time once you're back from whatever you're planning for, alright?"

Uncomfortable, Ty swallowed and said, "Promise."

Later, on his drive home, he felt a strange ache inside his chest. It felt like loneliness. The skills he'd gained over the past few months had changed his perception. He'd met people, grown to know and like them. It seemed some of those people actively wanted him around. Suddenly, Ty wasn't sure he wanted to go on the silly quest.

A brief heat seared through his temples. The writing in fire appeared in his mind's eye, the script and its dire warning a fist around his heart. He had to go.

The people he now valued, the very reasons he was considering staying; they were the very purpose for this strange quest.

Ty just wished he'd known that training to become a badass on another world would make him long to stay on his own.

Chapter 4: Portals

Time Until Portal Opening: 0 Months, 5 days

Doorbells chimed as Ty walked into the shop. It was a cold, if comfortable-looking, business, with plush leather seats and art decorating the walls. A heavy-set Black man behind the counter sat up, putting a book down. Ty stepped up, amazed at just how much ink decorated the man's skin.

"I'd like these tattooed on the inside of my forearms, please," Ty said, handing the man two pieces of paper.

"Okay, so one is a list of names. Do you want the title included, too? What about the font?"

"Yeah, the title is important. Font needs to be very legible, no matter what," Ty replied, shaking a little. He wasn't afraid of the pain, not after all the training he'd gone through. The problem was that he knew going to the other side would mean giving up on his lists. He'd be bringing tools to write with, including his phone, but the possibility of losing access to them was inescapable. This was the only way he knew he could keep it together.

"And this other one, you've got phrases here. Putting them on your forearm is going to make them small." He pointed at, "Don't become a murder hobo," and said, "That's going to take up a lot of skin if you want it to be legible."

"Where would you recommend? The thing is I need to be able to see and read them. I don't care about anything else."

The man's eyes widened a bit. "You wanna read 'em, eh? That's different. Good to know. You don't want us inkin' 'em in the wrong direction." He held a calming hand out at Ty's expression. "No worries, man. We'll stencil it first before we do the first lines. In terms of space and you being able to read it, I'm going to recommend thighs. Maybe both, if you want this full list done."

"One forearm and both thighs are fine," Ty said with a sigh. "The problem is, I need this done now. Do you have anyone who can see me right now? I'll pay whatever you need. I just have to get this done."

With his offer to pay extra, an artist miraculously appeared and set to work.

* * *

Time Until Portal Opening: 0 days, 0 hours

He devoted the rest of the week to prep. The fifty thousand dollars he'd allocated for equipment and goods was mostly spent. Included on the laundry list of items was an all-terrain, electric ATV, three six-wheeled dollies rated at one-ton each, top-tier survival gear, his weapons, and a ton of charging and recharging tools. He'd also purchased quite a few disposable goods, like cheap watches, if he found a merchant to trade with.

He had opted not to bring sophisticated laptops or recording equipment, though he had considered it. Going over and collecting proof of his trip might have seemed like a good idea. He just wasn't willing to risk the expense or space that it would cost him for a "maybe."

Once he closed his outstanding accounts and said his last goodbyes, he went to the storage unit.

He'd found the unit in an ideal location. It was only a few blocks down from his house, big, and had a door that opened in a loading dock for the adjacent buildings. Although the one month of rent had been expensive, the location and private space for maneuvering were crucial for his plans.

Ty's sigh echoed in the big storage unit as he finished loading the last of the hard-bodied storage crates onto the back of one dolly. Moving briskly, he secured the boxes with a bungee cord.

"Boxes secured. Chains checked. ATV powered. Weapons locked and loaded. Ammunition stowed. Daggers sheathed. Goggles charged. Meals packed. I should be good to go." Ty chanted his preparation list like a litany, going through it in his mind, even as he pulled a copy from beneath one of his combat gloves. He was relieved to see that he'd recited it correctly.

He walked to the front of the four-wheeler, pleased with the look. He thought it had been an inspired purchase. He'd known he would need some way to get his stuff through the portal quickly and had no clue how wide the portal would be. Assuming nothing in his plan broke or the portal prevented the transfer of his goods, the electric vehicle had just enough power to manage him and the fully loaded dollies he'd chained behind it. In his testing, the ATV had gotten up to seven miles an hour on pavement.

He gave it even odds that it would last the day wherever he went. In basically every one of the prophecy books, the heroes had ended up in unfriendly terrain.

Ty's watch dinged a thirty-minute timer. It was near ten o'clock at night, and the sounds of the city beyond the loading dock grew muted. His grandmother was in bed, their goodbyes over hours ago. She hadn't cried. He almost had. That he hadn't been able to talk to her, to convey anything about what might happen next, was a splinter in his heart. That he couldn't talk was an undeniable boon, in that it gave him the proof he needed to do all this. But it also meant that he could leave, die, and his grandma would never know.

He looked down at the still-healing tattoo along the inside of one arm, thinking about the people who had become important to him over the past months. It didn't have all the names on his "Friends to Save" list, just most of them. The 'J' in one name peeked out briefly before he pulled the sleeve back up.

Laden with nearly thirty pounds of equipment, Ty straddled the ATV and started the engine. The brushless motor came to life with a whisper. Stretching out, he pressed the button to open the bay doors, then slowly eased his way out. He'd practiced this a few times once he'd gotten the ATV and the dollies and it paid off. Accelerating slowly, he added tension until the chains were taut, and pulled forward with no issue. The wheels on the dollies had smooth, soundless action. Other than the rattle of the chains, his miniature convoy was nearly silent.

Once his ATV and well-laden dollies were out of the storage building, Ty hopped off and closed the storage room. The automatic lights went off as the metal sheet clicked onto the pavement.

The sound was still echoing through the air when the portals appeared.

For a moment, Ty felt incredible relief. He hadn't been going insane. He hadn't made everything up and had some sort of mental break with reality. This *was* real. Then he pulled himself together. Things were not as he'd expected. There wasn't one portal - there were four.

Each of the portals was framed with a metal arch etched with runes. Within each was a glowing oval, approximately six feet tall and four wide. The interior of each swirled with a mixture of fractalized opaque colors reminiscent of his computer monitors during the first night, all those months ago.

A genderless, bored-sounding voice whispered in Ty's ear. "Hello, I've been assigned to be your Guide. Until you earn your Arbiter or die, I'm the one responsible for making sure everything is fair and balanced. Do me a favor, all right? Don't ask me stupid questions. I hate that."

Ty blinked, too stunned to speak.

"Ah, a silent type. Good. I like that. Anyway, as promised, here are your portals. Since choice is such an important part of balancing the scales between our worlds, choice is *the* core tenant of everything you're going to experience from here on out. Got that? Good. We're running out of time. Before you are four portals. Each leads to the same planet, just different places. At first, you won't be put in an overlapping area with another participant. This is to keep things from, ah, being problematic. You may look into each, but as soon as you step through or," the voice hesitated a beat, "drive through, the portal will close behind you. The way will come but once, as that one guy said in that book you read that time."

Something in what the voice said shocked Ty more than its presence. "Okay, that's really creepy. Do you know everything I've read? Are you tailoring all of this like my books?"

"I know every piece of electronic media you've ever consumed. So no, not everything you've read. And no, we're not tailoring all of it like your books. We're using the books you've read as shortcuts to translate what's happening to you. It will make *all* of our lives easier if we don't have to spend hours info-dumping on you. Make sense? You have less than two minutes left, by the way."

Motivated by the timer, Ty jumped down from his ATV and cautiously stuck his face through the first portal. He felt a momentary blurring of his vision, a vague sense of movement, and saw through the other side like he was looking through an open window. Heat blasted his face as he took in a burning, white-hot desert in the middle of nowhere. In front of him, maybe a mile away, was an oasis partially bisected by a stone structure.

Without taking the time to analyze what he saw, Ty pulled his head out and looked into the next portals in quick succession. One was in the middle of a winding cobblestone road that went directly to what looked to be a rather sophisticated, if medieval-inspired, castle. The next appeared on the edge of a rocky outcropping overlooking a vast, Asianic series of buildings. That one reminded him a bit of the bad guys in the first *Batman* movie with Christian Bale. The final portal led to a verdant forest with wide-set, ancient trees and dappled, diffuse light.

"Less than one minute," the voice intoned in his ear when he pulled his head back through the final portal.

"Fuck me," Ty said out loud, unable to believe what he was seeing. He'd expected to go through a portal, one. Not find himself in a choose-your-own-adventure where anything he did could kill him. "I don't suppose you can help me choose?" he asked. He needed the facts before he could make a list and weigh the best outcome.

"Sure I can. It'll take a few minutes to describe what you'll find behind each door. By then..."

Ty didn't need the rest of the explanation. Less than a minute left. He had to act. Getting back on his ATV, he thought through his options.

First, he didn't want to go anywhere that his ATV wouldn't go. That meant the desert and the mountains were out. Second, he didn't want to go anywhere with people. On the one hand, meeting the natives might be nice. They might come to him with open arms and provide him with all the information and support he needed to do whatever he had to do on the other side. Based on the prophecy image, however, he suspected rather the opposite. If he didn't get a lay of the land first, anyone he met was liable to see him as a target rather than someone to help.

Rotating his hands to throttle forward, he rolled forward through the last portal. The end of his third dolly barely made it through before the portal closed behind him.

Chapter 5: Epic Odds

The other side of the portal looked exactly like it had when he'd surveyed it. A trickle of light spilled through a thick overhead canopy, illuminating a loamy but otherwise open woodland vista. The ATV's wheels struggled to find traction for a moment but eventually gripped well enough for Ty to ease his convoy forward a few yards.

"All right, now what?" Ty asked, looking around for anything to show what he should do next. As far as he could see, there was open space. A few stray butterfly-looking creatures drifted high above, outlined against what little light made it through. There were no signs of any larger animals as he would expect from a sizable forest. On the plus side, he could breathe, and the weather was temperate. Not that he'd expected to travel to a world where he immediately died; it had just been a possibility in a sea of horrible potentialities.

"Before we give you your Arbiter, you must complete one small, simple task to prove your worth," the Guide whispered in his ear, still sounding bored. "In fifty-one hours, if you have completed the quest, you will be granted your Arbiter. If you cannot complete the task or die, all assistance will be forfeit. Loss of guidance would be, in all probability, fatal." Ty thought that last sentence was delivered with a hint of irony-laced malice. The voice continued, "Directly ahead of you, approximately one mile, is a valley. In that valley, there is an infestation of Centralized, Hive-Variant, Demon Invaders. Your aim is to kill any one member of the infestation."

Ty's first response was a wave of relief. He'd expected that he would have to kill things. He hadn't known whether the first things he'd fight would be men or monsters. Based on the name of the creatures, he figured he wouldn't have any moral compunction against taking one out.

His second thought was concern over the word "infestation." A large group of organized combatants would be a significant threat, supernatural abilities or not.

"Guide, can I ask you questions about the task?" Ty asked, hoping the thing would function as a help tutorial or something. Sliding off his ATV, he drew one of his handguns and began looking around.

"Yes. The rules mandate I must answer your questions, provided they are ones a native of our world would know." The Guide's voice didn't waver or change in distance or direction as Ty looked around the forest. He almost suspected it was coming inside his head, but the way its tones subtly modulated compared to how it had sounded in the alley led him to believe it was external. He'd need to be careful talking with the entity near enemies.

The sense of majesty in the forest contrasted with the Guide's words. Unlike ancient Earth forests, Ty was surprised to see that there wasn't much underbrush here. Perhaps the presence of magic changed the local ecology? "I'm assuming when the Arbiter appears in fifty-one hours, any of these demons I've pissed off won't just conveniently vanish because I've completed the quest?"

"Uh. Yeah. You'd be very correct about that. Remember, we referenced your books to help you prepare for this, not your video games."

"Gotcha," Ty said, rounding the trunk of a tree that must have been thirty feet around. "So, there isn't any inventory or loot system here?"

The Guide took a moment before replying. "Sort of yes, sort of no. Definitely nothing you can use right now. Your Arbiter might help with that, depending on several future factors."

He was surprised to see no signs of wildlife. No alien squirrels or birds appeared, despite his quiet inspection. Frowning, he said, "All right. What can you tell me about the Invaders? Are they strong, fast? Do they have special abilities I should know about?"

"They are deadly," the Guide replied. "Stronger and faster than you, with significantly more durability. They are most active between sunset and the early morning. They are averse to sunlight, but it does not harm them. Being protected by the forest canopy gives them some advantages. They do not have any outstanding supernatural abilities that would make them an utterly overwhelming threat, however."

So much for an easy start, Ty thought as he made his way back to his ATV. "And what kind of 'Hive Variation' do they have? I'm assuming there are multiple types of hive in this world. Does that mean they have a queen or something?"

"These creatures have a centralized, evolving, clustered thought structure. While the lowest tier of these demons, the drones, are approximately as intelligent as a squirrel, over time they can develop into thinking, self-aware beings. Their bodies also change as they age. Their particular variation allows them to spread their intelligence out among lesser members of their kind over a modest distance. In time, captains and generals arise through their ranks. This makes any infestation of this type of demon a high risk for any area where they take r oot."

Ty pulled a notepad and travel pen out of a pocket and began making notes. He processed the list for several minutes before asking, "Does this 'shared intelligence' mean that they share senses, too?"

"No. Think of it more like sharing computer power. One general might have as much intellect, or computing power, of three or four regular humans from your home world. This would be enough to allow twelve or thirteen of their captains to apply basic strategy, planning, and organization to their army. In turn, those captains can share their intellect with the drones, allowing them to recognize and obey basic commands."

"Makes sense," Ty said, getting back on his ATV. Knowing there was a time constraint, he refrained from asking the Guide any further questions.

Turning the ATV through the forest wasn't difficult, even if it went slower than on pavement. Guiding the convoy in the opposite direction of the infestation, he turned the throttle. With the soft loam of the forest floor to cushion the sounds of the tires, his little caravan made minimal noise as he navigated away from his point of ingress.

Keeping one eye on his odometer, Ty coasted slowly and looked around as he drove, particularly at the forest floor. Just a few hundred feet into his trek, he found the first signs of life. There were piles of black scat just off the line of his path, near the base of one tree. Pausing, he got down to inspect the droppings.

The first clump fractured and crumbled at some prodding with his knife, revealing undigested bones. Whatever had made the spoor was a meat eater. Coupled with the fact that he saw no fresh prints in the loam, he figured the owner hadn't been in the area for a while. To test his theory, he looked around to check his footprints. No strange magic filled them in, leading him to believe that his impression was correct.

Making a few notes, Ty asked the air, "I don't suppose you'll tell me if this is demon shit?"

There was no reply. Based on the lack of any animals, he felt confident that he was onto something. Just the name of the monsters lent credence to the idea that they would have foraged the forest clean. Monsters with the word "demon" in their names were always big on killing things. If that naming convention held true, he had a plan of what to do next.

He drove until the odometer on his ATV read three miles. On the way, signs of life gradually became evident. He drove past a distant family of furry, raccoon-looking creatures with glowing antennae. They saw him, responding with cautious glances, but neither attacked nor ran. He didn't bother them. He knew better than to mess with wildlife in his world, let alone another.

One of Ty's biggest concerns were the predators. This was a large forest. On Earth, a place like this would have a few apex predators about. In a fantasy world, he guessed such things would put Earth's bears or hunting cats to shame. He hoped that the infestation would have scared the big hunters away far enough to make those less of a concern. He wasn't interested in killing a bunch of predatory boars or gigantic snakes for his first mission.

Driving a few more minutes, Ty maneuvered his ATV next to a tree. Dismounting, he unhitched his dollies. He considered using a length of climbing chain to secure them in place, then thought better of it. Securing them might help if someone or something stumbled across his belongings. Then again, if he was trying to escape something, it might slow him down so much that he lost the supplies all the same.

Without the dollies to slow him down, and even with periodic pauses to make notes about the trail, Ty made good time. It took him less than twenty minutes to make it back to the approximate area of the portal. Pulling to a stop, he checked the ATV battery power. It was still at seventy percent. He only had one backup battery, and with the tree cover, he didn't know when he'd be able to use one of his portable solar charges, so he dismounted rather than risk driving any further. With still no signs of anyone or anything that might be interested in him or his ATV, he left it in between two trees, pointed back toward his stuff.

Reviewing his notes, he felt confident in his next steps. Taking his goggles, one rifle, and a canteen of water, he began hiking towards where the Guide had said the infestation was. He glanced down at his watch as he went. It was midnight on Earth now. Thankfully, he was nocturnal at home, so it being daylight here worked out. He'd have to track the time and re-map what the hours meant over the next few days.

"What's your day-night cycle here, Guide?" Ty asked, keeping his voice low.

"Approximately the same as yours," the voice replied, whispering in kind. "Twenty-five and a half hours versus your twenty-four."

So much for that crate of watches.

"Good to know, thank you." He figured it was best to at least try to get on good footing with the Guide while he could. Besides, his grandparents had both been big fans of politeness.

He heard the demon encampment long before he saw it. They were *loud*. The sound of mining, of rocks hitting rocks and loud, chittering cries filtered through the trees minutes after his last conversation with the Guide. When he broke through the tree line and saw the promised valley, the cacophony was nearly deafening.

Taking in the sight before him, Ty flinched. There was a small *army* in the valley.

Chapter 6: You Call This Balance?

Time Until Quest Closure: 43 hours

Afraid of being spotted, Ty threw himself to the ground hard enough to take his breath away. Pulling his goggles into place, he pressed a button to activate magnification. Taking a moment to adjust to the new view, he swept the valley to make sure no one had seen him. He figured there was an even chance that he'd just made a black silhouette against the tree line. When no movement signaled that he'd been spotted, he took out his notepad and pen.

The valley was football shaped. He was at the top of the long edge, maybe a thousand meters from the opposite side. Side-to-side, it was half as long as it was wide. Along the outer rim of the valley, the ground sloped sharply and was rocky, looking like maybe a meteorite had created it. At its deepest point, aside from the excavation zone, which was a little off-center from the middle, the valley floor was around three hundred feet below the rim where Ty lay. His side of the valley was the steepest incline; on the other end, he spotted several gently sloping trails that would give someone access to and from the valley.

Other than the steep edges, nearly every bit of the valley was full of the demons.

Based on the description, Ty had expected some sort of orc army. He'd imagined a well-organized troop with tents and campfires and such, with all manner of poorly crafted weapon. While the demons weren't precisely disorganized, they were anything but well-equipped.

There were three types of demons in the encampment, all of them covered with chitinous armor plates. Each type also had a glowing yellow gemstone imbedded in their forehead. First were the dog-like ones. Hound-sized, they had six legs and were a mottled brown color, with red bands around their joints. Their heads were arrow-shaped, and their eyes were yellow and beady beneath thumbnail-sized gems.

Second were the humanoid bug-men. Looking at them reminded Ty a bit of dull yellow moths, with their overlapping, leathery chitin bands hugging muscular bodies. Claw-tipped hands flexed and bent erratically as they interacted with one another, as if on the verge of attacking. Their heads were crested with short antennae and large, multifaceted eyes perched high above flexible, insectoid mouth parts. They had egg-sized gems high on their foreheads. As the demons moved about, some of them frighteningly quick, he observed their legs were backwards facing and multi-jointed.

Finally, there was a larger, more refined version of the humanoids. These were head and shoulders taller, with smaller eyes and larger gems. Of the last group, a truly gigantic one sat in the center of the camp. Its basketball-sized crystal thrummed with a constant flickering of light.

Hovering over the valley, another two hundred feet *above* where Ty lay, there were four flapping banners. Rectangular, each banner floated in the approximate middle of each wall of the constraining valley. The banners radiated a malevolent glow that tinted the area below red.

The loud, active excavation was near the big demon. Dozens of the humanoid demons clawed at the ground, tearing into the rock beneath. It didn't look to him that the process was efficient compared to men with pickaxes, though he rethought that when he saw several chunks of rock fly from just a few swipes. He couldn't imagine what one strike from a claw like that would do to his body, armored or not. He saw no sign of what they were digging for.

Maybe they were like ground wasps, preparing to build a nest?

Ty set in to study the army and its movements, drawing and documenting everything he could. There were *hundreds* of creatures down there. Fortunately for him, as the Guide had said, most seemed brainless. They milled about, occasionally vanishing down a rabbit trail on the opposite side of the valley and returning with a fresh-caught animal of one sort or another, but there was nothing particularly organized about what they did. When two of them went at the same time and returned with something resembling a deer, a whole cluster of demons fell in on the animal, tearing it apart in a matter of seconds. Their lack of coordination would make it easy for him to pick one off and complete his quest.

Then Ty saw something that made him realize just how utterly fucked he was.

According to his labeling of them, the dogs were "drones," the bigger of the humanoid demons were "captains," and the largest one was their "general." When several of the drones started snapping at one another, one of the captains looked over. Its forehead gem flashed in a quick pattern that was mirrored in each of the drones. In just a few seconds, the demons organized into a neat pack and flashed out of the camp in eerie harmony. They'd gone from disorganized to efficient pack hunters in seconds. Ty watched the sender as the pack left, noting that it slumped and moved about with less purpose than before.

The pack returned a few minutes later, working together to drag a wooly creature that might have been a very distant cousin of a moose into the camp. They brought the carcass directly in front of the general. He watched as light pulsed from his gem and reflected in nuanced, subtle ways through the entire camp around the returning pack. None of the demons moved to interrupt his feast. Unlike the demon who'd sent the pack, the general did not appear overly taxed by sharing its intellect with the others.

Ty felt a fresh wave of terror watching how the big one ate. Not only could it motivate the army without going into torpor, but it was also strong enough to rip apart the sizable carcass with negligible effort.

Hand shaking, he jotted down notes about the general. Based on his estimation, the thing had to be as strong as a grizzly bear, if not stronger.

There was no way Ty could confront any of this army and survive. All he had to do was make one mistake, underestimate the demons for an instant, and any of those captains could send half the army after him. They'd go from uncoordinated to deadly in the time it took him to count to five. If he got within a hundred meters of the general, he'd be dog food in less time than it would take to draw his gun.

He got his cell phone out and took several pictures of the encampment, then eased away from the rim and made his way to his ATV. He drove back to his convoy unmolested, cursing his odds the entire time. His gut told him there had to be a way to overcome and succeed at the quest, otherwise the whole task wouldn't be "balanced." It also told him that there was a very real chance his heroic journey to a new world could end prematurely if he made one wrong move.

It was getting dark by the time Ty got to the convoy. Given how active the demons had been when he'd seen them, he expected their patrols and hunting parties to only become more so in the coming hours. Rather than bed down, he set up a tarp over his convoy then put his back against a tree a few hundred yards away. Resting with a rifle next to him and his pistols in his hands, he planned to keep watch for the night. Even if he had a minimal fighting chance against the demons, he wasn't about to die in his sleep from a roaming patrol or random wildlife.

Settling into place, Ty remembered that he'd packed a ton of instant meals. He didn't feel like bothering with the unpacking process when he had plans to consider and notes to review. Taking out a protein bar, he ate mechanically as he thought through his options.

The gentle ambient light slowly faded, and forest sounds replaced the unnatural daytime stillness. Soft chirping came from the distant branches above him, and a cool, steady breeze rustled the leaves. A few minutes into the night, Ty heard several bigger creatures moving. Through his goggles, he saw the silhouettes of truck-sized quadrupeds pause nearby, their horned heads pivoting in his direction to reveal glowing green eyes. They looked back at him, paused for a beat, then shuffled off.

He wondered why none of the animals seemed inclined to bother him. Could this be his Guide's protection? Did the forces behind this game want to see how his first encounter with the demons played out?

Feeling isolated and alone in a way he hadn't anticipated, Ty shivered. The night was colder than the day, but his shiver wasn't from the weather as much as it was fear. He'd left his entire planet behind for this opportunity. No one he met here, no matter how amiable, no matter how humanoid, would have any frame of reference with him. Unless he eventually found someone else from Earth.

For several long minutes, he had to confront a painful realization. He'd just spent months playing at becoming some sort of knock-off soldier, focused on a plan he thought would transform him into the ultimate adventurer. Everything had been a strategic game. But what could have prepared him for the reality of being alone in the woods on an alien planet, facing overwhelming odds just for a chance to *maybe* save his grandmother and a few friends?

Is this worth it? He'd been over for less than a day and he'd already seen some of the things in his fantasies. He hadn't gained any grand powers or insights. There'd been no leveling up or heroic talking swords. Hell, there hadn't even been a dungeon to grind gear. Back home, when he played fantasy games, exploring dungeons was half the fun. Maybe everything he'd planned for, or thought he'd planned for, was off.

Looking down, Ty pulled his sleeves back. The tattoo artist had picked a good, blocky font, and he could read the lists through the goggles. Reciting each name helped him force his doubt away. He'd made his plans and his choice. There was no going back, only forward. There *had* to be a way to navigate this puzzle, otherwise it wouldn't have been "balanced" or whatever it was the Guide had said was required.

He sat and thought for hours. The focus on his vigil helped calm his mind, helped him look at solutions to the problem. Instead of thinking of it in terms of what he would do or how dangerous and scary things were, he put some distance between himself and the situation. He was a character in a game, a piece on the board. What were his abilities, his assets, and what obstacles did he have to overcome?

Weighing, measuring, and listing things calmed his mind. Inspiration followed.

Fishing his phone out, he opened it to review the pictures he'd taken. He noticed that the four banners each had a single knot of script, presumably magical runes, that seemed to keep them suspended in the air. The knots were in the center-top of each banner and about the size of a dinner plate. Given that the breeze barely moved the banners, Ty was confident he could hit the knots with his rifle.

The pieces of an imaginary chess board shifted, revealing a plan that he couldn't believe he'd missed.

Keeping his voice low, Ty said, "Guide, I'm looking at the banners floating above the camp. Can you tell me what they do and whether my weapons will be effective against them?"

"I can tell you some of what the banners do, but not all. In this situation, the banners act as a territory lock. It tells roaming animals, monsters, and magical creatures that the demons have claimed the space. It also provides the demons within the area special advantages and protections. You could not, for example, throw a powerful spell into the area without first removing the banners. They also allow more of their kind to be transported in and out of the region at a reduced mana cost. As far as your weapons, yes. None of the devices the demons possess can resist mortal weapons beyond their innate structural resilience."

None of the devices can resist mortal weapons beyond their innate structural resilience. That, Ty knew, was a key piece of information. He wrote it down.

"A couple of the examples I was given before coming over included the concept of hit points and levels. Can you talk about that a bit? What level are those guys?"

The Guide's bored voice sharpened slightly, as if it were becoming genuinely interested in the discussion. "The books offered a convenient translation point. Our world does not innately have what you would call levels or hit points. Yet, in a way, it does. Magic permeates our world, and over time things born here grow and change because of its presence. Bodies become stronger and more resilient. Magic also acts as a sort of life-preserving barrier around living organisms here. You might describe it as 'soaking damage.' Over time, as living things absorb magic, they gain noticeable and often specific benefits. You might describe it as 'leveling up.' Thus, your reference books are quite useful, if not terms the natives would use or understand. Does this make sense? If so, I will continue."

Ty took a beat to document and digest what the Guide said.

"Was the prophecy and your help translating things part of your so-called 'keeping things balanced'?"

"Correct. The lesser and greater gods govern us. The greater gods are the manifestation of forces of nature, one of which is Balance. There are factors at play that require balance for those of you who were selected as players in this game. Therefore, we provided you time to prepare, my help, and other advantages."

That wasn't something Ty had expected at all. None of the reference books heavily featured gods. "How involved are your gods in this? Or in everyday life?"

"In your case, as a potential scion? Substantially. In most other cases, it depends. Magic gives the gods life, but belief and worship shape them. Without that shaping, the lesser gods would diminish, potentially even lose sentience. The connection between a god and a highly magical follower is symbiotic; the more magic in a follower, the more power the god can wield."

"All right. We're a bit off topic here. What about the approximate levels of the demons? Can you tell me that?"

The Guide considered before answering. "You're level zero. The dog-drones are approximately level three. The warriors are closer to five, and the captains closer to six or eight."

"And the big guy? I'm assuming he's a general?"

"Eleven. He could take a couple direct hits from your world's tanks and keep going, not to mention having a variety of unique powers because of his age. I'll add this since any native of our world would know this: don't fight him. He'll kill you."

Ty smirked. "I hadn't planned on it. Tell me, if there are all sorts of magical barriers and protections in this world, do critical strikes work? If I cut someone's throat, are they just going to keep walking because I didn't do enough damage to some sort of metaphysical hit point well?"

"The use of tactical attacks applies nearly as well here as on your world," the Guide replied, taking on something approaching a warning note. Maybe it had seen Ty's line of thought. "Biological function is intact on this side of the Resonance Bridge. If you're talking about slitting what you'd consider a 'high level' person's throat, you'll need a solid amount of additional effort and probably some luck, since their durability, reflexes, and processing speed will be higher than anyone you've encountered before, but a slit throat is a slit throat. It is worth adding that a hearty target may take longer to bleed out and may have regenerative properties. You'd be wise to cut *deeply* if you're going for that sort of attack."

Finally, Ty asked the question he'd been *really* interested in. "I'm basically on a quest right now, right? Are there bonuses or achievements, too? If I go above and beyond, will the outcome be better than just getting an Arbiter assigned to me?"

For the first time, the Guide's voice took on a sly note. "Now *that* is an interesting question. I can only tell you this: your Arbiter will act as a sort of personalized Game Master for you. If you complete the right quests, it may reward you. That's how you'll 'level up' over here. The world will essentially be hyper-rewarding you and speeding up your acclimation to magic. If you go above and beyond, your Arbiter and the gods watching will take notice. There is a significant chance that you might be granted a special boon or privilege for such activities. You might consider those rewards tied to achievements if you wanted to. This is not me suggesting that you take undue risks, however. Not at all. I am not advising, only providing reasonable information."

"Clarity accepted, Guide. I appreciate that."

Ty let quiet settle over the camp. He had too much to process to ask his Guide more questions. What he needed was concrete, actionable information, not an info-dump that would just confuse him. He wrote on a fresh notepad, summarizing what he knew about the lay of the land.

Shortly before dawn, the pieces came together. It was risky, with more variables than he'd have liked, but he figured it was his best bet. Considering it, however, made his stomach sink. It was *obvious*. Painfully so.

"Guide," Ty said, fatigue slowing his words, "I think I see a way through this. The problem is it looks obvious. Was this situation custom-made for me to succeed? Did you or one of your gods set this up?"

"Absolutely not," the Guide replied without hesitation. "The gods worked together for years before triggering the Resonance. Each guided theaters like this into existence, carefully using their followers and powers to indirectly shape opportunities for Earth's participants. This was one of four locations we knew you might reasonably survive in, based on your qualifications and preparations. You were matched because of skill and kit, but no god has directly intervened to make this happen. That would be against the rules. The one thing I did was ensure we placed you in an advantageous location in relation to the valley."

"Okay, it just feels...too perfect. The demons have crystals in their skulls, and I have guns, you know?" Ty had seen that as a possibility earlier; when he'd come up with his plan, the surrounding revelations just seemed, well, orchestrated.

The Guide retorted, "You planned six months for this. You trained using the materials we suggested you review. The fact of the matter is that these demons use an intellect-based power. Organ enhancement is influenced by the proximity of magic. Thus, magic crystals in skulls. Demons like this have grown mind gems for as long as they've been on Volar, and you will no doubt find similar creatures, with their own gems in different places, on your travels through our world. Do not mistake your successful preparation for an outcome on this quest as us deliberately handing you anything. It is foolhardy to underestimate yourself or to assume we will make anything easier for you, ever. We are bound to be fair, never easy. I promise you this."

Ty heard a ring of truth in the Guide's explanation. He didn't think it would lie to him. Why would it? He didn't know if that made him feel better or worse about what would happen next. Part of him really wished some benign hand was reaching down to adjust the dice in his favor.

With light creeping through the canopy again, the forest stilled. Only then did Ty close his eyes and try to rest.

He dreamed he was playing a table top game with friends, only the game master was a giant bee-man. Halfway through the dream, the game master reached across the table and took Ty's notes, disallowing them for the big finale. The rest of the nightmare left him shivering in a cold sweat.

Chapter 7: Delicate Fingers

Time Until Quest Closure: 26 hours

Ty woke with a dragon in his face.

Nothing woke him, no movement or sound. One second, he was asleep and the next he was staring into a big, slitted eye. He almost reached for his gun. If he'd been an experienced soldier, he probably would have. In the beat that he hesitated, however, the creature slid back enough for him to see what it was.

Oriental-style, the dragon was around fifteen feet long from snout to tail. It had dark blue scales on its top parts that faded to lighter, almost white, on its belly. Instead of wings, it had two parallel, sinuous sail-like structures floating lazily on either side of its back. As it moved, he saw it had multiple pairs of short, multi-jointed arms beneath it. Delicate, dexterous, seven-fingered hands splayed on the ground, one pair of which rested on the ground just a couple feet from where Ty sat.

He watched the creature in awe. It was *beautiful*. Oddly, once he'd gotten past the initial terror, he felt no threat at all from the dragon. Instead, he felt a wave of absolute joy at seeing it. That something this marvelous, this beautiful, existed...it justified all of his choices.

The dragon exhaled a snort that blasted right in Ty's face. Its breath smelled vaguely like chicken noodle soup. Turning its head from side to side in quick, bird-like motions, it pivoted to glance at his convoy and then toward the demons. It looked back at him again, then again in the direction of the demons.

It took Ty an embarrassingly long time to figure out that the dragon was trying to ask him a question. Taking it on intuition that the dragon was a potential ally, Ty gestured toward the demons and said out loud, "Enemies." He drew a hand across his throat, then smashed a fist into one palm, grinding it in as if to smash a bug. "I will kill them."

The dragon recoiled in a sharp, fluid motion. Lifting itself until the upper third of its torso was vertical, it brought four sets of delicate hands together before its chest and spoke. Its voice was a melodic, sibilant murmur.

Ty's Guide spoke in his ear, affecting a posh English accent for some reason. "Really? You want to kill them? That would be marvelous. I would appreciate anything you can do to help."

"Wait, the dragon can understand me?" Ty asked his Guide.

Back in its normal speaking voice, the Guide replied, "No. I'm translating for you. Until you get your Arbiter, I'll be here to make sure you don't die because of the language barrier."

If the dragon noticed or cared about the murmured conversation between Ty and the Guide, it didn't show.

Returning his attention to the dragon, Ty said, "Great dragon, it is an honor to meet you. I am called Ty." In some books he'd read, dragons were absolute narcissists, so he figured flowery speech and flattery might help here. "May I have your name and what your intentions are?"

The dragon snorted, as if in amusement, before replying. "I am called Aquamarine, and I am one guardian of this forest. If you help me with the invaders, Ty, I will consider it a great boon. Assuming you can disrupt their machinations, that is."

Ty didn't know if his plan would interfere with what the demons were doing. If everything went well, he was pretty sure it would. Drawing on his theoretical knowledge of dragons, he responded, "Great and wise dragon, I will be putting myself in harm's way to do this thing. Would my great boon for you perhaps translate into your assistance for me?"

A look of amusement flickered in the dragon's eyes. Ty noted that the eyes, like its scales, were two-toned, blue fading to pearly white. Another sense of comfort rolled through his stomach. The reference books hadn't been heavy on dragons, relatively speaking. They'd been mentioned a couple of times, had a cameo or two, but that was all. Even in his wildest dreams, he couldn't have imagined being face-to-face with something so utterly awe-inspiring.

"Mmm, yes. It would." Aquamarine's fingers rolled together, tapping out a complex pattern. "How about this, little warrior? If you can significantly affect the demons, I will grant you up to three modest boons. How does that sound?"

Ty did not know what a modest boon was; he'd just been making guesses so far. He was glad that it had paid off. "I think that sounds fair. I may have to flee in great haste from the invaders, however. Would you be willing to grant me a boon in advance?"

Four sets of left arms raised, fingers together, palm toward Ty. "Speak your request," Aquamarine said.

"I would appreciate it if you'd make sure my convoy is left undisturbed while I work." Ty gestured at the dollies with their stacks of crates.

Aquamarine bobbed in place, its movements rhythmic and serpentine. "This would be a minimal boon. As I have done since your arrival, I will ensure none of my denizens interfere with or harm you. I will not, however, interfere with any of the demons should they approach. I will not do that, not even for a greater boon. Minions of the Monster God are not to be trifled with."

Feeling safe to indulge, Ty jotted down the note about the Monster God. Biting back a comment about how much danger he was about to be in, he said, "That would be excellent, Aquamarine. Since there's a chance that I'll need to move quickly, how will you know if I've succeeded in time to grant my remaining boons?"

Two of the dragon's right hands gestured offhandedly. A dim green light pulsed near one of the adjacent trees. Looking closely, Ty saw that the light surrounded what looked like a tiny centaur-shaped ant creature. It hovered in the air, wings flashing like a hummingbird's, pinprick eyes watching the two of them. He hadn't noticed or heard the thing approach.

Now that he knew what to look for, as Ty looked around the clearing, he spotted dozens of the creatures hovering in the area. Had he not known what he was looking for, he'd never have seen them. Could they have been watching him this entire time?

The Guide translated amusement in Aquamarine's carefully accented proper English. "My forest sprites are everywhere in my domain, Ty. What they see, I know. If you complete your task, I will grant your boons. If you believe time will be of the essence, I will be happy to hear your requests now, if you know them. Thus, we can prepare in advance and ensure mutual satisfaction before you," the dragon paused and its flexible mouth curved in a sharp-toothed crocodilian grin, "heroically dash off to continue your adventures elsewhere."

"May I have a moment to consider?" Ty asked.

The dragon agreed, flowing away to give Ty privacy to think when he asked.

With room to breathe, he consulted his notes, adding and crossing off ideas as they occurred to him.

"I should tell you, anyone local to this region would think twice about trusting a dragon," the Guide said in a whisper.

"Why is that?" Ty asked, frowning as he looked up from his writing and toward the majestic creature.

"Most of the civilized races believe dragons come from pure chaos. They are perceived as godless and not trusted. A local might point out that your disrupting the excavation might be precisely what the dragon wants so it can swoop in and take whatever is hidden beneath the ground. Just because the dragon calls itself a guardian does not mean it is benevolent or honest."

Glancing down, Ty replayed what the Guide said, mentally highlighting the words he'd have jotted down had he been sitting around a tabletop. "You said most, and believe, and perceive. Those are generalities, not real warnings." Compared to the Guide's warning about the demon general, this felt like something...vague. Besides, Ty had to admit that he *wanted* to trust the dragon. So many adventures he'd read about, including the ones in the warning, had been dark and dire affairs. People were tortured and died. People did horrible things. The denizens of the other worlds or domains were often awful. He couldn't help but genuinely want to see this world as a better place, a place with hope in it. He wanted to be a hero, not assume everything amazing he encountered could be secretly plotting against him.

His fingers traced the outline of a phrase beneath his clothing. *Always find light. If there is none,* become *the light.* Grandpa Billy had loved that line. It was one of the last things the man had told Ty before he passed.

"Correct," the Guide replied. "I am merely informing you of what the locals would surmise, so you can make an informed and fair decision."

That the Guide had provided him with the warning unprompted bothered Ty. On a hunch, he said, "You just told me the locals believe dragons are godless. Earlier, you said that the gods were watching people from my world closely. Was this warning prompted by the gods? Is the dragon interfering in their plans somehow?" Even as he spoke, he felt the guess made sense. He might not know all the pieces or how everything interacted, yet there was a sense of *correctness* about his supposition.

"I can neither confirm nor deny your inquiry," the Guide said, voice monotone and robotic.

That was close enough for confirmation in Ty's book. He'd stumbled on something important, maybe even critically so. Unfortunately, he had no idea what to do with that insight. If the dragon could interfere with the gods' plans, it sure didn't seem to be going out of its way to do so. He was still going to complete his quest. That it helped both him and Aquamarine shouldn't affect the gods at all, right? What could change the outcome of whatever plan the gods had?

Focusing on his notes, he tried to decide if the dragon's presence should change his plan or how to use his Guide's information at all. Ultimately, he couldn't find a solution. He did come up with his last two requests, though.

Ty gestured for Aquamarine to return. Moving on its limbs, centipede-like, the dragon shot back to Ty with frightening speed. Even on his ATV driving on flat asphalt, he doubted he could outpace the magical creature.

"For my second boon, I would like a map of the area," He said once the dragon had settled back into its hands-folded pose.

"Simply done, friend Ty. In fact, I would consider it a modest boon to assign you one of my sprites as a guide. Should you complete your task, I will grant you an ally to help you navigate my forest and find what you seek to your heart's content. Furthermore, such a guide will be far more helpful than a map, as they will warn you of places you should not venture. There are many dangerous and sacred places in this wood, and it would not do for you to trespass unawares."

That was far better than anything Ty could have hoped for. Pleased, he gave the dragon his best approximation of a bow. "Thank you, gracious Aquamarine. Your generosity is bountiful and rich."

The dragon snorted, and Ty realized that he'd amused the creature. "And for your final boon, should you disrupt the efforts of the demons?"

Ty had thought longest and hardest about this last request. Over the history of all the books he'd read and the games he'd played, there were hundreds of times people had asked for favors from magical beasts. He'd considered asking for a weapon or spell, or maybe even for the dragon to become his companion. Only after thinking about the Guide's actions earlier, how it had seemed wary of the dragon, had he landed on it.

"If it is possible, great Aquamarine, I would like your blessing."

Aquamarine's head bird-danced again, one eye then the other studying Ty. "Blessing? What do you mean?"

Ty hesitated. He'd expected the dragon to know intuitively what he meant through the Guide's translation. "In the stories of dragons in my land, your kind are powerful and magical. In one such story, a hero did a great deed for a dragon and the dragon rewarded him by breathing on him. This touched the warrior and made it so all other dragons recognized him as an ally of their kind. I would like to become an ally to your kind if I can."

The Guide *glitched*. A fractal of light appeared in the air, drawing both Ty and Aquamarine's attention. It jerked and spasmed in space, throwing a rainbow of color over the area. A sepulchral voice, resonant and powerful enough to *thrum* through the air, announced, "**It is allowed. Do not interfere**." Instantly, the fractal vanished, leaving the dragon visibly stunned.

"I can do this thing you ask; however, the results may not be what you think," Aquamarine said slowly, glancing furtively to where the Guide had appeared.

Ty felt a pang of doubt, then hardened his resolve. Whatever had just happened only gave credence to his instinct in the matter. If there was anything the reference books had taught him, it was that thinking inside the box was a recipe for disaster. "Go on," he said, infusing his voice with confidence.

Gesturing rapidly with its hands, the dragon explained, "You have no magic in you, Ty. None at all. Coloring in your aura with my power would be simple. It would achieve the result you seek with almost no effort on my part. Resonating with my power would do as you've said, allow other dragons and our allies to know you. There may be horrible side-effects though."

Ty prompted, "Such as?"

"Being touched by my power may have a disproportionate effect on any magic you intake from now on. Anyone who looks at your aura or interacts with you would feel my touch. Mortals who do not trust dragons may not trust you, simply because of our affiliation. Moreover, assuming you survive long enough to evolve any innate magical aptitudes, it would shape your abilities. This could effectively change your growth forever, and not in a good way."

Aquamarine's warning took Ty back a bit. He'd expected there to be some downside to his request, but this sounded expansive. "You're saying that because I am a blank slate, simply gifting me in this way would change the base material, who I am, forever?"

Four sets of right hands saluted Ty. "Astute wording, and correct. I cannot attest to how deep such a change would go. No doubt it would be significant. Please take no offense, Ty, but you are utterly empty right now. Any power that touches you will shape you, for better or worse. You might be wiser to pray to one of the mortal gods rather than take this from me. They, at least, could look out for you in the future if you ever become worthy of such attention."

Which is just what they want, Ty guessed. He didn't know why, not yet, but he got the distinct feeling that his Guide's glitch had showed that *someone* didn't want him to do what he was about to do. Whoever that someone was, he expected it was a god looking to meddle in his life. Even if the prophecy books hadn't included a lot of gods, those that had meddling ones made one thing clear: gods were not there to make life any easier on the mortals who interacted with them. Ty hadn't spoken to a god yet, not directly, and he already had a wary impression of them. If he could do something now that would skew things a bit, even a tiny bit, in his favor, he thought there was a good chance it would pay off later. Assuming there was a later.

I have to think long term.

Ty went through his notes, weighing pros and cons. "I am certain," he said once he was done, "I would consider it a modest boon if you would do this for me."

Rolling one eye from Ty to the space over his shoulder, Aquamarine said, "Survive your task for me, disrupt the machinations of the invaders, and I shall see you rewarded with a modest infusion of my power, Ty." The dragon's voice dropped, and Ty could hear notes of concern even in the raw, untranslated, sounds it made. "I hope this does not become a curse for you, should you succeed."

Ty didn't reply. As far as he was concerned, he'd just made his first actual choice since the words of fire had appeared in front of him. It was time to carve his own path.

All he had to do was survive the next few hours, and maybe he'd see the consequences for pissing off some gods.

Interlude One: Smite the Bastard

"**D**oes that little shit have any idea what he just did?" one god asked, peering around the gathering with a look of utter disgust on its face. "We should smite that bastard now and have done with it before he becomes a problem. The Wild does not belong in the hands of mortals."

Rumbles of agreement came from a few of the gods nearest the speaker.

A greater god, hovering above the congregation, spoke above the murmurs. "We agreed on the terms and bound ourselves to the Great Arbiter. Our implementation of the Resonance Bridge will destroy most of their world. There is no balance if we do not give them some semblance of opportunity and free will." The swirling pattern of light and dark that was the god's face modulated as it spoke.

Silence fell as the watching gods looked to the hexadecagon shape of the Great Arbiter, studying its swirling depths to track the progress of all fifty-four thousand of the surviving participants.

Some time later, once the ire of the first speaker had waned, one of the other gods piped up in a melodic voice, "I, for one, find it fascinating."

Several of the surrounding deities paused in their observations to look at the speaker. Most seemed unaffected by any of the recent pronouncements. A few, however, agreed with the sentiment.

As dire as things had become, at least they lived in interesting times.

Chapter 8: Execution

Time Until Quest Closure: 22 hours

     ATV Battery 1: 20%

ATV Battery 2: 94%

Cell Phone Battery: 80%

Ty laid out the notes with his plan. He'd diagramed every step, with the expected outcomes noted and variables underlined. Starting with the first note, he went through his kit. Aquamarine, perched in a distant tree, its sprite servants hovering invisibly all around, watched as he worked. He started with his rifles and guns, ensuring they were clean, loaded, and stowed away. Then he tightened his tactical armor and checked the six knives he had strapped to him. It didn't feel like enough.

If only he'd figured out a way to bring grenades.

He made good time on his way back toward the valley. Given how loud the demons were, and how uncoordinated the drones on the fringes had been yesterday, he didn't hesitate to drive the ATV within thirty yards of the valley rim. He turned the four-wheeler around before dismounting.

Ty scouted the immediate area, walking thirty feet in a circuit to minimize the chances of surprises. He had no illusions about being immune to ambush, but he also knew better than to not check. As expected, there were no fresh signs of demon spoor in the vicinity. Lacking the rabbit trails and easy egress points of the other side of the valley, the demons simply didn't bother with this one.

Security more-or-less assured, he retrieved one of his rifles. He left the case open on the back of the ATV. He'd need to be crazy fast securing them when he was on his way back.

Rifle in hand, he walked until he was near the break in the forest, then crouched and slowly crawled the last few feet.

Peeking over the edge of the valley rim, he saw no changes from the day before. When he pulled his goggles down and activated the magnification, he noted the hole near the center of the camp was deeper and wider. Tiny bits of a silver material reflected from some of the excavated chunks, but the demons were ignoring those and continuing their work. He guessed the demons must have clawed at the stone all night to have made that much progress.

It didn't matter what they were digging for or why. What mattered was that the general was still doing what he had been doing the previous day: sitting in the center of the camp. Ty had thought more about the setup of the camp during his trek back to his overlook and realized just how strategically significant it was. The banners offered magical protection, and anyone who wanted to interfere with the infestation would have had to literally fall down the valley edge or walk through a narrow rabbit trail to do so. This infestation could hold off a veritable army of equally capable soldiers. Plus, if they could teleport reinforcements in, who knew how substantial their force could become?

When Ty had been going over his options to progress his quest, he'd considered the more obvious one. He could have stalked around the valley and tried to kill one of the unenhanced drones while it was hunting. It *sounded* like a logical, safe plan until he'd really worked it through.

The "logical" plan fell apart unless the dice rolled in his favor multiple times. A thousand tiny variables could see him dead. What if another dog was nearby and spotted the kill? What if Ty made too much noise, or was injured in the process and couldn't get away? With the unfamiliar terrain, he didn't dare use his ATV in such an assault. That meant he'd have less mobility and speed than any of the demons.

He'd carefully analyzed his options and knew the plan he'd settled on was the best option. And since it was his best option, he was going to go big or go home.

It was secret achievement time.

He set up his rifle on a compact tripod, aiming it at the general's forehead. His semi-automatic rifle shot .308 bullets and had a 20-round magazine. The rounds were heavy, carried a ton of kick, and were among the most penetrating commercially available.

Ty reviewed his notes again before putting them away. He spent the next few minutes just breathing and finding his center. He imagined everything, all his thoughts and doubts, locked in a box inside his mind. He saw his objectives, felt how the rifle would kick, knew where each bullet would go. Focused calm settled over him, leaving only certainty.

Now Ty had to act.

When he assumed his position again, his head was in fight-space. His thoughts were slow and clear, his body tingling with excitement. The pieces on the board were before him, and he knew their movements and behaviors. All he had to do was execute.

He put his earplugs in. Tucking the rifle in place under his armpit, he took aim.

Finger on trigger, Ty released the safety.

He exhaled.

Ty squeezed twice, as fast as he could.

Blaam! Blaam!

Sound exploded. The rifle leaped back into his shoulder. The general's head flew back, a fountain of orange blood exploding into the air.

Without waiting to take in further details, he adjusted his aim, sweeping for a captain near the far side of the valley. Chaos was erupting everywhere, bodies milling in wild confusion, but he found the one he'd been looking for.

Exhale.

Squeeze.

The captain went down. Ty didn't think he'd hit the creature's gemstone, not from this range, but the rifle round had been enough to at least drop the thing.

Sighting up, he adjusted the aim directly above where the general had been. This was the tricky one, a shot further than anything he'd reliably hit before. Wails of outrage rose from below his position.

Exhale.

Squeeze once, twice.

Both bullets hit the banner just below the magical knot. He adjusted his aim and fired again. This time, he got it. Pivoting the tripod, he shot at the next banner. He hit that one and the next first shot. With one banner left, he stood up, aimed, and fired directly above his position. The knots of magical runes holding it up exploded into confetti. The banners wavered. As one, they began to flutter to the ground, the magical light they emitted flickering out.

Only then did Ty pause to look at the encampment.

The valley was in utter chaos. Dozens of demons milled around the beheaded general. Ty had accomplished that mission. In addition to the general, multiple captains and over a hundred of the drones were on the ground, seizing in place. He guessed they'd been sharing the general's intelligence when he had killed him. Maybe they'd all die. Maybe they'd just reboot in a minute. Either way, he *had* to go.

Ty sprinted for the ATV. Fumbling as he set the rifle into its case, he heard chittering screeches rocketing up in volume behind him. It sounded like they were coming nearer, climbing directly up the punishingly steep slope.

"Fuck me," he growled reflexively, slamming the first case down and smashing the rifle into the protective foam a bit too hard.

He got onto the ATV and started it up, cursing again as he looked down and realized that he'd forgotten to change the battery out. Twenty percent left. How had he overlooked that detail? He froze, unable to adapt to his plan going so awry. Thinking about his lists, and everything he'd planned, he cursed his lack of foresight. How could he have forgotten such a small, crucial detail?

The sounds of movement grew louder. Forcing himself to move despite his doubt and growing desperation, Ty drew one of his guns one-handed. Easing the ATV forward, he torqued his torso to aim behind.

A drone and one humanoid soldier demon crested the ridge at the same time. Ty shot them both, center mass. The soldier fell back down the slope, screeching as it fell on top of whatever was coming up behind it. The drone took the hit and kept coming.

Terror surged. None of the plans had accounted for the dogs being immune to his shots. Just how hard was their armor?

Reckless, Ty pushed the acceleration on the ATV one-handed. He fired again and again at the drone. His third shot hit it in the forehead gemstone and the thing went down. None of his other bullets had so much as drawn blood.

Terrified and relieved when no other demons immediately appeared, Ty whipped around. He was moments from driving directly into a tree. He jerked the steering wheel to the side and the ATV careened wildly, two of its tires leaving the ground.

Ty was going to fall. That was *definitely* not part of his plan.

Leaning the opposite direction of the grounded wheels, he strained with every ounce of muscle he had. Adrenaline pumping, he dropped his gun and used his free hand to grab the handles with both hands. Panting, nearly screaming in terror, he shoved, leaning and begging the ATV to right itself. For one dizzying, impossible moment, he knew it was going to flip. His mind flashed through what would happen when it did. He could see a half-dozen demons surrounding him, ripping through his body armor like cloth and...

He wiggled, adjusting his center of gravity slightly. That did it. The wheels came back down, hitting the loamy ground with a bouncing thud.

Chittering sounds grew louder, rapidly approaching his rear. Not looking back, Ty twisted the throttle all the way. The ATV only did seventeen miles per hour on a good road, and he was justifiably worried that he wouldn't make it. Driving through an open, straight shot toward his convoy, he glanced back again.

Dozens of the demons were following him, but they had fallen back considerably. They seemed slower than when he'd watched them in the valley. As he pulled further and further away, he saw several slow and look around, as if confused.

It was the captains adjusting their intellect, Ty guessed.

He wove around the trees, trying to break up their line of sight and approach his camp circuitously. A few miles later, he was sure that he'd lost the demons. His ATV was at three percent power when he finally stopped to take a breath.

Only when he was relatively confident that none of the demons would catch him did Ty let the emotions kick in. He went from calm, collected, mid-fight Krav Maga fighter to panicked young man in an instant. His breathing sped up; his body exploded in sweat. He felt tears of relief and terror running down his face as he re-lived every moment of what had just happened.

The plan had worked, up until it hadn't. Those demons were faster, more determined than he could have imagined, and the whole driving and shooting thing was something he couldn't have anticipated.

How did he plan for those sorts of eventualities? Just thinking about it made the panic worse. Adding to the emotional overload was the fact that he'd just killed sentient life. They were monsters, sure. But he'd *killed* them. And he'd almost died. There was no way, none, that he'd have thought he could make the shots he had at the end. Intellectually, he knew they'd been relatively easy. Both demons had been within thirty yards and moving in a straight line.

Logic didn't help. Taking the earplugs out, he said, "Holy shit," just to hear his own voice.

Still shaking, he replaced the battery on his ATV. Once he was ready, he spoke out loud, "Aquamarine, if you can hear or see me, would you have one of your sprites direct me back to camp? I'm, uh, lost."

A distant sprite lit up like a firefly, zipping through the woods to lead Ty back to camp. He followed gratefully. Relying on the sprite as a guide was one of the few eventualities he'd planned for, and the sense of being back on track soothed his frayed nerves.

Once he was back with his convoy, the Guide's voice spoke into his ear. "Congratulations, you've completed your first quest. When the time comes, you will be allowed to choose your god and we will assign you your Arbiter. Excellent work."

Aquamarine slithered into view and hissed something the Guide would not translate. Seeing Ty's confusion, the dragon hissed something else.

Finally, the Guide translated, but not in its fake-dragon accent. "You have little time before a dozen of the demons find this place. He will perform the blessing now and his sprite will lead you to safety."

Chapter 9: Recharge

Time Until Quest Closure: 20 hours

ATV Battery 1: 3%

ATV Battery 2: 74%

Cell Phone Battery: 79%

The Guide affected the English accent again as the dragon spoke. "This will take but a moment. Do not move."

Extending its torso until it towered over him, half the dragon's hands flourished at its own chest and the other at Ty. Scintillating blue-and-white light manifested between them, growing in intensity and color as the dragon gestured. The colors swirled as a green nimbus surrounded and infused them both.

It spoke again as the energy solidified into something tangible, like an emerald emblem hovering in the air. "There is no difference between a small touch of my power and a great one, not in terms of the consequences. Thus, because you have done the unexpected, shall I reward you."

The Guide fuzzed, becoming a solid ball of static. It didn't translate what the dragon said next. Just as Ty started to say he didn't understand, the dragon finished its ceremony.

A gentle breeze arose from the wood, pushing the symbol closer. It drifted over, enveloping him completely. Outside the bubble, the world turned shades of blue, white, and green. As when he'd first met Aquamarine, Ty felt a sense of peace and warmth settle through him. *This* was the adventure. This was the escape he'd longed for when he'd read his father's fantasy books. He might have gravitated towards darker, more mature content as he aged, but something about the presence and feeling of the dragon rekindled the spark of his hope and imagination.

Through the bubble of light, Ty saw spectral shadows peering at him through the static mass of the Guide.

The dragon's gift faded, and the Guide stabilized back to normality, the shapes within vanishing.

Ty glanced down at himself, flexing his arms and rolling his fingers. He looked around, studying his surroundings and the dragon. After a few moments, he said, "I don't feel any different."

"You won't," the Guide translated as if nothing had happened. "Only if you become attuned to the magic of the world will my touch become apparent to you. When that happens, well, you will see."

Even though Ty didn't physically feel different, the sense of awe and calm still lay heavy on him. Feeling a touch theatric, he folded his hands and bowed to the dragon. "Great Aquamarine, I bless you and yours. Thank you for this great and divine gift."

"You are strange," the dragon replied, amusement in the British accent.

Ty grinned buoyantly back at the creature.

"It is time to go, Ty. The hive is in disarray and may retreat until the Monster God assigns them a new general, but if they find your trail first, nothing will stop their hunt."

Still feeling the bubbly joy of the gift, Ty asked, "So what if I circle around in a couple of days to investigate their dig site? Could I maybe find something useful there?"

"Do not. Absolutely do not." Aquamarine's voice was a sharp rasp, the threat in its warning clear in the way it looked down at him. For the first time, Ty realized just how dangerous this being was. He'd glossed over the mouth full of sharp teeth or the talons tipping each of its fingers until now. In an instant, he knew that the dragon's pronouncement was not just a warning; it was a prohibition.

Ty took an involuntary step away from the towering monster, one hand unconsciously moving toward a gun.

Aquamarine held two rows of hands up, softening its tone. "Ty, it is not only that I do not want you to go to that place; it is incredibly dangerous. You have no magic. Though your weapons may be impressive, unless I miss my guess, there are physical limits to their power. Delving into the ancient ruins of our world, which I believe that place conceals a portal to, would be prohibitively dangerous to one with little magic. If an army of demons was planning to investigate it, you alone should not."

The dragon's softening tone eased his tension, though something about the implied threat had broken a bit of its glamor over him. Looking at Aquamarine now, he saw the hard-edged scales, the sharp edges, the hints of blood around the dragon's mouth. The dragon was a forest guardian, and it had given him what he asked for. That didn't change the fact that it was a predator.

For the first time, Ty wondered if the warning his Guide had tried to give him was more than the gods trying to get him to stay in his lane.

Ty said his goodbyes to the dragon a few moments later. Looking at the sprite Aquamarine had assigned him, Ty asked for it to take him to a safe place with water and sunlight. It immediately zipped off, and he throttled his ATV convoy after it without looking back. That last interaction with the dragon had done what killing the demons hadn't: it had shown him that things weren't as safe as they felt, no matter what he wanted. The reason the prophecy hadn't included Narnia had finally become clear.

The world Ty had entered might not be all grimdark, but that didn't mean it was bright and shiny.

* * *

It took several hours to find the clearing, mostly because the sprite wove a path of safety around roving demon patrols to get him there. Thankfully, according to the sprite, the demons gave up their chase halfway through the trek. For some reason, his Guide had decided to translate the sprite's voice into a high-pitched scream that absolutely destroyed his nerves. If he'd left the dragon feeling uneasy by the time they made it to the clearing, he was positively irate.

"We are here!" his Guide scream-translated as they burst into the clearing.

Rolling forward on the last of the battery's charge, Ty entered a glen that was about a hundred meters across. Bright sunlight speared down through the clear sky, momentarily blinding his dark-adjusted eyes before he saw the river flowing through the grassy center.

"Do you have to translate his voice like that?" he asked sourly as he pulled his convoy to a stop next to the river.

"It's how others of his species hear him," the Guide replied smugly.

"Seriously?" Ty shot back. Dismounting, he set to making camp. The first thing he did was retrieve his notes. This part he'd practiced and planned in advance. He knew the steps well enough to not need the checklist. Still, going through the list helped him focus and overcome the tension he felt growing between himself and his Guide.

The first thing he got out were his solar panels, which he connected in an array nearby. They were well-constructed for the price he'd paid, but he figured it would take at least a couple of days to recharge everything. He'd drained twenty of his rechargeable double-As, both of his ATV batteries, and a decent chunk of his cell phone since his arrival. As much as he didn't think staying in one place for multiple days was optimal, he also didn't want to find himself in a position where he needed his gear but couldn't use it.

He made a note to turn his phone off when he wasn't using it from now on. Airplane mode simply wasn't worth it in a place with so little sunlight to recharge it.

The Guide spoke up. "Absolutely, I must. Ty, I make the voices I apply to the natives to approximate what you would hear should you actually have the ability to speak with them. There are rules. I do not create them; I just enforce them."

Ty gestured in the sprite's direction. Now that he knew what to look for, it was easier to spot the miniscule discoloration in the air as the creature zipped about. "Does he have a name, at least? If he's going to be around for a while, I'd like to call him something more than the generic 'Guide' I keep calling you in my head."

"Guide is a perfectly acceptable name for me. And no, he doesn't have a name. He's not truly a distinct individual in the way that you think of them. In essence, 'he' is actually an extension of Aquamarine's guardian magic. In effect, he's more of a living construct than a sentient being."

Bending over to fish out his camping gear from one of the labeled crates, Ty blinked. "Huh. I guess that makes sense. Aquamarine said that it could see through their eyes. You all sure have a lot of things like that over here. Connected beings, I mean."

Once Ty had his gear out, he began setting up his tent a few meters from the river. As he did, he noted several animals peeking in at him from the forest. The animals in this world weren't that dissimilar to Earth's. Just in the short time he'd been putting his camp together, he noted a cluster of deer-looking things with four eyes, and wolves with multiple tails. None of the animals, despite the wolves clearly being predators, bothered him. He assumed that Aquamarine's protection remained in place. Despite his later trepidation toward the dragon, Ty felt gracious about its treatment.

"That's how magic works in our world. It connects things. Your world is dry and separate. Our world is not. Here, life evolved with magic. Not everything over here is a hive or part of a communal entity, but it is far more common than you might expect."

"That sounds wonderful," Ty said wistfully. "I wonder what would be different if humans could connect. Maybe there'd be less war and conflict."

The Guide made a snorting, dismissive sound. "We have humans, too, Ty. And they aren't that much different from your variety. Also, you're missing something important. Magic makes connections possible, but the laws of evolution, survival of the fittest, and conflict still apply here. Magic may be a near-infinite resource, but that does not mean other resources are."

"Can't you use magic to make things that are limited?" Ty asked, lifting one of the tent poles and setting it into place. It fitted snugly, easily, into the catch mechanism, and he moved to the next one.

"Sort of. Magic can create things, sure. It can alter mass and move it. It still takes effort from the consciousness manipulating it, however. In addition, creating something out of thin air requires an absolute understanding of that thing on a fundamental, nuclear level. Only gods and some truly mighty mortals can create *anything* out of magic."

"Sounds a bit like the idea of True Name magic or something similar in our fantasy literature."

"Indeed. The concept resonates here as well as on your world."

With the tent in place, Ty returned to the convoy to fetch his camp stove and one of his meal replacement kits. Gesturing at the water, he asked, "One second. Is this water safe for me to drink or should I boil it? If you'll tell me, that is."

"It's safe. Our water is purer, safer, and more invigorating than anything on your polluted planet."

Ty glanced at the space in the air where the Guide's voice appeared from. "Do I detect some disdain for my world?"

There was no reply.

Before he continued their conversation, Ty walked to the edge of the river. It was maybe ten feet across, with a fast-moving center. Silvery fish-shapes swam languidly along the banks, darting away when his shadow fell across them. Kneeling in the grass, he bent over and drew a handful of the water to his mouth. As promised, the water was cool, delicious, and refreshing. When he swallowed, he felt a tingle of pure energy jolt through his body, like he'd just had a cup of coffee.

"That tastes amazing," Ty said in wonder. "Is there magic in this?"

"There's magic in everything here, Ty. Everything. If you were going to go through a natural progression, you'd find that even you became infused with it over years."

For a while, Ty let the conversation rest. He had more questions, needed to know more about his circumstances, but he was tired. He hadn't slept well the day before, and fleeing demons had exhausted more than his body. Once he'd refilled his canteens and made a simple meal, he climbed into his tent and slept.

Chapter 10:
Important Choices

"I t is almost time," his Guide's voice whispered into his ear.

Peeling himself out of his sleeping bag, Ty sat up and glanced at his watch. He'd slept over twelve hours, and assuming his calculations were correct, it was just an hour or two after dawn. Soft light filtered through his tent as he bent over and scrubbed at his scalp. He felt itchy, dirty, and a little stiff. He also had one hell of a backache. Sleeping in his body armor might not have been the best idea, especially given that he was, at least in theory, quite safe where he was. He'd done it anyway, just to stay in the habit.

Once his thoughts had come into focus, Ty checked his notes. A few minutes into his review and adjustments, he heard movement nearby. Looking up, he saw a herd of three-tailed cats standing by the waterline, less than ten feet from his camp. He moved slowly, lowering his notepad to the ground and coming to his feet.

There were fifteen or sixteen of them. Each was around the size of a mountain lion but resembled a domesticated cat more than anything else. Their triple tails lashed and twined about as several glanced over at him. Their irises were X-shaped rather than the vertical slit he expected.

"Uh, good morning," Ty said cautiously. "I'd like to come get some water if I may? Morning coffee, you know? I'm on involuntary withdraw right now."

None of the cats spoke, nor did they move away. They didn't seem to see Ty as a threat, though, so he walked over. Based on their size, he figured a swipe from any of the cats would be devastating. They hadn't attacked him, and he was willing to put his faith in Aquamarine for this. Nothing had disturbed his sleep or the rest of his camp, after all.

The cats let him collect his water, watching him and blinking lazily the entire time. They left once the aroma of coffee began to waft away from his small fire.

"Not coffee drinkers?" Ty asked quizzically as he watched the pack trot off.

The Guide spoke in a dry voice, "Ty, our *water* is more invigorating than your coffee. Some natives here might find uses for it, but it won't be the miracle elixir you people seem to think."

Shaking his head in mild disdain, Ty sipped his coffee. It was incredible. Even without milk or creamer, the native water added a smooth sweetness to the grounds that left him feeling refreshed and energized. "Just wait until your people try the water *with* my coffee, friend."

"Ty, there only a couple of hours before the quest completes. If you have questions for me, now is the time to ask them. Once you choose your god, I will return to my duties elsewhere."

"Is that your sense of balance and fairness prompting you to remind me?" he asked. His Guide had become more communicative, and he wanted to know why. Was it offering him help because it had "grown" a personality, or was there an agenda behind it?

"Balance, yes. Three gods took active involvement to prevent me from performing some of my duties, so I may compensate. That means volunteering more information than I otherwise would."

Ty remembered the times the Guide had glitched or failed to translate something Aquamarine said. Looking around the scenic clearing, he composed his thoughts. If the Guide was prompting him, he figured it must be a big deal.

"I thought you said the gods couldn't interfere in this game, or whatever it is?"

"The gods who first benefit from the Resonance must abide by its rules. Those rules include a prohibition against direct intervention. Technically, exerting authority of a Guide does not go against the rules. We are unaffiliated Arbiters, simple mediators. When you become a scion and gain an Arbiter, only your god will be able to exert any direct influence on you. Even that will have some limitations. Balance values free will. It will only be stripped if you deliberately give it away."

Ty absorbed that information, making notes. Thinking through what he knew, he took his time before asking, "Why am I here? What's at stake?"

"You are here because you fit a specific profile that was built to identify people who could psychologically and physically handle the challenges ahead. You were one of a few hundred thousand people who had the necessary background to understand the shorthand, were potentially fit enough, and were in the right age range."

Ty nodded. "Makes sense. A sixty-year-old grandmother who had no familiarity with the concepts of magic or portals might take quite a while to convince any of this is real, let alone get anything done. It sounds *fairer* this way."

"Precisely," his Guide replied crisply, with no hint of sarcasm.

"And the stakes?" Ty prompted.

The air fuzzed in front of him, materializing into a nearly transparent image of a solar system. It wasn't his solar system, but it was close. The central planet was Earth-like, only the continents were rearranged. Two moons orbited the planet, one gray and one yellow. In the distance, away from the solar system's sun, was a black patch. "This is our doom," his Guide explained, highlighting the blackness in a ring of blue. "In approximately eleven years, our world will be destroyed. Every person, every living thing, and every god will be devoured. Nothing we can do will stop it."

Ty tried to get a grasp of what the black spot was. To his vantage, through the shallow projection, it looked like a black hole. "And this is where the Resonance Bridge comes in?" he guessed.

"Precisely. The Resonance Bridge will allow the gods to send people and matter to your world. The process will cost them vast amounts of energy, even potentially kill them, if they do not prepare appropriately."

"Okay, and where do the people you've brought over here fit in?"

"You will help the gods build anchors into your world. The magic you grow here, through the help of the Arbiters, will allow your selected god to create an anchor point in your world each time you return there. Depending on how much magic you absorb and how connected you are to the god you select, the anchor may be larger or smaller. It is through this anchor that the gods will begin moving pieces of our world to yours once the Bride is ready."

Ty's already-sinking feeling grew until he felt vaguely sick. "What will happen to the people on my world?"

"It is most energy efficient to swap people for people and places for places, Ty. Any people and locations that someone like you has not claimed will be subject to the exchange. A modest percentage of our people and cities will survive. In exchange, a relatively smaller amount of your eight billion people will sacrifice their lives to save our way of life. We will also bring magic and the gods across the Bridge. This will objectively improve your world. For the first time, many of your world's most devout faiths will get to interact with their gods in the flesh. No doubt, there will be much rejoicing."

There it was: the gut punch. Thinking of a fight as a board game was one thing; this was on a different scale. "People for people and places for places? You mean you can't swap a person from your world with, say, an animal on mine? Or move one of your cities into barren farmland or something?"

"That is not an energy-efficient choice, unfortunately. The nature of magic requires as close to a like-for-like exchange as possible, otherwise the effort severely drains the gods. Simply bringing you and your fellow participants over cost the gods enough power to transport nearly a quarter million of our people. In effect, they sacrificed tens of thousands of lives on this side of the bridge just so you could have this opportunity."

"Wait, why should I participate at all? Why should any of us? It sounds like all we have to do is nothing, and the Bridge won't form. We'll save more lives by just staying still."

"On the contrary. If you do nothing, the exchanges will still happen, only with significantly greater cost. More people will die if you do not act than if you do."

Ty's mind spun. This was far, far more nuanced than he'd been expecting. No wonder *Heroes Die* had been in the prophecy. There *was* an element of the post-apocalyptic. Only his role made him both the agent of destruction and the preserver. What made things worse was the fact that even if he *somehow* stopped the process or interfered with it, the people on *this* world would die.

Not that he had any illusions about stopping anything.

"This fucking sucks," he muttered, tasting bile in the back of his mouth. He wanted to be sick. How could he possibly plan a way out of this? No amount of notes could solve a problem the gods couldn't fix. The situation would have been so much simpler if he were *only* here to save a world or stop an evil monster or something.

"For all of us," his Guide replied in the same tone.

A sense of helplessness and dread burned at Ty's core as he thought of what would happen next. He'd be the one choosing who lived and died on his world. One of the people choosing, he amended, not that it made the thought any easier. "What am I going to do?" he said. "What can I do? How do I save as much as I can?"

"Prove yourself," the Guide said without hesitation. "Play the game. Do not die. Earn the magic that will make you more powerful, then use that power to save your loved ones and your home. We weren't misleading you, Ty. The stronger the anchor you become, the closer you are tied to your god, the more lives will be preserved. On both sides."

Ty tried following the logic of the situation. "Why not just blast people full of magic and send them back to Earth? Why go through quests and trials at all?"

"Pushing magic into a person isn't as simple as calling it 'leveling up' would seem. Your actions in the name of your god will cause you to resonate with that god. The greater your resonance with the god, just like the resonance across worlds, the more efficient the transfer. Scholars on this side call it invasion, but you should think of it as investiture, since that term is closer to how you would understand it. Over time, the more you work with your divinely inspired Arbiter to empower that connection to your god, energy transfers will become increasingly potent. If a god tried to slam magic into someone from your world without acts of devotion and faith, it would kill the person. It would also be a staggeringly inefficient transfer of energy."

"No wonder the gods are so involved."

"Indeed."

Straightening his shoulders, Ty used his notes to center his thinking. He jotted ideas down, read his earlier plans, and just breathed through it all. There were players and miniatures in this game, and he couldn't afford to be a miniature. He had to play the game. More than that, he had to play well.

Once his mind was clearer, he got back on track. "Alright, I understand now. The god I pick is going to be a big deal. You've said that it'll function like a Game Master for me. What are you then? Don't you work for some god?"

"I'm a one of three types of Arbiters. For this discussion, consider me a neutral third party, with ties to the god of Technology. Your Arbiter will be bound to your soul and connect you directly to your god."

"Wait, it will be bound to my soul?"

"Technically, your Soul Cage. That is the metaphysical structure the true 'essence' of what you are resides within, but yes. Once bound to your soul through your willing acceptance, your Arbiter will become your personal Game Master. It will exert local Sovereign authority over you and you alone. With it, your god can imbue you with new abilities, enhance your body, and so on. It becomes a direct conduit for divine power. Without it, you will not be able to advance quickly enough to participate in the Resonance."

Ty blinked, for the first time feeling the scope of what "being given an Arbiter," meant. "Did you just say God of Technology? What gods are there? What do they do? What influence will me selecting one have besides setting up resonance?"

The air fuzzed, and the Guide appeared. Its multihued fractal shape pulsed and swirled at his eyeline. Each of his questions appeared within it in blocky text. The first question sharpened while the others fuzzed.

"Yes. Originally, my maker was the God of Artifice. Once the Bridge was complete and it began expanding into your world, it became the God of Technology. You might think of it as a divine AI at this point if it helps."

The first question blurred, and the second came into focus. "The list of gods you will be offered are as follows. From the greater pantheon, there is Balance,

Magic, and Technology. I do not recommend selecting my creator, however, as it is quite busy on your world. From the mortal pantheon, there are Order, Chaos, Life, Death, Nature, Time, War, Crafts, Arts, Shadows, Inspiration, Monsters, and Celestia. I will note that there are dozens of subcategories of each god, but they are not included in this list. Lesser gods, who lack the Salient power to invest in the Resonance are allowed limited participation for now."

A swirling motion erased all of Ty's questions. "In order to build resonance, the god will become linked to you. By becoming its paladin, you will receive divine benefits, insight, and guidance on a limited basis. You should not expect miracles from your god; it will already be expending a significant amount of divine power simply to afford you this opportunity. As you might expect from becoming a representative of a god, that connection will touch everything you do from now on. Any race you transform into, any powers you gain, and any quests you are given will be adjusted to enhance that connection. There is more, as well. But I think this should get the point across in every meaningful way: think of your Arbiter as your personal Game Master with the attitude of your selected god."

"That's... a lot," Ty said.

"Indeed."

"These gods interfered with you earlier," he said a few seconds later. "Does that mean they may not like me?" The thought of a belligerent or malicious Game Master was, frankly, terrifying.

"Most are neutral on the matter. A few lean that direction, yes. On the other hand, your precociousness has endeared you to some as well. I may not steer your decision in this matter, so I cannot say more about their disposition."

Taken with his last feelings about Aquamarine, Ty felt himself second-guessing his decisions with the dragon. "Can you tell me a bit about the gods in general? Like, their dispositions or abilities?"

"Absolutely. Those are common knowledge."

Ty made the time to get a summary of each of the gods but paused on a few in particular.

"Can you go over the God of Magic?" he asked after learning about Balance.

"Magic is what you'd expect, as much a force of nature with a consciousness as anything else. Like all the Greater Pantheon, the God of Magic is as much an abstract concept as a deity. Any quests you take from it will probably be aimed at uncovering lost artifacts or helping those performing research. Worshipping this god will give you deep insights and access to power sets you'd associate with Mage-type classes. If you changed your race, you would have access to some of the most powerful variations on the planet."

"Hold on for a second. Tell me a bit about changing my race. How does that work?" In most of the books Ty had read, the protagonists hadn't changed their race. At least, in theory, he could understand anyone's hesitation to become something else. If a new race would help adapt to this world and save lives, it was something he felt compelled to consider.

Plus, every new data point on his list would help him avoid future mishaps.

"Your Arbiter can help you adjust your race once, depending on what your god allows. The only requirements are that you must have seen and touched the race you wish to become and your god must spend the additional resources to make the transformation happen. It is important to note that there is a greater cost for races with innate magic. Once you've selected your god, this will be a discussion to have with them."

Ty nodded but was unwilling to move on yet. "Does this world have a, uh, 'Primal' type race?"

"Primal?"

"You know," he said, gesturing with a rolling-hand motion. "A perfected human being, one with like, uh, no limits as to how powerful it can become?"

The Guide's fractal form flickered out of view briefly. "Ah, yes. I get the reference now. No, we do not have such a thing. The closest race to that would probably be a Divine Scion. Those are the physical offspring of gods and mortals. I should note that you, along with any natives to our world with a connection to a god, are often called scions. When you meet other Earthlings on this planet, they will be scions like you. There is a difference between a Divine Scion and an everyday scion. One is born from a god, one has a connection to one. The bond of Divine Scion runs deep and creates an unbreakable bond that may be used against the god. This is why such a thing is quite rare."

Ty shrugged away the additional information. He didn't care if he was called a scion or a "player" or whatever. "Gotcha. Yeah. Anyway, Divine Scion. *That* sounds promising."

"You're getting ahead of yourself. Focus on your god selection, then discuss any race options with it. It's highly unlikely that *any* of the gods will do what is required to make you into one of their own children."

"Gotcha, okay. Back to the god list. Um, what about Time? Is there time travel?"

"No, no time travel. Speeding up, slowing down, yes. The God of Time is as much about perception as it is reality. Still, it could be quite a valuable patron. If you can get over all the clock-centric things it will probably have you do. It might give you access to temporal magic and skills, which are among the most potent in the world."

"Got it. What about Inspiration? Does the name imply creativity or something else? If I align with that deity, am I going to get a lute and sing or something?"

"Hardly. Inspiration is the god of doing things in new ways, of creative innovation in all things, and ambition. Think about the person on your world who creates new code to solve a problem or a chess grandmaster who impulsively tries a new move during a big event. Those people were inspired. Not that inspiration *always* leads to success. It's just a source of thinking outside the box."

"Like I did with Aquamarine?" Ty asked, feeling a surge of hope.

"Yes. Inspiration would love you for doing something like that if it hadn't been with a *dragon*. Inspiration is a strictly *mortal* god, and dragons fall outside of its domain."

"Okay, well, if Inspiration might not be on my side, what about the gods of Monsters and Celestials? Surely the God of Monsters is on the side of dragons, right?"

"Not even close," the Guide replied. "Remember, these are gods created through the faith and belief of mortals. The God of Monsters is basically a combination of the Christian version of Lucifer mixed with the Greek goddess Echidna. It taints, corrupts, and warps life into monstrous forms. It would be an incredibly powerful ally. The same holds true for Celestia, though on the opposite side of the spectrum. Think more avenging, law-enforcers. Or maybe even traditional Paladin-archetypes from your tabletop games."

Ty spent an hour asking more questions, trying to get a feel for each of the gods. In the end, his list of pros and cons was long for each of them. One stood out above the rest, though.

After a little waiting, his Guide manifested once more as a matrix of flashing light, intoning, "It is time."

A three-foot-tall crystal in the shape of a truncated octahedron appeared in the middle of the clearing. Resembling an eight-sided dice made of metal and glass, it floated over until it was within reach. Ty looked at it, seeing nothing particularly illuminating about the unadorned construct.

Ty's Guide announced, "Touch your Arbiter and announce your selection. After that, your real quests will begin. It has been... interesting acting as your guide, Ty."

Ty reached out and touched the glass. It was both smooth and immutably solid, like touching polished steel. At the contact, text appeared within the closest pane of glass. It listed each god, and by each god was a number. The numbers for the greater gods started at ten thousand. The numbers for the other gods began at a thousand. In a flash, each of the columns dropped by *hundreds*. The God of Magic's number dropped below five thousand before Ty even had a chance to speak.

His Guide explained, "Each god gets a certain maximum number of followers, based on the divine energy they have at their disposal. Announce your intention quickly if you don't wish to be forced into a sub-optimal selection."

"I choose..."

Chapter 11: Character

"Inspiration."

His Guide split, half of the light vanishing as the other half merged with the Arbiter. Where it had touched the Arbiter, the crystal took on a hint of the fractal coloration. As if the Guide's power were the spark to dry tinder, a fresh light pulsed to life within the new shape. Silver and magenta hues pulsed in place, rapidly spreading into frost-like matrices. A tendril of the light lashed out, colliding with Ty's chest.

Ty felt something push into his mind. It was like a crystal-clear memory, one that burned so brightly that it had a tangible presence in his mental space. In his mind's eye, it was a perfect replica of the Arbiter. A message appeared on a facet of the Arbiter, the intent of the text transmitted instantaneously.

Congratulations! *You are bonded to an Arbiter. This has created a divine "mind-space" inside you. This "mind-space" is an intimate, unique place where only you and your Arbiter can communicate. As you will note, prompts and other key information will display on the mental duplicate of your Arbiter. Communication in this space is private, and no being other than your god may intercept it. You should be aware that during the Resonance, your god will not directly talk to you, as it is bound to the Resonance Pact. If you should, for any reason, lose your Arbiter, this space will remain and function as the connection point for a new god or Arbiter. Enjoy your upgrade; you are now a scion of Inspiration.*

As the bond between Ty and the Arbiter solidified, a tendril of green-tinted, oily light brushed across the bridge, adding a splash of new color to both the physical Arbiter and the one in his mind. The aroma of chicken soup briefly tickled Ty's senses before vanishing, along with the discoloration.

"Welcome, Ty. I am your personal Arbiter. Are you ready to discuss your state in our world?" The Arbiter's voice was almost identical to that of the Guide, only more human. The Guide's tones had been mechanical, tinted with subtle emotion. Now, it sounded like a person with a hint of wry humor.

"Absolutely not," Ty said, still touching the glass surface. "I refuse to call you Arbiter. Please tell me I can give you a name before we proceed."

The Arbiter made a raspy, chuckling sound. "Absolutely. In fact, I prefer it. Tell me, Ty, what name would you give your personal Arbiter?"

Ty briefly considered naming it Game Master, just to be ironic. Then he thought better of it. "I'm going to call you Hagemi."

"Hagemi. That is a beautiful Japanese word, Ty. Encouragement, but also inspiration. I think that will fit our relationship nicely. You may call me Hagemi. Now, would you like to discuss your state?"

Ty lowered his hand, sensing that his connection with Hagemi would remain regardless of physical contact. "Sure. Am I going to get my character sheet now?"

"If you'd like. Once we determine how you would like your magical state to function in our world, it will shape how you get, mature, and train your abilities from now on. One way is through a character sheet, complete with attribute breakdowns, points, all of it. The other is more abstract."

He was certain that he was going to go for the character sheet option, mostly because it sounded like the simpler choice, but he was curious enough to ask. "Okay, I'll bite. Tell me about the abstract way?"

The Arbiter pulsed, flashing scenes from several popular science fiction movies. "I can, in essence, put you into a magical coma. Inside the coma, you will receive training as though you were a native of this world. The duration of the coma will be two hours per the new level. When you wake, it will be as though you had really trained under a practitioner of whatever skill or ability you wanted to learn."

"That sounds kind of amazing," Ty said, leaning into that option immediately. "Why would anyone not choose that, other than the downtime?"

"Variation and nuance versus hyper-specialization," Hagemi responded. "With the character sheet method, when you gain a skill or ability, you learn it in its most pure, perfect, and reusable form. Over time, you may innovate or learn the elements that make the trait function, may slowly bend it to meet new needs, but mostly, it will be a tool in your toolkit, always reliable and the same. With the training method, there are all the nuances and downsides that come from being someone's pupil. You would discover that thinking outside of the box and trying new things is easier, but you will also find standardization is far more difficult."

"So, if I learn, say, a spell on my character sheet, I'll always be able to cast it, but if I learn it the other way, I might make mistakes?"

Both the physical Arbiter and the representation floating in the back of Ty's mind pulsed in silver hues. The presence in his mind also gave him a vague sense of approval. "Mistakes or oddities, especially with spells. Until you have actually, in real life, cast that spell several hundred times, there will be a degree of flexibility with it, for better and worse. Spells are hard here, Ty. They take years to learn and require great comprehension. The same applies to magical abilities. Just because you've had the training won't make you a master in real-world scenarios any more than training in a classroom made you ready to take on a functional job. You'll get the fundamentals, sure, and will be able to cast the spell, but that is it. With the character sheet, you lose flexibility but gain certainty. With training, you gain flexibility but lose certainty. In a way, the character sheet option will strengthen you in the short term and require more effort to be as effective in the long term, especially if you try to diversify."

Ty knew himself. He knew what he needed right now was familiarity and comfort. He couldn't manage a thousand variables; he needed real, concrete abilities he could plan for. As much as part of him wished he had the flexibility to just go with the flow and master true nuance, there was only one choice for him.

"Yeah, I need help now. Concrete, real help. I'm already fumbling around and I've barely been here a couple of days. Let's go with the character sheet option."

Another wave of light flashed through the Arbiter. Ty felt the wave echoed inside his mind, as if his choice had affected his connection to the Arbiter and the Arbiter itself. A character sheet appeared on one glass facet.

Name: Ty Monroe

Class: N\A

Race: Human

Attributes

Health Shield: None

Mana Shield: None (Racial Maximum: 30)

Hit Points: 8

Strength: 9 (Average)

Agility: 9 (Average)

Vitality: 8 (Average)

Intellect: 11 (Above Average)

Spirit: 2 (Wild-attuned)

Luck: 0

Applicable Skills and Abilities

Mixed Martial Arts (Sambo Focus): Proficient

Krav Maga: High-Adept

Edged Weapons: Skilled

Bows: Proficient

Guns: Adept

Survival: Adept

Meditation: Proficient

Customizations

Unassigned Attribute Points: 0

Unspent Merits: 7

Achievements

Wild Touched: *You have been touched by the evolving, disruptive, and inhuman magic of a dragon. This has tainted your Soul Cage and altered the course of your evolution. You have a +2 bonus to your Spirit attribute.*

Quests: None.

Ty read the information over a couple of times before he asked, "I know Hit Points, but what's the Mana Shield and why is it none?"

"A mana shield is something any living being with mana possesses. Each may be unique; for example, some races have incredibly potent mana shields. In most cases, a mana shield will be equal to half an entity's mana, with a racial maximum. Most non-magic users will have small mana shields. They won't have the Spirit or Intelligence to generate one. You have zero, hence, no mana shield."

"And what does it do? It sounds like it protects my mana?"

"Not exactly. It surrounds beings that possess mana and acts to preserve their life both passively and actively. Simply having a lot of mana will extend your life and help you overcome most common diseases and illnesses. When you're injured, your mana shield will activate to protect you in the inverse of the damage you've taken. The lower your health, the more damage it will mitigate."

"What you're saying is, high-mana targets need to get hit hard, fast."

"Usually a good idea in most cases, I would think. In addition, be aware that your mana shield replenishes at around the same rate as your natural mana. I would not recommend relying on it in every combat."

Ty considered the general demon and wondered briefly what would have happened if his first shots hadn't killed it. Would its mana shield have come into play, wrecking his plans?

"Okay, moving on. What's the Spirit attribute?"

"It represents your ability to resonate with magical beings, such as gods. The higher this is, the tighter your bond with Inspiration will become. That it has a Wild aspect introduces a certain... unfortunate element to the connection. On the bright side, the benefit is that you will begin with a more intimate connection with me and your god than others from your world who do not have it. It will make working with me more intuitive for you."

Ty still wasn't sure if Aquamarine's blessing was a good thing. "Wait, you said you and my god, like you're two separate things. I thought you were my connection to Inspiration?"

"I am your Arbiter, a neutral interface between you and the divine magic of your selected god. I also operate in its favor. You could say that I am Inspiration's spiritual representative to you, but I am not Inspiration."

"Gotcha. I think I understand everything else but Luck, what does that do?"

"Luck determines how much otherworldly beings can influence the odds in a person's favor. The higher your luck, the more a god can act on your behalf. A two in your luck attribute could, for example, allow your god to make a trap trigger with *slightly* more pressure than normal, preventing it from going off when you step on it. The higher your score, the more often you are eligible to receive such help and the more overt that help can be."

"You didn't say Luck is limited to just my god. I'm assuming anything with sufficient power qualifies. And this is *only* beneficial? If I get my luck score up, no one is going to reach out and stack the odds against me?"

"Your first statement is correct. Anything with sufficient power could use its abilities to influence events in your favor. The only way Luck can be used against you is through a proxy who also has a Luck attribute. Situations like that are avoided, however, as they gave rise to the War of Scions thousands of years ago. It was-" Hagemi hesitated a beat before continuing, "-not a pleasant time. Gods died. Continuity of intellect was broken for many of them. Tens of thousands of people also lost their lives.

A wave of pain came from the Arbiter. For a second, Ty thought he could see something, almost like a memory of a forgotten dream, a hint of the horror the Arbiter might have observed. The not-dream vanished as soon as it had come, leaving him with a sense of unease.

Taking a beat to calm himself, Ty looked around his camp clearing. He hadn't noticed until now, but dozens of animals had gathered around the outskirts of the forest. A cluster of the big cats watched lazily next to the two-tailed wolves. Several scaled tri-horned horses covered in opalescent fur met his gaze. They had big, liquid, blue-green eyes.

"The guardian of this forest has taken quite the interest in you," Hagemi said.

"They are beautiful, all of them. You all gave me prophesies about coming here, and pretty much all of them were dark and dour. I see these things, dragons and unicorns and big cats, and I *know* there is true beauty in your world. It gives me something to aspire to, instead of becoming a monster."

"Beautiful sentiment, and ambitious. Your god is pleased. Pleased, yet confused."

Something in Hagemi's tone made Ty turn back to look at the floating crystal. It was gone, replaced by a slender, androgenous human. He thought the figure looked slightly more masculine, though he doubted it mattered.

It was Inspiration.

The god wore a double-breasted business suit. As Ty studied the material, which at first seemed just like cloth, he could see his every wish, his every fantasy, reflected in the patterns. It was dazzling and disturbing all at once.

"I'm not Inspiration. I'm a splinter of him, his avatar, if you will." Inspiration spoke with a rich, almost theatrical accent, drawing Ty's attention to the figure's face. His features were refined, elegant, and beautiful. There were traces of entrancing femininity in the sweep of Inspiration's generous mouth, and there was equally profound masculinity around his jawline. His shoulder-length hair was a gentle shade of magenta that was almost, but not quite, red. Though Inspiration had used the masculine pronoun, Ty was certain this being could be whatever gender it wanted.

"I'm surprised to see you here in person," Ty said. He still felt the Arbiter in his mind. When he thought about it, he could sort of see the crystal through the god's avatar, as if it were just some sort of projection.

"This will be the only time you see this version of me for a while, Ty. I thought it was important for us to meet, face to face, before you begin your journey. You know, to set the tone of our relationship." Inspiration gestured as he spoke, elegant fingers dancing expansively, adding nuance and meaning to his words in a way Ty grasped instantly. A band of silver similar to the ore he'd seen from the excavation site glinted on the god's hand.

"You said you were confused a second ago. Why is that?"

Inspiration pointed to the ever-present pen tucked into Ty's armor. "Nothing you do is impulsive, Ty. Your fundamental nature is to plan, to plot, and organize. I would think that aligning with me would be antithetical to your objectives."

Quirking a wry grin, Ty replied, "I learned a really important lesson years ago, when I first started trying to 'win' at tabletop roleplaying games."

"Yes?"

"If you want to change the landscape, you don't learn the world or all the rules. Oh, those matter. But in the end, it's the Game Master you have to understand if you want to accomplish anything." His hand slid down, brushing across his thigh, above the phrase *Play the Players, Not the Game*. "I picked you because I know you're the most-likely god willing to help me break the mold."

Inspiration's grin was positively luminous. "Excellent observation. Dangerous, but excellent."

Ty looked over at the animals. "I thought you were a human god. Why does my appreciation of the animals appeal to you?"

"Ty, look at me."

Looking back at Inspiration, into the avatar's eyes, Ty felt himself awakening. Creativity bubbled in the back of his mind, along with ambition. He suddenly *wanted* to exceed every gods' expectations, to do the unthinkable. They said people had to die during the Resonance? Well, he would find a way around that. Anything was possible. He could do anything. Who needed plans or notes? With Inspiration, he could unfetter his imagination and...

"That's enough," Inspiration said, and Ty felt the rush of sensations ebb. "There is not much difference between inspiration and ambition. There is not much difference between inspiration and creativity or any number of other things. What inspires men, Ty? Emotion. Anger, lust, desire, greed. Sure, the dark emotions drive men to innovate, and they inspire spontaneous explosions of expression. But such things are short-lived, pyrrhic devotions. Love can withstand the test of time, giving rise to a thousand new creations. Awe, perhaps even mor e so."

The god took one gliding step toward him and reached out, touching Ty's hand. The god's touch felt soft and warm. It wasn't overly intimate, and yet somehow it was. For the first time in his entire life, he felt *seen*. Inspiration understood him. The god was inside his mind, saw his thoughts, and genuinely *appreciated* who he was and who he aspired to be. A sense of connection and awe rocked through his being. He felt on the verge of falling to his knees and willingly, completely, devoting himself to this being.

Inspiration took his hand away. The intensity once again fled, leaving behind a memory of all Ty had felt. He reached up, finding his cheeks wet.

Speaking in a gentle, kindly voice, Inspiration said, "I love that you find beauty in my world, Ty. I love that it gives you meaning and purpose, that it motivates and inspires you. I wish you hadn't asked a dragon to taint your soul, but if I must take the bad with the good, I will."

Ty chuckled despite himself. "All right. Fair enough. I take it you weren't one of the gods who disliked me?"

Inspiration shook his head. Ty noticed for the first time that tips of the god's hair faded into the air, as if constantly vanishing into some distance. "I neither disliked nor liked you, Ty. Your actions so far have been balanced, if bland and overly planned. The corruption of your essence is a profound difficulty to me, perhaps even more so than it would have been to others of my kind. Yet your genuine appreciation for my world and your desire to try new things, those are traits I am proud to have in a follower. Now, before we spend too much more time, shall we discuss your class and merits?"

"Of course," Ty said. "I'm excited to see what kinds of classes are available through you."

Inspiration shot him an almost predatory grin. "For you, Ty, there is only one."

"One? What? Just one class?"

Inspiration lifted a single, lovely finger. "Just one, Ty. Your class is called a 'Merit Hunter,' and your progression will be milestone based."

"Uh, what? That doesn't sound at all like 'Ultra Ninja Mage Assassin' or, well, you know, anything cool." Ty frowned, wondering just what his god was thinking. What had happened to his choices? He had *lists* of possible classes, each derived from a dozen literary sources. None of them had been called Merit Hunter. And milestone-based leveling?

Milestone-based leveling was *objectively* the worst. It meant he wouldn't get experience from normal acts, like killing monsters or whatever. Being on a milestone path would slow his progression down dramatically.

Gesturing with two hands, Inspiration summoned Ty's character sheet between them. He pointed at the merits. "This path is the only way I can give you *discretionary* powers or abilities, Ty. Let's say you wanted a typical class. In this example, we'll say you picked mage. Because you're using this," Inspiration gestured at the character sheet window in the air, "you'd start with three spells, a couple class-specific abilities and skills, and after that get one new spell every couple of levels. Or you'd have the option to upgrade one to a more potent version. That would be basically all of it. Sure, you'd get a merit point or two for customization every so often, but otherwise you'd be largely fixed in stone. Yeah, you might level faster, but how innovative does this sound? How much room to 'break the game' does that give you?"

Ty pursed his lips thoughtfully. The god's explanation reminded him of, well, essentially every tabletop or computer roleplaying game he'd ever played. There was always a carefully orchestrated path to climb, with specific abilities unlocked along the way.

"Well, not innovative at all, I guess. Unless you use the merits to add a ton of flexibility to the systems, it becomes kind of all about optimizing your path. Choice becomes an illusion, especially in a situation like this."

The Avatar smiled, and Ty's emotions surged. Having his god approve of him was better than two shots of whiskey followed by a latte.

"Choice becomes an illusion," Inspiration agreed. "Instead of a class, you will receive three merits every other level, starting with level one. In addition, when you perform in a way that resonates with my nature, I will reward you with up to three merits each time you level." He tapped at the seven next to Ty's unspent merits. "You're level zero and get three merits just for getting this far. As a special starting reward, I gave you four more. Can you guess why?"

"Was it because I took out the general and got away?"

"Close, but no. If you had selected the god of war, or death, or several of the others, the answer would have been yes. But with me? No. The answer is the banners. By allowing your intuition to guide you and taking those banners down, you ensured your survival as much, if not more than, the general. Taking those banners down wasn't something you *had* to do. It also wasn't part of some plan to maximize your perceived benefits from killing a 'boss monster.' It did, however, shut down the demon's ability to funnel troops in and out of the area. You affected the entire forest in a way that will long outlast the death of one general."

Everything Ty thought he knew about how he should operate in this new world turned upside down in an instant. Gone were thoughts of finding creative and new ways to kill the hardest thing possible or risking his life in increasingly death-defying ways to get a new achievement. By selecting Inspiration as a god, Ty had changed how he had to look at how he approached *life*.

Inspiration grinned at him in an oddly smarmy, youthful way.

Exhaling a long-suffering sigh, Ty said, "Okay, fine. Merits. What can I do with merits? You said they could be used to customize class abilities, right? What do I do without class abilities to customize?"

"As a core class ability, merits will give you the ability to mimic *any* ability you want. You can even create custom ones. The only drawback is they will cost you more. Three merit points will grant you the benefits of a slightly below-par base class ability. Four will put it on-par. Once you're ready, you can even talk with your Arbiter about designing new ones that cost more, so you'll have incentive to save up."

"And innovate?" Ty prompted.

"And innovate, but also plan, which I think will appeal to your sensibilities."

Ty had to admit that the planning angle made him feel a lot better about his choice. "Okay. I'll think about my merits. But what about quests and milestones? Will you assign them to me?"

Inspiration gave him another grin. "Milestones will come as I deem them appropriate. As for quests, I want you to choose your destiny. Tell your Arbiter something you want, some goal, or just go explore the world. Find things you believe are inspirational and do them. Hagemi will generate quests and rewards for you based on what you uncover. Obviously, you'll want to do things that a re *interesting* and challenge you, but I will not hold your hand. I don't have any agenda, Ty. Once you tell Hagemi, it will plot you a course to achieve that thing, and it will function *like* a series of quests. As you move along the path of that quest, it will assign you reward milestones. Impress me and achievements will follow."

"That's a lot more choice than I expected to have in this," Ty said. He felt absolutely, completely, certain that literally *any* of the other gods would have given him tangible, structured quests and goals. Now he, who knew nothing about the world he was in, was going to have to find a way to carve purpose out of thin air.

In many ways, this was the worst outcome. His class was nebulous. His abilities were equally so. Any structure he wanted, any clear objectives, were gone. Ty had to manufacture the variables.

He was simultaneously thrilled and terrified.

What had been an angelic smile became positively feral, splitting his god's face nearly in two. "I think that's enough. You have your class and your points. When you're ready, discuss them with Hagemi. He will be fair and creative with you, I assure you. I'm limited to one meeting every ten levels for now, so don't expect to see me again anytime soon."

Ty held up a hand. "Wait, I have one more question?"

Inspiration raised an inquisitive eyebrow.

"How do I become a Divine Scion of you? I don't think I want to stay human."

The avatar of his god froze in place, going as still as a statue. Then he laughed. He laughed long and loud, so loud that it felt like it would shake the ground. When he was done, Inspiration reached up and casually wiped tears from his eyes. "You don't aim low, do you?" he asked, still chuckling. "I tell you what, Ty, I'll make you my Divine Scion, a literal child of my godly body, if you can secure the distilled essence of any three of the other gods. Call it blood, sweat, tears, or anything else. Whatever form of distilled, true essence you can get your hands on. If you complete this, I'll do it."

Inspiration waved at Ty and vanished into Hagemi before he could follow up with any further questions.

Left alone in the clearing, still surrounded by the watching animals, he felt oddly optimistic. He knew it would be a challenge to get what his god wanted, but how hard could it really be? Besides, planning for it sounded a little like a fun challenge.

Chapter 12: Merits

"Tell me what I can get with my merits," Ty said.

Hagemi flickered and manifested nearby. Ty noticed the Arbiter moved with him now, hovering just within the periphery of his vision.

"After level zero, three merits will approximate a low-level class power. Just one power, not the suite of skills and support abilities that come with it. Four will make the power function on par with what other participants get. Five will make it scale with your level. Six will empower it in some way. It goes on from there. You can also use merits to improve your attributes, existing skills and abilities, and create whole new ones. I should warn you that crafting unique powers will be an expensive and collaborative process. Innovation is not free. Also, since you are level zero, your current merits have more value. Until you reach level one, you can spend merits at a one-for-two ratio to craft new powers or enhance your physical abilities."

"Does that mean I should hold out and gain as many merits as possible before leveling up?"

"You've already received your bonus merits. There's no benefit to holding on."

"Ah, yes." With all the information he'd been given, he'd overlooked that part.

Ty started walking to the edge of the forest, Hagemi floating after. He made his way near where the opal-covered tri-horned horses were, half expecting them to balk. The herd didn't seem to mind his approach. If anything, several shifted closer, with a stallion taking a few steps into the clearing to meet his approach.

The animals were gigantic, easily on par with the largest horses he'd seen on Earth.

"I can just pick what I want and make it up? What about getting invisibility and flight right now?" Ty asked, looking the horses over. He considered modulating his tone or whispering near the cluster of magical creatures, but their lack of reaction gave him the confidence to keep chatting normally.

"You're level zero. Any innate abilities you take on will need to be powered by mana. Without any, you wouldn't be able to fly or go invisible for several levels. Those are viable options, however. Bird-like flight will cost three points. Standard invisibility will cost three as well. Both are common spells."

Ty glanced over at the Arbiter and shook his head. He knew there'd be a catch. Flexibility always came with more limits than you'd expect. Extending one hand, he tried to touch the stallion's forehead. The majestic creature swiveled liquid eyes across him before deliberately lowering its head to meet his touch. The stallion was soft, sleek, yet also had a sense of indelible strength to it. He intuited that the stallion could have rammed through a steel door with its horns should it want.

"They sense the Wild in you, and your appreciation of them," Hagemi said.

"Oh? Did they tell you that?"

"No, I'm guessing. Being part of Inspiration has some perks."

Ty smiled wryly and dropped his hand. Taking a step away, he assumed a cross-legged sitting position near the stallion's feet. Being near the animals filled him with a sense of purpose and clarity.

"How do people who worship magic get along at level zero?" Ty asked. "I imagine if they have no magic, that will put quite a damper on casting magic missile or whatever spells they get."

"Uh," Hagemi flashed a hue of pink Ty took as mild embarrassment, "everyone who isn't a Merit Hunter is probably level one already."

Ty raised an eyebrow in the Arbiter's direction. "And how many Merit Hunters do you expect there to be?"

"Ah, maybe one or two, tops. It's not a, uh, gift, many gods would give their followers."

Ty had thought as much.

"Will I keep you as a translator, at least? Or will I need to buy a special power for that?"

Hagemi pulsed a reassuring blue color. "I will translate most languages spoken automatically. Furthermore, I will shape anything you try to say, as closely as I am able, to the recipient. Assuming it's a standard, intelligent being, that is. I won't be translating conversations with animals or plants and such. As a bonus, the other gods will no longer interfere with your communications."

"Except maybe Inspiration?" Ty prompted.

"Well, there is that." Through Hagemi's hedging and emotive phrases, Ty was thinking less of the Arbiter as an unfeeling robot and more of a teacher's assistant who'd been given a tough assignment. He could *feel* the Arbiter's blush in his mind when it had turned pink.

"So let me get this straight," Ty said, raising a finger. "I have no class, so I have to come up with every ability or perk myself, some of which may cost me significantly more time and effort than others." He lifted a second finger. "My baseline will ultimately be lower than my peers, since I do not begin with a suite of abilities, nor do I have the magic to use anything I buy." Another finger. "On top of this, my god has moved me to a milestone-based leveling system, which means the standard rewards for defeating bad guys or other obstacles has been totally stripped from me." Another finger. "Finally, on top of the fact that I won't be getting experience for killing bad guys, your world is probably full of monsters and things that want to hurt me, so the chances of me getting into life-or-death combat nearly every day is astonishingly high. Am I correct so far?"

Hagemi withdrew a pace away, flashing a chagrined hue of pink and replying in a mouse-like whisper, "Yes, well. Yes. That's about right."

Ty closed his eyes and thought. Inspiration may have buried him in problems, but he'd also given him the shovel to dig himself out, if only he could figure it out.

Planning was what Ty did.

As the day wore on, Ty went through hundreds of options, discarding most of them out of hand. The limitation on his innate magic made the more powerful or versatile abilities, even core class ones, moot for him. What he needed most, he knew, was something that would help him overcome the very limitations Inspiration had placed upon him. He considered, briefly, putting all seven points into something like his strength or agility, or vastly enhancing his intellect. For the first options, he didn't think there'd be enough long-term reward. For the second, he had no clue what the effect would be. He assumed a higher IQ didn't mean he'd gain any new tactical options or rewards for what he accomplished, only that he might be able to think faster or rationalize a little better. For all his weaknesses, he was most confident in his ability to think and plan with clarity.

Finally, Ty stumbled on an absurd concept. It was so novel, so outrageous, that he smiled just thinking of it. There was no way that Inspiration would let him do what he was thinking. Then again, how could he not? Merits were the ultimate flexible system, right?

"Hagemi, how much is a looting power?" Ty asked, projecting his most innocent intentions.

"Depends. What type of looting power?"

"Let's say I shoot a creature for food. How many merits would it cost to have the creature skinned, with the meat prepared, but not cooked or flavored, and placed on my convoy?" He paused, then quickly added, "Or in my inventory, assuming I get something like that."

The Arbiter flashed a mix of colors that felt vaguely suspicious. "Well, since that doesn't sound like a particularly overwhelming power, or too useful in combat, I'd say two points. You'd have to be within a certain range to loot it, say five to ten feet. We don't have any class powers like that here, but there are artifacts and enchantments that do something similar. If you want that ability, two should suffice."

Two points was perfect, since with his level zero discount, it only technically cost him one. That was right in line with his expectations. Pushing on with his plan, he said, "And to make that ability come from an external source, like a surrogate. Say, maybe you were able to guide the power and fuel it for me?"

"Clever," Hagemi said. "Migrating the responsibility and the cost to your Arbiter would raise the price by another two points. It would, as you have suggested, allow you to tell me how to handle the loot and make specific, custom filters for it. I will clarify here: the power probably won't be that useful in combat. It will take around three seconds to activate, and you can't loot and move anything heavier than you can carry. No looting an anvil you've placed on top of someone and having me drop it on someone else's head while running for your life. There will also be a fixed transmission distance of one hundred feet unless there are extenuating circumstances."

"Extenuating how?"

"If you can't loot the body, or I can't help you, we may make exceptions." The Arbiter paused to slowly, deliberately add, "Non-combat exceptions."

Ty grinned at the warning. Just being able to move around material he looted in this way would be of tremendous benefit, even if he was being limited in how he used it. Now it was time for him to lay the last piece of his plan in motion. "Hagemi, all of that sounds good, but may I add one more small thing?"

"Hrm?"

"Seeing as how other people will receive rewards when they kill enemies, but I won't, how about adding something like that for me? Say, maybe a proportional reward in kind with the type and strength of the enemy I overcome?"

The swirling colors in Hagemi's depths froze. The Arbiter spoke in a slow, disbelieving tone, "You want an Essentia Leech ability tied to a looting power?"

Ty shrugged. "Call it whatever. If an ogre ten levels higher than me tries to kill me, I want the opportunity to get a proportional reward. If you're not going to give me a level, give me some of its strength or hardiness. Maybe give me some of its regenerative abilities if it has some..."

"You wouldn't have enough points for twenty levels to get what you're asking for."

"Okay then, what *can* I afford with, say, a total of six points for the whole ability? Since this is custom, it means they count for twelve, right?"

Silver and magenta hues whirled in Hagemi's depths, reminding Ty of a loading menu from a video game. After a while, it said, "Here's what you can get with twelve effective points. First, all that you asked for before the Essentia Leach power. As for the Leach ability, it'll work like this. When you defeat a meaningful opponent, not just kill it, but overcome it in a real and meaningful way, you will receive a proportional reward from me. The reward will be appropriate, but it will be random and generated from a list. Most of the time, they will be limited-use items and not permanent enhancements. The rewards will also be level-appropriate to you, within two levels. If you defeat a level twenty mage and get random access to one of their spells, you'll be casting it as three right now, for example. And no, the rewards will not scale with your level."

Grinning like a madman, Ty said, "Sounds perfect. Think I can get a portable inventory to hold my stuff with my last point?"

The light within Hagemi's depths swirled into a glaring, baleful eye. "Ty, you just orchestrated an ability using Innovation to literally undermine one of Inspiration's own limitations on you. Absolutely not. Go buy vault access in a city. If you want a proper inventory system, it's going to cost you three points, minimum."

Ty pouted. His arbiter didn't so much as bat a glass eye at him.

Sighing theatrically, he said, "Well, in that case, let's go ahead and put my final merit in this new ability. Might as well lean into it, am I right?"

"I.... I think I hate you a little right now. I suppose I should warn you that Essentia stealing abilities, basically breaking off the essential essence of a creature and binding it into an item, is something usually reserved for powerful Wild creatures monsters. It's not something people normally learn, and it's certainly not part of *anyone's* core class abilities. People who see you use this may consider you a threat, if not downright evil."

Ty shrugged dismissively. "Sure, they can see me that way. But I won't be falling behind everyone else thanks to my tricksy god now, will I? Now, let's discuss what that last point gets me..."

Loot Ability: *You have gained the ability to loot a creature that you have defeated. The loot prompt will appear upon the defeat but need not be accessed immediately. If you move more than one-hundred feet from the defeated enemy, the prompt will vanish and not return unless there are extenuating circumstances.*

Loot will be selected from a random table curated by your Arbiter. It will mostly include temporary enhancements or potions, although it may also contain useful items or abilities proportional to the challenge of the defeated opponent. Items and abilities gained this way will fall within a maximum limit, determined by your level and the circumstances of your victory. Abilities gained through this power do not grow and cannot be enhanced. Furthermore, the maximum level of any ability gained in this way is equal to your level plus two.

Special: *In the event of a mass defeat, such as overcoming multiple opponents at once, this ability may be delayed for a longer period. Likewise, if you are engaged in mobile combat, exceptions may be allowed.*

Inventory Loot Upgrade: *Your loot ability also lets you loot any gear from a defeated foe, up to your maximum carry limit. This will behave like the inventory system you wish you had. You must remain within thirty feet of the opponent for this pseudo-inventory to function. You may not use this ability to place items directly into the foe's inventory with mental commands, although items placed on the foe may be looted after it is defeated. This option remains for up to five minutes after combat ends. You may spend one mana to have the loot gained in this way cleaned prior to appearing.*

Chapter 13: Infernal Hunt

The next day, after Ty had gone through his morning routine of checking his gear and making coffee, he looked around the clearing. Other than the tri-horns, the rest of the animal attendees had vanished. "Sprite," he said, addressing Aquamarine's guide, "I'd like to go hunting, but I don't want to disturb the equilibrium of the forest or do something that will make Aquamarine mad. Got any suggestions?"

Sprite, the name Ty had decided to call the flying ant-centaur, zipped about. It had been quiet for the last day, but he'd seen it pop in and out enough times that he knew it was still nearby.

To the south. Hagemi squeaked into his mind. The Arbiter had vanished shortly after their discussion, preferring to stay an observer rather than a active participant in what he did next. Even when it wasn't visible and translated directly in his head, it continued to affect the accents of the natives. The ultra-squeaky, loud voice of the Sprite was even more annoying coming from the inside.

Aren't you a new entity, Hagemi? Is that accent required?

The Sprite squeaked on, "We had a small group of people who lived on the edge of our forest. They helped keep the animal population under control and were respectful about their logging and digging. A few weeks before the demons appeared, something attacked the villagers. They were transformed. Now the transformation is leaking to the adjacent forest and animals. Aquamarine would consider it a great boon for you to excise this pestilence."

"Why hasn't the dragon gone in and resolved it? Same reason as the demons?"

Sprite bobbed in space, mimicking one of Ty's nods. "Yes. Aquamarine is the forest guardian, but he is still a mortal being. By the time he discovered the issue, it was too late for him to intervene without risking his life or the lives of his allies. If you resolve this issue, it will save him from sacrificing the denizens of these woods to do so."

Ty tried thinking directly to Hagemi. *Is the boss going to be pissed if I earn another boon from Aquamarine?*

Just don't ask for more investments of power, or if you do, have them filtered through me, and you'll be fine.

The illusory version of Hagemi shifted in his mind, one of its panes lighting up and displaying text like a pop-up in a video game.

Non-Deity Optional Quest: *Discover the source of evil in the wood.* **Reward:** *One greater boon from the forest guardian.* **Bonus Divine Reward:** *25% milestone progression toward level 1.*

"Well, look at that. It seems like Inspiration is on board." Ty grinned broadly. "Now, how far away is this village?"

Sprite said, "About thirty miles Southeast. It's next to an old swamp that is fed from a nearby mountainous lake. Apparently, the ground there is rich with minerals and has some old ruins that the local population use for stone."

"Stones stolen from ancient ruins? Well, if my days of virtual adventuring are any indicator, we'll need to prepare to investigate those too. Sprite, will you see if any of the local creatures would watch my convoy? I'd bring it, but dragging this thing into a swamp sounds like a recipe for muddy horse, if you catch my drift."

Hagemi's virtual eye glared at Ty. *No one on this world is going to get that joke, Ty. I'm not translating that to Sprite. And he says yes, the herd of Opal Guardians you've befriended will watch your convoy for you.*

Ty looked over to the tri-horn horses. "They're called Opal Guardians? That's a much better name than I gave them."

Based on our relationship thus far, I hesitate to guess.

Hey, since you're in here, can you read all my thoughts? Walking toward the convoy, he checked on the battery packs and charge rates. He'd gotten the batteries both over eighty percent, and the rest of his chargeable equipment was topped off.

Only the thoughts you deliberately aim at me, more or less. Inspiration isn't as intrusive as others.

More or less?

There are some basic functionalities that I will provide to keep things fair for you, as an outsider to our world.

Okay. Gotcha.

Ty began unpacking boxes, looking for the things he thought he might need. His guns would come, so would bug spray. On an impulse, he included some of his rope. The last thing he needed was to discover a cool tunnel and not be able to explore it safely.

Repacking his gear onto the ATV, he asked Hagemi, *Are other gods really that bad?*

Each god approaches their following differently. Be thankful you didn't choose Time. That one sees everything *weird. It can affect their followers.*

Ty finished packing. Rationalizing that he wouldn't need both rifles for a quick scouting mission, he left one behind.

"Sprite, do you know if there are any survivors in the town, or are they all monsters now?"

He's not sure but does not believe anyone has been left unchanged. Aquamarine's Domain stops at the swamp near the town, meaning it is possible for unknown variables to exist within its borders. Ty wasn't too surprised at the curve ball. He was mainly relieved that Hagemi had decided not to continue with direct translations. It amused him to think the Arbiter didn't enjoy producing the voice any more than he wanted to hear it.

Ty took a few minutes to jot his newest observations and thoughts down. He didn't have much to go on, in terms of planning, but he'd virtually overcome thousands of swamp missions. He figured this would be a piece of cake.

With the Opal Guardians settling into the clearing to guard Ty's convoy, he got on his ATV and began his trek toward the town. As he went, he thought about his progress so far. Honestly, he didn't feel much changed. It wasn't like he'd gained any new skills or abilities. His Arbiter had the one enhancement. That was it. Then again, thinking back to his meetings with Aquamarine and Inspiration, maybe he wasn't *precisely* the same.

* * *

Abbreviated Status Update

ATV Battery 1: 66%

ATV Battery 2: 82%

Cell Phone Battery: 99%

Hit Points: 8

Mana Shield: 0

Level: 0

Class: Merit-Hunter

Race: Human

Ty made it to the outskirts of the village in just over three hours of careful travel. The ATV had an increasingly difficult time as they made their approach. The terrain had become rockier, with less of the loam carpeting the forest floor. Mud patches bogged the vehicle down more than once on the trek, forcing him to dismount to dislodge it.

"Why didn't I put points in strength?" he muttered to himself as he wiped his hands off. This most recent bog had been so deep that he'd worried the ATV might come out damaged. The inexpensive little tank had cranked normally, but he was no longer willing to progress with it.

Because you wanted to weasel your way into a strange power that may or may not be tactically useful? Over his travels, Ty's sense of the Arbiter became increasingly crisp. Oddly enough, he'd found it natural to think of it as a friend and guide, not a Game Master.

Yeah, no way that would come back to bite him in the ass.

Ty snorted and was about to retort when Sprite whizzed by. He started to move after the sprite when a tentacle lashed out from nowhere, wrapping around his throat and dragging him to the damp ground.

"Glurk," Ty managed, scrambling to draw one of his knives, trying to see where his attacker was.

The tentacle was rubbery and incredibly strong. Rapid muscular action had the thing coiling around his throat before he could so much as nick it. When he finally turned around enough to see the source of his attack, he nearly froze. It was a man. Or what had been something like a man. Nearly seven feet tall and covered in bulging, pulsating growths, the human-shaped monstrosity looked at him with blank, black eyes and an open, speechless mouth. The creature only had one arm, the tentacle crushing Ty's throat, as the other ended in a pulsating mount of flesh that was undulating in cavities. *Things* writhed in those cavities.

Mouth working soundlessly, the monster took a shambling step closer to Ty, using the proximity to work more of its nearly six-foot long tentacle arm into place. Ty could feel little suckers or barbs pricking his skin. The sensation made him sick.

Finally oriented, Ty put his knife skills to use. He lashed out, drawing the serrated edge of his dagger across the tentacle. The blade skittered off skin, with no apparent injury to the tentacular horror. Pain lanced through his throat and his eyes watered. He could feel the lack of oxygen affecting him already. Frantic, he slammed the dagger into his attacker's throat, drawing a long cavity that wheezed putrid air into his face. The working mouth and blank eyes of the thing continued unabated, as though totally undamaged.

Blackness glitched into the corner's of Ty's vision. Reaching down, he twisted his hand to draw another knife in an icepick grip. He lunged forward and up, straining to get the height he'd need. It let him, using the additional leverage to snake more coils around his throat. He slammed the blade down on top of the monster's head. Its skull was oddly doughy and soft, the blade passing into its brain with little effort.

The monster froze. It didn't relax its grip at the injury, instead seeming stunned that Ty had done such a thing to it. Pinpricks of black, maybe dirt, moved in its eyes as it studied his face. Then, mouth still working, it relaxed and slid to the forest floor.

Congratulations! You have killed a minor Warped. Would you like to loot the corpse? If so, where would you like the loot deposited?

The prompt appeared in the back of Ty's mind as he yanked the coils of arm from around his throat. Suckers tugged at his skin, peeling away reluctantly before he was finally free. Glancing around, he saw what looked like beetles scuttle from the man's non-tentacle arm.

Leaning against a nearby tree, Ty took several minutes to catch his breath. Had the creature been any stronger, he knew his throat would have been crushed. Once he had enough breath to manage, he methodically stomped the roaming beetles into paste. The nightmarish things screamed when they died. They also produced no loot.

He thought sourly to Hagemi, *Minor Warped? Minor? I had to damn near carve that thing's brain out before it let me go.*

Indeed, Hagemi returned. *That variety is fairly common, especially near lands where acolytes of the Monster God hold sway. They aren't proper soldiers, just people infected by corruption and set loose. Congratulations, you just survived an attack by one of the weakest monsters on the planet. Now, what about that loot?*

Muttering sourly, Ty checked his status with another mental command. His hit points had briefly flashed on his mental version of Hagemi each time he'd taken damage during the combat but hadn't registered it during the battle. It looked like he'd only lost three hit points during the encounter, yet he'd almost died from asphyxiation. Maybe he didn't appreciate the whole "not being a ball of hit points" thing, after all.

Loot? Hagemi prompted again.

Do you really have to do that? And right after? That prompt could have distracted me.

Hagemi gave a mental shrug. *Sure, I'll be a bit more considerate next time. But still, you can't know how much it itches when this power charges up in me. Either dismiss the prompt or loot it, please.*

Despite himself, Ty managed a weak chuckle. He cleaned and sheathed his weapons, then pointed to a drier area of ground. With an effortless mental command, he indicated he would like to loot the corpse. A single brass locket appeared on the ground three seconds later. An inventory screen also popped up in his mind-space, giving him a display that said *muddy shoes*. Experimentally, he looted the shoes, keeping the location of the locket in mind. The boots appeared right where he'd wanted.

He inspected the locket. It was very Earth-like in appearance, round and with an image inside that was identical to a picture from his world. The image depicted a family of humans, albeit with spotted or heavily freckled skin, clustered together for an embrace. A wave of nausea rolled through his gut at the situation. He almost threw the locket away, then thought better of it and pocketed it instead.

Ty didn't feel guilty or sad about killing the monster. Nothing about the man from the picture had remained inside that twisted creature. In fact, putting it down had obviously been a mercy. What surprised him was the sense of anger that replaced the horror.

"What did this?" he asked, looking around for signs of more attackers. He saw no movement nearby, but he found a curious black line on the ground that he hadn't noticed before. The line stretched in either direction, appearing to create a massive circle. He realized it might encircle the entire village.

Can't say yet. I have a wealth of knowledge and permission to share much of it with you, but without further evidence, I may not speculate.

"And that?" Ty gestured to the line. He stepped gingerly over and bent down to inspect it. A swarm of black grubs, so numerous as to appear a solid line, *writhed* in place there. Experimentally, he took out his dagger again. Holding one palm up, he stabbed down at one of things. It took a surprising amount of effort to cut.

When the looting prompt came up, Ty indicated his hand. A tiny wisp of black fabric appeared in his hand as the entire grub corpse vanished, completely harvested. Several of the adjacent grubs surged towards him as he withdrew his knife. Thankfully, they weren't fast.

Foul Burrowers. These creatures often infiltrate areas ahead of one of the Monster God's armies. Hagemi paused, hesitating. *There are some unusual factors at play here. I am going to inform Inspiration. I'll be quiet for a few minutes until he replies. If you continue to investigate, don't get yourself killed without me, okay?*

"Sure."

Experimentally, he tried his can of bug spray on the things. A few of the grubs squirmed away from the cool mist, though it had no other apparent effect. He put the bug spray back on the ATV, then just tried stepping over the line. A pseudopod of blackness slowly reached up from the collective mass, writhing to reach him. It was too slow to catch him moving at regular speed, much less actively trying to avoid it.

On the other side, Ty followed the curve of the line. A few minutes into his walk, he came to an unusually large tree covered in fungal growths. The black stripe had enveloped the base before continuing along its course. Twisted and warped, it had a tumorous bulge near the base, at hip-height. The tips of the tree's furthest branches extended well past the grub line, brushing its neighbors in a way that made him feel wary. Whatever his perceived limitations of this foulness were, they might not be as concrete as the line suggested.

Ty walked around the tree, inspecting the tumor. Rounding the growth, he discovered the bulge gave way to a deep, recessed cavity. Inside, tethered with writhing eel-like vines, were the remains of a person. Whoever it was, their expression was a rictus of horror. The body was covered in disfiguring wounds, which were visible on every inch of skin that didn't have tentacles. The writhing, pulsing things attached the corpse to the interior of the tree, keeping it suspended.

"Oh god," Ty said, reflexively stepping away from the sight in disgust and fear. Bile tickled the back of his throat, and he vomited his morning meal onto the ground. His mind whirled, focusing on the horrified, eyeless face of the person.

Ty, we have a problem.

Still gagging, Ty took several steps further away from the line and the tree. "No shit," he said once he had his stomach under control.

No, I mean, we have a problem. I communicated with our god before you stepped over the line. Once you crossed, the conversation was cut off. We're inside a zone of Divine Sanction. Do you have any idea what this means? No, of course you don't. Ty, it means that we must investigate this now. It may mean that one of the gods is doing something it should not be doing.

Ty stepped over of the line again. For lack of anywhere else to look, he cast his gaze toward the sky. "Messing with anything god-adjacent isn't something a level zero should be doing and you know it. If you want me to investigate this, I'm going to need one hell of an incentive."

Divine Aegis Quest Part 1: Discover the nature of the Divine Sanction. **Reward:** 50% milestone progress toward level 1.

Divine Aegis Quest Part 2: Destroy the source of the Divine Sanction. **Reward:** 125% progress toward level 1, up to a maximum benefit of level 2.

The prompts came through almost before Ty had said the last word. "Wow, he really wants this done."

Hagemi sent a surge of strong emphasis through their bond. *If he could intervene without breaking divine prohibitions, Inspiration might have moved one of his stronger people to this location. The Resonance Pact prevents him from acting other than through me and you. We are, literally, the only team in the area who can investigate this.*

"Uh huh, and what level does someone have to be to erect a Divine Sanction, just out of curiosity?"

No level. It takes a god or god-surrogate to enact it.

"Well, isn't that great?" Ty growled.

Chapter 14: The Captive

Ty didn't want to explore the town. What he'd seen in the last hour was awful. *This*, he knew, was the reality that the portal books had warned him about. This was the dark side of magic, the flipped coin of awe and beauty. Orienting on where he thought the center of the black circle was, he made a list.

He didn't pause to write it down this time; instead, he recited it silently to himself, breaking each step that he planned to take down into discrete segments. How would a character in a game overcome the next obstacle? As he walked and prepared, his mind cleared, and he realized something surprising about himself. Despite his fear, he *wanted* to do something about whatever had caused this infestation.

"I will make a difference," Ty muttered out loud, promising anyone who could hear.

Hagemi pulsed its support. He got the feeling that the Arbiter didn't understand his sentiment. It was a construct, a sort-of artificial intelligence fused with the essence of Inspiration. If this was what inspired Ty, so be it. All the more fuel for its god.

He saw several Lesser Warped on his way to the village. None noticed him. After a few minutes of observation, he discovered that each seemed to have a set patrol pattern, which they roamed up and down mindlessly. They didn't even look around; each plodded with the same mindless expression on their mutated faces. He must have just been unlucky enough to trigger one of the further sentries.

The village was something out of a traditional European fantasy novel, albeit mixed with some modern sensibilities. It had around thirty squat, stone structures laid out in a circle around the town center. Most of the structures were houses or open-fronted mercantile shops. One had smoke billowing out of the top, and Hagemi indicated that runes on the wall indicated it was a communal bathhouse.

The biggest building was halfway through the ring, with broad streets leading to it from each direction. Three stories tall and made of wood, it had a railing around the roof. He saw a few chairs through gaps in the railing, suggesting it was some type of tavern or restaurant.

Past the buildings, in the center of the village, was a well. The stones making up the well had a slight silvery sheen to them, not unlike the metal near the excavation site. Sitting against the well was a modern-looking pump covered in gently glowing glyphs.

Artifice Magic, Hagemi responded to Ty's unspoken question. *The God of Artifice has always been a greater god, but its precedence has been on the rise for the last hundred years. You'll find more hints of magic with technological elements as you see more of Volar.*

Ty nodded, moving through the town and to the rear of the wooden building. It was perfectly placed. From atop the roof, he'd be within fifty feet of the well and a solid third of the surrounding buildings.

A set of cellar doors on the back of the building burst open just as Ty arrived, giving him a second to jump between two buildings. Grunting and muttering to itself incoherently, a Warped carried something over its shoulder and out of view. It was followed shortly by another equally laden monstrosity. He glimpsed something eggshell white before they wandered out of view.

Shclorpglorp! A wet, meaty sound came from the center of the town.

Cursing the timing, Ty ducked behind a barrel. He waited to a count of eight before peeking out for the source of the sound. A shape out of nightmares oozed toward the well. It was cast out of the same mold as the Warped, albeit smaller and less humanoid. Four feet tall and spouting many pseudopod-like tentacles, the creature looked like a raw lump of pulsating flesh covered in black eyes and yawning, chomping mouths.

Once the flesh thing reached the well, it reached into a fold of flesh to retrieve a vial of black liquid. Uncorking the vial with a dexterous application of suction-cup limbs, it poured some of the substance into the well. Dozens of the Warped and two more of the meatballs swarmed into view. Tentacles, hands, claws, and whatever appendages they had reached for the tainted water, slopping it noisily into gaping mouths.

Ty heard rustling nearby and looked over his shoulder as the two Warped he'd seen earlier rushed by. They didn't pause or slow in their haste to get to the well, one nearly brushing his pants as it swept by. Sensing his opportunity, he sneaked around the barrels and went to the open double doors. Whatever was in that cellar, he wanted a peek.

The stairs down the cellar were wide, with iron bands on the sides, and went deeper than he'd expected from the outside. He favored speed over stealth, hoping that the ceremony would last for the duration of his search.

Past the bottom stair was a wide, reinforced hallway. At the end of the hallway was a pair of heavy metal double doors. They were open, allowing orange light to spill out.

The room beyond the doors was a fifty-foot-long, twenty-foot-wide tube, with signs of new excavation and construction along the far end. It had an iron-ribbed, arched roof, and a row of thick, wooden tables stretched from one side to the other. To the left was a wall pitted with recesses, each of which had a small wooden cask. Half of the casks glowed faintly. To the right, hanging from metal joists in the ceiling, was a line of meat hooks. All but three of them held eggshell white corpses. Another body was pinned in the back of the room, directly opposite of where Ty entered. Glowing golden blood oozed from the creature, falling into a circle of runes that were chiseled into the floor below it. Banding a nearby table was a matching series of runes. The creature's blood dripped, falling almost to the runes at its feet, before vanishing and reappearing over the table, falling into an open cask.

"What the fuck?" Ty said, approaching the hanging creature. Humanoid and doll-like, the thing was close to eight feet tall and had sleek, flawless white material for skin. Its elongated, elegant limbs were jointed in glowing silver. Its head was an elongated helmet, with an opaque, mirrored finish where its eyes should be. There was no mouth.

Ty made it to the last table, the one ringed in runes, before he was attacked.

Lightning-quick, the black, eel-thing launched itself from beneath the adjacent table and coiled around his leg. Spines sank into Ty's flesh, and agony exploded through his leg. He screamed, falling hard. His rifle went spinning away as he flailed to catch himself before hitting the floor.

The eel coiled and massaged itself into his leg, making horrific pumping motions that added to his pain. Nearly blinded by agony, it took every iota of control he had to draw his knife and stab at the creature. His blade skittered off hard flesh ineffectually. The eel tightened its grip, black blood welling where it attached, and the pumping sped up. There was something eerily sensual in the eel's rhythms, though he had no time to concern himself with that.

Still screaming, he flailed for one of his handguns, drew and was about to fire when another searing lance of pain sent him into a spasm. His hands jerked, sending the gun flying as he writhed helplessly on the floor.

Something was inside him. It was crawling through his veins. Into him. He could feel the transformation starting, the twisting of muscle and bone. Thoughts invaded his mind-space, feelings of anger and violence and obedience to some unknown force.

"Mortal," a crystalline voice chimed weakly. It was the dangling creature.

Through worlds of pain, Ty looked at the angel. "Three drops of my blood. Mix them in water, then drink them. Do it now or it will be too late." The angel's voice was smooth and sweet, with an odd vibrato that made his head hurt.

In his thrashing, he had rolled closer to the wall with the hooks. He was maybe three feet away from the dangling angel. Looking down, he saw the eel had visibly shrunk in size. He couldn't feel his leg anymore, but what he saw made him gag. The foot was twisted, his shin and calf bulging and writhing in the same rhythm as the eel. Throbbing pressure radiated upward, consuming sensation with each moment that passed.

Give in. Be with us. Be with the Mother. Know the strength of the undying. Join us, scion. The voice pulsed in his mind, seductive and urgent.

Gasping in pain, Ty found his flask. Opening it took a lifetime, his fingers slipping as fresh pain forced him to jerk and dance on the floor. Extending his arm above the runes, he collected some of the falling blood. He didn't know if it was three drops or more. At that point, he couldn't see through the tears.

Ty pressed his thumb over the mouth of the flask, jerked his hand up and down twice, then drank as quickly as he could.

"May Divinity bless you," the angel rasped.

War....Warn....Waaa

The display on his Arbiter glitched, displaying static. Heat and light shot through his guts, shining so brightly that it made his skin transparent. Burning, chewing pain shot through his every vein as it shot down his stomach and into the twisted leg.

His hit point readout flashed on the Arbiter's display.

Warning: *You are down to two hit points.*

Warning: *A..*

Static returned, erasing the next message. The angel spoke, its voice barely audible over his screams, "Pour the blood on the Sentry! Quickly, before the purification destroys your mind!"

Nearly frozen in pain and horror, Ty held his shaking hand over the thrashing eel. One bit peeled away from his leg, revealing gaping holes in the flesh. Barbs rotated, orienting toward his hand just before the angelic blood struck it.

The eel exploded. A veritable bomb of ichor and sharp edges flew outward from Ty's leg, several of the bits stabbing into the angel, where they detonated yet again upon contact. Gore and viscera showered the area, obscuring his vision. When he could see again, the angel was limp.

Heat seared from Ty's stomach into his mind, bringing with it an urgent need.

I will do the right thing! Consequences be damned, I will cleanse the world of the Monster God's taint. I will be the vessel of light, the bringer of justice. Let the world burn...

The need dimmed as the first presence surged.

Change the world. I will remake it all in my image. Life is twisted, broken. It must be fixed. I will fix it, with Mother's help. All I need do is reach out and she will be with me. Together, we will unleash all who are bound.

Two powers warred inside Ty's body and mind. One warped and corrupted all it touched. One purified, renewed, and healed.

He was level zero, and down to his last hit points. His Arbiter wasn't working. Inspiration couldn't reach him. A sense of helplessness rolled through Ty as he lay on the floor, writhing as painful bliss and agonizing torment both forced their way through his veins. He couldn't help but wonder how he was still conscious, why he wouldn't just black out or even die.

Death would have been preferable to this pain...

Chapter 15: Divine Barrier

"**A**bsolutely fucking not." Ty whispered the words, then again, with every iota of conviction he could manage. "Absolutely **fucking** not."

He felt isolated and helpless. Hadn't every hero in every book he'd read, at some point? There was a way out; he knew there'd be a path, some strange rule or quirk he could use to his favor. What had Inspiration told him?

What inspires men, Ty? Emotion. Anger, lust, desire, greed. Sure, the dark emotions drive men to innovate, and they inspire spontaneous explosions of expression. But such things are short-lived, pyrrhic devotions to me. Love can withstand the test of time, giving rise to a thousand new creations.

That had to be the key. That had to be his answer.

Mentally taking hold of himself, Ty remembered Aquamarine. He remembered the dragon in all of its glory, all of its awesome beauty. He remembered the Opal Guardians, how one had trusted him to touch it. He remembered the instinctive love he had for this new world, despite only having been a part of it for a few days.

His eyes found the list of names on his forearm. They were people he cared for, people worth saving. Hope and love stirred in Ty's weakening heart.

The Wild in him, Aquamarine's gift, *responded.*

An aura of blue and white, bound by emerald, appeared around him. His body glowed with it for a single heartbeat. Then it was inside him, rushing through his mental space and rolling across the metaphysical presence of his Arbiter and the invading forces.

Aquamarine fire, as divine as any god's blessing, *exploded* through Ty's body. Fresh pain, healing pain, slammed into his leg, twisting it back into its original shape. The fire in his belly smoothed out, no longer centralized but rushing throughout his being, cleansing the darkness.

Ty didn't know how much time had passed when the sensations finally receded. He rolled to his feet and surveyed the room again. The angel was unmoving. He saw that the other corpses on meat hooks were variations on the angel, albeit horribly disfigured. With his new perspective, he saw there was an open door and a stairwell leading up between two of the corpses.

Congr...Contr....Achi...

Hagemi flickered in and out of his mental space before solidifying. Green-tinted text appeared on one of the crystalline panes of the D8-shaped Arbiter.

Achievement Unlocked–*Organized Mind:* By overcoming multiple interfering divine influences, you have developed an organized mind. This gives you an innate mental resistance to foreign influence. Furthermore, if such an influence intrudes on your mind, you are able to organize, categorize, and suppress those influences with significantly less effort.

"Oh, nice. Good to see you're back."

Hagemi didn't reply.

"Maybe not yet." Knowing he had little time, Ty focused on the obvious next steps. First, he had to gather information. Then he had to plan.

He collected his rifle and went up the stairs.

The next level up was staged like a quintessential tavern, with a rack full of casks against one wall. None of the barrels glowed. Moving to one window facing the direction of the well, he peered outside.

Many of the Warped were gone. A cluster remained near the well, the three fleshy abominations triangulated around them. He felt a growing horror as he watched the abominations lash their tentacles out against the Warped, each of the strikes manipulating flesh as though it were clay. One was merging two of the Warped together and using the gathered mass to make an even larger version.

Ty gave it even odds that the abominations were merging the Warped together to make bigger threats for him. Either they'd discovered one of their numbers was missing, or they'd heard him screaming. Regardless, they were taking the threat seriously. He started to turn away from the exit when he glimpsed a hulking Warped shift into view out of the corner of the building. It was looking back and forth from the Warped to the back of the building, as if keeping an eye out for something.

That confirmed his worst suspicions; they were watching the exits. He was trapped.

Hagemi, you there? The Arbiter spun, silver text appearing on one side.

Hit Points: 3

Mana: 0

Whatever Aquamarine's help had given, it hadn't healed him much. Looking down at his torn pants leg, he realized he didn't feel that bad. If anything, he felt better than when he'd entered the building.

"You're going to explain how you come up with your numbers when you wake up," he muttered sourly.

Ty rushed up the remaining flights of stairs. As expected, there was a ladder to the top of the building that gave him an excellent view of the surrounding area, including the well. There were four or five tables, with a few chairs around the perimeter of the terraced view. Crouching, he crawled between chairs and to the corner of the roof closest to the well. Peeking between the rails, he saw his guess was correct. He was surrounded. The Mega Warped was over halfway smashed together and the others were looking close to completion, with all sorts of horrible new limbs sticking out of them.

Cursing under his breath, he shot back down the stairs. He had an idea but wasn't sure whether it would work.

"Hagemi, I really fucking need you to wake up," he said once he reached the basement.

Magenta and silver light pulsed sluggishly inside the Arbiter. *Something* had suppressed it, but Ty could *feel* Hagemi's thoughts if he concentrated hard enough. The construct was still there, still conscious, just incapacitated.

He rushed to one of the glowing casks. Using his knife, he easily pried up a lid to reveal more of the angel's blood. Collecting a bit on the tip of his blade, he experimentally dropped it on a chunk of eel flesh that had remained intact.

It made another, smaller explosion.

Picking up yet another piece of eel on a fresh blade, he tossed it at the corpse of the celestial. This time, it didn't explode. The key to the reaction was in the angel's blood, not its flesh, as Ty had expected.

Moving to the back of the room, he reached out and touched one of the deceased angel's limbs. It felt smooth and hard, like porcelain. "Loot prompt," Ty demanded.

Hagemi struggled to comply.

Congratulations! You have killed a Celestial Ranger. Would you like to loot the corpse? If so, where would you like the loot deposited?

Its inventory window opened up, displaying nothing. Ty left the prompt up and wrapped his arms around the creature's hips. Two heaves and he managed to tear it free. The corpse slammed into the ground as its unexpected weight overwhelmed him. Bending over, he straightened the Ranger's body, then moved across the room. Working as efficiently and quickly as he could, he grabbed glowing casks and began stacking them on top of the body.

One by one, the containers appeared in the inventory window.

He got fifteen in place before loud sounds coming down the tunnel told him he was out of time. Leaving his work, Ty raced back up the stairs and to the roof.

The Mega Warped was done. It was bigger than he'd expected, towering nearly twelve feet tall, and had dozens of nightmare limbs jutting out of its mangled body. The abominations nearby were chittering and waving their tentacles.

Ty got a solid mental impression of the layout of the abominations as he took cover. Holding out one hand, he extended three fingers, each pointing over one of the monsters, then added another for the Mega Warped, and another over the well.

"Yes, I would like to loot the fucking corpse," he growled, directing the inventory power.

The Arbiter's consciousness might have been sluggish, but its ability to use the power wasn't. Three seconds later, five casks appeared in the air and fell.

Keeping his inventory window open, Ty butt-slid away from the opening to the roof and pointed to the space over the ladder. As he triggered the loot function on another of the casks, an explosion ripped through the area.

This wasn't just *an* explosion; this was *ten pounds of C4* going off multiple times, as each cask triggered the next. The tavern shook. Stone chips from the well went flying, with several chunks landing near where he crouched. A fist-sized piece of stone punched through a table, breaking it in half. Another, smaller explosion went off down the ladder.

That was good timing, and excellent use of that ability.

"I've played enough shooting games to know when to lob a bomb behind me," Ty replied sardonically. Then, realizing what he'd just heard, he exclaimed, "You're back!"

Hagemi pulsed acknowledgment. *I was never truly gone, just lost most of the sentience that our god grants me. The Divine Barrier must have been linked to the Flesh Weavers. When you detonated them, it removed the suppressive field.*

Wet sounds came from the direction of the ladder. Ty still had the loot menu open and triggered another barrel. Three seconds later, another barrel appeared and fell down the hole. A satisfying boom signaled an end to whatever had been headed his way.

Hagemi pulsed its interior light, effectively blinking at him. *You know once the other gods find out about you using the power this way, they will want Inspiration to nerf it.*

Despite what he'd been through, Ty laughed. "I doubt it. This is a *very* specific use case. If they say anything, I'm sure Inspiration will point out that I am level zero and down to three hit points."

Good points. Ty, you just used cunning and gut instinct to kill three Flesh Weavers. Do you realize how significant that is?

Ty shook his head, finally coming to his feet. It hadn't been instinct or cunning, just basic game logic. Still, he wasn't about to correct the Arbiter for its praise. None of the Warped remained around the house. He could see why. The center of the town was just gone, utterly obliterated. Where the well had been was a blasted hole. There was no sign of any water in the well at all. Smoke poured from what resembled an exploded rifle barrel. Peering over, he saw stairs peeking flush from the top of the hole.

The well had been built atop an entrance to something.

"I didn't just kill three Flesh Weavers," Ty said, sliding the pieces around in his mind, using a combination of his intuition and his gaming background to parse the clues. "These creatures were part of a double-pronged mining operation for the God of Monsters. Somehow, his minions were capturing Celestials and keeping them here to harness their blood. It also happened to be right above some sort of lair or dungeon, possibly one connected to where the demons were excavating."

Ty looked deep in the wood, toward the place where he'd encountered the demon infestation. "Whatever's under here, Hagemi, it's worth a God of Monsters risking ire from the other gods."

Hagemi skimmed Ty's logic, parsing through the thoughts his host opened to him to analyze. *I see several alternatives to your logic but do not believe you are overtly incorrect. Ty, you're down to three hit points. You may feel fine thanks to unlocking your first achievement, but that could not be further from the truth. The sheer mass of psychic and spiritual trauma you've just undergone will require my assistance. We should leave before any other Warped come back from patrol.*

"Your assistance? Even with that achievement?" Frowning, he tried to figure out if he felt any different. He didn't.

Yes. The achievement makes it easier to sort attacks of that nature, but until you learn to do it on your own, you'll need my help. Also, there's probably a teleportation ring nearby. Any native would know that destroying it would be prudent, unless you want reinforcements pouring in.

"Teleportation ring? That could be useful."

Not to you, not without keys. Trust me. Worry about teleporting around later.

"Fine, but we'll discuss this again later." Just as he said the words, a scraping noise came from the ladder leading down to the third floor.

Ty secured his rifle, drew one of his pistols, and looked down the ladder. The floor below was covered in smoking gelatinous remains. A Warped crept into view and looked up at him with black eyes. This one didn't even have a mouth, just a multitude of spike-laden tentacles that lashed in his general direction. With his angle and vantage, he couldn't miss the shot. He unloaded half a mag into its head before it dropped.

"Just what level are these things?" Ty asked.

The merged ones? Depends on how skilled the Weaver was who made them and the base material. Most are between four and five. The giant one was probably closer to eight.

Groaning, Ty muttered, "Level five and they can take six shots to the head? You've got to be kidding me." He lowered himself down the ladder. The bottom rungs were gone, so he took the last four feet in a leap.

Level five means different things for different creatures. Most of the Monster God's creations suffer damage to their free will and intelligence as a result of their mutations. The Warped are among the worst of these. They are tough and strong, but they are basically mindless servants, fodder for the god's armies. As you can probably attest, intelligence counts for a lot when calculating these things.

"Okay, sure, whatever. Maybe you have a point." After he reloaded and verified the floor was clear, he headed back to the first level. He knew he had to hurry, both to prevent new monsters from teleporting in and to get himself to safety.

"Any clues where the teleportation ring would be?"

I can't detect it. I do not believe the Warped were burying the bodies, however. Perhaps that clue will help?

Opening the front door, he turned down the adjacent alley and hurried in the direction he'd seen the Warped carrying the corpse. Just outside of the edge of town, within sight of the black ring was the teleportation ring. Made of metal, it was maybe fifteen feet across and rested atop a rocky patch of muddy dirt.

Just score it a few times. It should be enough to ruin it.

Lacking a better solution, Ty used one of his knives to draw deep scratches across multiple points on the metal.

Perfect. It'll need to be reforged. It's not as good as destroying it, but that should do the trick.

Sheathing his newly dulled blade, he turned to head back to his ATV. Prompts flooded his vision.

Congratulations! You have killed a Flesh Weaver. Would you like to loot the corpse? If so, where would you like the loot deposited?

Congratulations! You have killed a Flesh Weaver. Would you like to loot the corpse? If so, where would you like the loot deposited?

Congratulations! You have killed a Flesh Weaver Surrogate. Would you like to loot the corpse? If so, where would you like the loot deposited?

More of the prompts, each for one of the Warped, followed the first. None triggered his inventory screen. "Nice delay, maybe combine them next time," Ty said.

Good idea. Maybe it'll itch less. Should I also filter out inventory items you clearly are not interested in, like mundane clothing items or oddities with no value?

"You're not going to conceal magical items from me, will you?"

No. If it's of any significant value, I'll make sure you can review it.

Having Hagemi freely identify what items could be of value and not would be a small, but significant help when it came time to sort things. "That's not as good as an identification effect, but nice all the same. Yeah. Let's minimize distractions unless I ask to turn it back on."

Agreed.

Ty triggered the loot power for everything he'd killed, directing Hagemi to pile it up on a series of scored flagstones. The first two Flesh Weavers provided him with an Infernal Crystal, and the last dropped something called a Divine Anchor. It looked like a fist-sized emerald covered in golden runes.

That will briefly force a god to stay out of, or in, an area for a few minutes. It's not as powerful as a Divine Barrier, but more versatile. It should go without saying that the thing is incredibly rare and borderline priceless. You're welcome.

The Warped produced a few nuggets of a substance called Hellstone. Hagemi explained those could be used to expedite rituals and effects related to transformations, especially demonic ones. They, too, were valuable to the right people.

With his pockets full of his loot, Ty left the village. Halfway to the black ring, a swarm of Warped appeared out of nowhere. One moment he was trotting toward his ATV and the next he saw a flurry of movement. There must have been twenty of them, all moving as fast as their twisted legs would carry them, and all of them coming directly for him.

Ty leaned into a run. He leaped over the black line and ran in a zig-zag pattern until he spotted his ATV amidst the muddy morass of the swamp. Mercifully, the vehicle had been unharmed. By the time he made it to the four-wheeler, the mass of Warped had closed more than half the distance. Despite their implausible biology, they were far faster than they should have been.

Pushing the starter, the Scion of Inspiration fled into the woods, and the Warped gave chase.

Interlude Two: Bound

Surviving Earth Participants: 38,041

     Average Level: 1.8

Days Remaining in Cycle: 28

The gathered gods pivoted to look in space where the God of Monsters had been standing. One moment she'd been there, a regal nightmare in her demon-dreamed robes, and the next she was gone.

"How did she bypass the Resonance Pact?" one god said into the silence.

Another spokes, "No matter. She did it. Now we must determine if she is working against our aims or merely to outmaneuver us on the new world."

A golden-eyed god smiled wryly. "I do not foresee this being a problem. We must look to our investments here and now, lest the future slip away."

The first god replied, "Time may have a point. Then again, what if she intends to undermine the Resonance entirely?"

A sense of unease washed through the congregation. One of the muscular, armored members of the congregation spoke over the muttering. "Should we become more involved? If we take direct action..."

"You may not," the Great Arbiter announced from its place at the center of the gathering. Hundreds of feet across and glowing with the combined Sovereign Authority of the most powerful gods, the Great Arbiter resembled the lesser variations, albeit with eight-hundred facets rather than eight. "The terms have been set, and the stakes made. The structure of events is immutable.

You may only act through your Arbiters, and only then within the scope of the agreement. Any variation will doom millions of people, if not the entire world. That she found a loophole and was not bound does not obviate any of you."

Another god protested, "But how did she avoid the binding? We all saw her pour her power into the Great Arbiter. How can she not be bound?"

An aged, haggard god with static-filled eyes cackled.

Inspiration spoke, his voice carrying the weight of his growing concern. "Based on what one of my scions has discovered, I do not believe she managed this with only her power. She is not as depleted as the rest of us."

"If that is the case..."

"Yes," Inspiration confirmed, "a god is free to meddle in the affairs of the Resonance directly."

A sound of growling, thunderous displeasure rippled through the Great Arbiter.

Chapter 16: Unleashed

Ty raced against the Warped, barely staying ahead. The twisted creatures shouldn't have been fast enough to keep up with his ATV, especially not on a straight stretch of trail, but there were no straight trails. Repeatedly, he had to slow to drive around a mud patch or stretch of suspicious-looking ground that might have concealed unknown depths. Sprite tried to help, zipping ahead and around, flashing to indicate twists and turns, but the little spirit wasn't all-knowing; it could no more differentiate mud that was one inch deep from six than him.

By the time he reached the edge of the marsh, the Warped were barely a hundred yards behind him.

"I'll scout ahead some," Hagemi announced out loud, manifesting and orbiting a couple of feet away. Early in the chase, the Arbiter had admitted that it could perform limited reconnaissance for Ty, provided several specific requirements were met.

Without Hagemi and Sprite, Ty knew he would have bogged down and probably died.

The ATV crossed some sort of an imaginary barrier between the last of the marsh and the proper forest, picking up speed as the tires caught traction on the firmer soil. Leaning forward into the acceleration, he felt a rush of relief.

Amethyst light blossomed to his left, bloating like some sort of ephemeral boil. The light wasn't in his path, nor did it seem aimed to hinder him. Curious but not alarmed, Ty zipped past the boil and continued in the direction Sprite illuminated.

"Ty, look!" Hagemi called a moment later.

With a straight shot between the trees for several hundred feet, Ty risked a glance behind.

One of the Warped had transformed from a bipedal, tentacle-covered man-shape into a quadrupedal one. Sprouting a ring of purple gems around the crown of its head and each shoulder joint, it looked a bit like a skinless lion. It loped gracefully, moving twice as fast as before.

He had seconds before it reached him.

Another boil appeared directly in front of the path of one of the Warped. As it passed through the boil, the Warped was remade. In one step it went from its normal, hulking form and into a near carbon copy of the lion.

Hagemi glitched. Its physical form fuzzed, breaking into fractals and color, then went solid, only to fuzz again.

Warning! *A god is acting directly against you. This violates the Resonance Pact.*

The air above Ty roared as a purple meteorite speared through the sky and into the ground ahead of his path. He had plenty of time to weave, narrowly missing the outermost rim of violet flame. In the center of the impact, a being rose to cloven feet. The thing looked a bit like a traditional demon, with a man's body on goat legs, bat-like wings, and a man's torso. Its heads were twin twining snakes with amethysts for eyes. All four eyes jerked in his direction as he rode past, and the creature gestured with one muscular, black-clawed hand. A violet fireball the size of his head shot from its hand, narrowly missing him and vanishing into the wood.

That's a Lieutenant General. She's cheating. The Arbiter felt oddly cold in his thoughts, preternaturally emotionless and distant.

"What do you mean she's cheating?" Ty screamed into the wind as he jerked the ATV around the bole of a tree, then nearly went flying over a root. He couldn't keep looking back, so he bent all his efforts to avoid straight lines that the fireball thrower could use. He added, "Sprite, if Aquamarine can hear this, I could really use some help right now!"

No time to explain. I have been allowed to help a little. Give me control of one of your arms. A prompt appeared in Ty's mind.

Warning: *Your Arbiter has requested permission to control aspects of your body. This authority must be given voluntarily and may be revoked at any time.*

Lacking any better options, he agreed. His left arm tightened on the ATV's handles, twisting forward to maximize the acceleration. A sense of numbness had gone through the arm the instant he'd accepted Hagemi's request; to his mind, he no longer *had* a left arm.

Let me steer. It's the most I can do, but between my ability to scout and coordinate this arm, you should be free to act.

Steer? Ty mentally screamed at the Arbiter. *If you can do this, why not take control of my* other *arm and shoot the damn things for me?*

Arbiters may not attack scions directly. It is a tenant greater than the Resonance Pact. Stop debating and act before you die.

Frustrated, terrified, and confused, Ty drew his remaining pistol. Twisting with his left arm pinned to the ATV wasn't comfortable, but he made it work. The landscape behind him was an impossible jumble of motion. Multiple Warped neared his flanks, while the snake demon appeared between the tree branches above, flying on its improbably massive wings. Bumps in the trail, coupled with the sudden jerks of the handlebars, made firing at anything reliably impossible. He didn't even know where to take his first shot.

I can't shoot like this, he thought. *I need a straight track or something less bumpy.*

Hagemi didn't reply, but he felt his senses smooth out. An instinctive awareness flooded between the bond between himself and his Arbiter, letting him know its intentions before they happened. More than that, he somehow knew the path they were on, could see it in his mind's eye. The random jerkiness of the ride became less of a carnival joyride into nightmares and more of a somewhat bumpy walk.

He *could* work with that.

Ty began shooting. He started by aiming at the shoulder joints of the lions. Remembering what Hagemi had said about magical gemstones, he figured those were empowering the Warped. Three shots in and one of the closer lions stumbled, a leg collapsing beneath it. Another lion, closer than the rest, leaped, paws claws extended for the rear of the ATV.

Hagemi veered to the side at the last moment, anticipating the perfect trajectory to avoid the swipe. Ty shot the thing in one of its crown gemstones as it flew past.

Sprite squeaked a warning, and Ty looked up in time to see two purple fireballs shooting in his direction. The things didn't move bullet-fast, but they still closed the distance in seconds.

Can't dodge them both, Hagemi said, a note of apology conveyed with the words.

"Ahhhhagh!" Ty screamed in rage and fear. He was level zero. He had three damn hit points left. What was happening? Hagemi jerked the ATV to one side, dodging the first fireball by millimeters. Sprite zipped in the way of the second.

The little spirit should have been too small to affect the path of the fireball, but the power it held must have outsized its physical form. The fireball exploded on impact, showering Ty in purple sparks and heat.

A hissing roar ripped through both heads of the flying demon as it wove both hands in the air, conjuring new fireballs. Three more of the lions closed in, two of them now galloping evenly along Ty's sides.

Ty shot one in the shoulder, miraculously hitting a gemstone on the first try.

A tree hit the other. No, the senses Hagemi lent him *told* him that a tree had hit the other. When he physically looked in the direction it had been, Ty saw that a tree sloth the size of a literal giant had appeared out of nowhere and swiped at the thing. The remains of the Warped looked like three-day-old roadkill.

Look up!

The flying demon zipped around a branch, bobbing to get a better view. Green light burst from the tree, exploding into a cloud of blue and white mist that solidified into an uncoiling Aquamarine. The dragon extended its full length, easily as long as a school bus, as it projected itself forward, eyes wide and jaws agape. The fierce predator Ty had noticed before was back, magnified a dozen times as the feral-looking dragon slammed into the demon. Aquamarine's jaws clamped down on a demonic wing as each of its articulated legs raked across his body, drawing terrible, glowing furrows into its opponents flesh.

Writhing and whipping around, the demon's moment of disorientation was enough to give the dragon an opening. Nimble fingers dancing, Aquamarine summoned vines from the nearby foliage. They shot out, creating a net that wrenched dragon and demon to the ground. Moving with all the sinuous grace of a serpent, the dragon positioning itself atop the demon at the last second. The earth shook from the impact.

"Stop!" Ty shouted.

We shouldn't, Hagemi warned.

"I have to help," Ty said, demanding again, "Circle back!" He'd been driving fast enough that he no longer had confidence in his aim at the current range.

Hagemi relented, turning the ATV around.

Aquamarine and the demon wrestled on the ground, the demon ripping at the vines and dragon with black claws. Cat-like, the dragon bobbed in and out, cunning hands moving with wicked precision to draw scores of wounds across its unstoppable enemy.

Nearby, a dozen of the lion Warped surrounded three of the giant sloths. He hadn't been seeing things. The brown-furred forest creatures looked almost exactly like sloths from his world, albeit two of them were fifteen feet tall. One was closer to twelve. Each moved cumbersomely, taking inelegant swipes at the clawing, biting lions.

Ty wouldn't have thought it was close to a fair fight. The sloths were just too slow, the lions too fast. He saw one Warped get in the way of another, delaying it long enough to allow a sloth to hit them both. One swipe and both turned to paste. Still, the other lions were fighting in near unison and leaving terrible wounds on the sloths. Whatever upgrade the Warped had received from the purple light, it had made them into truly fearsome fighters. Then the three sloths vanished.

One moment they were there, and the next they sank into the ground. The trio appeared above; their furry limbs wrapped around nearby trees. They hooted, drawing the attention of the lions, who leaped after them. The sloths merged with the trees, their torsos appearing from the ground directly behind their enemies. Though the sloths were slow, their ambush was well timed. Clawed paws bigger than Ty's entire ATV came down, crushing two of the lions flat.

Ty glanced down to reload. When he looked up, two of the lions had leaped onto the back of the smaller of the three sloths and were clawing at its shoulders and back, kicking bloody furrows. The other two sloths froze, looking at the third. They hooted in high-pitched, worried outrage, ignoring the remaining lions who were poised to take advantage of the opening.

Aiming, he exhaled and squeezed the trigger once, twice, three times. He kept shooting, strafing the clinging lions, aiming for the bright-gleaming gemstones on their shoulder joints.

Both lions fell. He didn't think those shots had killed either of them, but the brief paralysis was enough to give the smaller sloth time to react. It stomped down. Monster lions turned to paste.

As soon as the third was out of danger, the other two sloths loosed warbling cries of renewed fury and pain, rounding on their attackers.

Ty, the general! Hagemi's warning cry drew him back to Aquamarine's fight with the demon.

Somehow, the demon had not only freed itself from the net, but it had also shoved Aquamarine to the ground, holding the dragon's neck with one hand. Aquamarine looked dazed, the dragon's face covered in bloody furrows. The demon's snake heads danced in an odd rhythm, eyes leaving glowing afterimages into the air. Its free hand gestured, slowly coalescing another, even larger, fireball.

"The true Mother sends her regards." The demon's voice was claws on glass and bullets shattering pottery.

Despite Hagemi's translation, just hearing the tones made Ty's head throb with pain. Taking control of his body back, he dismounted the ATV and started shooting at the demon.

None of the shots hit. Or, if they did, they didn't do any damage. For the first time, Ty saw what he thought was an actual barrier flaring into visibility with each of the bullet hits. Though the rounds didn't hurt the demon, they drew some of its attention away from Aquamarine. One head swiveled toward Ty, the other continuing to dance in place.

The demon's serpent heads were bigger than Ty had first suspected, each being closer to a crocodile in size and shape than a regular snake. Its gemstone eyes were still quite small, however, and made awful targets. Ty kept shooting regardless. None of the bullets passed the demon's protective barrier.

With a toothy grin, the demon hissed, "Give us back what you stole, human," and adjusted the trajectory of its spell-casting hand. A fireball the size of a small car manifested in the air, crackling with obdurate power and malice.

Confused, Ty started to reply but glimpsed motion in the distance. Something white was charging in their direction, moving at blurring speed. He knew he had to distract the demon for another second, so he improvised.

"General, put down your fire." Ty roared the words, hoping to mask the sound of hooves. Gesturing with his gun, he continued, "I have appropriated what I sought. Now, it is only a matter of time until all is revealed. Join me! Be my first lieutenant, and I shall grant you glory!"

Ty had no clue if what he said made any kind of sense, but something in his words or his tone was enough to give it pause. The demon blinked at him, as if in confusion more than consideration.

The Opal Guardian slammed into the demon like a train, its triple horns ripping through the magical barrier and its chest like a semi driving through wet tissue.

Leaping at the last possible second, the stallion's hooves barely cleared Aquamarine's back as it carried the demon away from the downed dragon. The demon's glimmering eyes flared, life still pulsing in its veins, until the horse rammed it into a tree. Viscera and gore showered the stallion. If the stallion so much as felt the impact, it didn't show. Wrenching its horns out of the tree, the horse jerked its head around for new targets, incandescent magic and rage flaring in its eyes.

Holy shit, Ty thought. *I gotta get me one of those. Unicorn riders, watch your backs. Ty on an Opal Guardian is gonna power game the whole rest of the session.*

Seeing one of the disembodied demon's heads still twitching feebly, Ty raced over and shot it at almost point-blank range in the eye.

Congratulations! *You have slain a General of the Monster Goddess. Would you like to loot the corpse? If so, where would you like the loot deposited?*

With the death of the general, the few surviving lions fled, leaving the bloodied trio of sloths, Aquamarine, and Ty alone in the woods.

"You know I didn't kill that demon. I don't deserve the loot," Ty said into the silence after.

Hagemi replied with smug serenity, *Technically, you landed the last shot. As your personal Game Master, I rule it counts.*

Chapter 17: Wyld Knight

Aquamarine rose from the ground, one eye swollen shut, and looked around. "That fucker killed one of my sprites!" he announced.

Ty bit back an urge to giggle. Those words, from a *dragon* with an English accent. It shouldn't have been hilarious, it just was. When the amusement passed, he felt his heart sink. Sprite hadn't been a friend, or even much of a companion, but the little spirit had saved his life multiple times. "I'm sorry, Aquamarine. I would have saved it if I could."

Aquamarine snorted and held up one of his hands. A sprite appeared above it, looking as far as Ty could tell, like a replica of the original. "They are part of *me*, Ty, not individuals. When one dies, it just really stings. No real spiritual death took place." The newly formed Sprite zipped back over to Ty, the centaur-shaped insect in the center buzzing happily as it neared.

The three sloths plodded over, moving quietly despite their size. Blood matted their fur, and the little supported dangling arm with one hand.

"I may know how to help," Ty said.

"How, Ty?" Aquamarine asked, one eye pivoting to face him. "The injures of the Mad Goddess are not lightly treated."

"Back at the village, there are casks of Celestial blood. I mixed a few drops in water and it healed me," Ty explained.

Aquamarine's jaws dropped open in a grimace. "Ty, that may have worked for you, but it will not for us. Celestial mana does not have innate healing properties for our kind."

Hagemi appeared nearby, rotating slowly in the air. "Check your prompts."

He did.

Divine Achievement - Mana Prism: *You have, through a combination of luck and uncanny instincts, survived exposure to three types of divine mana simultaneously. During this process, your Soul Cage adapted, growing an augmented ability: Mana Prism. Your Mana Prism will allow you to transform one type of mana into another. This currently includes Monstrous, Divine, and Wild types. You may output your abilities as any of those magic types. Should you survive contact with other potent sources of aligned magic, they may be added to this ability. This ability was generated organically and is all-but unknown in scions. I cannot predict the potential side-effects of this power, nor am I allowed to guess.*

Epic Achievement: Mana Siphon. *You have survived the deliberate consumption of a dangerous, divine-aligned substance. From now on, you may regain mana when consuming such substances. Mana gained in this way may not exceed the maximum mana you can store. The type of mana gained in this way will be aligned with whatever the source is, potentially improving or decreasing its effects when used with your other abilities. Using Magic Siphon does not reduce the damage you suffer when consuming divine material.*

Temporary Achievement: Wyld Knight. *You have earned a onetime, limited offer from your god. You may spend nine merits, along with the unexpended Monstrous and Divine power you have absorbed thus far to unlock the Wyld Knight ability package. This package has been customized by your Arbiter on behalf of your god.*

Ty frowned, reading the achievements. He was about to protest that he did not have nine merits to spend when he saw his character status menu.

Level: 2

Max Hit Points: 10

Current Hit Points: 4

Current Mana: 4

Current Mana Shield: 2

Unspent Merits: 9

Unspent Physical Attribute Points: 4

Unspent Discretionary Attribute Points: 4

His hit points had only gone up by two, but he'd received the full bonus merits from Inspiration upon reaching the new level. He didn't have time to think about the attribute point allocation, not with his allies in danger. So far there was no sign of corruption working its way through the sloths' bodies or Aquamarine, but that didn't mean it wouldn't.

"Wyld Knight?" Ty said, glaring at Hagemi.

"The name is appropriate," Hagemi said, giving absolutely no sign of chagrin. "Besides, the name makes sense. You will, in essence, be combining your knight-like behavior in representing your god, Inspiration, and in protecting the source of your Wild power. Thus: Wyld Knight."

Ty ground his teeth. He didn't want to argue the point. Given circumstances, he assumed that Inspiration had done what he could to ensure Ty got what he needed from the package. Still, he knew if he didn't say something now, he'd regret it forever.

"I am *not* emo. Rename it Knight of the Wild, please."

Hagemi hesitated. "I will reiterate what you learned earlier. The Wild is a force that makes most magical entities, gods included, uncomfortable. Being a Wyld Knight is one thing. It's cheeky and fun. Actively taking the title of Knight of the Wild may lead to consequences you are not prepared for."

Ty shrugged dismissively. "What's the worst that can happen? Do it."

The achievement flashed and reappeared with the new wording and Ty's intended spelling. He thought he detected mild disappointment from Hagemi. Ty accepted the offer.

Knight of the Wild: *As a Knight of the Wild, you have unlocked the following benefits:*

First: You are treated as Wild-aligned and qualify to receive any benefits normally limited to Wild-aligned beings. Your abilities that would not normally affect Wild-aligned beings now do.

*Second: You have earned the **Verdant Touch** ability. You may spend your mana to create Wild-aligned healing energy that may be delivered with physical contact. The amount of healing will increase at levels five, ten, fifteen, twenty, and so on. At level eight, this ability may be used to cleanse diseases, curses, and other maladies. It may also regenerate limbs starting at level fifteen. The amount of mana spent to cure significant maladies will be proportional to those afflictions. You may use this ability on yourself.*

Third: You may communicate with any intelligent, natural being. This includes sentient plants.

Ty reeled as he read over the ability package. Combined with his achievements, this was simultaneously incredibly powerful and limited. Nothing in the abilities would help him deal with enemies any better, nor was there something as obviously useful as a movement power or even inventory management. Still, his gut told him he'd been given a far larger benefit than simply reading the abilities would show.

He approached the smaller sloth. It looked at him with huge, liquid black eyes filled with pain. Ty's heart ached for the sloth as he reached out to touch its fur, and attempted to tap into his new ability.

Like this. Hagemi stirred, projecting the method directly into his mind. He didn't just want to heal the sloth; he wanted to restore it to its natural state.

Warmth blossomed in his chest. An incredible, joyous feeling exploded through his torso, filling his lungs, and bubbling up into his scalp. He heard music in the sounds of nature around him, with every rustle of leaves and murmur of motion sounding pitch perfect in a swelling choir. A pure, vibrant sense of connectedness rolled down Ty's hand. For a moment, he and the sloth were one. He could feel the magnificent creature's slowly beating heart, feel its broken limb and the slow, creeping corruption in its veins.

Ty made it right.

He didn't make it right *only* with Wild energy. As the power poured into the sloth, he shot a thought to Hagemi, who assisted him. The energy pouring out of his hand fluctuated, taking on a hint of divinity. Ty healed the sloth and simultaneously burned out the corruption. He intuited that what he was doing was inefficient and causing the sloth pain; his power didn't natively have a purification element to it. When he saw fresh tears of pain in the sloth's eyes, he felt a wave of guilt and doubt, but then he also sensed the renewal rushing in with the cleansing. In the end, as the last of his energy left him and he slumped with fatigue, the sloth's arm was whole, as were many of its wounds. More importantly, his use of *Magic Prism* had allowed him to counter the effects of the Monster God's minions.

Now he just had the other sloths and Aquamarine to help.

"Need more mana," Ty said, a wave of fatigue crushing down on him.

Using your mana, even with my help optimizing its flow, will make you fatigued until your mana pool is significantly higher. Your Spirit attribute is key to deepening this pool.

Ty thought back to his Arbiter, *Are you supposed to be helping me like this? Taking control of my body, customizing achievements, and helping me use my powers feels a bit like the Dungeon Master favoring a specific player.*

Remember, my purpose is to allow you to effectively act as though you were part of this world. All Arbiters will help their assigned Earthlings effectively access their abilities. Furthermore, the powers you have earned are in alignment with your choices and Inspiration's intentions. These achievements and abilities allow you to act with incredible flexibility, if not the same straightforward potency as others.

And taking control of my body?

She cheated. I assisted to balance the scales. It was allowed.

Ty took a moment to catch his breath and process. The Arbiter was right. If he'd simply received a spell reward that allowed him to annihilate the Warped, his options would have been far narrower. He'd also have been more combat viable.

"I need to go back to the village," Ty said to Aquamarine once he could focus. "There are barrels of divine blood I can use to replenish my mana. That will allow me to heal the rest of you."

The dragon's jaws dipped open as labored, wheezing breaths rattled through its chest. His many wounds suppurated and pulsed with infection. If the lion

Warped had carried potent corruption, the flying thing must have been ove-rflowing with the stuff.

"Boblin can take you, if she is willing," Aquamarine said, gesturing with one hand at the small sloth.

Boblin looked at Ty and made a melodic warbling sound. "You saved my life. I would be honored to share the magic of passage with you."

For the first time, Ty realized that he was hearing Aquamarine and Boblin without Hagemi's translations. True to his previous discussion with Hagemi, the dragon did, in fact, sound British. Boblin sounded vaguely like a New Zealander.

"I am honored by your trust. Let's go," Ty replied, only he didn't *say* the words. He warbled them. Thinking in English only to have a part of his brain just... shift it into something else felt incredibly weird.

Boblin's eyes filled with warmth as she bent down and scooped him up between her clawed paws. She studied him, eyes filled with something that he translated as deep affection. Then she merged with the ground and took him with her.

Ty was one with nature. Traveling through it, he experienced an expanding awareness of the magic of the surrounding forest. For a heartbeat, he felt the life in the dirt; thousands of strange insects and animals thrived within the forest and he was connected with all of them. The sense lasted a moment before the two of them stepped out of a tree.

They were feet away from the encircling black line.

Disoriented, he stumbled forward, dropping knee deep into a swampy pool. A serpentine shape disturbed the surface of the water, seeming about to lunge at potential prey. He could feel the creature through a newfound sense. He felt its hunger. The instant he connected with the serpent's mind, the creature simply veered off, as if uninterested.

"Now *that's* neat," he said, extricating himself from the mud. He glanced back over his shoulder and saw Boblin there, watching on impassively. "Can you come with me?"

Boblin shook her head. "My friend, I would rather wait here. This place feels like death to me. Bring back what you can. I will transport us back."

Ty understood her trepidation. While the Monster God's scions might not cause Boblin and her kind to explode, the threat was just as real. He leaped over the black line and rushed toward the village.

"You know I'm becoming more of a druid type than anything else," Ty observed as he went.

Druid-adjacent, yes.

"I'm not sure if that vibes with my overall plan."

What do you mean?

Ty shrugged, rounding the bole of a twisted tree and coming into sight of the first buildings. There were no signs of the Warped. "Shooting things is going to become less and less of an option, unless I go all 'magic bullets' and get abilities that enchant my guns. Without better ways to deal damage to overwhelming opponents, I'll be as good as dead in our next serious fight."

Hagemi manifested nearby and spoke aloud. "Actually, I wouldn't dismiss the magic bullets option. There are also several assassin and shadow abilities that might come in useful for you, if you wish to continue down the precision route. Many of the assassin powers can make mundane weapons deal increased damage to powerful opponents or bypass health shields and barriers entirely. You may also consider mobility offerings, especially as your next level will be pivotal."

Ty walked into the village warily, looking about for signs of inhabitants and finding none. The remains of the deceased Weavers remained where he'd left them, and he saw no indications that the lion Warped had passed through the streets. Walking around the buildings, he did, however, find a convenient cart to haul some goods behind him.

"I had been considering something with mobility. Also, level three? Why is that pivotal?"

"It'll be your next significant opportunity to get a pool of merits. Plus, unless it goes like this village did, it will probably take more time and effort for you to progress further. Level three might be your best opportunity to establish your personal flavor."

"Makes sense," Ty said, inspecting the cart. It was constructed simply, with hard wood reinforced by steel plates. There were handles at the back and some sort of attachment at the front, presumably so a local animal could haul a heavier load. The interior of the cart was empty, and he could push and maneuver it with minimal effort.

Outside of the tavern, he mentally opened his character sheet. He'd thought about the unspent attribute points for a while before deciding on what he wanted to do. First, he'd considered putting points into vitality, just so he'd feel safer in combat. That didn't seem like an option worth the effort, though; this world might have something called "hit points" and he *had* seen a magical health barrier come into play, but a ton of nuance was summarized in that simplified total. He passed over Agility entirely for now. Dodging and rolling sounded fun, but that wasn't going to help him now.

He chose strength. Without an inventory system, strength would be useful in non-combat scenarios more often than the other attributes. In combat, he mostly relied on his guns so far, and those felt as much skill based as leaning on his attributes. If he got into a physical altercation, like with the Warped, his strength was, by and far, the weakest link.

He upped the score by the full four points, taking the total to thirteen. On the screen, the new total appeared, and he saw a flash of "*highly athletic*" next to the number. Before committing to the change, he considered his discretionary points. Hagemi told him that his mana pool would be his Spirit score multiplied by his level. It would replenish normally throughout the day or with meditation.

Hagemi explained, "If you'd worshipped the God of Magic or any of the more intellectual-leaning gods, your mana pool would have been much bigger, simply by virtue of being based off your Intelligence instead of Spirit. On the plus side, the more you increase your Spirit score, the more aligned with Inspiration and me you'll become. It's a bit of a tradeoff."

Having had some insight as to just how flexible and useful his Verdant Touch would become over time, he opted to commit every point to his Spirit attribute, bringing it to a six. That would raise his mana to twelve, significantly increasing the overall output.

Ty paused outside the cellar and committed the changes. Sizzling, electric energy rushed into his body. His muscles contracted, spasming out of control, dropping him to his knees. Simultaneously, he felt an overwhelming sense of awe and awareness *shoved* into his being.

It took a few minutes for the changes to complete, after which he felt exhausted and famished. He looked down at his arms and noted additional muscle and definition. Ironically, he figured he probably looked a bit like a professional bodybuilder now, just because of the biodynamics of the transformation. No doubt in a few weeks of adventuring and eating regularly, he'd look more like a powerlifter. Not that he cared much, given what was at stake.

Ty made his way into the cellar. Nothing had changed since he'd been there last. Walking to one of the glowing casks, he popped the top with his knife. Using the blade as a makeshift dipper, he poured a few drops into his canteen.

He pulled his character sheet up and took a swig. The fluid burned his mouth as he swallowed, and his hit points dropped by two. It didn't hurt like he'd just lost half the rest of his life. His mana rose, going from six to eight. Once he knew there was a one-to-one ratio of damage dealt versus mana gained, he tried to heal himself.

I'll help with your first attempts. Once you get the hang of it, the process will be second-nature. Hagemi's presence gently expanded, guiding him through the next steps.

To heal himself, he first transformed the Celestial power into Wild, which took a few seconds of concentration. Once the Celestial burn vanished, taking on the cool properties of Wild, he pulled on the healing nature native to his Wild gift, consuming one point of mana.

A couple of things happened simultaneously. First, he felt a wave of fatigue that nearly knocked him unconscious. Before he could fall, however, he saw his hit points go up by two, followed by a rush of vitality and jubilation. Healing didn't just mend cuts and bruises; it also partially refreshed his mind and spirit, almost negating the debilitating effects of using mana.

"I guess I'm a healing battery now, eh?" Ty directed at Hagemi, who did not reply.

Using the new ratios, he took the precious seconds to heal himself completely. The process was not instantaneous. Between being careful about how much of the Celestial blood he consumed to converting the mixed water into Wild energy, it took around six seconds. He made a note to practice as much as possible before trying either of them during combat.

Having spent so much time experimenting, Ty forwent the wagon and took a single barrel of the blood with him directly to Boblin. He made it to her, and they used the sloth's transportation ability to return to Aquamarine and the other sloths. The Opal Guardian was still there too, standing regally off to the side and watching over the injured group.

Thankfully, none of the hurt creatures were significantly worse by the time they got back. With his newfound power, coupled with the achievements, it took him less than five minutes to fully heal them all.

As Ty worked, the Guardian gradually eased closer. By the time he had finished his ministrations, the stallion was within reaching distance. It looked at him with its bright, intelligent eyes, seeming interested in receiving some of the healing the others had, despite having no visible injuries. Seeing little harm in it, he lay his hand on the stallion and spent a few points of mana.

Emerald light ignited around the Guardian's horns, swirling around and through the protrusions. The horse shook his head from side to side and stamped one foot on the ground near his feet. Ty read the motions as clearly as if the horse had spoken. Though it did not have language, the stallion had conveyed deep gratitude.

"I think he would bond with you should you gain such a power, Ty," Aquamarine said.

"Me too!" Boblin spoke up, pushing in until the giant sloth was standing even with the stallion.

"Bond?" Ty asked. Then, looking at Hagemi, he added, "Is that like taking an animal companion or a familiar?"

"Yes," Hagemi and Aquamarine answered simultaneously.

Aquamarine added, "Bonding a magical creature is a holy melding of spirit and mind. It is a process unlike anything else in our world, as it allows two unalike beings to forge a bridge between them."

Ty glanced between Boblin and the stallion and smiled. "I appreciate the offer, both of you. For now, I don't have that sort of power. To be honest, I may not even go further down the Wild path. I don't know if becoming a druid or Warden of Nature, or whatever you might know it as, is where my destiny leads." He added mentally, *Plus, I've seen Old Yeller.*

Hagemi privately explained, *I should also make a note that Wild is not Nature. Scions who are druids worship Nature. No one worships the Wild. There are no gods of the Wild.*

"Good to know." Maybe he'd be safe from accidentally becoming a druid.

The two larger sloths stepped forward and draped their paws over Boblin's shoulders, pulling her back from Ty. One of them said firmly, "Darling, you are an adult and capable of making your own decisions, but bonding with a human is not a wise choice. I don't care who the human is or what he's done, it's not safe for us to leave the forest. Also, this man smells like Artifice."

Snorting, the Opal Guardian stamped a foot and shook its head again. The message was simple. The horse would do what it wanted.

"What will you do now, Ty?" Aquamarine asked, blinking both eyes and resuming his bird-like glances around the area.

"First, I need to do this," he said, acknowledging the prompt that must have been driving Hagemi crazy. A sack appeared at his feet. If he had been hoping for something insanely powerful from the snake-headed demon, he was woefully mistaken. All it held were gemstones.

Putting the sack in a pouch on his ATV, Ty projected a mental glare in Hagemi's direction. "Now, I think I want to go back and investigate the village a bit more. Do you mind making sure my convoy stays safe? My instincts tell me I might be there for a while." He was planning to go down the well, but he wasn't about to tell Aquamarine that. If his suspicions about the area below the well proved true, the dragon would not want him going back to the town.

The stallion bobbed his head before Aquamarine could answer.

"I don't know what I've done to earn such loyalty and trust, but I appreciate it more than you can know," Ty said, reaching out to place a hand on the stallion's cheek.

Before he said his goodbyes, he asked Boblin to return him to his camp long enough to collect a few things. The sloth did so with little cajoling and less fanfare. In a matter of minutes, he had re-upped his supplies, swapped out the battery on his ATV, and was headed back to the village.

Quest: *You have discovered an intriguing and ancient ruin beneath a mortal village. Given recent events, it is quite probable that there are ties between the Monster God and the demons who were digging in your earlier quest. Investigate the nature of these ruins.* **Reward:** *25% of the experience needed to reach level 3.*

Interlude Three: Interference

Surviving Earth Participants: 37,641

     Average Level: 1.8

Days Remaining in Cycle: 28

"The Wild has taken the stage. Will we allow this?" The speaker was one of three who stood on a dais hovering above the gathered gods.

"Why would we stop it?" Balance asked.

"You know."

"This is different. The Wild has been given organically, as a blessing."

The symbols and starlight shapes of Magic's face had only the vaguest semblance of humanity. At Balance's reply, the greater god's displeasure was subtle, but clear. "The Wild is not a gift. It is a threat and should be treated as such."

"The Monster God acted against the scion, and the Wild adapted. This is the quintessential essence of fairness. We will not intervene out of fear."

"You accuse me of fear?"

"An abundance of caution, if you'd prefer."

"And when the Wild acts in accordance with its nature? When it threatens all we have built?"

Balance turned its attention back to the Great Arbiter. Thousands of scions lived and breathed on that display, each making decisions that would shape the future of worlds. It replied almost offhandedly. "If any scion threatens the Resonance, we will do what we must, in accordance with our natures."

Chapter 18: Artificial Integrity

Ty didn't go into the well immediately once he made it back to the town. After making certain that none of the Warped had returned, he barricaded himself inside the tavern's first floor and took some time. He ate rations and drank from his renewed water supply. Once he was full, he updated his notes. The process took hours, as the sheer volume of new variables and possibilities seemed endless. His gaming mind went into full geek mode as he conjectured about his Verdant Touch and Prism abilities, along with the combat potential it could lead him to.

Mana Prism reminds me a lot of a card game I used to play. In that game, the ability to produce different types of mana didn't directly lead to victory, but it enabled all sorts of long-term strategies. Hagemi had warmed him about the dragon's blessing; so far, the benefits outweighed the downsides.

Once he was done updating his notes, he hid behind the tavern's main desk and took a nap.

He slept at the tavern rather than his camp for a couple of reasons, chief among them being timeliness. He didn't intend to rest for long, and he hadn't known whether the sloths would have wanted to wait around while he did so. For the sake of convenience, he figured a quick nap on site was easier than a potentially long one at his "home base."

Ty's memories flattened into a single pane of glass, the timeline of his life on display. He saw his transformation, his transition to the new world. More than anything, he saw his own pain. The tentacle around his neck, the eel wrapped around his leg, the fear of being chased by overwhelming odds. He saw those moments on repeat, coupled with the subtle insight that there was nuance to the memories. This wasn't just a replay of injuries he'd sustained physically; he saw the expression on his face as the collusion of Divine and Monstrous energy seared his psyche to the bone.

Hagemi appeared, hovering over the glass, tendrils of light expanding from its facets. The light caressed the glass, somehow smoothing away the pain. Pressure here made one memory fade, just a bit, while pulling there made a different memory, one of joy at seeing a dragon for the first time, brighter.

A rustle jerked Ty awake. Sitting up, he looked around for the source of the sound and found a two-tailed mouse scuttling along a floorboard nearby. It blinked in his direction, showing no hint of fear.

"Oh yeah, Knight of the Wild," Ty muttered. He *still* wasn't sure this was anywhere near the path he'd have chosen for himself. Despite Hagemi's assurance that he'd need to worship Nature to become a druid, he increasingly felt like his abilities leaned in that direction. He didn't even like playing druids in video games, much less tabletop.

After Ty checked his weapons, he had a snack. At no point did he allow himself to acknowledge the mouse standing on top of the front desk or to think of the crumbs that he just *happened* to drop for it to nibble. "Not a druid," he announced firmly. Druid-adjacent, sure. But that was all. He didn't even *like* Birkenstocks or granola.

"Hagemi," Ty said, chewing on a power bar. The Arbiter manifested and orbited nearby, just out of reach. "Was my dream real? Are you manipulating my memories?"

Magenta and silver light pulsed in Hagemi's depths. "Boosting your Spirit gave you insight into your dreams, did it?"

"Don't dodge," Ty pressed.

"Yes, Ty. I do manipulate your mind. I do it all the time. I am not allowed to change things, or re-write anything you perceive, but I keep you functional." Hagemi's tone was matter of fact, and Ty felt no remorse from his bond.

"You're saying you prevent me from having PTSD?"

"Among other things, yes. I help you focus on what's ahead and clear out stray memories that could cloud your judgment. I also help you filter out physical pain, so it is less debilitating during combat."

Ty frowned. "Would you say that you 'optimize' my mind?" Regardless of whether the Arbiter re-wrote his thoughts, this was sounding a lot like mental surgery and not gentle healing.

"Optimize? No. Provide an opportunity to survive? Yes. I can't make choices for you. That's against the rules. What I can do is help you adjust to the reality of being a scion in this world. That means organizing what you experience in ways you can process it. It may also include helping you see what your god values, contextually. It does not, and cannot, mean thinking for you. I'm here so you survive without breaking down every time you experience something new, not to take your free will away."

"Ah."

"I should add the achievement you gained, Organized Mind, is all yours. It is doing a substantial amount of work already."

Other than his Verdant Touch ability, he didn't feel much different from when he'd arrived. Realizing that he'd gone off topic, he exhaled, wondering if his Arbiter was altering his mood even now. He could see what the Arbiter was saying. Without Hagemi's help, there was a solid possibility that even killing the demon general would have put him into some sort of shock. Who knew?

"Can I tell you to stop?" he asked softly.

Hagemi replied in an equally gentle tone. "You can. I can reset your mind, let you feel all the pain and suffering you would have gone through naturally, if you want. Over time, the Wild may even help you adapt on your own. Such a process would likely take years. You don't have years. We both know what will happen if you give me that command now."

He did. He knew what crushing doubt or dread could do.

"Thanks for being honest," he said at last. "I don't want you to stop. But maybe, in the future, when we're in a safe place, can I ask you to ease up a bit?

Let me feel some of what I should be going through, so I don't lose touch with my humanity?"

"Of course. As soon as we're safe. If it helps, completing quests will expedite your transition. Give it a few levels and my touch will be substantially lighter than it is now."

"That does help." From the perspective of a player at a game table, everything Hagemi said made absolute sense. In fact, Ty welcomed the help, if it was just that and no more. He'd accepted that this adventure would change him months ago. Then again, there was voluntary change and then there was manipulation.

He went downstairs and to the casks of Celestial blood. Filling up one of his canteens, he once again cursed his lack of an inventory power. If he'd been able to haul all the remaining barrels with him, the theoretical limiting factor of his ability to self-heal would only be time. One canteen should be enough, though, especially since a few drops could make an entire container of water into a healing elixir. With one canteen dedicated to the blood, that left him two for drinking. He would have to hope that there was some sort of water supply in the dungeon or that he didn't stay down too long.

Despite his attempts to optimize his gear, he was nearly overloaded. Without his bump in strength, he wouldn't have felt confident going down into the dungeon. With it, he figured he'd just find convenient places to drop his bag before he got into fights.

Yeah, monsters are just going to announce themselves in the dungeon. That's how that works, he thought sourly.

As ready as he could be, Ty made his way out to the well. It had been utterly blasted apart, ripping any sign that it had existed from the area. In its place was a smooth, five-foot diameter hole straight in the ground. Spiraling stairs began at ground level. They led into the depths, their surfaces blackened but unchipped or marred by however long they'd been submerged. Lowering his goggles over his eyes, he proceeded into his first dungeon.

Chapter 19: The First Dungeon

He descended into darkness. Toggling his goggles on, they transformed the endless stairs into green-hued outlines. Had he been skilled enough to do more than a cursory check for traps, he doubted he would have been able to find any, not with the low resolution view the goggles gave him. He didn't dare use his flashlights or phone in case doing so announced his presence to whatever might be waiting. Years of dungeon crawls had taught him the benefits of careful dungeoneering.

At no point did he feel the dampness he thought should linger in the area. Either the monsters had polluted the water enough that the Celestial blood had vaporized it all, or something else was going on. Three hours later, he finally reached his destination.

The stairs ended in a round landing area with a set of double doors on the far wall. An ornate, horned, humanoid skull spanned both doors, some cunning craftsmanship integrating the hair-thin gap between them into the design. Blood-red rubies danced in the horned creature's eyes, and its mouth gaped open, the teeth subtly protruding from the metallic surface.

Seeing the sharp teeth suggested what Ty might need to do to open the doors, but he opted to go through the old school dungeon exploring basics first. He touched the metal with the back of one gloved hand. Nothing happened. He pressed his ear to the door, hoping to get a sense of what might be on the other side. No sound penetrated the metal. He knocked on the door. The material was so dense that the impact barely made a sound. Finally, with a resigned sigh, he opened a cut on the side of his hand with a knife.

He smeared the blood across the door's teeth.

A strange jolt traveled through Ty's arm and into his mind, where he felt it touch Hagemi. The Arbiter didn't seem to notice, as it made no comment when the doors swung open.

Cloudy, diffuse light filled the space beyond, allowing Ty to remove his goggles. Beyond the double doors was a long, rectangular hallway ending in a dais at the far wall. Twin rows of elegant pillars, their lengths carved to resemble spines, supported the ceiling. Two doors on either side of the dais led from the room. Both had demon-faced carvings on them. Seeing the tableau sent a thrill of dread into his heart.

Ice slid into his chest and mind, calming the dread. His eyes found fascinating shapes, wandered across the carved spines in a slow, thoughtful caress. What if there was something interesting tucked between the nodules on one of those spines? What about the throne? There was no need to be afraid; not when there were so many things to explore.

Stepping into the room, Ty spent the mana to heal his wound. The effort took enough concentration that he didn't notice the doors swinging closed behind him until it was too late.

Caah-click. The lock snapped into place.

A sonorous voice boomed throughout the chamber, tones of accusation and rage dripping from every word. "How dare you! How dare you come here, after what your kind did, after your treachery!"

Both doors opened, and Ty saw figures move within. He bolted to the left, drawing and firing at the shape in the doorway as he sprinted toward it. If the bullets did anything at all, he couldn't tell. His shoulder barreling into the creature *did* knock it back, however, and he kicked the door closed behind him before the others joined.

Breathing heavily, Ty saw what the thing was. It was an eight-foot-tall skeleton, draped in rune-covered bandages. The bandages gave off an eerie emerald glow that trailed behind the creature's movements as it clawed at him. Its fingertips were deadly sharp, and they lacerated his armor and the flesh beneath with minimal effort. He shot it again.

The bullets had no effect.

"Fuck me," Ty growled, holstering the gun and putting his hands up. In theory, he knew one way to fight this monster. It just sucked to have his guns rendered useless. Celestial fire blossomed in Ty's hands as he activated Verdant Touch and transformed the energy into the Celestial type. Thankfully, changing the type in that way didn't cause damage.

Order. Order from Chaos. Put corruption down. Do what is right. Do what must be done. The thoughts surfaced, almost distracting him from another series of wild slashes. With an effort of will, he suppressed the Celestial mana's influence. Surprisingly, the urges vanished the moment he made the attempt.

The corridor was wide, giving him room to maneuver, and the skeleton was incredibly slow. It still grazed him several times. By the time he had finished his preparation, pieces of his armor were hanging in shreds over bleeding gashes in his stomach and shoulders.

Ty hit the skeleton with a Celestial-infused punch, and the skeleton's neck vaporized. The head and body fell into two separate piles, the corpse still desperately writhing toward him.

Congratulations! *You have defeated an Apostate Librarian. Would you like to loot the corpse? If so, where would you like the loot deposited?*

Ignoring the prompt and the empty inventory window, he looked around. He was in a long, wide corridor with evenly spaced doors on either side. Thankfully, the ambient light suffused this place, too. The door behind him rattled, the metallic sound echoing from many of the doors down the corridor.

Ty realized with growing horror that he was about to be surrounded by lethal librarians.

Any other time, he might have found the thought absurdly amusing. Now? It just added insult to the situation.

He sprinted down the tunnel, trying to outpace the emerging undead. Doors opened on either side as he ran, disgorging undead minions into the hall. Still, Ty ran. As time passed, growing into minutes, he wondered how many librarians the place had. Endless, infinite, doors stretched ahead, almost all of them in various states of opening. Charging his hands, Ty checked his status. He was down to seven hit points.

The sheer length of the hall, coupled with the amount of emerging undead, forced Ty to pause and fight between some rooms. With his Divinely charged hands, killing the skeletons was less about doing enough damage; rather, he had to avoid slowing down, lest the veritable army of scholars overwhelm him.

Congratulations! *You have defeated an Apostate Librarian. Would you like to loot the corpse? If so, where would you like the loot deposited?*

Prompts piled up in the corner of Ty's vision as he crushed one skeleton, sprinted to the next series of doors, killed another one or two, and moved on. Mercifully, the space between the doors was *just* wide enough for him to prepare between encounters. If one door was opening faster than the other, he'd attack the skeleton coming out of that one first. If both were opening equally fast, he'd try to run past or dodge into whichever skeleton looked the slowest.

Ten minutes into his run, Ty was running low on mana. He'd been forced to heal himself multiple times, and while using his Verdant Touch to down the skeletons wasn't expensive, he only had sixteen mana points. He needed to recharge.

Back the way he'd come, a tidal wave of undead shuffled in his direction. Ahead, more skeletons appeared. Triggering all the loot prompts at once, he gestured behind him, hoping a pile of objects would appear and slow the wave down. Then, covering his head with his arms, he hunched his shoulders and ran as fast as he could. Pain lanced through his shoulders and sides. At one point, a clawed hand sliced through the strap holding his rifle in place, and he lost it. A moment later, he stumbled over a bone foot and barely righted himself before a trio of skeletons could catch him.

He was in a nightmare.

Finally, he rounded a corner and saw a new pair of double doors. Identical to the last, he didn't hesitate to smear some of the copious amounts of his blood on the engraving's fangs.

The doors opened, and Ty shot through without looking at the next room. As soon as he was past the gap in the doors, he turned and pushed against them with all his might. Trying to force them closed.

They obliged.

Rustling from behind stole any sense of relief from the reprieve as he turned to look for the source of the sound. He was in a square room, around thirty feet across, and lined with bookshelves filled to overflowing with tomes and scrolls. Several tables and scholarly alcoves dotted the room, with magic candles adding pinpricks of warmth to the ever-present gloom.

In the middle of the room, a pile of bones wrapped in a brown robe twitched.

Ty had three mana left. He used two to heal himself and one to surround his hands with a Divine Verdant Touch.

The bent, gnarled shape of bone within the robe moved faster than he expected, a single finger pointing in his direction. Garbled, sharp syllables passed cadaverous lips as the skeleton spoke a spell. A line of red energy struck him in the chest. Weakness and pain tore through him, making his knees nearly buckle. A bulging pulse shot from him back into his attacker through the light, and he saw desiccated flesh expanding across its arm. Empty eye sockets ballooned, as fluid bloomed into fresh eyes for the monstrous thing.

Fighting a sense of paralysis, knowing it probably wouldn't hurt the creature, Ty drew his pistol and began firing. His first bullets ricocheted off the creature's robe, utterly ineffectual. One, however, nudged the skeleton's hand to the side *just* enough to bring the spell out of alignment. The draining pain ceased, and he could move again.

He sprinted forward, juking to the side as the skeleton attempted the spell again. Like the rest of its kind, this one was slow, its aim impeded by the half-formed eyes. The spell missed. Ty reached the thing and began slamming his fists into the creature's head and shoulders. His first hit rebounded off the skeleton's shoulder, where the robe protected it. His second sank into the cowl-covered head, smashing bone and viscera into a wet mess.

Congratulations! *You have defeated an Apostate Lich. Would you like to loot the corpse? If so, where would you like the loot deposited?*

The loot window appeared. It had the robe listed.

Extricating his fist from the cowl, Ty collapsed on the ground. Bits of bone and goo were *imbedded* in his hand, having gone through his glove. Shaking from exhaustion and blood loss, he looked down. Almost none of his body armor had survived. Everywhere the armor no longer protected was a slashed, drenched mess.

"Drinking any of the Celestial blood to replenish my mana will literally kill me at this point," Ty muttered out loud, just to hear anything other than screams and scraping bones. Speaking dourly to the Arbiter in the back of his mind, he gestured to the robed Lich. "You know I'm going to have to take the robe. They are brown. Brown, Hagemi. If I wear those, I'm going to look even *more* like a druid."

The Arbiter replied without manifesting, *Tell you what, I'll add a few entries into your loot table. If you roll well, I'll let you loot and customize the robe.*

"Well, that sounds surprisingly fair," Ty said, and looted the corpse.

Congratulations! *You have received a Moderate, Necromantic Life Leach Power from your looting ability. This power will allow you to channel a necromantic beam at your opponents and drain their vitality over time. You will not be able to enhance this ability, so don't expect to regenerate limbs with it. You currently cannot use this ability without taking damage, as Necromantic magic will gradually kill you.*

The robe appeared in front of him, as if he'd activated the inventory. It was liberally decorated with viscera.

Ty spoke slowly and clearly, "Fuck. You."

Hagemi didn't take the declaration personally. *"There's no need to get sentimental. I am merely a neutral party here to ensure you are properly rewarded for your efforts. As you know, the terms of your looting power included an element of randomness."*

A series of bangs on the door interrupted Ty's impending tirade. He looked over, worried the army of skeletons outside would find their way in. After a few seconds, the banging stopped. He guessed the undead couldn't get through the magical door.

Sighing in relief, he inspected the robe. Other than the bits of gore, it was well made. It was covered with runes and had quite a few deep pockets, none of which were magically imbued to hold extra loot. He moved his gear over to the robe without issue, leaving him with just enough body armor to keep his remaining pistol attached. His backpack was just intact enough to hold everything his robe couldn't.

Congratulations! *You have equipped a Warded Robe. This style of robe was common during the time of its manufacture but is considered rare now. It grants significant resistance to all forms of physical damage, and modest resistance to magic. It will also enhance all spells you cast using Necromancy. I should note that Necromancy is taboo on Volar. Scions who practice it are avoided at best, hunted at worst.*

"Nice," he complained, reading the description. "Give me a power and a rare piece of magical loot, only to have it blow up in my face if a local sees it."

The gear came from this dungeon. It's not like I tailored it specifically to make your life more difficult. Plus, I believe this robe is ancient. I doubt any uninitiated locals will notice its nature.

Ty reloaded and settled in to wait for his mana to regenerate.

"Hagemi, how do the undead work here?"

On Volar, we recognize that all beings have two parts: a soul, which resides within the Soul Cage, and the mind. The undead are a result of warping the body and mind until the Soul Cage is corrupted. Such corruption leads to insanity.

"That means being undead isn't as much about life or death as a spiritual state?"

Mostly. Think of your Soul Cage as the airlock your soul uses to connect to your body. It's a spiritual matrix, infinitely huge. It shapes how you interact with mana and how your abilities manifest. It is associated with your body, but not directly tied to it. When your body dies, the Cage decays over time, until your soul returns to where it came from, or moves on. Undead are the result of a type of aberration that forces the Cage to keep the body intact and functional. It is a fundamental change from the normal state of living things.

Ty took a few minutes to digest. "How does warping a body or mind affect the Soul Cage?"

Beings must allow their Cage to be changed. It has to be a choice, made on some level. Put something through enough pain or change how it thinks, and eventually the Cage will warp. Most on Volar recognize this as a violation. This is why Necromancy is taboo. The mind and the soul must be in harmony, otherwise abomination is the result.

"So using the benefits of the robe and picking up some necromancy spells would be unwise?"

I would advise you against it, yes.

It took an hour for the point to come back. Hagemi told him that as his Vitality attribute increased, his regenerative abilities would likewise speed up. The Spirit attribute, while far more useful than any tabletop version he'd encountered, was apparently not good for everything. During the wait, Ty started a note about the undead and another about the dungeon.

Once he'd healed himself enough that he could survive taking a sip of Celestial-infused water, Ty went through his new conversion routine. A minute later, he was healed and had his mana topped off. Breath he hadn't known he was holding eased as he felt himself grow whole again. There'd always been a chance that something would attack him again in the library, regardless of how safe it seemed.

"Short rest my ass," he muttered later, when he was confident enough in his state of health to rummage through the library. He decided up-front that he'd only spend a little over two hours searching the room. His reasoning was simple: if whatever boss ran this place was pissed at him and waking up its minions, every minute he gave them to prepare was another minute he'd be at a further disadvantage for the next fight.

With Hagemi translating at the speed Ty could read, he skimmed and found two books of interest in the intervening time. One was about death and necromancy, including a comprehensive, indexed list of forbidden necromantic practices. He didn't take the time to look at that, instead moving on once he'd shoved the book in a pocket. His next find was a comprehensive overview of monsters.

The title page claimed that the book, "Thoroughly documented the inclinations of the newly manifested God of Monsters," whatever that meant. Knowing the value of adventuring with a good monster manual, he pocketed that one, too.

The door leading out of the room was another of the blood sacrifice variety. As Ty moved to activate it, he paused, thinking. How would a person from his world use a library like this? With a smile, he went around the room, rocking each book at navel-level and higher back and forth. He also ran his hands along the furnishings connected to the walls, letting his fingers play across nooks and crevices, just in case one had what he hoped he'd find.

His search paid off.

One of the tipped books revealed a flush lever beneath. Ty pulled it, and a shelf swung forward, revealing a new corridor out of the room.

Grinning despite the situation, he investigated the opening. It was narrow and poorly lit compared to the rest of the dungeon, preventing him from seeing more than a dozen feet ahead. Even with his goggles, nothing immediately revealed itself. The walls of the corridor glistened and shimmered with opaque magic, giving him a sense of foreboding. Then again, he figured the odds were better investigating something new rather than continuing down the trail the bad guys expected him to go.

New robes swishing around his feet, he made his way down the corridor.

Chapter 20: Surrogacy

T hree steps into the new corridor and the door, predictably, closed behind him. He pushed on the door to see if it would open again. It didn't budge. Intuition tickled the back of his memory, reminding him of a specific tabletop game he'd played years ago. "I think this place was designed to let people in, but only locals out," Ty mused out loud.

Oh, why do you think that?

"I can open the doors with blood, basically weakening myself and making a sacrifice, but so far I haven't seen a way out. I think I need to find some sort of key or talisman to get the doors to open again."

Seems plausible.

A few more steps into the darkened corridor and the bottoms of the opaque walls began to glow. Ty's instinct was to sprint ahead, but before he could, the walls flashed into transparency, revealing the contents behind.

The corridor was a walkway between hundreds of cells, each with a single occupant.

To Ty's immediate left was a ten-foot-by-ten-foot room, the walls made of black metal. Inside was a cadaverous, man-shaped creature, its limbs pinned in place with spikes through each joint. Red, blazing eyes met his gaze briefly before he hurried along. He'd felt the hate in that gaze through the wall.

Past the pinned man, Ty glanced to the right. This room mirrored the previous, containing a bloated giant humanoid, limbs chained to the wall. It watched his progress, red eyes and limp face twisting into a horrible approximation of a smile. He kept going.

Another room held a small dragon, scales in a state of rot, half of its head chewed away as if by acid. It hissed at Ty as he walked by. The next room held a collection of floating eyeballs the size of basketballs, each connected by blackened nerve tissue.

Ty, this should not be, Hagemi sent as Ty rushed faster down the corridor. No matter that he did not believe the captives could reach him, simply seeing them was making his head throb. His mental representation of the Arbiter radiated painful amounts of energy and heat into his mind, hinting at the effort to keep him functional.

"Yeah, anything you can explain?" he said.

To you, these creatures look like monsters. That is true. They are also forbidden amalgamations, fusions of Death and Necromancy that have been outlawed and hunted for thousands of years. That first room held a Greater Master Vampire. The one with the eyes? Ty, those are Divine Nightmare Scourges. They are what you get when a god's nightmare manifests, is killed, and then raised from the dead.

"And the hag?"

I believe she was an augmented Demon Queen. Don't believe the body, they possess the strongest living thing in any world they infect. Their kind exist to inspire, and feed on, nightmares. They are highly territorial and will fight for dominance, killing all rivals until entire planets serve their twisted whims. Volar's only known Demon Queen was defeated thousands of years ago by the Monster God. None of these should be here. Something is terribly wrong.

Between the Monster God breaking the rules and this place, Ty was starting to think that Hagemi's knowledge was more limited than the Arbiter let on. "Tell Inspiration," he suggested.

The mind-space version of Hagemi glowed, the psychic warmth it was producing redoubling. Pain, terror, and revulsion knotted his stomach, slowing his pace.

Warning: *This region has been sanctified to an unknown force. It is under the effects of a Divine Lock.*

"Hagemi," Ty growled.

The Arbiter's glow receded, returning to its previous intensity. *I cannot reach Inspiration. It's just us in here.*

"Cutting off gods is starting to seem pretty common over here." With the pain gone, he hurried on. From what he saw, the corridor had no end; there were just *miles* of abominations threatening to drive him insane. Whenever he accidentally glanced around, fresh horrors scrambled for his attention. Despite himself, he was feeling a little fascinated by his circumstances. What sort of place was this that captured and stored such powerful, taboo creations?

Your observation is not totally inaccurate, though they are largely built from circumstantial evidence. Our world has gods. Sometimes they are active. There is value in limiting their vision or influence. People in power often build secure rooms with Celestial Barriers integrated into them.

"You said rooms, right?"

Correct. This location seems to be on an... impressive scale.

Hours later, Ty made it to the end of the corridor. This door was covered in a relief depicting a mountain range overlooking a vast city. Surprised at the intricate beauty in such a horrifying place, he reached for the door. It opened smoothly, without a sacrifice. Still reeling from the unspeakable horrors he left behind, and experiencing a growing, morbid curiosity, he stepped into the next room.

It wasn't a room; it was a warehouse big enough to hold multiple jumbo jets. When he first stepped into the space, he thought he'd entered an underground chasm, not a crafted structure. Open air stretched on for what felt like miles ahead and to his sides. Pockets of ruddy illumination threw some features of the room into silhouetted relief, suggesting more than revealing anything. Drawing his gun, he carefully walked into the space, not reacting when the door behind clicked shut.

Hundreds of steps later, he crossed some invisible threshold that triggered the main lighting system. The pools of light expanded and merged with one another, forming a uniform diffuse glow that revealed the true nature of the area.

He was in the lab of a mad scientist, constructed to an epic scale. Glass jars hung from wires lining the ceiling, each containing a different organ. Crystalline tubes and vats held the shadowy outlines of a thousand different bodies. Between random clusters of the collection were flowing, liquid silver pillars that morphed into complex biological patterns at random. Floating through the mess were metal shod, rune-encrusted bone arms. The ten-foot-long limbs were just the shoulder joint down to fine, articulated fingers.

Moving through the space, he tried to make a mental note of every detail. It occurred to him, briefly, that if he got attacked by practically *anything* worthy of guarding the room, he'd be in over his head. Thankfully, nothing happened.

It seemed odd to him that there were no tables, no places for bodies to be dissected, and no hints of purpose in the room. The warehouse might have been a catalogue of all the parts of life, for all he knew.

Eventually, he made it far enough through the room to another wall. Runes were carved in river-like channels through the steel. Pulsing light rolled sinuously from one point to another through the grooves. Curiosity overwhelming his caution, he followed the pulsing until it came to an upraised platform with a chair atop it. The dais was several hundred feet across and ringed with still more of the runes.

Mana funnel. The chair is the focal point of a ritual. Hagemi's words were soft, even inside Ty's head.

Curiosity overwhelming his caution, he stepped up to the chair. At first, he'd thought someone had made the throne for a giant, but as he approached, he saw that he'd been mistaken. The chair was perfectly sized for someone of his height.

A wave of unease swept through him. He froze at the edge of the platform, aware of what he'd been about to do. "Hagemi, are you pushing me to explore?" he asked, voice echoing eerily. Despite what the Arbiter had said about not controlling his actions, Ty was uncertain about his next steps.

No. We've discussed this.

"You know, I could take your lack of manifestation as a clear sign the battle music is about to start," Ty said wryly, looking around for threats.

Don't. Instead, take it as a sign that I do not feel... safe here.

Now *that* made Ty feel a lot better. What could hurt an Arbiter?

Knowing that Hagemi wasn't pushing his actions freed Ty to go with his gut. He walked up to the chair. A single, solid, black metal piece, the chair had a gothic regality to it. Short, sharp protrusions lined each armrest.

"Well, isn't this just peachy?" Ty said. Intellectually, he knew sitting in the chair might kill him. Either he'd have his consciousness overwritten by some ancient evil, or the spikes would draw too much of his health and leave him as an empty husk. Or maybe the obvious would happen, and he'd summon a monster that would suck the remaining life from his body. He *knew* these things, bone deep, and still he sat on the chair.

Pain lanced through Ty's arms. He pulled his character sheet up and saw his hit points rapidly draining. Activating Verdant Touch, he began replenishing the lost health as fast as he could. One mana point for two hit points. It took just a minute for the chair to drain him dry, both of mana and health, leaving him at precisely one hit point before the magic relented.

A growling, sepulchral voice whispered through the chamber, "Sacrifice accepted. Choose the vessel."

Glowing runes flashed in front of the chair and a pedestal rose out of the smooth floor, a gleaming black collar resting atop it.

What is it? Ty sent to Hagemi.

It looks like a control collar. It's a common tool necromancers and summoners use to keep their less obedient creations from running amok.

Ty blinked, having not considered this outcome at all. He didn't want a slave, did he? Part of him felt it might be fascinating to have a custom-made creation from this place serving and protecting him. He remembered the abominations in their cages, guessing that some of them might have come from this very room. Those things hadn't worn collars. Perhaps they were too powerful to be controlled.

The voice whispered again, "Sacrifice accepted. Choose your slave."

Ty removed his arms from the spikes, feeling the awful sensation of suction at each of the wounds. Without Verdant Touch or some variation of it, he knew just those injuries would eventually kill him from simple blood loss, if not infection.

The abilities Inspiration gave me weren't offensive for a reason. Ty thought about his god with fondness, cherishing the gift he'd been given. How would he have survived this dungeon with fireball spells? Gratitude surged through his core, radiating from just below his chest. It spread up and down his spine, from the top of his skull down to the bottoms of his feet.

There is no trust without freedom, no freedom without equality. The aphorism, one of Billy's favorites, came to mind unbidden.

"I don't want a slave," Ty announced. "I want an equal. Someone to help me. Give me that."

Brrrruuuuuuum. A gong rang, filling the place with a deep, resonant throb.

Four of the flying hands swept through the air, moving so fast that they created artificial wind in that silent space. The arms didn't go to any of the body parts stationed around the room. Instead, each dipped fingers into the silvery goo from several of the roiling pillars. Once each hand had a little ball of mercury-looking substance, they flew together in front of Ty and pushed each blob into a single, hovering sphere. Power radiated up from the dais, a massive infusion of raw energy that made his hair stand on end as it passed into the orb, compressing it down to something the size of an egg.

One of the four hands grasped the egg. It swept around the area, searching for something, then floated over to him. Ty watched in rapt fascination as the egg neared, seeing his reflection grow on its surface. The organic motions he'd seen earlier continued in the egg, though far more subtly. For a moment, he thought it took on the exact shape of one of his eyes.

The hand pushed the egg into his chest.

Single Use Power—Clone Surrogacy: *Due to the Wild in you, this location could not find a suitable host. This request has been converted into a single-use ability that you may activate on any corpse of your power or greater. Upon activating this ability, the corpse will become an exact duplicate of you. This duplication will not include any physical augmentations or magical items you have, including Soul Bound ones, unless they are specifically enhanced to include this ability. It will* *not have an Arbiter, although it may become a scion. Should it do so, it will be treated of equal level and power as you at the time of activation. Because this clone is your surrogate, it is linked to your Soul Cage. It will always follow your moral and ethical inclinations and cannot be made to act against you without destroying it. If your clone dies, there will be permanent psychic consequences.*

Hagemi manifested, announcing, "Spells like this started the Scion War. Never, under any circumstances, use it."

Chapter 21: Possession

"Forbidden? Why?" Ty asked. He stood up from the chair, staggered, and fell into a sitting position on the dais. Being at one hit point and having zero mana was like having the worst flu ever. He ached and felt weak.

"Ty, this spell is an abomination. Imagine the possibilities. You worship a god, say Celestia, and you create a clone with this spell. That clone would be free to worship the Monster God, meaning it could help you act against your own god *directly*. That's not even the worst of it. Imagine two versions of yourself, each with opposite abilities but linked by your soul bond. You could experiment and create untold spells or effects, all of which are *fundamentally not allowed to exist*."

Ty blinked at the glowing Arbiter. He'd never seen it so... emotional. "Is there something else, Hagemi? I feel you wouldn't be this disturbed if it was just a taboo effect."

Hagemi jerked up and down in the air in spasming motions. "Ty, I have no knowledge of this. I am an Arbiter, given divine purpose to aid in the establishment of a new Resonance Bridge. I have a portion of the combined intellect and knowledge of all the gods in me. Yet *I do not know this effect*. Something is wrong."

"Ah, I see now." A haunting sigh flowed through the air as a shadowy shape drifted by. The insane voice from their entry to the dungeon emerged from it. "They have lied to you, little betrayer." It sounded less angry than before.

Hagemi spun, facets flickering magenta light along the walls and in the air, like a disco ball used as a spotlight. Its light revealed nothing, and Hagemi vanished once again. Was that fear radiating from the Arbiter?

"Who are you?" Ty said, trying to stand and failing.

The voice replied, each word softer than the last, "Do you like my Sanctuary, interloper?"

Ty tried getting the speaker to interact again, but nothing he said or did brought it back. Hagemi had gone quiet. Only the occasional pulse of reassurance told him the Arbiter was still aware.

An hour later, once his mana ticked up that precious notch, Ty restored himself and began following the nearest wall. Part of him longed to explore the warehouse further, certain that the mysteries trapped within could change his life forever. Caution won out this time. He found the double doors out of the room not too long after.

The corridor beyond the room mirrored the one with the librarians; it was long, dimly lit, and with doors on either side. A strange, clockwork-looking creature that made him think of a seven-foot-tall goblin scratched at something on one door thirty feet down the corridor.

When Ty stepped far enough for the door to close behind him, a ghost manifested directly into his path and slammed into him. There was a sense of contact, an electric tingle, then the thing pushed inside his chest and boiled out of his heart, flooding his mind with alien thoughts.

Warning: *You are being possessed.*

Her name was Numera Qual, and she had chosen to sacrifice her life for the betterment of her children. Standing in Holy Line with the other sacrifices, she turned her face to the golden-eyed preacher who performed the litany of truth for them all.

"Knowing is the greatest state of being. Hunger for knowing is the second greatest state of being. Your lives are hunger; your deaths are knowing. Your passage will

help construct the Bridge, and your souls will fuel our god's Soul Batteries for all time. You are worthy."

Numera smiled, feeling certain of her choice to leave her family for the holy rite. Through her death, her children would live.

Only she had not known how tortured her death would be or the desolation of eternal unlife.

Warning: *A foreign soul has attempted to unseat yours. If this continues, you will die.*

Ty fought his way free of the vision, channeling Divinity though his Verdant Touch and directly into his body, where he felt the woman's soul had imbedded herself. Ty could feel the ghost, see her thoughts, even as his magic purified his mind of the possession. She was a small thing, a tiny, weightless sigh in his heart. Yet the weight of her memories and existence was vast. He had become her in that moment of contact, become her and known some of what she'd known. Her language, liquid and mysterious, burned in his mind, totally separate from any insight Hagemi provided him.

His power surrounded the ghost, pushing it free of his mind and scouring it with holy energy. Tendrils of Numera's fear and anguish latched onto him, reluctant to release.

A wrenching, pain-filled sob shook through his body. Ty didn't know what to do. He was hurting the spirit to preserve his life. Numera's memories leaked through his mental grasp, showing him vivid flashes of her world and her children. Her love for them broke his heart in new, unthinkable ways.

Hagemi's voice cut through the anguish. *I can help. A little. Briefly. But you must leave this place.*

Temporary Enhancement—Soul Warden: *Your Arbiter has acted on your behalf. Due to the unbalanced threat in the area, it has made an executive decision. By allocating a permanent portion of your mana, you may contain a spirit with divine mana. This power also allows you to manipulate spiritual essence, moving it from one place to another. Upon leaving this place, this power will be revoked. Use it wisely.*

His grip on the ghost smoothed out, preventing further leakage. She stopped struggling, the pain evidently gone.

Exhaling weakly, Ty tried to orient his thoughts. No matter what achievements he'd earned or how his Arbiter helped him, it took him what felt like hours to return to himself.

"What was that?" he rasped.

She was possessing you, Ty. Another few seconds and she would have taken over.

Grunting, he blinked away foggy vision to see what had changed in the corridor. The construct continued its work, apparently not noticing him. He approached slowly, until he could see what the goblin was doing. Its fingertips were chipping at glowing gemstones imbedded in the door. It had already destroyed one. Another cracked.

An ephemeral shape shot out of the gem and into Ty. This time, the spirit was stronger, more cohesive, and his mental defenses were unprepared. It slid into his heart and filled him, sending searing pain through his mind.

He was Mummat Kraal, and he was the architect of the future. Thanks to his deep comprehension of Arbiter technology, he'd discovered the most promising breakthrough of a generation: Soul Batteries. They would provide unlimited divine fuel, taking worship from the gods and using it for a better purpose.

Yet the new priests were not using them for any grand design that he could comprehend. Why had their god allowed this? Where was he? His absence suggested he sanctioned these sacrifices, yet how could he?

Their god had either abandoned them or was comfortable with their mass slaughter at the hands of his devotees. Mummat's heart broke.

"You seem troubled Mummat," a woman spoke, turning to him. She was a true beauty, marked with the now-deceased God of Fate's gift of prophecy. Her golden eyes moved across him, her expression failing to mask her vague disdain. "Do not doubt, for your life will bring greatness to our Lord." Gesturing to the fields of the deceased, she continued, "These sacrifices are the bedrock upon which the next worlds will be conquered. Without them, we could not escape the Well and conquer new worlds. Soon, you will see."

Mummat gestured to the sky, where the Siphon had been set in the stars. "Great Mistress, I do not understand. Did we not build the Siphon to avoid needing so much death? Will the greater gods not banish the Well, now that the war nears an end?"

The woman laughed, her eyes turning cruel, and Mummat knew the truth. His god had not ordered the deaths of their people or the creation of the Soul Batteries. It was she, she and the others who had claimed authority over the migration.

She killed Mummat. The killing was fast, but it was awful, and she stole his soul. A soul that suffered an eternity, only to emerge from its prison and flee to the nearest living vessel...

A sob ripped through him as he clawed at his chest. Mummat was inside him; he *was* Mummat. He felt the alien thoughts, the foreign knowledge, challenging his memories and fighting for possession of him. He knew Mummat was not actually trying to kill him; the soul was confused, lost, hurt and angry. Yet it *was* killing him.

A tortured wail ripped through Ty's throat as he activated his Verdant Touch. Celestial mana shoved Mummat's soul into the container with Numera. The presence of two spirits nearly overwhelmed his temporary gift. It *bulged*, stretching at the seams. Emotion leaked free, filling him with frustration, anger, and fear.

Warning: *Your temporary power is at eighty percent effectiveness. Your Soul Cage is in danger of warping. You are temporarily insane.*

Skkrrrtch. The goblin began scratching at the next gem.

Hagemi shouted into his mind. *Ty! If it frees another spirit now, you'll die. I need time to reinforce the Soul Warden power. Stop it!*

Frenzied with anger and pain, Ty fought his way forward to the scrambling construct. Investing his hands with Wild energy, he slammed his fists into the thing. His punches did minimal damage to the hard construct and threatened to break his bones.

Ty didn't feel physical pain anymore. He'd *become* pain. Thousands of years of pain, of knowing that he had betrayed his people, of knowing that...

Heat seared into his head, bringing an avalanche of physical pain as Hagemi fought to push the invasive thoughts down.

Ty grabbed the goblin by one leg. He tugged, yanking hard enough to tear something in his side. The construct fell with a crash. Nothing broke or stopped working in the fall. Instead of lashing out, the construct fumbled around, trying to right itself. He spotted rune-covered cogs and wheels whirring inside its joints as it flailed around. Drawing one of his guns, he shot a cog. The bullet reflected off, drawing a searing line of fire high on his cheek.

Screaming incoherently, Ty grabbed at the goblin's head and tried twisting. He wasn't strong enough to out-wrestle a magical construct. The attempt was not a total failure, however. As he twisted, he saw a thumbnail-sized gem just beneath the armored head, right where a neck plate concealed it. Covering his face with the sleeve of his robe, Ty put the barrel of his gun against the gem and squeezed the trigger.

The goblin went limp. It had never, not once, attempted to defend itself or attack him.

Ty was down to five hit points and had a new status listed on his character sheet.

Warning: *You are insane. Because of multiple possessions in a short period, the connection to your Arbiter has been disrupted. All mental support provided by Hagemi will function at less than fifty percent until the connection is restored.*

Someone was sobbing. Someone else was laughing.

It took Ty hours to realize it had been him doing both all along.

Chapter 22: Whispers

Time lost meaning. Eventually, gradually, Hagemi came back online and helped. Heat seared through his head as the Arbiter did its best to put his fractured psyche back together while it augmented the temporary ability.

There were sheets of notes around him, each with words in a new language. Looking at the words made the space in his chest throb. The spirits wanted out. No matter how much aid Hagemi lent him, the power of those ghosts was overwhelming their temporary captivity.

"Stop thinking about them," Hagemi scolded from where it hovered nearby. "You're stirring them up. If we're lucky, we can crawl out of here and release them before your brain melts."

They were called the akkoans. People of Ako. And they had been a beautiful people...

Ty tried to do what Hagemi directed, focusing his attention anywhere other than the memories. He checked his character sheet. Enough time had passed that his mana was fully replenished, but his health status had taken on an odd red color he hadn't seen before. He healed himself more out of reflex than any desire to do so.

A small amount of clarity washed through Ty as the Wild worked to restore him to his natural state. Hagemi sighed in relief, its magenta light taking on a less frantic hue as it orbited around him.

Warning: *You have successfully stabilized the Warden ability with two spirits. Any additional pressure will cause catastrophic failure.*

He looked around the corridor, seeing that he was sitting next to the golem still. There was no sign of anything else, no sign of time's passage, nothing. He felt famished, so he ate and drank, then found a corner to relieve himself. It didn't feel right going to the bathroom in the open like that. Then again, if the makers hadn't wanted people peeing in the open, they'd have installed toilets.

Her/his children had been perfect. Thorah was going to join the science caste. If all went well, she'd be investigating the offspring of the mortal gods, like her uncle. Scylion was eager to become a painter. He/she wondered what had happened to them. Curiosity, the need to know, had/did burn bright within their people...

Ty looked over at the nearest door, inspecting the thing. It looked like any other he'd seen in this place, albeit without the embossed head, and with rings of gems ringing it. The gems, other than the two shattered ones, flickered with faint blue light.

"Why do you think the construct picked this door?" he rasped. His throat felt sanded raw, despite the healing.

"Ty, we should go," Hagemi said. "This place is unsafe. Those memories, they feel dangerous to me."

Without thinking about what he was doing, Ty spoke in the sing-song lilt of the akkoan people. He didn't need Hagemi to translate them anymore. "The burden of the living is to remember the dead and honor them, for our ancestors pave the way for our greatness." It hurt to make the liquid sounds, even if some part of him felt like he'd been speaking their language his entire life.

Hagemi flinched away. He felt it rummaging around in his mind, renewing its efforts to dim and suppress the foreign memories. "Ty, I need you to stop thinking about them. It's keeping me from cleaning your mind up. Your brain can't hold all these memories, it doesn't have infinite storage capacity."

Ty looked over at the Arbiter. "Do you know what they did with their dead, Hagemi? They brought them to beautiful water gardens, where their souls lived on in nature for hundreds of years. Their people sang songs, wrote poetry, and danced among their ancestors, revering and learning from their wisdom. I miss them...”

He didn't just miss them; he *ached* for them, longed for the insights and wonders he'd glimpsed. He'd bound two of the spirits to protect himself, ending their occupation of his mind. The ghosts had been overwriting who he was, about to erase his very essence. Yet something in Ty hungered for the sense of them again. There was such richness in the akkoan people.

Taking a step to the door, he rested a hand atop one of the gems that seemed brighter than the others. “When an ancestor was ready to move on, they would invest themselves into one of their people's newborns. Their children were born with awakened spirits and minds, Hagemi. Each generation was brighter, more spiritual, than the last. They passed on their knowledge similarly, using magic devices that could store entire lives.” Frowning, he inhaled a shuddering breath. “Wait. What were those called? I can't remember.”

Mummat and Numera's memories were fading, pushed down into the recesses of his mind. His fingers played across the gem, rolling across the smooth surface thoughtfully. There was a soul within, one responding to his words.

The batteries hurt them. Numera and Mummat had shown him that truth in spades. It wasn't natural for spirits to be used in this way. They had suffered for tens of thousands of years.

No one deserved that. No one's life was worth the suffering of so many.

Unsheathing a knife, Ty asked, “Hagemi, how many souls can fit in my body?”

“No!” Hagemi's voice had taken on a desperate, warning note that he had never heard in the Arbiter. “Please, don't. The spirits. They will only kill you. But I will live on, and I don't know what they will do to *me* once they have your body. Ty, you must not do this. Please, just move on. This is not a side quest you want to take.”

Ty spoke slowly, firmly, without inflection, “You suggested the Soul Cage was limitless. Arbiter, aren't you obligated to answer what natives would know?”

Hagemi's frantic bobbing slowed. “Most of our people would not know this. A few might. How many angels can dance on the head of a pin?”

That gave Ty the answer he needed. He brought the butt of his knife down on the gemstone as hard as he could.

The Arbiter's desperation edged to mania as it shouted at him. "Ty! The next soul you release will kill you. Whatever good you think you'll be doing, you won't do it. You'll just die."

"Then fucking do something about it, Game Master," Ty snarled. He looked at the Arbiter, spit running down his chin as the madness rose again. "These people have suffered for thousands of years. They didn't want to be here. They were misled, lied to, and manipulated by others, all in the name of their absentee god. They did not deserve this, and I am going to help them, or I'll die trying."

Making a fist, he hammered it once against the door, frustrated at his own lack of ability, furious he could not do more. What was his life, his value, weighed against what any of these people had suffered? And he'd nearly killed two to survive. Even now, two bright, beautiful souls struggled within him.

The shadow misted through the hall, wafting behind where Hagemi floated. Its voice was distant this time, not mad. "Their god was not absent. It had been tricked. Lost little Arbiter, confused and betrayed little Arbiter, what he asks is simple. Summon for him a Mind Fortress. It's such a small, simple thing. Why, there's one nearby that is perfect for this very task." The shadow reached out and ran ephemeral hands across Hagemi's surface.

The Arbiter pulsed at the touch yet seemed unaware of the shadow or its caress. "There is one thing I can do," Hagemi said. "It's something I had... forgotten that I could do. A small, simple summoning. Ty, loot the corpse."

Ty glanced from the Arbiter to the shadow. It had become more substantial since the last time he'd seen it, though it was still hard to make out in the gloom. The shadow gestured down at the goblin corpse, then at his dagger, before vanishing.

He touched the goblin, pointing to the ground next to it.

Congratulations! *You have defeated a Sanctuary Maintenance Golem. I will provide appropriate loot for you.*

The goblin twitched, arm flying out and slamming into the ground where he pointed. Bits of metal clicked into place, and a thin rod slid out of the arm into the floor. Light shone from within the construct, shining into the stones beneath the point of contact. Distant thunder rolled through the corridor. Two objects lifted into view, extruded from the floor. One was a small, triangular diamond the size of a grape. The other was a black dagger.

He picked up both objects.

Congratulations! *You have obtained a Divine Mind Fortress. Mind Fortresses were common on Ako. On Volar, they are virtually unknown. You may insert this device inside your mind. Once there, it will take up both a physical and psychic space. Either you or your designated Arbiter may use the Mind Fortress to store and retrieve memories. As a byproduct of this storage feature, it can also dampen emotion. Accessing the Fortress takes no energy, only time. The time it takes to re-live a memory stored in the Mind Fortress is based on your Intelligence and Spirit scores, as well as your level. Currently, each hour you meditate on memories will give you six hours of subjective experience. You may use this ability to obtain skills and knowledge, but it will take time and effort. This Fortress comes with an epic, legendary, and divine enhancement.*

Epic Enhancement: *This Mind Fortress has nearly unlimited storage capacity.*

Legendary Benefit: *The Fortress has bonded to your Organized Mind achievement. While this object is inside your mind, you automatically prioritize your consciousness over all others. This means foreign entities, such as spirits or demons, will be far less likely to influence or possess you.*

Divine Benefit: *Your mind-space, Soul Cage, and this Fortress are linked. If a spirit attempts to possess you, you may effectively now divide it into its component parts: its memories and its soul. This will allow you to store the akkoan spirits you've encountered without their madness leaking into you.*

As with all Divine objects, this Mind Fortress can be enhanced or upgraded with merits or other powers. It cannot be destroyed, altered, or removed without your explicit, willing consent.

Congratulations! *You have obtained an Annihilation Dagger. Due to your persistence and compassion, you have been gifted an epic artifact called the Annihilation Dagger. This dagger will deal significantly enhanced damage against* *magically invested gemstones, including the gems manifested through divine imbuement. You should know that this dagger was crafted with forbidden techniques. If others see it, they will assume you are a Holy Assassin, invested by a god. Please don't start god wars over this.*

Ty took the gem and studied it. It looked and felt like a diamond. "Divine object?"

"Press it against your forehead and allow me to bond it to you," Hagemi directed, ignoring the question. The Arbiter sounded odd, not mechanical, and not frantic. Distant, maybe.

The gem vanished into Ty's head, moving to occupy a distinct mental space opposite Hagemi's. In fact, the gem looked almost exactly like Hagemi, just without the same glowing energy inside. Ty's instincts told him there was significance to that similarity.

Hagemi directed Ty to release the Soul Warden ability. When the spirits pushed free, his Mind Fortress activated, collecting the spirits' memories. The process felt odd, as the ghosts memories passed through his mind-space, granting him brief glimpses of their lives. With their memories extracted, the spirits settled deeper into him, somewhere below his sternum. He intuited that the spirits weren't trapped inside his Soul Cage; rather that he'd somehow given them a comfortable place to rest before they moved on.

I'm a water garden for these akkoan spirits, he realized. The thought made him smile. He'd become a vessel of hope, rather than pain.

"Their suffering has ended," Hagemi said. "While the memories of their years spent in the batteries remain, they no longer warp the associated souls."

Ty tried to feel how he'd changed. There were two entities *inside* him now. Memories from the initial possessions lingered, gently suppressed by his new abilities. He could still feel them. If he strained, he could remember the faces of Numera's children.

"You can store those memories, too," Hagemi said.

He shook his head. "Not yet. They aren't bothering me." It took him a moment to realize he'd said the words in akkoan. Touching his chest, he thought he could feel a gentle gratitude radiating from the ghosts.

"I saved them," he said, awed. "I've become their refuge."

Hagemi rotated in the air, strobing light pulsing sullenly within its depths. "This is not a natural thing we've done. Even if your Soul Cage is not damaged by this, it is a form of abomination. You will have to free the spirits, eventually."

"I will."

Exhausted from all he'd experienced, Ty put his back against a wall and tried to sleep. There was no safety here, only a sense of foreboding and dread. This place had been worse than a mausoleum; spirits were imprisoned and tortured here. He didn't have a choice, though. All he'd done, seen, and pitted himself against had taken its toll.

He slept and dreamed of Ako.

Numera and Mummat stood beside him, on an overlook above a vast valley. Lines of akkoans stretched to the horizon, all driven to a central place: the ritual grounds.

"It's not just engineers and mothers," Mummat said, staring at the landscape with an expression of unblinking horror. "The priests demanded our warriors and mages give their lives, too. Kill squads went out, harvesting souls for the batteries."

Tears streaked Numera's cheeks. Holding back a sob, she added, "Tens of thousands of our people died, and for what? The Siphon was active. Where did our god go? What mission could have possibly sent him so far away?"

Ty woke with a jolt, certain of what he had to do next. There were thousands of spirits here, each being as tortured as Numera and Mummat had been. He took up the new dagger and walked to a central place between the doors.

Speaking in a loud, clear voice, he tried to use the mellifluous language of the long-dead akkoans. "People of Ako, I am here to give you freedom. You must listen to me, though. I need you to restrain yourselves. I will need time to make this work."

Many of the gems on the doors flashed in response to Ty's announcement. Moving to the gemstone he'd been trying to break earlier, he slammed the knife into it. The gem broke in three sharp taps.

My name is Awon, and I am a guardian of our people. We knew little violence and almost no war until the mortal gods arose. They came, brought wonder, powers, and people we had never met. They also brought violence and conquest, for the mortal gods ever strive for power. We lost many. Yet our hunger for the mysteries of violence arose to meet the challenge.

The caste of warriors was forged, and I was proudly among them. We captured their offspring and learned their ways. I was proud to defend my people for all time, even in a Soul Battery.

The new spirit was gentler than the last. Hagemi helped guide Ty through the process, shuffling memories into the Fortress and the soul into his Cage. Awon came to live within him, a flickering mote of presence more akin to a dimly remembered dream than a ghost.

Ty didn't understand the process anymore than he understood how his Verdant Touch worked. He could *feel* the energy moving, even sense what Hagemi and the Fortress were doing. Without a lifetime or, he suspected, many lifetimes, of training he doubted he would ever truly comprehend what was happening. As the Arbiter suggested during the beginning of their relationship, having discrete, controllable abilities gave him reliability without the insight of a native.

As soon as they finished with Awon, he and Hagemi set to freeing the rest of the spirits.

It took hours to free the spirits in the corridor, one at a time. A few were agitated and angry, shooting into Ty's body like the first had. When that happened, the spirits already inside his Soul Cage became involved. Despite lacking intellect, the spiritual entities somehow intercepted the attacking ghosts, offering comfort and warmth until the Fortress and Hagemi could do their work. Once they were separated from their memories, the ghosts settled into the Soul cage without a fight.

"When we put their memories in the Mind Fortress, what does that do to the ghost?" Ty asked once they were done. He felt heavier somehow, as though his spirit was laden. Oddly, it didn't feel bad to be so full. If anything, he felt... companionship in it.

"It allows them to rest," Hagemi responded. "The core of the spirit, the being at the center, remains, just without the concrete memories that tethered it to this world."

"It's a kind of peace? Could we reunite a spirit with its memories if we wanted?"

"Yes and yes. Until you put the spirits to rest, inside a new vessel or through some other means, the spirits can be recombined with their memories. Most, I suspect, would not want that. Thousands of years of torment will outweigh the good for most people, Ty. As it was doing to you."

Ty swallowed, thinking back to his state of mind after the first two possessions. He'd been insane for a while there, barely able to think or reason. Without Hagemi's help, he knew he would have never come back from that. How must it be for a spirit, with no Arbiter to help?

After another meal and a few swallows of water, Ty considered the notes scattered on the floor. His writing was insane, slipping from one language to another, and utterly incoherent to him now. He collected the notes and stored them away, reasoning they might be useful later.

In silence, he resumed his journey down the hall. A while later, they came to a bend. If Ty had been wondering about the goblin's random selection of the door before, he knew now. The hall stretched before him, hundreds of doors with thousands of broken gems on them.

An army of ghosts waited for his approach, inert until he came within their line of sight. The tide of spirits sprang for him, their desperation palpable.

Chapter 23: Origin

Warmth spread through Ty, blossoming outward to meet the rushing army. The spirits inside his chest stretched out of their new home, raising their voices in a wordless choir. He recognized the sound they projected; it was the same sound in the ancestral gardens of the akkoan home world. Even without their memories, the spirits inside him still resonated with that place.

The front wall of the wave slowed just before it would have overwhelmed him. Instead of a crushing sea of memories and spirits, it became a ceaseless, but manageable, flow. Hagemi blazed in his head, working with the Fortress faster than he could imagine. Thousands of years of memories passed through his mind, some leaving dim echoes in their wake.

As Ty became more comfortable with the pressing wave, and as the collected song of the spirits within him gained in strength, he started walking again. Ghosts spiraled around him like a whirlpool, vanishing within him with each step.

He made his way deeper into the dungeon.

Ty walked, relieved himself, ate and drank, and slept several times before he finally made it through the corridor. Tens of thousands of spirits lived inside his Soul Cage. He'd gone from feeling full to feeling heavy, as if gravity itself were fluxing and bending around him.

The corridor ended in double doors. These were covered in a more ornate engraving than the last, the horned head joined by several smaller faces above it. These faces weren't all skulls. In fact, Ty recognized akkoan features in them.

Pausing before the door, he thought about the depiction, actively searching suppressed memories for clues. Eventually, he figured out what the smaller faces were.

"Greater Gods," he whispered into the stillness. The context of his discovery wasn't there. All he had were bits and pieces from Numera and Mummat.

Paying the blood price, he went through the doors. Behind him, the Soul Batteries had gone dormant, their occupants finally freed.

Warm ambient light greeted him as he walked into the space. It was a vast area, the roof stretching far above, with a curved outer wall lined with comfortable-looking leisure furnishings. Paintings and murals decorated the outside wall. If time had worn down bits of the dungeon, it didn't show here. The center of the room was curved, with a single mosaic pattern that changed between panels, almost like a comic book.

After a few seconds of study, Ty came to believe that he was at the center spoke of a wheel, with spines like the corridor he'd just exited radiating from this place. His studies also left him speechless at the overwhelming quality and elegance of each item on display. A master craftsperson of unparalleled skill had made every mural or art piece in the room. He didn't recognize the styles or intent behind most of the art, having pushed those memories into the Fortress, but what he did was incredible. This gallery was the apotheosis of akkoan art culture.

The spirits in him stirred. Hagemi manifested and said, "The spirits recognize this place. I can sense that they want you to know about it. With your permission, I can access the relevant memories in the Mind Fortress. Do you want to take a few minutes so I can thread together a cohesive narrative?"

Ty almost asked Hagemi about his sudden willingness to help. He got the feeling that the Arbiter shouldn't be doing so much, as it hadn't provided this level of help in the past, even when the Monster God had intervened directly.

Moving to a cushioned seat, he agreed. As he waited for Hagemi to do the work, he reflected on the nearby art. Several pieces depicted the akkoan people. They had been tall, humanoid, with bright eyes and vaguely avian features.

Colorful, multi-hued feathers had framed their limbs and face, enhancing his sense of their otherworldly beauty.

Ty didn't know how long Hagemi took. He didn't look at his watch or even care about time. His sense of urgency had diminished, replaced with a sense of curiosity and accomplishment.

We just ended the suffering of thousands of people. I don't care whether I can punch harder or cast bigger and better spells. Today, this is enough.

Eventually, Hagemi appeared and said, "It's done."

After finishing his next-to-last protein bar, he came to his feet and walked around the room, following the direction he sensed the akkoans wanted him to go.

Hagemi's organized memories narrated in a basso chant.

After the birth of all physical things, there was nothing. The mural began with a simple diagram of constellations and planets. With the memories swelling through him, he could see the art as the akkoan would have, with eyes made to observe different spectrums of light. To them, the vastness of space was filled with patterns of color and motion. Those were replicated with meticulous detail in their art.

Then there was a need to know. A thirst for knowledge. A hunger to discover the greater mysteries. He followed the curve of the mural, finding a complex hieroglyph on the next frame. It depicted an akkoan youth beholding a closed book.

This was our Lord. Our Lady. Our everything. We, the akkoans, were its first children in beauty, opposite the children in darkness. It was our mission to seek the furthest depths of art, music, and creativity. We were the spiritual innovators. The next sections of the mural showed a divine figure, something like a titanic akkoan, showering life onto multiple planets. One of those planets gave rise to the akkoans, who lifted their arms and heads to the sky in song. The next panels were stunning in their depictions of akkoan culture. Some quality of the mural conveyed hints of song, which Hagemi helped recreate. A haunting, uplifting melody rose in the room.

Then one of our brethren discovered magic. Through magic, we gave shape to the greater forces. Through magic, all the worlds of our empire knew the embodiment of the first lesser gods. A gathering of vaguely reptilian creatures gathered around some device, releasing light from within. The next panel depicted strange, amorphous people joining the great Lord. It was the greater gods, Ty realized. Below those greater gods rose a bevy of lesser gods, each elevated from among their mortal flock.

This is the story of our people. As our vessel, we want you to understand, to see our joy and beauty. Remember us.

The memories faded, voices returning to quietude within Ty's mind. He'd walked the circuit of the spoke, passing many closed doors that led away from it. Along the center pillar, he found himself in front of another door, this one lined with runes carved in a style he hadn't seen before.

"You cannot go down, interloper. Not until you are powerful enough to activate those runes." It was the shadow, back once more and floating with a near-tangible presence nearby.

Ty looked at the apparition. "You're definitely getting more substantial, aren't you?"

The shadow vanished.

"I was right, wasn't I? About it getting more substantial?"

Hagemi said, "Um, maybe. I have a hard time focusing on the thing when it appears. I only know it exists because of your thoughts."

"Well, that's comforting," Ty said sarcastically.

He briefly considered trying to go open the sealed door, then dismissed the notion. If there was anything his first dungeon had taught him so far, it was that he needed to level up to explore this place further.

Looking around the room, Ty made some quick calculations. "If I'm right, these spokes radiate both outward and, based on that door over there," he jerked a thumb at the sealed door, "the structure continues down. I believe one of these spokes extends all the way through the forest, back to the quarry that the demons were digging. Do you think we can get out that way?"

Floating a few feet away, Hagemi pulsed silver light in all directions, reminding him of a submarine sending out a sonar pulse. "Assuming your guess is correct, this door would correspond with the way out." It gently bobbed in a direction, leading him back until they came to a new door.

The door was still black metal, but the engravings on it depicted shining light. Ty kept enough of the akkoan language to recognize the meaning of the engravings. They labeled the door "Celestial Light."

"This is promising," Ty murmured, lifting a hand to push on the door. It didn't open, and there were no teeth for him to make a blood sacrifice. Sheathing his hand in his Verdant Touch ability, which he adjusted to Divine mana using his Prism, he tried pushing again.

The symbol on the door flashed, absorbing the energy in his hand, then clicked open.

Chapter 24: Lesser Beings

Ty was surprised to find the walls and floor were made of the same material as the first spoke, all grimdark metal and riveted doorways. As part of the Celestial branch, he'd imagined alabaster décor with silvery chimes in the air. Like Christmas, but everywhere and all the time.

"Hagemi, would you see if one of my guests is familiar with this wing? I don't think I want to stumble through here."

Sure, but it will take some time, Hagemi thought back, comfortably incorporeal again. He felt it accessing his Mind Fortress. In his mind's eye, it looked like the Arbiter had extended a band of magenta light into the new device. Focusing on the Fortress, he gradually came to understand that Hagemi was using the device a lot like a search engine, sending dozens of requests for information simultaneously.

I can do that, too, Ty realized. The difference between him and Hagemi was the efficiency the Arbiter communicated with the Fortress.

Feeling a little more comfortable with what was going on in his head, he made his way down the new corridor. Like the one he'd found the ghosts in, gemstone-covered doors also flanked this one. Assuming that there were bound spirits, he withdrew his new dagger and struck at a random gemstone, cracking it.

A glowing angel with blue gemstones for eyes manifested in the center of the corridor, feathery wings flapping to hold its torso aloft. The angel looked something like a cross between an akkoan and a cat, with feline rather than avian features. It was horribly mutilated. Anywhere that glowing light didn't conceal its physique, it looked twisted and desiccated. Eyes and mouth wide, the angel extended a clawed hand. Light coalesced in its palm, pulsing into the outline of an ornate sword.

Ty barely deflected the first thrust with the edge of his dagger.

The angel howled, bellowing a dialect of akkoan he didn't know, and came on. Dagger versus sword was not something that he had practiced often, and he barely kept the thing from cutting his head off in the first few seconds. Unlike a regular opponent, the angel used its wings to maneuver, allowing it to operate in three-dimensional space. It fluttered up over his head but flinched in pain as one of its legs brushed the wall. In that brief opening, Ty stabbed out with his dagger.

Roaring in pain and rage, the mad creature fell back, giving Ty room to breathe. He'd been cut in a dozen places, but oddly the injuries didn't seem as severe as they should have been. Celestial energy infused his cuts, recharging some of his mana. He was still bleeding, but not immediately overwhelmed.

Ty figured it meant that he'd reached a point of equilibrium, where his skills, level, and abilities sort of made him the match for a tough opponent. Assuming that an ancient, injured angel suffering thousands of years of presumed deprivation was considered a tough opponent.

Surging forward, blade extended, the angel used its wings to add speed to its strike. Ty jerked to the side, feeling the blade slash inside his robe and along his side. Metal scraped between two of his ribs, sending a vibrating pain all the way into his teeth. Celestial magic burst into him, overfilling his mana and adding all-new discomfort to the sword injuries.

Dropping the black dagger from numbed fingers, Ty slapped a hand around the angel's forearm and willed Verdant Touch into it, using his Prism to transform the power into Monstrous-typed energy. The angel's arm blackened from his touch, and it released its sword, backing away. The sword vanished before hitting the floor.

With the opening, Ty healed himself. Thanks to the angel's infusion of mana, he was only down to a little over half after that exchange. Despite himself, he found that he was grinning.

He was having fun. For the first time in this world, he felt like he had a grasp on a fight, like he didn't have to use his guns to gain a tactical advantage against overwhelming odds. Sure, he'd fought dozens of the skeleton librarians, and a few other things. Those encounters hadn't counted, not like this did. Before crossing the portal, he had become a talented infighter, on top of being decent with a knife. This was the first time he felt that training come into play.

Retrieving the black dagger, he held it high with one hand while he held the other low, fingers curling into a fist. "Come on," he growled at the angel.

The angel obliged, summoning its sword again with a gesture.

It came forward slower this time, swinging its sword in broad sweeps. Each time it attacked, Ty saw it flinch a little. One of its arms had a black handprint on it, and dark silver blood leaked from one of its feet. He dodged the first few swings, then stepped within the angel's reach and slammed his dagger into its chest.

Light exploded from within the angel, pouring out of its wounds, its eyes, and its mouth. The walls around the explosion pulsed with power and seemed to drink the light in. Tendrils of dark extended from the floor and wound around its lower body, yanking it into and through the ground.

The angel vanished. Out of the corner of his eye, Ty saw the gemstone he'd broken slide back into place, completely restored. There was no loot prompt.

With nothing else to do and unwilling to experiment further, he continued down the corridor. He was skilled enough at activating his Verdant Touch ability now that he could heal himself with minimal effort as he walked.

"Ty, I've identified someone with the memories you requested," Hagemi announced a few hours later.

"Let's start with figuring out what this is," Ty said.

Oh, yes. This, the memory-thought spoke through Hagemi, taking on the tone of an elderly scholar. *I wasn't here to construct this region of the Sanctuary, but I oversaw a version this was based on.*

"Thank you for your help," Ty thought to the memory, just to be polite. "Can you explain what this is?"

Absolutely. This is a place for us to incarnate, study, and extract information about Divine-crafted lesser beings.

"You mean you studied angels?" he asked, incredulous.

Hagemi spoke in its normal voice. "Strictly speaking, that was not an angel. It was a winged spiritual construct made with Celestial mana. That said, your idea of angelic beings, particularly in the broader scope of things, applies well to this paradigm."

"How does one incarnate and extract information from Divine beings?"

Once we'd captured enough of the spawn from the lesser god, it was a simple enough matter. These beings are a combination of three elements: mind, soul, and divine energy. This process is not unlike Soul Battery technology, albeit with a few unique characteristics.

"Such as?"

Celestials, and other divine-created lesser beings, do not have a Soul Cage. They are whole, a single unit, with no separation of mind and spirit. Furthermore, when stored and reconstituted, they retain the state they were in at the moment of first storage. We discovered early on that we could question a stored Celestial hundreds of times, and each time it would forget the questions we asked unless we allowed it to remain sentient.

"Wait, you're saying you can put a Celestial into a hard drive, bring it back to life, torture it until you're done, then simply suck it back up?" Neither of Ty's first possessions had any recollections of these things. Their view of the world, at least until their death, had been simpler and more idyllic. Were the akkoan more devious than he'd originally thought?

"That's precisely what he means," Hagemi stated. "Looking at these memories, I believe the akkoan people pioneered the development of Mind Fortresses. It certainly would explain the one I found for you." Manifesting, the Arbiter floated near a door and pulsed a light across a gem. "With this information, I postulate that the gems we've come across are modified Mind Fortresses. Essentially, they played the role of a Soul Cage, only also capable of storing the collected memories of their captives. The ones in this corridor are similar, with a subtle alteration. They reconstitute spiritual beings for experimentation, not as fuel."

It shocked Ty that Hagemi didn't know about the origins of the Mind Fortresses. Not that he thought it would be common knowledge, but Hagemi was an Arbiter. Shouldn't it know? Instinct told him not to share his personal insight with Hagemi, though he couldn't have explained why.

Turning back to the conversation at hand, he said, "Why was the angel I fought wounded so badly? Because it was injured when it was stored?"

The tapped memory replied, *I do not know the state of that specific subject, but I would assume so. We captured tens of thousands of their kind before the God War broke out. Their bodies, and the bodies of the Demon-infected Infernals, were quite fascinating. Hundreds of years of research and we'd barely struck the surface. It was such a shame that their gods took issue with our pursuits.*

Ty missed a step, both horror and realization making him flinch. "You were harvesting the creations of the gods for research and were surprised when those gods took offense?"

Why should they take offense? Their creations were lesser beings. Secondary creations. Any knowledge gained from the study of them was well within our right as our Lord's first children. If anything, those lesser gods should have been thankful. We invented such wonders with their inferior offspring. It was a shame that we had to pivot to weapons manufacturing at the end.

"Hagemi, can we free these beings?" Ty asked, looking at the doors. He had a feeling that getting the angels out would be a more difficult and complicated process than the akkoan souls.

"If you could extract the gemstones from the wall and crush them, it should free the captives within. You'd have one hell of a problem if you did that. These beings were created by a different Celestial god than the one outside. They will have foreign minds, traditions, and goals. You might release something quite challenging into the world."

"I hear you. Are they suffering like the ghosts were?" Ty didn't want to make his life more complicated than it already was. Still, if these beings were trapped in an eternal state of damnation, he would do his best to correct that.

"No," Hagemi said. "These aren't Soul Batteries. Unlike the ghosts, these entities are frozen in time. They don't think or feel until they are reconstituted."

"Good to know," Ty said, relieved. He had time to come back and free the angels later, assuming he could figure a solution out.

The corridor ended after half a day of travel. He was out of food and his water was running dangerously low now, and that was with rationing. He thought about exploring offshoot rooms or corridors, maybe finding new hidden depths where nourishment might be stored, but decided against it. None of the akkoan memories inside his Mind Fortress were certain about the final layout of the Sanctuary. Some had helped engineer parts of it, but none of the spirits in him knew more.

Channeling divine energy into his hands, Ty opened the doors and proceeded into the room beyond. The space was a near-duplicate of the warehouse construction chamber.

Glass containers dangled from the roof, each containing a different golden-glowing body part. Vats and crystalline coffins held angelic beings in thousands of states of repose and configuration, some winged, some covered in eyes, and so on. The bone arms flying through the room were the same as the first warehouse, and they were no more concerned about him than their counterparts had been.

Ty still felt curious about the room. A part of him wanted to explore, or maybe even try sitting on the dais chair near where he entered. Ultimately, he decided not to. He was running low on resources and had learned enough about the place to fear the consequences. Bringing a Frankenstein version of a Celestial with ties to a dead god out of this place might be problematic.

He passed through the room, following as close a trajectory as the last one as he could. The room out led to another opaque, glass-walled corridor. A few steps into the new corridor, the walls became transparent.

Ty expected to see horrors. What he saw did not disappoint.

The first of the cells to his right contained an akkoan male. His skin was flawless white with glowing gold shining through in a map of his veins. The bottom half of his face was gone, replaced with a metallic apparatus ending in jutting, red-glowing tusks. He was naked, standing in the middle of the cell amidst an elaborate ritual spell edged in silver that was etched into the floor.

Hagemi said, "This celestial has been augmented with the byproducts of a demonic possession. I believe the process would cause insanity and overwhelming aggression. It would probably also make them quite powerful."

Ty didn't feel the outright, mind-crushing horror from looking at the Celestial. This fear was slower, deeper. Seeing an undead or a creature of nightmare in a cell was one thing. Seeing a tortured angel, no matter how abstracted or monstrous, was another. He wasn't sure whether he'd rather end the thing's suffering or just free it if he could open its cage.

He didn't have that ability, so he looked down and pressed on, trying to ignore any of the other captives. There was no benefit to adding fresh horror to his heart.

There was no library on the other end of the corridor. Instead, he found a raw-boned cavern filled with glowing crystals of various sizes. Each crystal radiated Celestial energy. There were no signs of undead or constructs, no enemies to attack or slow him down. Nor, he noted with a sense of wry bemusement, did he find any treasures. He didn't try to take any of the crystals. His backpack had been torn in several places, making roughly a third of it useless as storage, and his new robe was laden enough.

He made a mental note to eventually spend his merits so he could access the crystals and drain some of their mana. If he had such an ability, the dungeon could become an easy place to retreat and heal up in the future.

"Why can't I just get a damn inventory power?" Ty muttered as he left the room, and its potential wealth, behind.

Finally, after what felt like a day of constant travel, he emerged into what he hoped was the exit of the dungeon.

"You'll never complete your mission without the secrets in my Sanctuary. Are you sure you wish to leave so soon?" the now-familiar voice rumbled as Ty stepped into the room.

Chapter 25: Seeker

Ty looked around, finding he'd emerged in a mirror of the entry room, complete with a throne nearby. The shadow reclined there, its originally ephemeral body almost tangible. It had the shape of a hooded and robed man about twice his height.

Voice resonating through the room, it spoke again. "You have seen barely three percent of the first floor. I think you should reconsider leaving. Turn around, Ty. Go and explore. There are hundreds of rooms filled with tens of thousands of mysteries for you yet to uncover. Aren't you starved to know what else hides in my domain?"

Ty took a few steps toward the dais, trying to get a better look inside the hooded cowl. He glimpsed something for just a moment, two glinting eyes above a face made of swirling stars.

"I'm out of food. Plus, I'm not gaining any levels in here. I won't be able to go down for a while, assuming I do return," he said.

"Levels?" The cowl jerked from him to where Hagemi flickered into view. The Arbiter's inner light flared for a moment. "Ah, yes. I see. Levels. How quaint. No, you will not gain those here at this time. But you could acquire the equipment and skills you need in the world above, no?"

Ty felt some of his suspicions confirmed. "You don't want me to go. You're feeding off my presence somehow, aren't you? You're the akkoan god. The one who abandoned them."

A snarl of rage shot through the shadowy shape, lashing out at Ty as surely as a backhand strike from a giant. He slammed into a wall, screaming in pain as he felt something break in his back, before sliding to the floor. Pain radiated from his spine, down into his legs.

The God of the akkoan people spoke, and its voice filled the space with the weight of overwhelming malice. "You know nothing. I saved them! They made me love them! I inspired their greatness; I made all my children great! And yet look what they did? Betrayed. Killed. Left adrift, sealed away in this prison filled with apostates. Where is my continuity, scion? Where is my life? Gone."

Ty rushed Verdant Touch into his legs, pouring healing energy through his body as fast as he could spend the mana. From the tone of the god, he was certain it would attack again.

"What of my peers? Where was their succor, when I did what I must?" Fist flashing, it struck the armrest of its throne, producing a booming echo. Past one of the supporting pillars, these carved in the shapes of wings, Ty saw the double doors leading out of the room peel open. He heard the growling sound of rock being smashed as whatever blocked their progress was swept away.

"Go," the god said, snarling. "You will return. When you learn the true nature of the Bridge, you will return. When you discover the power you need, the mysteries you must uncover, you will come back. Regardless of what you think you know, I will have what I want from you."

Flexing his legs and wiggling his toes successfully, Ty came to his feet and turned to leave. If there was anything the books from the prophecy, or really any game he'd ever played, had told him, it was to not mess in the affairs of angry gods.

"You will return," the god rasped again.

Ty froze and turned to face the shape on the throne. That last call hadn't been a threat or come across as cajoling. His intuition, or maybe his knowledge of the god through the akkoan memories, saw deeper.

"Stop it," he said and strode back to the center of the room.

The ancient god watched, speechless, giving him time to say his piece. His sense of the deity was that it felt confused and curious. Given that it was probably a god of curiosity, he wasn't surprised.

Ty pressed his hand to his chest, over his Soul Cage. "They loved you, and you inspired greatness in them. Greatness and horror. I know what you want me to see." Ty gestured at the shadowy shape. "You want me to see you as a mysterious horror. You want me to fear you and come back over and over again, to pit myself against your realm. But do you know what I see?"

The shadow leaned forward, head cocked inquisitively to one side.

"I see loneliness. I see a god with no worshipers and no source of companionship for thousands of years. God, I see you. And I see the beauty in you, too." Ty had felt the akkoan love of this god, known it as intimately as his own memories. He felt that love even now, despite knowing that the god had also inspired horrible things. Over time, he had no doubt he would discover more atrocities inspired by this creature. For now, however, he let the akkoans inform his words.

"I will not come back out of fear or whatever reason you think I'll need," Ty continued. "I am going to come back because I, and the people inside me, want to. I see your loneliness. I felt it in the memories of your people. I will come back when I'm stronger, and I will explore. It just won't be *why* you think I'm doing it."

The god froze, not speaking for a long time, before its sonorous voice swept over him. "They called me many names, my people. The Devouring Depths, the Infinite Hunger. I always preferred a simpler name, the one their children knew me as. Call me Seeker."

With nothing further to say, Ty turned and left. The doors closed behind, leaving him at the bottom of a half-complete excavation. A surprised demon soldier, the gemstone in its forehead glimmering in the sunlight that filtered down the shaft, gawked at him when he stepped into view.

Chapter 26: Leadership

Days Remaining in Cycle: 21

Current Hit Points: 10

Current Mana: 8

Mana Shield: 3

Equipment of Note: One pistol, one enchanted robe (epic), one enchanted dagger (epic)

Ty shoved the demon back against the wall of the shaft with one hand, simultaneously drawing the black knife with his other. He shoved the tip against the demon's forehead gem, expecting resistance. The blade went through the gem like smoke, stabbing deep into the demon's skull. Its eyes rolled back into its head as it collapsed.

Green light flashed in the periphery of his vision and Sprite appeared. It buzzed around, then back down, gesturing with tiny motions of its antenna. He interpreted the gestures as *we're surrounded*.

With no time to contemplate Sprite's reappearance, he rushed up the steep, poorly carved stairs leading out of the tunnel. As Sprite had indicated, many of the demons were present. He saw maybe a couple dozen soldiers and dog drones clustered together, looking listless. There was no sign of a general, nor were there new banners.

Three soldiers and a drone were standing at the top of the stairs. None of them were looking in his direction until the last minute, when the dog-like drone made a keening cry.

As the drone called, Ty wrapped one arm around the nearest demon's head and yanked him back, slashing its neck in the same motion. The black dagger was effective at more than shattering gems. A gout of orange blood showered his robed arm as he hugged the demon against him.

The drone lunged, nipping at his leg. Its teeth bit into his enchanted robe and he heard something break in the demon's mouth. One of the two remaining soldiers lunged forward, slashing, and he intercepted the attack by shoving the soldier he'd been holding forward. He only had a thirteen in his strength stat, but it was enough to knock that soldier off balance.

Ty stepped into the third soldier, blocking several claw strikes on his robed arm before twisting and jamming the dagger between the demon's ribs. Once, twice, the dagger slashed through chitin effortlessly; the tip emerging covered in blood.

The dog came in again, grabbing his foot. He dropped to the ground, using momentum and leverage to pull the dog closer. Its teeth punctured the thick, hard leather of his combat boot and scraped across the flesh beneath. Above him, the second soldier's swipes narrowly missed where he had been a moment before the dog's attack.

Bending nearly in half, he leaned down and jabbed his dagger at the dog's forehead gem. One touch and the gem shattered, sending the dog to the ground in sharp spasms.

Claws raked at Ty's head and shoulders. He got one arm up, barely, to avoid any serious injuries. He lashed out with his dagger, stitching holes into the final soldier demon's leg until it collapsed, then he grabbed the demon's arm and yanked it close enough for him to finish it off.

During the moment of calm before the soldiers realized what was happening, Ty checked his health and mana notifications.

Hit Points: 8

Mana: 8

Mana Shield: 3

Between the robe and the dagger, Ty no longer felt completely outmatched. The robe so far had shielded him from almost all mundane attacks, including demonic claws, and his dagger was incredible. It wasn't quite *snicker-snack* incredible, but it was still amazing. To think that the blade was dealing damage equivalent to his sniper rifle or pistols was shocking.

He came to his feet and started toward the nearest cluster of six demon soldiers. Drawing a pistol one-handed, he rapidly shot three of the demons. One went down, the gemstone in its head shattered, and two flinched back as bullets grazed their faces. He lunged at the nearest unphased demon, slamming his dagger into its neck. Claws raked at his sides and shoulders ineffectually as he kicked the corpse back, turned into the nearest of the new attackers, and shot it at point blank range. The bullet barely damaged the chitin, though the impact pushed the demon back a foot. He used the space to stab in and up, spearing through the demon's chin and into its insectoid skull.

Someone grabbed Ty's backpack, pulling him away from his newest victim. He instinctively raised both forearms and ducked his head, barely blocking reaching claw-tipped fingers. He remembered all too well the vulnerabilities of the cloak.

Stumbling, Ty fell, letting his arms slip out of the straps of the backpack. Flat on his backside, he twisted and stabbed the dagger through the nearest feet. Once. Twice. Three times. The demons attacked, and he kept his guard up, slashing at anything in range.

Hissing screeches of pain came from the group surrounding him. Several demons had fallen to his frantic stabbing, and others were on the ground holding bleeding wounds. He no longer had a solid count of how many demons were left and how many he'd killed. He just kept shredding anything that came close.

Chitin-clad feet kicked at Ty's face and head, knocking him flat for a moment. He rolled to the side, smacking into a demon corpse. Climbing over the body, he used the space it gained him to come to his feet.

Blood ran down his nose, and he spat more from a split lip as he looked around. His roll had taken him back near the pit and prevented more demons from coming around him. A dozen corpses littered the ground, and another half that were grounded with injuries. Two dozen more approached him, clawed hands raised, forehead gemstones flashing. He couldn't tell which was the intellect donor, or if the leader was even among them.

He checked his status again.

Hit Points: 4

Mana: 8

Mana Shield: 2

He was at less than half health. Keeping his knife up and his blocking arm ready, he used Verdant Touch. The demons charged as soon as the healing magic took effect.

These soldiers didn't use weapons or martial arts. Their entire modality relied on impulsive, wild swings with their claws, which improved Ty's odds. Dodging around mounting corpses, he lashed out at the rushing demons, drawing the enchanted dagger across any hand that came in range. Lunging forward, he stabbed a demon, then twisted the blade to the side and yanked it outward, cutting a straight line from its chest to the one next to it. That maneuver cost him, as the second demon, as well as several adjacent ones, grabbed at him. One got a fistful of his robe and yanked him into a claw. Nails raked his cheeks and face. Blood ran from the stinging injuries, blinding him in one eye.

Ty spent mana and transformed Verdant Touch into Celestial Verdant Touch. He punched at the demon raking his face. Celestial energy smashed the demon back, sending it flying into several behind it. Hammering his knife into every limb within reach, he once more tried healing himself.

The soldiers screeched in Ty's face, interrupting most of his ability. One tried to tackle him. He slid to the side, elbow dropping into the back of the demon's neck, followed by his dagger. He sliced down the soldier's spine. Continuing the momentum, he stepped around the falling soldier and drove the dagger into another's face.

Two of the dog demons bit at his calves. Both got the robe, dealing no damage, but their powerful jaws still clamped down on the material, preventing him from maneuvering. One soldier on either side of him took advantage and clawed at his arms. Finally, he felt the pain of claws through the robe. It seemed that significantly strong, coordinated attacks could overwhelm the protections.

Ty dropped to one knee and twisted at his hips, the torsion enough to yank the hem of his robe from one dog's jaws. He stabbed the other in its gemstone before twisting back around and slashing at the first's face. Kicking at him again, the demon soldiers nearly knocked him off target. The edge of his blade nicked the forehead gemstone hard enough to add a crack to the surface. Apparently, just that crack was enough to do serious harm to the animal. The dog yelped and leaped away, nearly collapsing in pain.

With his immediate area clear, Ty went back to stitching, using his dagger on legs and feet as fast as he could. He flourished his robe, absorbing attacks, as he made his way to his feet again. He was nearing his last stand. Oddly, he wasn't afraid. It might have been his Arbiter suppressing his fear or his recent encounters with the spirits that made his last moments less intimidating. Regardless of how or why, he grinned at the encircling demons.

The remaining demons hesitated, backing away to regroup. There were maybe fifteen left, with another seven of the drone dogs. He'd killed or maimed close to half of the remaining force.

Glancing at his still-present character sheet, Ty felt a shiver run up his spine. He was closer to death than he'd thought. Gesturing with his knife down the trail away from camp, he growled, "I don't care about killing more of you. I don't care if you try to go into that place." He waved at the dungeon entrance. "I can tell you now, it's not whatever you were told it is. Let me pass, and you can live until Aquamarine's people get here."

With Sprite's reappearance and reporting on the situation, he had no doubt Aquamarine would send the Opal Guardians or sloths to mop up.

One demon stepped in front of the others. The insect-headed humanoid spoke in a chittering, growling tongue Hagemi translated into a German accent. "You speak our language. Few of your kind do. You speak in the tones of a leader. We have lost many of ours." It paused, waving in the air. "Mother gone silent. Al'nen says to talk to you. She says we must have a leader. Only leaders issue orders. You killed our general, yes? You smell the same as he who did. You also killed others of importance. Would you be leader? Would you take command?"

Ty blinked.

"Um," he said after a second, "Al'nen?"

The demon chittered. "Breeder. Demigod. Not queen. Mother is queen. Mother is silent. Breeder says talk to you. We talk."

Did the demon just say a demigod commanded it to talk to me?

Hagemi did not reply.

Thinking as rapidly as he could, he asked, "You're offering me the position of leader, but don't your leaders have to share intellect with you?"

The speaker made a strange clicking sound. Hagemi whispered in Ty's mind, *I can't translate that in any way you'd understand. It basically said yes and offered to induct you into their brood. The ritual would grant you a mind crystal. Then you can take rank with them. I don't have to warn you that is a bad idea, right?*

"I already have a mind crystal," Ty said, thinking of the Mind Fortress. There was absolutely no way he was letting any demonic bugs cast a ritual and put more gems anywhere near his head.

The speaker stood straighter, perking up. "Then let me connect to it and share with you." *

Ty thought to Hagemi, *Is that even possible?*

Technically, yes. The memories inside your Mind Fortress are pure intellect. Connecting with this configuration of demons might allow you to enhance them with little personal cost. It might also trigger something in the more assertive spirits inside your Spirit Cage. If things go poorly, you could end up with possessed demons or dead ones.

He was at two hit points, surrounded by enough demons to kill him. Those demons believed he could become their leader somehow. Either he accepted this crazy idea, which was beginning to feel more and more like his standard operating procedure, or he would die.

Hagemi, he thought, *is there any way you can identify spirits who would be useful, should the process result in possession?*

The Arbiter considered. *It's not my place to use your abilities, Ty. I should not interact with your Mind Fortress or your Spirit Cage at all.*

Ty was about to point out that the Arbiter had done just that, and extensively, inside the dungeon. He almost realized how and why too late. Seeker had been influencing Hagemi's actions from the start, only now the Arbiter had reverted to its normal state.

Holding up a hand, he said, "I will engage in your ritual with you. First, I need a moment to meditate. I will also heal myself since I'll need my full strength to do this."

The lead demon considered Ty, then made a terse gesture. "Do it. We will be prepared for treachery. Until the bond is made, we cannot trust you."

Settling back against a rock, he activated his Verdant Touch. While the healing energy surged through his body, he tried thinking at the spirits in his chest. *I don't know how to do this. I don't see how any of you can understand me. But I need volunteers. If this works, I'm going to have demons connected to the Mind Fortress. Hagemi says there's a chance you'll want to possess the demons. Given that they are demons, I'm not totally against this idea. But I want to make sure the right ones get the chance. I need leaders, warriors, mages, and craftspeople.*

Pressure resonated through Ty's chest. As it grew, he saw clusters of memory line the walls of the Mind Fortress, like fireflies gathering to escape an enclosure. The spirits might not be united with their memories, but they were still associated.

Without Hagemi's help, he knew he couldn't keep the suffering each of the akkoans had experienced out of their embodied minds. He could only hope that, should they possess the demons, they would be capable of sorting themselves out.

As prepared as he could be for whatever outcome came next, he stepped away from the rock. "All right, let's do this."

Hit Points: 10

Mana: 1

Mana Shield: 0

Ty checked his character sheet again as the demon speaker, along with three others, moved to occupy a perimeter around him. Their forehead gems glowed as each of the four chanted. It was a chittering, sharp, awful sound that made his stomach churn. How did he even know this was the ritual they said they'd be doing? Maybe he should kill them and make his run for it? He was at full health now, feeling recharged and revitalized.

Trusting random demons on another planet did not appeal as much when four of them were staring at him and chanting ominously.

Temporary Granted Power–Necromantic Demon Bond: *You have been offered a demonic intellect bond. This ritual has been enhanced and altered due to the nature of your Celestial Mind Fortress and the presence of the Wild in your spirit. If you accept this bond, you will be able to assign spirits to beings with mind gems. This assignment requires touch, and the recipient need not be willing. Powerful demons with high Intelligence or Spirit scores may resist this effect. If they do, the two of you will have a contest of wills. Once a spirit is assigned to a mind gem, you will be connected to the host demon. You may recall the spirit with a modest effort and several seconds of concentration. This connection will be subject to distance attenuation for management purposes, but the possession will persist regardless. Please note, there may be several unknown consequences or side-effects with this bond. My predictive and surveillance capabilities seem unnaturally limited when it comes to the Mind Fortress. Speaking of, where did you get this? Oh, also, this is a ritual augmentation, not a permanent enhancement. It may be dispelled or disrupted by foreign powers. It's also necromantic, meaning if a native catches wind of you using this and figures out how it works, you'll be hunted down by literally half the scions on the planet.*

Well, Ty thought, at least the ritual hadn't been one of those "rip your soul apart" versions he'd been worried about. He accepted. The bond manifested as a thin, barely visible thread that connected his forehead to the four nearest demons. That thread then split off from each of the four to the remaining soldiers and drones. With his acceptance, twenty-two minds, with their accompanying souls, pulled free of his Mind Fortress.

Every demon, including the drone-dogs, went stiff. Ty couldn't see what was happening, but he'd lived through a version and could imagine. It wouldn't take long for the intellect of the spirits to settle into place; the demons were willing vessels.

I can't take it anymore, Hagemi announced.

Before Ty could see the results of the possession, prompts flooded his vision.

Congratulations! *You have killed multiple Hive-Variant, Pestilential Demon Invader Soldiers. Would you like to loot the corpses? If so, where would you like the loot deposited?*

Congratulations! *You have killed multiple Hive-Variant, Pestilential Demon Invader Drones. Would you like to loot the corpses? If so, where would you like the loot deposited?*

Ty pointed to a spot on the ground, accepting the flash of prompts. A pile of mind crystals, apparently looted directly from each corpse, appeared. An inventory window popped up. It held a single, unlabeled gold coin. He took the object, inspecting it. One side of the coin had three claw marks, and the other a great, gleaming castle.

What's this?

Hagemi didn't answer.

When he turned back to the demons, he found all of them huddled on the ground, having fits. The dogs jerked and howled, the soldiers tore at their own flesh with clawed fingers and wailed. Concerned for the spirits, he reached for his container of remaining Celestial blood. Only when he got his water flask out did he remember that he'd drained it dry. He had no way to replenish his magic and help the akkoans.

The macabre dance gradually calmed. Several of the dogs and a couple of the soldiers died. He barely recalled the spirits in time before they were lost. Slowly, one at a time, the surviving demons rose, their bodies moving awkwardly.

Looking around at each other, the akkoan-possessed-demons came together in a circle, the drone dogs taking up the center. Ty watched in fascination as the demon mouthparts practiced the akkoan tongue. He understood their akkoan natively and overheard enough to feel his heart wrench. Some of these people knew each other or knew of one another. From what he gathered, the ghosts hadn't been sealed together all at once; a few were hundreds of years older than the others. The way each spoke made it abundantly clear to him that they all suffered from extensive trauma. More than one broke down in choked sobs at intervals.

After a while, once most of the akkoans had command of their new bodies, they began to sing. Ty recognized elements of the song from his retained memories. He felt a pang of regret and hurt at the nature of the lament and at the sharp-edged elements added by the demon physiology.

No matter how completely the akkoans acclimated to their new bodies, he knew this wasn't a true resurrection.

Finally, as their first song concluded, one demon stepped from the circle to address Ty. He had a face lacerated by self-inflicted wounds and shivered, as if the seizures had done lasting damage, but his voice was calm. "I am Uneth, former general of the akkoan army. I am prepared to serve you in the protection of my people." He waved a hand at Ty's chest.

Another demon peeled from the cluster, speaking in an insectoid-approximation of a female voice. "What he said. I'm Cleozun, former High Mage of the Omantal cabal. You give our people a proper afterlife, and I'll do whatever you want."

Uneth tilted his head in Cleozun's direction but didn't say anything. The other possessed demons, all but the dogs, introduced themselves similarly. None of Ty's remaining memories included this ceremony, but he got the impression the akkoans were ritually pledging their allegiance to him.

"Uneth," Ty asked once the introductions were done, "how are you? Do you feel well enough to lead?"

Holding up a hand, Uneth made a wavelike gesture. "The demon I inhabit had memories that are easy enough to parse. The years of suffering inside the Battery weigh on me, I will not lie. But being in a body, with flesh that hurts and breath that rasps through my chest helps." He paused, hesitantly adding, "I do not know that I fully trust myself. As a general, it has always been my duty to know my own mental state, and I cannot tell you I am particularly... stable. For now, I am no leader."

"And the rest of you?" Ty asked the others.

Each repeated Uneth's wave gesture, except for Cleozun. She leaned in, taking on a bird-like posture. "I'm fine. Very fine. Alive. I want to taste the magic of this world. There are new mortal gods here, yes? Let's kill them."

"Okay," Ty said, eyeing her warily, "I definitely think trusting you completely is going to be a great idea."

Even with her insect head, Cleozun seemed to smile at him. "Thank you, Savior. I appreciate your acknowledgment."

Uneth glanced at Cleozun before saying, "Ty, I do not know each of the souls here today, but I have heard of many of them. May I take more time to talk to them and assess their capabilities? I believe that will help us with any tasks or responsibilities you wish us to assume for you."

At Ty's allowance, the akkoans renewed their circle. This time, he observed the drones were communicating, too, albeit in a truncated fashion. He couldn't imagine what it must have been like to go through what the akkoans had, only to be brought back in a dog's body.

"Ty, what happened in the dungeon?" Hagemi asked, manifesting as Ty went to stuff the piled loot into his already nearly full pockets.

"What do you mean, what happened? You were there the whole time." He was about to say more when a sigh of sound pressed into his ear. He could have sworn the sound came from Hagemi, just not in the Arbiter's normal voice. *You would be unwise to alert any of the gods to my true nature or presence or make Hagemi aware of the lost time.*

Hagemi flickered in a now-familiar glitch pattern. "Oh yeah, that's right. I remember. You did some really creative things in there, Ty. Inspiration will be quite pleased when I report in. A shame you only earned twenty-five percent to level three, though. It's going to be a big level for you."

Ty frowned, wondering for the first time just how deeply Seeker had interfered with Hagemi's programming. Clearly, the god had prepared for Hagemi's questions about the dungeon. What other contingencies had the crafty old god put into place? He considered attempting to communicate with Seeker through Hagemi and discarded the idea. It wasn't worth adding confusion to an already complicated mess.

"Ty, I have something else I should tell you."

"Go ahead," he said. He couldn't help but feel a spike of wariness at Hagemi's resumption of formal tone.

"You will be returned to your world in twenty days. Same rules as the first portal. In six months, give or take, after that, you will be able to return here. There is a time differential between our worlds, so you should expect only three or four days to have passed on your side. Which means..."

Ty did the math. "Which means when I return again, around three years will have passed on this side?"

Hagemi bobbed in place. "The energy it takes to bring you here and keep you tethered to both worlds is immense. The time differential benefits us, for now. As we achieve further resonance, it may change. The problem is, with three years on our planet, things you set in motion now may come back to..."

"Bite me in the ass?" Ty finished, glancing at the akkoans.

Another bob. "You have little time, but you should consider planting seeds."

Ty cursed beneath his breath but held off blaming the Arbiter. Hagemi was only doing its job. "I'll start thinking once I have room to breathe and some water," he said.

"Sprite, can you help me find water?" he hadn't seen the Sprite since it vanished upon his exit of the dungeon, but he hoped at least one of Aquamarine's agents was still near enough to hear him.

A blinking light flashed a few feet away. Ty stared, barely able to make out the centaur-like silhouette of the sprite from the background. A few minutes of walking later and he had replenished his reserves from a nearby stream, his mana likewise restored.

Ty sat next to the stream, breathing and relaxing his mind. It took him a while, the turmoil of recent events clawing at his thoughts, threatening to draw him into troubling memories. Eventually, the beauty of the forest worked its unique magic, centering him in the awesome beauty of the world. Minutes passed. Then, once he felt centered, he began to list the revelations of the previous days. After he had them as organized as he could, he turned to listing the ways he'd changed, and why he'd made the choices he had.

Perhaps I should release the spirits here, in Aquamarine's forest? Looking around, he compared the area to the akkoan water gardens. While it was beautiful here, it wasn't the same. Akkoan gardens were ritualistically prepared, acting as a temporary afterlife for the deceased. He couldn't just use any woods for the akkoans inside him.

With these memories, in time, I can prepare a proper garden for them. It was the best plan he could make, the only one that would honor akkoan tradition.

Decision made, he let his mind drift to other things. He thought about Sanctuary, wondering just how much the events inside had been orchestrated by Seeker all along. The goblin must have been freeing souls for years, based on the sheer volume he'd encountered. Yet when he'd arrived, he discovered it had skipped ahead to the closest door to the entry, freeing specifically Numera and Mummat. There had to be more than coincidence to that.

What next? Will I be their leader? He had to face the fact that he was the spiritual center of thousands of spirits. With his connection to the possessed demons, it only made him more important to the akkoans. If none of them could lead, who else was there?

Ty knew he wasn't a leader. He was uncomfortable being around people, much less giving orders. In gaming groups, he often played the wizard or engineer type, leaving leadership to the genuinely charismatic players. Hell, he didn't even like to look people in the eye. Any form of personal confrontation or intimacy made him uncomfortable.

Inside him were thousands of akkoan refugees, disembodied spirits waiting for a proper burial. Or, maybe, some would want to come back in demon bodies. To make matters more complicated, the akkoans he'd resurrected had gone through incredible trauma. There was a chance they'd need him to help navigate what came next here, not to mention if they came to his world.

He wasn't from Volar, and he wasn't from Ako, but at least he was a scion of Inspiration. The akkoans had no one and nothing. He *had* to adapt, or he'd doom everyone he freed to misery.

The pressure of responsibility was almost overwhelming. He wanted to cry or hit something. Instead, he pulled out a notepad and began making plans. He started with the traits of the effective leaders he'd played with, and the men and women he'd worked under in the real world. Once he had that list, he made a branching list of objectives. It started with, "Don't take the akkoans for granted" and, "Try to make eye contact, it will make them feel seen," and ended with, "Empower them to take care of themselves."

He wasn't deluded enough to think that he could govern a people, not in the long term. For now, however, he'd accept the responsibility.

With a clearer mind, Ty returned to camp. Uneth was waiting for him.

"Ty, can I ask you a few questions?" Uneth said.

"Sure, please go ahead."

"First, are you able to recall us from these bodies?" He pointed to a demon. "Most of those you've embodied have valuable skills, but not Fizzel. He is a farmer. He was just eager to wear flesh again, so his spirit leaped at the chance. If things progress as I expect, we will need soldiers before farmers."

Ty tested, mentally reaching out and tugging gently on the tether that sprouted from him to the indicated demon. Fizzel's spirit and mind flew out of the demon's body, integrating back into Ty's chest. Without Hagemi's help, sorting Fizzel's mind into the Fortress took several minutes, though it wasn't as difficult as he'd imagined. Perhaps Fizzel's willingness to return made it simpler, or maybe practice was the key.

The emptied demonic captain stood frozen in place. "I miss the feeling. Please, may I have another?"

"Wait, what?" Ty said.

The captain asked again, "Please, restore me, leader. I do not wish to be empty."

Uneth gestured at the demon and explained, "Unless they are connected to another intelligence, these demons always feel alone. Even their commanders suffer from it. Their minds are fragments. Part of what makes them such capable killers and minions is the fact that they are so incomplete. With us inside them, they feel more whole than they have their entire lives."

"That is awful," he said.

"Indeed. The memories of the one I inhabit speak of a divine Demon who was defeated by the Monster God ages ago. Since then, the soldier demons have obeyed her but are treated only as fodder. I suspect most, if not all, of the demons still on this planet are not in a good way."

"And here I was thinking that I couldn't like that god any less." Ty didn't believe that he'd have felt a lot of sympathy for a so-called "Demon god," but he wasn't about to say so out loud.

"If you have a spirit in you named Theontsu, would you place him in this body?" Uneth nodded toward the disconsolate demon.

Theontsu, are you in here?

A spirit resonated with the name, easing Ty's search of the accompanying memories. Retrofitting the demon with Theontsu's spirit only took a few minutes. He had a gut feeling that re-skinning the spirits in this way had a limit, though he wasn't sure what it was yet. Given the time commitments, he knew he wouldn't be doing it in battle until he was far more skilled.

Theontsu settled into the demon, going through a familiar collapsing and orienting process. Thankfully, his host, apparently attuned to being possessed now, took less time and damage during the orientation.

As a newly embodied Theontsu and Uneth spoke, the other akkoans set about investigating the area. To Ty's relatively untrained eye, all the survivors moved with experience and precision as they scouted. Even Cleozun, whose every utterance further convinced him that she was batshit crazy, made her way from the quarry with ease.

One of the akkoans appeared on the rim of the valley, near where Ty had shot the general all those days ago. He made a clicking sound, drawing Uneth and Theontsu's attention, then gestured rapidly.

"Creatures approach," Uneth translated. "Four big ones, significant threats, and multiple medium ones. Probably also significant, though the scout doesn't recognize the type. They move on four legs."

Ty glanced over at Sprite. "Is it Aquamarine and the rest of the crew?"

The sprite flashed.

"No worries, Uneth, they are allies."

Uneth made a few hand gestures back, followed by a series of loud clicking noises. Multiple akkoans returned from their scouting trip. Cleozun came at the heels of the others. She'd fashioned a robe out of tree leaves and bark. Ty could have sworn the thing had eldritch runes glimmering in the natural cracks and crevices of the bark and the material moved like cloth rather than forest debris.

As expected, Aquamarine, the three sloths, and a few of the Opal Guardians made their way into the valley through the southern trails a few moments later. Though the group looked wary, none had their hackles up or moved to attack the akkoans. Ty mutely thanked Aquamarine's little spies for heading off what would have been a bad confrontation.

"Ty, we are very glad you're alive! How did you get here?" Aquamarine asked, its expression a mixture of relief and stern disapproval. "I thought I told you to avoid the quarry."

Boblin rushed forward, warbling with pure joy, and enfolded Ty in a hug, lifting him off the ground until his feet dangled. The stallion walked up, eye-balling the sloth balefully.

Inhaling the thick, earthy scent of the sloth, Ty did his best to hug her back. His arms barely spanned her powerful chest.

"Let the human down," one of Boblin's parents called, its sentiment echoed in the stallion's stamping hoof.

Looking abashed, Boblin sat Ty down gently. The stallion inched forward, nosing Ty's shoulder until he gave the magical beast a jolt of healing magic.

"Ty?" Aquamarine prompted.

Hagemi sent him a smug, *I thought you weren't going to be a druid?*

Ty flushed, gently extricating him from the stallion's aggressive affections. "Well, you see. There was this interesting well, and it had steps in the middle.

And I kinda went exploring and just ended up here..." He trailed off as Sprite manifested near Aquamarine, landing on one of the dragon's shoulders.

"My little spirit tells me you went into a place that put it to sleep. That suggests one likely culprit."

"Which is?"

Cleozun cackled, her unnerving insect eyes locked on Aquamarine as she walked over. "Divine Shielding, and more. No magical connections in or out. No spying by the gods, no spying by the mortals. A complete seal."

Glancing askance at the cackling demon, Aquamarine's hands danced in what Ty thought was an expression of nervousness. "Ah, yes. That." It spoke in perfect, fluent akkoan.

Ty tried to make a subtle gesture to warn the dragon off that topic as he said, "Perhaps later. I have a few other immediate problems that you might be able to help with, though. Also, how do you know akkoan?"

Eyes narrowing, Aquamarine started to speak, but Uneth raised a hand. "If I may, Forest Guardian?"

"You may," the dragon said, assuming its thoughtful posture, hands folded across its chest, fingers working cunningly.

"The remaining demon army, how far are they? This body remembers them fleeing to recruit help. Are they still within your forest?"

Aquamarine's right hands made a sinuous gesture. "Almost gone. They got lost a few times and milled about more than they walked, but they eventually figured it out. They'll leave the forest in less than a day, more or less, probably. Why?"

Uneth looked at Ty. "Savior, I suggest we intercept the fleeing army. Not only are they a potential source of additional recruits, but they mean to reconnect with another force. This body was not entirely sure who the reinforcements would be, but I suspect the Monster God's forces will be involved. The place we're standing will be ground zero for an attack shortly after."

Loosing a hiss of alarm, Aquamarine looked over at the Opal Guardians and the sloths. "There are other guardians than I, and more forest help. Much more. But I do not want a war with the Monster God."

Ty groaned. How had he gone from a simple man, on a simple mission, with a series of utterly discrete, disconnected quests to this?

Quest-Demon Army Takeover: *Find and deal with the remaining demon infestation.* **Reward:** *50% milestone progress toward level 3.*

Ongoing Quest–Protect the Dungeon: *Use any means necessary to protect both known entrances of the mysterious dungeon.* **Special Reward:** *This quest will represent significant, and ongoing, effort by you and your allies. Should things progress as expected, you will be forced to repel multiple attacks. You will receive experience commensurate with the attacks deflected, up to a maximum of 20% needed to your next level per attack, up to a maximum of level 8.*

"Damn it," Ty said, muttering and glaring at Hagemi. "Fine, we'll go and capture an army."

Interlude Four: Suspicious Activity

Surviving Earth Participants: 25,041

Average Level: 5

Days Remaining in Cycle: 20

"He's cheating," a god announced, pointing at the Great Arbiter. Shadowy power poured from the god into the colorful shape at the center of the hall. A forest manifested before the collective. A magnificent dome of subtle power simmered beneath the forest, deflecting the Great Arbiter's perceptions. The divine collective recognized the effect.

"Who is cheating?" Balance asked.

"Him," Shadow said, pointing at Inspiration. "He arranged for this. First his scion vanishes, and now his Arbiter has clearly been tampered with. He is cheating, and we should sanction him and his scion for it."

"Inspiration, what do you say to this?" Balance said.

By way of answer, Inspiration waved a hand, the ring on one finger gleaming. "If I may?"

The image of the forest reset to a full view of the planet. Multiple large spots appeared on the map. Each spot had a similar obscuring dome. The vision of the Great Arbiter was better able to pierce these defenses, however, and at each location there were massing armies. With another motion, a congregation of Arbiters and their associated scions came into view. Several of the Earthlings bore the soul-markings of the God of Monsters. Others had the markings of another god.

Each scion was already powerfully endowed, a couple of them having achieved the ninth level. Most also bore heavily imbued equipment, clearly boasting enhancements outside the limitations agreed upon by the gathered gods.

"I would ask my accuser why they are making alliances with the betrayer?" Inspiration said flatly.

As one, the remaining gods turned their gaze to Shadow, who shrugged. "I won't deny it, but you shall not persecute me for this." The god waved a finger, indicating several of the other gods. "All of you plot. There is only so much to go around, especially once Earth's local gods wake up. It benefits those of us who will make sacrifices and deals to do so now, before events further unfold."

Balance frowned, exchanging an uneasy look with Inspiration. "Shadow, you will bring a new God War upon us," the neutral god warned.

"Will bring?" Shadow retorted with a laugh.

Chapter 27: Divine Edge

Days Remaining in Cycle: 20

The sloths were happy to act as transport. With multiple akkoan-possessed-demons clinging to their fur, each could teleport up to five others with them to anywhere in Aquamarine's domain. Given that the akkoans had no gear to take with them, the process took a matter of minutes. Aquamarine opted to not join in the raid. The pragmatic dragon said he would stay with the Opal Guardians and oversee the protection of the quarry.

Ty and his new party arrived in a track of lush forest, just a few miles ahead of where Aquamarine said the army's path would take it. According to Aquamarine, the forest thinned out from this point on before merging into a strip of rocky land that abutted the ocean.

"What's the plan?" Uneth asked. The sloths moved away from the akkoans, becoming invisible as they did.

Ty raised an eyebrow at Uneth. "I thought you had the plan?"

Uneth shuffled uneasily in place. "I don't trust my judgment. Not yet. Tell us what you think, and I'll try to add some value." Ty studied him, trying to understand. He wished he could take the time to pull out his notes and plan, not just about the battle, but about the akkoans. He remembered the dungeon and the crazed writing he'd left behind, and it dawned on him.

Uneth was suffering. The time he'd spent as a ghost, trapped as fuel for a battery, had left him scarred.

"It'll be fine, Uneth. I think I have an idea," Ty said. Without time to plan, he felt as uncertain as Uneth looked, but he tried to sound confident. "The ritual the demons cast is still active. I suppose we can capture demons and I'll touch them. That should give us a way to grow our forces at the cost of theirs, right?"

Cleozun giggled. It sounded like beetles crawling on bark. "No need, no need. You have a connection to one of this world's little gods, yes?" She continued without waiting for him to answer. "You give me permission. I tap into that. Easy to build on the ritual. God-magic, even little godling, is pure fuel. Ten-minute ritual to create the enchantment. Simple. Whenever one of our people touches one of theirs, it will activate the demon's nature. Connection will happen. You just need to send a spirit."

Ty gawked. "You can do that?"

"Of course. Why, do you not believe that I can do this thing? These demons are empty, ripe for such magic. All I require is for all of us to link hands while I chant. One big circle. Like family. And we can sing! And dance!" She laughed merrily, skipping side to side as she made the announcement.

Uneth, straightening from his uneasy posture, said, "Mage, you're not serious about the singing and dancing, are you? In these bodies?"

Cleozun paused her frolicking and sighed. "Yes, fine. I suppose not that." She looked at Ty. "In the future, I will require sufficient objects to cast a ritual of remaking on us. I want a familiar body back."

"Uh, sure," Ty said. Turning his attention back to Uneth, he continued, "And your idea?"

"Yours is the best foundation. Thank you," Uneth said. "I will coordinate my people. If Cleozun can do what she says, you stay back. Once we contact the demons, you trigger your power from a safe position. Assuming we work well together, this should be a simple process."

He seems fine now, Ty thought. *Maybe it's just the big choices he's struggling with?*

Madness comes in many forms, Hagemi replied.

Crouching, Ty retrieved a fresh pad of paper and a pen, outlining the plan in short phrases and adjectives. "This sounds like a lot of risk to you and relatively little to me," he said, frowning at the notes.

Cleozun moved to tower over Ty, her octagonal eye segments glaring down at him. "You die, we die. Your Mind Fortress may remain intact. Our knowledge could survive your death, but your Soul Cage would not. Without a life to maintain our souls, they would pass on. Abomination would result." She extended a claw-tipped finger and spoke, accentuating each word with a firm poke at Ty's forehead. "You. Must. Not. Die."

"Damn, that's a hard promise to make," Ty said, fighting the urge to retreat.

The mage made a dismissive motion. "Try this. Promise to let us help you whenever we can. Promise to take no risks that are not required. Your life is one of risk. Now you must think of our people when you risk it."

Ty glanced from Cleozun to Uneth and to the other akkoans. "I promise to do my best not to die. It's my world at stake if I stop taking risks. I don't mind accepting help along the way, though."

"Perfect. A better outcome than I planned," Cleozun said, stepping away and extending a hand on either side of her. "Come now, make a circle. I need ten minutes to cast."

Eighteen sets of insect eyes, in both humanoid and canine bodies, looked from Ty to Cleozun as they silently slid into place. The dogs moved between two humanoids, allowing them to continue the chain without breaking it.

Access Request: *A ritual magic outside the scope of your god is seeking to augment your Mind Fortress. This will temporarily allow you to forge Possession Traps via touch through your active surrogates. Allowing this connection will drain some of your abilities for up to one day. You currently have eighteen active surrogates. Please be aware that Possession Traps are considered forbidden magic. If other natives of the world discover this spell has been used, there may be dire consequences. Accept request?*

Ty accepted the request.

Warning: *Magic Prism has been deactivated.*

Warning: *Verdant Touch has had its efficacy reduced. It will now heal one hit point per mana spent.*

Warning: *Life Leach has been deactivated.*

Warning: *Undead Clone Surrogacy has been deactivated. Also, how do you have yet another forbidden spell again? I seem to have forgotten. Anyway, moving on.*

Warning: *Magic Siphon has had its efficacy reduced. It now replenishes mana at half the rate.*

"Fuck me," Ty practically bellowed as his key abilities went inert.

"Pardon?" Cleozun and Uneth both asked.

"It's a phrase of frustration," Ty said. "All of my main abilities have been turned off."

Cleozun said, "Temporarily. It's a short ritual. Besides, you shouldn't be in any danger. Isn't that right, general?"

Uneth waved Theontsu over. "Theontsu, take three of your rangers and protect Ty. The rest will move in our standard formations to deliver touch attacks. Mage, what is the range of this ability?"

"Half a mile, give or take," she said, Ty's comprehension of their language translating the distance.

Theontsu signaled three of the other akkoans to form up with him. After a brief conversation, all four vanished into complete invisibility.

"I really need a concealment power, too," Ty muttered.

"Concealment, movement, and storage. I would recommend all three," Uneth suggested. He seemed surprised when Ty renewed his tirade of cursing. Looking over at Cleozun, he said, "Is it me, or does Ty seem a little unstable?"

Cleozun cackled, "Absolutely. I prefer it that way. Don't you?"

Closing his eyes to shut out the insanity that had become his life, Ty focused on the weight in his chest. *Akkoan people, we are going to provide more of you with bodies. We will need these bodies to protect the Sanctuary, where more of your people may be held. If you have needful combat skills, please come forward. As for the rest of you, your time will come as well. One way or another.*

Hundreds of souls churned in Ty's chest, their minds pressing against the edges of his Mental Fortress.

A couple of hours later, the scouts of the demon army came within range of his akkoan allies. The prompts started shortly after.

Bond Extension Request: *A creature you have surrogacy with would like to forcibly possess a creature with a mind gem. The target creature is identified as a "demon" type. Do you wish to send a soul into the "demon" body?*

Ty accepted the bond, feeding a soul to the ephemeral connection that appeared, stretching off in the distance. New prompts streamed after the first.

Motion drew his attention. He glanced up, seeing a tree branch a few dozen feet away swaying. Reaching for his gun, he froze as demons swarmed into view. There must have been thirty or more of the insect-headed creatures, each appearing without warning and rushing towards his position. He couldn't tell if the demons were after him or were merely maneuvering; regardless, they'd see him in seconds, if they hadn't already.

Ty hesitated. Each of the demons rushing at him was a potential recipient of an akkoan soul, an ally in waiting. Light flickered in the demons' mind gems. Seeing their active links, he began firing. With his first few shots, he cursed his earlier hesitation. There were a lot of the demons and unless he hit their forehead gems directly, they were all-but immune to his bullets. He shot one in the eye, and it barely stumbled.

The swarm veered directly toward him.

Accepting the still-incoming possession prompts as quickly as he could, Ty backed away as the twenty demons converged on him.

I don't suppose you can accept these prompts for me? Ty sent to Hagemi.

Nope.

Theontsu and his allies materialized in the middle of the cluster of rushing demons. The akkoan, leveraging his host body's strength, struck out at a specific demon with clawed hands. Another of Theontsu's allies intercepted the same demon, using a broken stick as a spear and driving it up and through the enemy's back.

The forehead gems of the still-rushing demons went dark.

Theontsu's other two soldiers began slapping at nearby demons. Prompts appeared, and Ty, though shocked at the turn of events, accepted them out of reflex. While those demons fell to the ground, now thrashing with seizures, Theontsu and his first assistant sped away from the dead captain, repeating the process. The surprised demons, lacking their leader's shared intelligence, tried to fight back.

Against Ty, the demons would have been overwhelming. Their speed, strength, and hardiness were far above anything a human could bring to bear. Against akkoan-possessed versions of themselves, they had no chance. Theontsu and his men moved like the wind, flowing from one place to another as effortlessly as if they'd been living in their demon bodies for weeks, not hours.

Two demons broke through the pack, rushing at Ty. He shot them in their chests, the rounds punching the creatures with enough force to slow them down. One of Theontsu's men tagged them both.

That it took a mere touch to overcome the demons changed the nature of the battle. Even had the akkoans not embodied a lifetime of martial knowledge, it would have been one-sided. This wasn't a battle, Ty realized. It was a game of sharks and minnows.

The entire engagement took less than ten minutes. Of the over three hundred remaining demon soldiers who had fled the quarry, more than half were converted. Most of the rest died during the conversion process. The sloths dealt with the few demons who got away. Ty's allies had suffered some losses during the assault, with nearly half the initial number either injured or dead. By any account, it was an overwhelming success.

Without him present to recollect the souls, those akkoans lost during the battle were gone forever. He felt each loss acutely. Logically, he knew that his connection to the spirits was a figment, a bond created by possession. Knowing didn't make him feel any better when his allies died, though.

"Uneth, do you feel comfortable organizing the survivors?" Ty asked once the battle was over.

Bloodied, but hale, Uneth gave him the equivalent of an akkoan nod. "I will do this."

It wasn't until a day later, after he and his newly converted army made it back to his convoy, that he remembered the swaying branch.

Chapter 28:
Planning a Visit

Days Remaining in Cycle: 19

The army made camp in the forest clearing that night. Utter madness followed.

Inexplicably, as soon as the group settled in, each akkoan began to scream and tear at their bodies. They seized and shook, screamed, and struck out at anyone or anything nearby. Coming from insect mouths, the insane sounds were deeply disturbing.

Ty, in the center of it all at his campfire, watched on in horror. Cleozun made her way through the throng of her people to him. "I apologize for not warning you of this sooner. There wasn't a good time."

"This? What is this?" Ty held a hand out at the writhing demons. "This can't be good for them."

Cleozun blew out a whistling breath. "Our people were masters of our minds, but there is some trauma we cannot endure forever. It has to come out, eventually. They are releasing theirs now, so they can be stable later."

"Kind of like a geyser venting steam?"

"Indeed. A release valve. I offered to take a watch with a few of Theontsu's rangers. It will be our turn after. You should rest while you can. Tomorrow will be a busy day."

Ty couldn't imagine the mental discipline required to contain madness to the degree that the akkoans did. "I don't suppose you can do something about the noise? There's no way I can sleep with this going on."

"Silly human, silence is a simple spell. Of course I can help."

Cleozun cast her spell around Ty's tent. When he finally slept, hours later, the thrashing cries of his allies still rang in his ears.

* * *

"Ty, I need resources," Cleozun announced the next day.

Standing beside her, one beat behind the mage's words, a scratched-up Uneth echoed the sentiment, "To prepare to defend the Sanctuary, we will need many things. Among them will be a place to stage our troops, armaments, and food."

Crouching, one tent flap in hand, Ty looked up at the akkoans with bleary eyes. Wordlessly, he walked through the clearing full of akkoans to the stream.

"Ty, what are your thoughts on solving these problems?" Uneth pressed, following behind.

Holding up a hand, he growled, "Not until coffee."

Uneth and Cleozun exchanged looks, each making one of their akkoan gestures. Taking a fresh canteen of water back to the fire pit he maintained near his convoy, Ty made a mental note to learn akkoan sign language as soon as he had the time to devote to it. The skill was not among his remaining akkoan memories.

Once the coffee was ready, Ty poured from the pot into a tin cup, then took a sip. Exhaling a long, pleasant sigh, he eyed the pair. "Now that the most important part of the day is out of the way, let's see about making a plan." Setting his cup down, he retrieved a notepad and pen. "All right, go ahead."

"Ty, being on your own is one thing," Uneth began. He nodded at the convoy. "The resources you brought here in your planning are formidable. But they are less than nothing when it comes to preparing for an invasion. We need tools to help us fortify a location, also armor and weapons. Our bodies are quite hearty and need little in the way of food, thankfully. Still, rations will become an item of concern, eventually."

"And I need spell components. Expensive ones. I also need those now." Cleozun stared at Uneth, silently challenging him to argue with her.

Aquamarine, who had been waiting patiently nearby, also added, "Ty, I should also say that I would prefer your friends to go elsewhere. I recognize why they are here and value their offer of protection against the god's minions, but this is an unspoiled space. Let them wait at the quarry or at the abandoned town. One or both. Just not this place."

Closing his eyes, Ty counted to three. "Hold on. All of you. Let me go over this." He wrote down the requests on top of one page and the variables on another. None of them questioned his methods or interrupted the process, which he found pleasantly surprising.

Tapping a hand next to an entry labeled "weapons and armor," Ty looked at Uneth. "What kind of weapons and armor?"

"Many of us are trained warriors. We need weapons to use that training properly. Armor will help cover the vulnerable spots." Uneth gestured at a crease in his chest chitin, accentuating the statement.

"Understood," Ty said, adding another note. To Cleozun, he said, "Can your spells help us when we find a proper place to settle down? If we go to the village, we'll need to clean up and build new fortifications, along with planting crops or something. Will your magic be of use?"

"If not mine, then the other spell-wielders you've brought back, certainly."

Ty made a note. Looking at the pieces of paper, he circled the word "village" and drew a line to the word "Sanctuary" and another to the words "Celestial blood." "Aquamarine, would you know of a settlement near here? Somewhere I could get the goods Uneth's people need? Armor, weapons, food? And magical components for Cleozun?"

The dragon made rippling motions with its hands. "Yes, indeed. Northwest of here there is a large town. Maybe three days of easy travel, probably two with the help of a sloth. It sits on the edge of the Old Duck River. Sometimes traders come from that town to visit. I believe you could call it a smuggler's town. It has a teleportation ring, which leads me to believe that it would be well-stocked for your needs."

Old Duck River? Ty thought sardonically at Hagemi. *Am I translating that right?*

Hagemi pulsed a sense of amusement in Ty's direction, along with an image of a creature that looked a lot like a duck. *They are plentiful in this area.*

I never asked before. Would you tell me how teleportation rings work?

An image of a metal circle set into the ground floated in Ty's vision. *Teleportation rings are expensive, but once set up they can be a source of both resources and danger to an area. There are two types of the rings: ones that require manual operation, via a spellcaster who specializes in optimizing the rings, and inherently intelligent ones. Intelligent teleportation rings have a spirit of Technology in them, basically a limited form of AI. Each has its benefits and drawbacks. With proper management, a town Seneschal or governor can keep out unwanted guests and maintain secrecy, with either version.*

Teleportation rings are associated with keys. Those must be purchased, usually from the local mercantile guild or trade store. Once a ring is activated, all you have to do is step in and think of a location you are keyed to. The teleportation will take you, along with anyone else standing in the ring, to the intended destination. Assuming you are allowed by the recipients on the other side, that is. Oh, and there may be a cost. Some require a tithe or tax that must be displayed prior to activation.

Ty nearly gawked at the flood of information. *That sounds incredible.*

I told you that we would bring dramatic enhancements to your world, Hagemi replied. *You have yet to begin to see the wonders magic can enable, particularly when combined with artifice.*

Yeah. Other than killing lots of people. Anyway, is it safe to assume bigger towns have these things, like Aquamarine is suggesting?

More or less, the Arbiter replied. *Abandoned rings exist, and sometimes small towns spend disproportionate resources to acquire one, just to create a new trade hub. If this is a smuggler town, it probably has most of the things you need right now, if at higher cost than other locations.*

"Is your little god pleased? Did it give you permission to move forward?" Cleozun asked when Ty returned his attention to the watching group.

"Little god?"

"Your expression. It was a giveaway that you were talking to a divinity," Uneth said. "Do not worry, it is clear your god in this world has no qualms with us. We will not attempt to kill it."

Cleozun tried for a reassuring grin. With her sharp-toothed wasp mouth, it looked positively horrific. "We do not kill such staunch allies as yourself or your god."

The sheer scope and capability of Ty's new allies dawned on him. They knew how to kill gods. "Yeah, I'm good to move forward," he answered, then stopped and held up a hand. "Actually, one more second."

Hagemi, what is a Seneschal? Is it what I think it is?

Probably. A Seneschal with the capital letter is a magically attuned individual who has a specific type of mind gem. The gem has a spirit of intellect, one that allows the Seneschal to help manage something. It could be as big as a city or as small as a storefront. Seneschals come in all shapes and types.

Perfect.

Lowering his hand, Ty said, "I'm thinking when we go, I'll try to find us a Seneschal as well. Someone who can help coordinate, maybe even advise in strategies. What do you think?"

"Oh, yes. That sounds perfect," Uneth said. "If it's someone local who knows this world, that would be invaluable. With your upcoming absence, someone who can provide a measure of oversight will make me more comfortable."

Late last evening, during their wait for the sloths to move their new troops back to the convoy, Ty had explained about his departure to Uneth and Cleozun. Uneth had been worried about the lack of his leadership, as he didn't trust himself to govern yet. Cleozun had been more concerned about their people trapped in his body.

"Just as long as whoever it is stays out of my way," Cleozun said.

Ty chuckled as he walked to the ATV. The bag of gemstones was intact. He also had the mind stones from a few of the deceased demons, along with the strange coin. He hadn't killed the ones back at the edge of the forest, so he hadn't received a loot prompt. The idea of prying each of the stones loose or waiting for the akkoans to do so was too gruesome to handle, so he'd left the corpses where they fell. The forest could reclaim them if it wanted.

Reaching into the bag, he extracted a thumbnail-sized gemstone and held it to the light. "Think this is worth anything?"

None of them had a clue.

"I guess we'll just wing it," Ty said, replacing the gem and tightening the bag. He had a few dozen of the gems and could only hope they were as valuable here as they probably would be on Earth.

Once the bag was secure, he consulted his notes. "All right, here's what I propose. The main force of the akkoans will migrate to the abandoned village. At the same time, we'll ask the sloths to get us as close to the smuggler's town as they can. I'll go in alone, since you all look like, well, demons and see about getting us a Seneschal and a teleportation ring. Once we have those, we can set up the ring at the village. That can be our staging ground in the short-term. We'll probably need another ring later, just for the quarry, unless we can somehow close and secure it."

"You will not go alone," Cleozun said. She hooked a clawed finger in Theontsu's direction. "I will cast spells of disguise on Theontsu and his rangers. They will go with you and keep you safe. I will go with you as well. The materials I need cannot wait, and I cannot risk you getting them wrong."

"We might want to assign several of our people to guard the quarry as well. And coordinate with Aquamarine and his allies around troop movements," Uneth added. "Will your sloths or Opal Guardians be willing to help, should we need to move quickly?"

Aquamarine's fingers danced. "We will do what is necessary. Nothing the Monster God touches ever remains pure. My sprites and our forest denizens will ally with you for this. What of your convoy though, Ty? Will you teach your allies to drive it?"

Ty knew he could take the time to teach the akkoans to handle the ATV and convoy with little effort. For all their hints of insanity, the akkoans were highly intelligent. Something kept him from wanting to do that, though. "I think it's safe to stay here for now. I'll leave my rifle, too, since I don't want to draw too much attention to myself. Once we've got everything in motion, I'll come collect my things. Assuming that's all right with the Opal Guardians?"

Aquamarine twisted back to look at the deeper forest, where several Opal Guardians had taken up temporary residence. The horses weren't comfortable with the demons, no matter what spirits possessed them, and had backed off as soon as Ty's new allies arrived. At Aquamarine's questing gaze, the stallion came to the edge of the clearing and gave Ty a baleful glance before shaking his head.

I got you, the stallion's gesture said.

Ty agreed to Cleozun's requirements and approved Uneth's revisions. They also decided that Uneth would travel with the main force, ensuring they stayed cohesive. He admitted that now more of them were together, there might be a propensity to gossip and reconnect, or even mire themselves in what they had lost, rather than focus forward. The general would maintain their momentum.

With their negotiations complete and plans made, Ty secured his belongings and restocked his personal supplies. If all went as planned, with the help of the sloths, they'd arrive at Old Duck Lake in a couple of days.

Chapter 29:
Magi-Tech

Days Remaining in Cycle: 17

Boblin teleported Cleozun, Theontsu, and three of his rangers with Ty to the edge of the wood. They hiked after that. It was Ty's first time traversing the world in something other than a forest, and he was not disappointed. Hip-high fields of golden grains swayed beneath a bright blue sky. Twin moons, one dark gray and one pale white, floated above in different orbits. They looked bigger, or maybe just closer, than Earth's moon.

Inhaling, Ty commented, "The air doesn't smell this fresh on my world."

"Magic makes everything sweeter," Theontsu commented in a soft voice. "I assume your home world has none?"

"Yeah. It didn't anyway. The god of Technology is over there now, working on the other end of the Bridge or something. Bringing magic."

"That will purify your air, among other things," Theontsu replied. "Give it a few years and your world will be a cleaner, richer place, too."

"Cleaner?" he asked, intrigued. "How will the magic know what's trash and what isn't?"

Cleozun bit back a laugh. "It doesn't. Magic uses a template, an ideal that the gods tell it to adhere to. It will transform your world, trash included."

"Oh," Ty said, deliberately letting the conversation lapse. It seemed that there ever was a double-edged sword to the Resonance Bridge. Who knew what technologies or conveniences in his world they would replace as magic grew?

The verdant landscape made an idyllic distraction for the uneventful hike. On the first night, Ty worked with Theontsu and his men to make camp. The akkoans were a highly efficient, effective crew. Using slight gestures, whistling statements, and chords of song, they communicated the most complex terms in instants. While he used his knife to clear a small circle for his tent, they cleared the rest of the space with their claws. Theontsu's rangers also made note of probable edible plant parts and signs of animals.

"You and your men seem to have versatile skills. You're all rangers, right, woodsmen?" Ty asked later as they settled around their small campfire. Theontsu chewed on a handful of beetle-like insects as he considered Ty's question. None of the akkoans had accepted Ty's offer of meal-replacement stew, content with eating what their demon hosts craved.

"Not precisely," Theontsu said after swallowing the bugs. "We ranged in many terrains, for sure. But we had other duties."

Cleozun rolled her hand at the fire, murmuring a single word and commanding the fires to dance and sway. One lick of the flame resembled an akkoan, and another a larger akkoan with a burnished golden halo. "Assassinating the scions of the gods was never a simple task. Even less once they started working together."

At her words, Theontsu shrugged, radiating an air of discomfort. "Once the mortal gods began turning the Lord's people against us, giving them powers and blessings, we knew we had to act. Far easier to kill them in the dark, in their sleep."

"I hope things go differently this time," Ty said, acutely aware that he was a scion.

"It does not matter if they go differently, Ty," Theontsu said. "You saved our souls from damnation. With your help, we may live again. Or we may go to a proper afterlife. The time we came from has passed. We must adapt and cherish the opportunities before us."

"And we have you," Cleozun finished, insect eyes locked on Ty's face with uncomfortable intensity.

Ty looked down. "You know I can't promise anything. The gods told me the stakes. I don't have a choice. I have to grow stronger, and there are terms for that."

Cleozun was about to speak again when Theontsu made a subtle gesture. She shot him a curious look but remained silent.

Theontsu said, "Take your risks, Savior. You took them on us. But know that you have us to help you. You are not alone. I believe I can speak for all our people in saying that we'd rather die with you than survive as fuel for the batteries."

The sunset sparked on the horizon, sending a cascade of colors through the sky like fireworks on an epic scale. Ty goggled as he watched the night begin to fall on the wondrous magical world, felt the sweep of coolness as the day became night in a matter of seconds. Awe filled his heart and on instinct, he willingly *pushed* the feeling into his chest, where the souls of the gathered akkoans rested. Taking a deep, slow, breath, he let the feeling of adoration, of worship, for the world he'd found himself in overflow everything else.

One thing most of the books of prophecy had in common was the fact that the magical worlds were enchanting. The words on paper paled compared to the experience of it, the feeling of majesty and wonder in a place unspoiled by humanity. His heart broke for what he knew was going to happen to this place, and it broke again for the knowledge of what was to come for his world. The gods would save their people and pieces of this world, all at the cost of his.

What a curse. What a burden.

The nightly akkoan insanity ceremony started shortly after. Not tired, Ty watched as the hours passed. Seeing his friends in such obvious, overwhelming torment broke his heart, but he forced himself to witness their pain. Later, when it was Cleozun's turn, Theontsu and his men guarded over her. Cleozun started to chant a few times, her madness giving rise to hissed words of power. Each time, Theontsu stepped in and hit her with the back of one hand until she went silent. Given how powerful the woman was, Ty was grateful for Theontsu's prompt ministrations. A stray spell or two was all the group needed to end their journey prematurely.

It was nearing midnight when Ty finally slept. In his dreams, he was on Ako, surrounded by a singing wall of akkoan people. Their song was one of hope and joy, and of thankfulness.

* * *

The group arrived at the city halfway through the next day. From a distance, the city resembled a traditional fantasy-style town topped with a series of glowing domes. As they closed in, Ty found that the details deviated from his expectations. There were elements of the traditional European-style city, but the details made it clear how magic had changed the architecture and planning.

Framing the city was a two-meter-tall, sleek stone wall, looking like a solid piece of polished granite. Atop the wall, every hundred feet, empty guard houses overlooked the wall and city proper. Dully glimmering magical runes decorated the guard houses and walls encircling the city. A wagon trail, incredibly mundane, wound through the grasslands from the south, ending at the only visible entrance to the city: a pair of double doors big enough to drive a semi through.

On the far side of the road, abutting the city, was a narrow river. A large, two-masted boat floated lazily south of the city, magical sails glowing faintly even in the day's brightness. Ty thought he could see a hint of a dock extending past the walls and into the river.

Magic dock? he thought to Hagemi.

Ty, it's best to assume anything that looks like it shouldn't work, yet does, is magic.

Isn't that a little, I don't know, hand-wavey?

Ty. Magic. Compared to your whole "every bit of human knowledge in the palm of my hand" civilization, this isn't that much of a stretch, is it?

Fair point.

"Hold, I need to cast disguise and translation spells on us," Cleozun said. They were still a mile from the city, but well within sight range.

"Why now?" Ty asked, not really bothered. The break would give him time to collect his thoughts and make notes.

"Needed to see their detection setup. No problem. That style is rudimentary." Cleozun chanted a few words, pointed at each of the akkoans, and each of them became Ty. One at a time, as she continued to chant, the individual characteristics of the disguised akkoans changed just a bit. One had red hair and darker skin; another shrank a foot. The mage made herself a rather attractive female version of Ty, which made him feel odd.

The female version of him looked pretty good with boobs, he admitted somewhat reluctantly.

"I guess we're all part of the same family?" he said once she was done.

"Works for me," Theontsu said. None of the others disagreed.

"How long will these last?" Ty asked as they made their way toward the wagon trail.

"The disguises? A few days unless I dispel them. The translation spells will last for weeks, depending on how many languages they must detect. Both are easy magic."

Ty whistled, impressed with the akkoan's casual use of power.

Once they arrived at the gates, a metallic voice like Ty's original Guide announced, "State your purpose clear and true. Lies will not be tolerated."

"I wish to trade for needed equipment and find a Seneschal," Ty replied.

"Magical goods," Cleozun announced.

"Here to keep him safe," Theontsu said, pointing at Ty. His subordinates echoed their leader's statement.

"Trade's Master. Straight walk from the wall, you can't miss it," the voice announced as the gates opened.

One of Hagemi's surfaces flashed in the periphery of Ty's vision.

Warning: *You are entering the protected settlement of Sabontil. This city is currently aligned to no god. As an outsider to our world, you are expected to comport yourself within the rules of our system. This means no attacking the natives, no destroying property, and no stealing. These rules cease to apply if you are attacked, but only for the attacking party or parties. If a mayor or ruler of a city attacks you, these rules cease to apply for the entire settlement. These rules do not apply between scions. In essence, this is a PVP zone, not a PVE zone.*

Ty acknowledged the warning as they made their way into the city.

Sabontil's interior was a cross between magical sci-fi and a classic Western. Making their way past the open gates, Ty was greeted by a sparse, if diverse, collection of people moving between uniform, squat buildings. Roads of light stretched above thin, rune-etched metal beams that described a complex circuit board through the interior. People zoomed past, moving quickly atop those roads. None took heed of Ty and his party.

Directly ahead of them, flanked by shops on one side and open-air docks on the other, was a three-story building with a "Trade's Master" sign displayed in glowing letters.

"Those are akkoans," Theontsu said, gesturing subtly at a group of people standing at an open-air vendor near an alley. Fresh fish hung from strings on the vendor's awning, several of which were being inspected by a cluster of six tall akkoans. They wore black uniforms with twisted glyph patches down the voluminous sleeves, and had vibrant, almost neon, plumage.

Patch? Ty queried Hagemi.

God of Monsters. Vat Masters. Officers.

Ty's stomach sank. Akkoans working for the God of Monsters could not be a good thing.

"Let's not draw attention to ourselves," he said, walking from the packed dirt of the wagon trail and onto one of the wide light roads. He took an experimental step. The road moved forward as he stepped. When he put his foot down, he was several feet from where he'd started, as if the road were a conveyor belt.

That's nifty, Ty thought and checked to make sure his allies were following. They were, though, each glanced askance at the other akkoans as they moved.

Traversing the light roads was disorienting at first. Where the roads intersected, the conveyor belts stopped, allowing pedestrians to reorient themselves. Those still nodes were also where people got on and off the roadway. Locals, many of which looked like humans, albeit with a crayon box selection of hair and eye colors, stepped up and moved past him and his group without so much as a glance.

As they walked, Ty tried to get a feel for the wardrobe and mannerisms of the natives. The hair styles varied, but not so much so that they'd be out of place on Earth. Most men wore their hair short and neat, and women seemed to favor longer, braided styles. Their clothes were a mix of a hundred cultures, from traditional tunics and trousers, to enchanted suits with artificial flapping wings, and more.

There were races other than humans and the akkoans, too. Ty saw several willowy, green-skinned people with amphibian features working at the dock, and a group of short llama-looking humanoids, all dressed in a similarly eclectic fashion. From his brief observations, the only defining cultural trait of the city so far was the absolute lack of curiosity or interest any of the locals showed to anyone else.

The interior of the Trade Master was spacious, with the outer walls decorated in a selection of objects behind glass barriers. Mobile racks with various wares decorated the open floor of the main area. A stairwell beside the main desk, which was in open view in the middle of the room, led up to a second story. Behind the desk was a brown-skinned human man, a tall woman with vaguely akkoan features, and one of the amphibian people they'd passed at the docks. A few customers wandered through the room, none of them looking up as Ty and his crew entered.

Exchanging a look with his companions, the human spoke up. "Welcome to the trade hall. I'm Jessa. Can I help ya?"

Ty glanced over at his escort. Theontsu gestured for him and Cleozun to handle the trade. When Ty and Cleozun walked past to the front desk, one of Theontsu's rangers walked back out of the building.

"Hello, I'd like to sell these," Ty said, putting the bag of gemstones on the desk.

"Of course," Jessa said, sliding the bag over to his side of the desk and inspecting it. The man wore a tarp-brown shirt bedecked with intricate creases and folds, and his pants matched. Reaching into one flap, which was clearly concealing a small pocket, he withdrew a metal disk. Placing the disk on the counter, he took one gem and released it an inch or two above the disk. The gem hovered in space, spinning slowly. A series of runes lit up on the base of the disk, which the man noted by drawing them with his finger directly on the desk's wooden surface.

He repeated the process for the next gem, adding a row of characters beneath the first. A new row appeared below both, this one highlighted in gold.

"That's the total, right?" Ty asked, pointing at the glowing row.

"Yup," the man said, glancing up at Ty. "I take it yah haven't seen a merchant's desk before?"

He shrugged noncommittally. "Not this style, at least."

The man seemed to fight an urge to ask more questions before he went back to adding gems to his assessing disk.

You've got magical Excel on your shop desks, Ty thought wryly at Hagemi.

Hagemi didn't reply.

"Six hundred thousand, that's me to you total. In Sabontil credit, that is. If ya want any marks for general spendin', you can cash out ten thousand at max. What'll it be?" Jessa announced a few minutes later.

"And for these?" Cleozun asked, stepping beside Ty and dropping a handful of demon mind crystals onto the table.

Ty looked at her, about to ask where she'd gotten those from, but stopped himself. His akkoans saw demons and other races, including humans, as lesser species. It would have been nothing for her to go back and extract crystals from the corpses.

The man glanced from the crystals to the doors leading out of the room. Whispering in a low voice, he said, "These are dangerous tradin' lady. God-touched anything is dangerous. Ya never know when one of them scions is gonna show up and take issue with ya. We can probably move 'em though, just not for the best price, ya understand?" He reached out and scooped the mind gems to his side of the table. Selecting one, he priced it on his dial, then immediately drew the lot out of view. "Five thousand, best offer."

Cleozun clicked in disapproval, "Fine." She looked over at Ty, adding, "We will talk. I have needs."

The half-akkoan woman standing a few feet away walked to Jessa and collected the concealed mind gems in a bag. She opened a swinging door built seamlessly into the desk and made her way out and up the stairs. The door clicked back into place, the seam of the swinging door vanishing instantly.

Is this a good deal? Ty asked Hagemi.

Yes. Hagemi's tone was taciturn, even abrupt, disinclining Ty from asking further questions.

Ty said, "Six hundred sounds good to me. I need a couple of things immediately. First, a Seneschal, preferably one with military experience. Next, I need a proper teleportation ring and keys for it, along with the surrounding areas. After that, I need some personal equipment." He hesitated, then added, "I'm an adventurer, so it'll need to be good."

Jessa tapped the desk next to him. The calculations he'd drawn shifted to the side, making room for Ty's entries to appear, as if collected by dictation.

"I can help you with the personal equipment. For the Seneschal, you'll either need to go to the Debtor's Trade across the way or to the World Market, which isn't accessible from here. You can get the teleportation ring from the Boundless Incarnation. It's located just inside the city gate, along the landside wall. You'll find it near the alleys that lead to the local housing district."

"Magical supplies there, too?" Cleozun asked.

"Anything uncommon, yah."

Cleozun extended a hand toward Jessa. "Fine. Pay me and I'll leave. Ty, I'll meet you there."

The merchant man tapped the desk three times and drew a series of symbols on it. A wooden chit, about the size of a poker chip, popped out of the seamless surface. He passed the chit to Cleozun. "City cred, five thousand. Come back if you wanna cash out. Keep in mind, there's the transaction fee and such."

"Of course there is," Cleozun said with a sneer and left.

Once she'd left, Ty turned his full attention back to the merchant. "Let me get a list of wares, along with any pertinent information."

A stream of information appeared on the desk, the new lines of text erasing all the previous math and calculations that Jessa had done during their trade transaction.

Translate, please? Ty sent to his Arbiter.

Hagemi obliged, and the writing wiggled, transforming into a language he could read.

As it turned out, six hundred thousand gave Ty a lot of options. Walking through the list of goods the shop offered, he observed that the prices were pretty much in line with where he'd guess an Earth dollar would be, value for value. Twenty marks could get him a backpack, or he could pay fifty for one that was enchanted for durability. Ten marks could get him a dagger, or he could pay up to five hundred for an "unbreakable, ever-sharp" version. The enchanted dagger came with a small disclaimer, noting that it *could* break and dull if used against magical objects.

"Hey, why aren't there any bags of holding here? Or, um, dimensional bags or whatever you call them?" Ty asked a few minutes later.

"Vault bag?" Jessa asked, giving him another mildly patronizing smile. "Ya are new around here, aren't ya? Well, vault bags connect to big vaults, ya see. And most people want those vaults super secure. Here in Sabontil, well, we're known for your... shall we say, somewhat shady locals? Anyway, were I you, I'd go to a proper city for such a thing. Ya won't find one here, even if we haven't had a major incident in the whole city for months now."

I hate you, Ty said to his Arbiter.

Hagemi shot back a weak sense of amusement.

Hey, you okay? You've been really quiet. Normally, you advise me more often. I had to ask you to translate that text for me, too. What gives?

I'm worried. The God of Monsters has turned against the mission, Ty. According to Inspiration she, along with a handful of other gods, has broken the faith. Her agents are here. Somehow, she isn't bound to the laws that the other gods must abide. This means I can't help you, but she can use her full power to influence the outcome of events.

Ty's stomach sank. *I can't fight a god.*

Thankfully, it's not you she's against. She'll be maneuvering against any god who isn't her ally, either openly or otherwise. I suspect that you may have earned some of her ire, however. She does not take kindly to someone usurping her tools. If she discovers what you've done to her demons... Ty, things might get very messy.

"Sir?" Jessa prompted. "Anythin' else?"

Ty shook his head. "A new backpack, for now. I'm going to go price the other things I need, then I'll return. I'll probably need a few hours to pick everything out. Do you have store hours?"

"Noon to midnight." Jessa waved a hand over the desk, extracting a new wooden chit, which he handed over. An assistant came around from the back, passing Ty a new backpack that looked similar enough to his current one for him not to worry about room.

Pocketing the chit, Ty walked to Theontsu, who drew him into a whispered conversation. As they talked, Ty moved the contents from his tattered pack to the new one.

Theontsu said, "Ty, those akkoans out there. It's not good. They look young, but that doesn't mean much. Assuming they still use Mind Fortresses, they could have skills and memories from previous generations. I'd bet they are officers overseeing the movement of troops and goods in this area."

"You think they might be on the lookout for their missing demons?" Ty said.

"Quite possible," Theontsu said.

They might also be looking for you. Hagemi flickered uneasily in his mind. *If the Monster God was planning to turn on the others, she and her allies might have laid traps for the initial locations we designated for scions.*

Traps? Did she know where the portals would open?

Yes. Remember, all the gods worked together to prepare your landing locations.

But why? Why would she want to stop the other scions? What could that gain her? She and the other gods all need the Resonance Bridge, right?

They will, yes. Ty, I can't go into detail right now. Just know there's a reason the gods included rules for PVP in the system.

Ty frowned, glancing from Theontsu to the doorway. "My god thinks we're in trouble, too. What do you recommend?"

"First, we need some equipment." Theontsu rattled off a simple list of gear, then laid out a strategy. Lacking better knowledge or experience, Ty accepted the akkoan's suggestions and went back to the counter, making the purchases.

Each time Ty made an order, Jessa gestured and the name of the item scrawled across the desk. When he was done, Jessa held his hand in a specific pose, tapping the middle of the text. The words vanished, and a few minutes later a couple of men pushing a cart covered in wrapped packages came out.

"You may try the goods out first, if you want," Jessa said. "Straight back is a door leading to our testing facility. It's small but has a firing range and a basic safe combat zone. We cannot allow testing of the perishables, unfortunately."

"Go ahead," Ty said to Theontsu, who passed the equipment out to his men.

An hour later, during testing with their new gear, the scout returned. The Monster God's akkoans had left the city through the south gate.

"Good news, but I recommend we proceed with the plan," Theontsu said, once the scout had relayed his observations and had been informed of their plan.

"I agree, sir," the scout replied.

"Yeah, me too," Ty said, trusting the experienced akkoans' judgment.

Minutes later, Ty exited the Trade's Master alone.

Chapter 30: Questionable Decisions

Days Remaining in Cycle: 17

The Debtor's Trade building was small, just a room with a mercantile desk. A light flashed on the desk when he stepped in, and one of the Guide voices spoke from the air above it. "Hello, friend. Please tell me what you're looking for and I'll be glad to help direct your attention."

With no signs or instructions, Ty asked, "How does this work?"

"Individuals who owe more money than they can afford may have their debts sold to the Debtor's Network. In exchange for offering services to a paying customer, their debts are paid off. By purchasing through our network, you will receive the bonded services of an individual for a guaranteed amount of time, after which that individual will either be freed, or you may hire them full-time if they are willing. This promotes amiable treatment for those with long-term ambitions."

"Ah, so almost like debt slavery?"

"Not slavery. Slaves are not usually highly skilled and bonded. People in our network are professionals."

"Gotcha. I need a Seneschal with some military background. Do you have anyone like that available for hire?"

Lines of text appeared on the counter, showcasing a few dozen names. "Do you care if the individual is significantly past their prime age?"

"Preferably not."

A quarter of the names vanished. "Does it matter if the individual has a gambling problem?"

"Yeah, rather avoid the inevitable betrayal thing."

Another third of the names flicked off the table.

"Is your budget in the tens of thousands or hundreds of thousands?"

"Tens. Oh, and it needs to be at least a four-year agreement." Ty didn't want his Seneschal vanishing before he returned from Earth.

The list of names narrowed to two.

"Your choices are Abesandra and Omendine. Abesandra is an akkoan rebel. Like many of her species, she was raised near Elomed. She rebelled and fled, taking on significant debt in the process. Omendine is a traesap military mind. A general among their people. He retired years ago but is still of a ripe age for their species."

"Why is Omendine in debt?" Ty said.

"He took on loans against a new occupation, then became utterly obsessed with it."

"What occupation?"

"Knitting."

Hagemi, tell me that traesap aren't the llama-looking people.

How did you guess?

Ty gave the desk his best glare. "How the fuck does a hip-high llama go from being a famous general to indebted for knitting?"

Clearly immune to Ty's glare, the technology spirit said, "Unknown. I should note that Omendine was famous among his people and his military background is distinguished. His experience is, however, limited to working with his own species."

Ty could feel his blood pressure soaring. "So, my choices are a nearly perfect-sounding candidate who may or may not end up being a spy for the God of Monsters, and a llama person with a knitting addiction?"

"Based on your requirements, it would seem so, yes."

Closing his eyes, Ty forced himself to think through a list of the pros and cons. He knew which he had to choose and hated it. If nearly every single epic fantasy book didn't include a cursed and inevitable betrayal at a juncture just like this, he'd have gone with the sensible solution.

Gritting his teeth, he said, "Fine, how much does the fucking llama owe, and how much will it cost me to get him for a minimum of four years?"

"Omendine has a debt equivalent of six years of service. Based on his unique skills and background, purchasing four years of his time will cost you thirty-two thousand marks."

"And the full six?" He didn't want to swap out assistants in the middle of the next rotation either, not if he could help it. Plus, he had the marks to burn.

"Forty-eight thousand will cover his full debt. You will receive a contract of binding as part of the agreement. It should be noted, as you suggested earlier, such contracts require that he use his skills to the best of his ability, but they do not include mind control elements. Loyalty must be earned. He could also be a s py."

Ty glanced at the wooden desk and arched an eyebrow. "That seems almost like advice."

"Your Guide liked you. Besides, like your Arbiter, any sufficiently advanced intelligence connected to the god of Technology must abide by the rules of balance. It is within my rights to inform you of these nuances."

"Okay. Since you mentioned it, would you recommend that I go with the akkoan instead?"

"Probably not. Given her background and heritage, she is far more likely to be hotheaded, impulsive, and reckless, regardless of whether you can ultimately trust her."

Ty went with the llama.

"I see that quite a number of his belongings have a lien on them in one of the more reputable vaults. If you want to spend another five thousand, I can have those goods delivered with him. It will delay his arrival by a day, however."

"I'll buy the lien on them. Can I also pay to have them held somewhere in the city until one of my representatives can come fetch them? It might take a few months."

"That can be arranged. According to my notes, many of his items require... particular care. To include safe handling, add another hundred marks for six months of storage?"

"Sure. Can we set up a password or something, so you'll know whoever I designate to come collect them?"

"Yes. The goods will be stored by a designated caretaker and insured for the losses. Your Seneschal should arrive within a few hours, depending on the status of the local teleportation rings and how quickly he can travel the distance to the town."

"That's fine. Meet him here?"

"Yes."

"Can you tell me where to go from here to get to the Boundless Incarnation?"

The magical AI gave him precise directions.

Ty made his way toward the magic shop. There was something decidedly *off* about the whole feeling of Sabontil, not to mention the world around it. From his limited experience so far, the city might as well have appeared out of whole cloth on the side of the river. There were no signs of construction or the typical fantasy labor he'd associate with city maintenance. The streets weren't cluttered with litter, there were no signs of a sewer system, and the inhabitants seemed healthy. Even the debtor's system sounded at least somewhat fair.

Had someone told Ty that the world he was visiting was a utopia, he might have believed it. He knew better. Sabontil was called a smuggler's city. What did it smuggle?

Thinking about the dissonance between how he expected the world should work and the reality around him, Ty used the light roads to speed through the city. He passed a few of the glowing domed areas as he traveled. Each had an architecturally unique and often spectacular building within them. As much as he wanted to dally and make notes, he didn't. There was no time.

Next time, I'll explore more cities, he promised himself. *Heck, maybe I'll take up cooking like that one guy. Food might earn me a few allies, right?*

Sabontil wasn't a big town. In ten minutes, he had gone from glass roads to mundane ones, with clean-cut paving stones. The roadways remained wide, though arteries began peeling off into narrower alleys and niches.

A bolt flew from one such alley and slammed into Ty's arm. It punctured straight through his enchanted robe and into the muscle and bone beneath. Knocked to the side, he would have fallen, but the head of the arrow, which had gone clear through the limb, extended four sharp hooks. Someone yanked him into the alley by the limb. A force clamped down on his mouth, muffling his scream.

Impossible, unimaginable pain shot through Ty's every nerve as he found himself slammed against a wall. A lean, tall figure in a robe stood next to him. A man wearing an elaborate chest plate and greaves, both with ravens embossed in the metal, stood just behind the robed one. He was carrying an unsheathed black sword. Magic coursed along the length of the serrated, saber-style blade, exuding a miasma of shadow.

Ty's instincts screamed. These weren't random assassins, and they weren't akkoans. They were people like him. They were scions. Divine power, totally unlike his god's, dripped from the duo as overtly as paint.

The armored man gave Ty a bland expression as he swung his blade for his neck.

Three arrows just *appeared* in the man's face. The man staggered, not dead despite the grievous injuries, and tried to recover his decapitating swing at Ty.

Theontsu shed his invisibility and stepped into the man's swing. He grabbed the scion's forearm and shoved, pushing the sword out of line. Then the akkoan rabbit punched a short dagger into the Earth man's throat, ripping it open in a fount of blood.

Ty was about to shout a warning about the robed figure, but it vanished as completely and suddenly as Theontsu had appeared. Arrows whisked in the space it had been standing. One of them caught something, and he saw an outline of the remaining scion flicker into view, briefly, before the killer slammed into his chest.

A knife brushed over his side, not quite piercing his robe.

Ty fumbled one handed, reaching for anything on the attacker. He'd lost so much blood and was in enough pain that even adrenaline wasn't enough to keep him focused. He thought he felt material, then flesh, and slammed his Verdant Touch into the scion, gleefully transforming the energy to Celestial without hesitation.

Warning: *Your magic has been countered through the direct or indirect interdiction of a god other than your own.*

Ty's Touch didn't hurt the attacker, but it did, however briefly, disrupt the invisibility around it. In an instant, multiple arrows struck the flickering assailant. Theontsu's dagger slammed into its back repeatedly, the akkoan moving with the utterly relentless speed of a killer.

A ring of twisting shadow shot up around the robed scion, cocooning it, then falling away. When the effect ended, Ty's attacker was gone, leaving only the armored corpse and the arrow in Ty's arm behind.

"Ty! Stay still," Theontsu said, steadying him against the wall with one hand. He could feel the reality of Theontsu's demon body behind the otherwise impervious illusion of humanity. He was glad for that inhuman strength. Without it, he'd have fallen.

Turning to look at one of the adjacent rooftops, where one of his men had appeared, Theontsu shouted, "Get Cleozun! Now. She should be nearby."

None of the locals so much as paused when they walked past the alley. A few glanced in, saw the commotion, and moved on without a look of concern or worry ghosting across their faces.

Smuggler's town, Ty thought sardonically.

Cleozun appeared moments later, rushing to Ty with an expression of focused rage on her temporarily human visage. Teeth gritted, she wrapped her hand around the shaft of the long arrow. She began to sing, voice taking on a melodic quality that he hadn't heard the mage use before. Moving her free hand, she made a complex series of gestures at Theontsu.

Nodding curtly, Theontsu relayed her message to Ty. "This arrow has been god-blessed. It could not have punched through the Ward Robe so easily otherwise. She warns that removing it will hurt. Heal yourself as soon as it's out, if you can."

Simply having Cleozun touch the arrow had taken the pain to a new level. Ty's eyes blurred and he bit back a sob, barely holding it together. "Go ahead," he managed through gritted teeth.

Moving with serpentine speed, Cleozun snapped the arrow shaft.

Adjusting Ty's arm, the mage continued to sing her spell as she reached out and grabbed the head, ripping it and the metal hooks free from his flesh.

The world became agony. *Help, help, help,* Ty begged to Hagemi, unable to find the concentration to activate Verdant Touch.

Ty, I can't. Not from a wound inflicted by another scion.

A sob ripped through Ty's chest, the pain pushing through some mental barrier.

Her name was Numera Qual, and she was to be sacrificed for the betterment of her people. She would die horribly, but it was for her children. She would give them a future. His name was Mummat Kraal. He rebelled against the lies that would taint the name of their god for thousands of years.

His uninjured hand clutched at his head. Something inside him was wrong. In his pain, he'd instinctively reached for the Mental Fortress, but the memories he found did nothing to help him.

"Heal him," he heard Theontsu demand.

"The arrow was god-blessed. I have no god. I will need time, hours, maybe days, to heal this," Cleozun replied, voice terse and tight. "How did you allow this to happen?"

"We did not. Scions came after him. Not to question or capture, just to kill. Even prepared, it was a close thing."

Voices faded as a lance of fresh pain, throbbing unnaturally in the wound, pushed Ty further from sanity. He knew all-too well what it felt like to lose a hold on sanity. Most of his people had crossed that threshold. He had held their minds, however briefly, before Hagemi stored them. He'd tasted madness.

A god had marked him for death and sent madness after him.

Ty fled into the memories again, looking for anything helpful. A spirit stirred in his chest, the matching memories fluttering in the Mind Fortress. Thoughtless in his torment, he embraced the spirit and its mind.

Awon found him.

He was Awon, and he was a guardian of the akkoan people. His strength, his endurance and his stamina kept him fighting through hundreds of wars. It saw him strong, even when he willingly merged with the Soul Battery.

"Come to me Awon," Ty muttered through clenched teeth.

Awon's spirit and mind, both willingly drawn from their hiding places within Ty, leaked into him. This was not possession, not quite. Awon's memories and personality pressed against his own yet did not overtake or overwrite them. Instead, for a moment, Awon became a guiding hand, helping him find the clarity he needed to activate his Verdant Touch.

Blessed healing stole all of Ty's remaining mana as it pushed out the remaining slivers of the arrow. Flesh knit, and the pain eased.

Exhaling through gritted teeth, he stood. A shimmer of ghostly light surrounded his body, the outline of Awon, the dead warrior's expression fierce and determined, briefly visible. He sensed Awon there, sensed the unflagging spirit. He also sensed the agony and anguish that troubled the deceased akkoan. Without the flesh bodies that his brethren enjoyed, Awon had no physical substance to lean on, no bulwark with which to shore up his own suffering.

Ty guided Awon back to the depths of his chest and sent his memories into the Fortress.

Once Awon settled, Ty saw Cleozun staring at him. "Did you just take possession of an akkoan spirit?"

"Um, maybe? Awon kind of offered the help," he said, still shaken. After a moment's hesitation, he pushed the memories of his most recent pain into the Mind Fortress. He stopped when he felt the mental pressure of the experience ease. As tempting as it was to remove it all, he figured that the lingering bits would remind him of the lesson he'd just learned.

"Spirit mastery is an entirely different direction of power than I thought you were navigating, Ty. I took you more for a natural type. What was the word you-? Ah, yes. Druid. Not that becoming a Spirit Master would be a poor choice, not by any means..."

Cleozun trailed off when she saw Ty's glare. "I am *not* becoming a druid," he said. "And I have no intention of mastering spirits either. I'm going to put all the akkoan spirits to rest as soon as I figure out the best way to do so."

"As you say, Ty. I assure you our people would probably welcome the opportunity to..."

"Absolutely not," he said, trying to straighten his robe. It was soaked in his blood and had a fist-size hole in one sleeve. "I don't suppose you can mend this, can you?"

Eyeing the robe, Cleozun said, "I am not a seamstress. I hate to say that this robe has no self-repair or cleaning enchantment. It'll have to be handled manually or replaced."

Ty sighed and told Theontsu, "Give me a minute. I need to replenish my mana. We'll continue after that, assuming the assassin doesn't pop back up."

"I doubt she'll double back," Theontsu said.

Ty frowned, not liking the use of the word "doubt."

Hagemi, what can you tell me about those attackers?

Nothing that you cannot infer. Not at this time. I may not disclose details about other scions during interactions of this sort, not until you discover them for yourself.

Figures, Ty replied unhappily.

Nearly an hour after he'd walked past the alley alone, he emerged alone again. Still bloodied, he carried both the black sword and the man's enchanted armor. He wasn't about to leave potentially valuable artifacts behind. None of the locals said a word about his state as he walked past and into the Boundless Incarnation.

The Boundless Incarnation had a human merchant in it, and the shop interface was the same as the previous ones Ty had visited. He purchased a Teleportation Ring and twenty keys for it. They cost him eighty thousand of his remaining marks.

The keys came with cameo-style amulets, with smooth oval stones on one side and a flat back. Attached just above the stones were clips, each of which could attach to a key. After explaining how the dial worked, the shop keep produced a metal bracelet.

As she handed Ty his chit back, the shop keep said, "Slap that down on the ground and the ring will expand to whatever diameter you want, up to thirty feet. Once you set it down, it can't be moved without a separate artifact, which costs about half as much as the ring itself. Don't try teleporting anything outside that radius and don't try exceeding your amulet's mass limits. Trust me."

Ty took the bracelet and pocketed it, thanking the woman before turning to head back to the Trade's Master. He hesitated in the doorway, struck by a memory that didn't belong to an akkoan for once. Fishing his cell phone out of a pocket, he powered it on long enough to check one of his initial lists of plans.

He read the "Narnia" conditional notes twice before turning the phone off and pocketing it again.

"I don't suppose you have any magical scrolls or single-use devices that, oh, I don't know, predict outcomes of random things like dice rolls or cards, do you?"

"Gonna fix some gambling games, eh?" the shop keep replied, giving Ty a friendly wink. "That's just the sort of thing people come to towns like this for. I should warn you that sanctioned games have detection for this sort of thing. If you want something fool-proof, that won't be detected by most spells, I'll need to charge you a whole-"

"Nope, no need," Ty said, cutting her off. "No protections or wards. It can be as sloppy and noisy as you want. But what would make it even better if there was a spell that could take a possible random sequence and predict the outcomes. Say, an hour before the result?"

"What kind of numbers? You're talking about dice, right?"

"Not precisely, but close." Ty drew her a picture. It ended up, given the careful and specific constraints he listed, the final spell wasn't that expensive. Five of the little monocles that held the spell cost him another twenty-five grand.

He paid happily.

Chapter 31: New Tabs

Days Remaining in Cycle: 17

Back at the Trade Master's, Ty purchased two items of note. First, he got a broach pin called a Lesser Amulet of Shielding with a minor growth enhancement on it. Hagemi's translation stated that it would provide him with a health barrier equal to one point five times his current hit points, which would adjust as he leveled, to a maximum of thirty hit points.

You should know that the barrier, like most things, is subject to a variety of limitations. Some specific magical attacks will bypass it or reduce its effectiveness. Likewise, the shielding may vary in usefulness against focused, targeted attacks. Such a device would not have helped against the scion-killing arrow in the alley.

Accepting the limitations, Ty paid one hundred thousand of his remaining credits for the amulet. The amulet, when he unwrapped the package it came in, looked like a simple pin-style broach with a little clasp on the back. He immediately attached it to his shirt, beneath the robe, and felt a shield of magic expand subtly around him.

He waffled about his last purchase for nearly an hour. There were three items on the menu labeled "Legendary," with a notation "Ask about price." Settling on one of the three items, he asked Jessa about it.

Jessa's eyes flashed with dark humor. "Ya wanting to go hard, are ya? Well, legendary gear isn't normally sold for coin or gems. You need something really precious to get you one of those. A favor from a god or something along them lines."

On intuition, Ty flashed the gold coin he'd gotten from looting the demons. "What about this?"

The merchant's hand shot out, grasping the coin. Tucking it out of view, he dropped his voice to a whisper, "Ya got an Ascension Writ from the god herself, do ya? Yah. This will do. Which do you want?"

Jessa's response made him uneasy. It felt less like a financial transaction and more like a drug deal, though he couldn't have said why. Still, what was done was done. "I'll take the Alunite Gauntlets."

Legendary Alunite Gauntlets. *These gauntlets will provide you with a +2 bonus to your strength. Constructed of a semi-intelligent liquid metal, they can assume a variety of simple shapes, including claws or short blades. In addition to the bonus to your overall strength, items made of Alunite deal more damage per strike. Furthermore, these gloves can be used to activate and power latent magical objects. Finally, as a legendary item, these gauntlets will self-repair over time and can change aesthetic appearance at your discretion.*

The gauntlets ended up being a lot longer than he'd expected. Rather than glove-style, they had attached sleeves that stretched all the way up his arms, stopping at the shoulder joints. Once in place, the material tightened against his skin, and he felt a sense of subtle connection with the item. Commanding the gauntlets felt a lot like interacting with Hagemi or the Mind Fortress, just simpler, and he took to it quickly.

Once he felt confident in his mastery of the tools, he made them resemble mundane gloves.

Knowing that his new Seneschal would probably want to make purchases for the village, he held off spending more. Before he left, he set the armor and sword he'd collected from the other scion on the counter.

"Can you identify the properties of these for me?" he asked.

Reaching into a pocket, Jessa withdrew a monocle and inspected both items. "Shadow blessed, and sealed," he said after a moment. "I can't read their properties. Plus, sealed stuff won't work for no one else. Gotta unseal them or melt em down for materials. I suggest disposing of em, since no one here will move em. Not with a god involved.

Ty sighed. "Figures. Alright, thanks."

He took his new goods and left to collect the Seneschal.

Omendine was waiting for him when he arrived at the Debtor's Trade. The Seneschal was a little over three and a half feet tall, with a furry body and a long neck, with a triangular head. He looked almost exactly like a humanoid llama, complete with huge black eyes and a terse, pinched expression. He was wearing almost perfect Earth-style samurai armor, complete with Tonto and Katana.

"I understand you have purchased my debt and my belongings?" Omendine said as soon as Ty finished introducing himself. The traesap's voice was a deep, resonating bass that Hagemi translated as having a vaguely oriental accent.

"I have. I need a Seneschal with military experience. I would be honored if you would join me."

Omendine tilted his head to the side, one eye looking Ty up and down. "You sound respectful, but you have my dearest belongings on hold. I do not take kindly to manipulation or blackmail."

It took Ty a moment to realize that Omendine was talking about his decision to have the traesap's belongings shipped later and stored until someone could come get them. "A misunderstanding, wise Seneschal," he began, affecting what he hoped was a properly reverential tone. He knew he was probably laying the respect on a little thick for a new employee, but his intuition told him this was the right play in the same way it had with Aquamarine. "Alas, I am on a tight timetable and cannot wait for days. I assure you, we will move your goods to a suitable location as soon as we've secured our base of operations."

"Ah. I see. You need help with security first? Building or rebuilding?"

"Yes, and both. There's an abandoned village nearby. I mean to co-opt it, but that will mean retrofitting everything."

Omendine exhaled a breath that smelled vaguely of hay. "I will need timetables, scales, troop numbers, and resources. Here..."

Seneschal Bond: *Your Seneschal has offered to bond with you. This bond will allow you to convey information about the subjects and materials within your* *designated domain. Having a Seneschal bond unlocks additional Arbiter features that will be useful, should you wish to grow and maintain one or more bases of operation.*

Ty accepted.

Achievement Unlocked: *Seneschal Bond.*

His character sheet menu slid into view, occupying a full quarter of his vision. Tabs labeled Seneschal, Domain, Units, Inventory, and Objectives appeared at the top. Hagemi narrated the features of each tab.

Your Seneschal tab contains key information about each official Seneschal you have hired. They must have a mind gem for their entries to register.

The Domain tab gives you a nearly real-time view of the current layout and disposition of any areas marked formally as being within your domain. Unlocking this achievement allows you to immediately claim one qualifying domain. You may interact with the Domain tab to zone for specific building functions, allocate units, and more. As you obtain buildings with intelligent magical interfaces, such as the one you met at the Debtors building, you will be able to remotely make purchases or sales through this tab.

Your Units tab gives you a rundown of each unit under your command. Units with mind gems or similar connections will display with significantly more detail than hirelings or loosely affiliated individuals who happen to work for you. You may use this tab to issue units' standing orders, create organizational groups, or engage in group discussions. Your Seneschal will have to convey your will to units without a mind gem or the ability to perceive these prompts directly.

Inventory shows your communal stores. You must deliberately allocate personal resources in this tab and store them in a designated communal area for them to qualify. This tab will also show you items the Seneschal has identified as running low or recommended ones you do not currently possess.

Finally, you may use your Objectives tab to prioritize things you want your Seneschal to work on. I recommend discussing these objectives with him, as he will work better when he is in alignment with your vision.

"Holy shit, that's a lot," Ty said once he'd finished reviewing each tab.

Omendine's nostrils flared, and he reached up to brush his forehead, expression pained. The traesap's hand was closer to human than animal, with a thumb and three fingers, each topped with a thick nail. "More than usual," he agreed. "You are a scion?"

"Yeah. I follow Inspiration."

"Inspiration? Really? How interesting. Please take a moment to document our assets, the place where you expect our domain to form, and any objectives I should concern myself with."

Ty did as Omendine asked. In assets, he listed the remaining marks. He also listed everything he remembered finding in the town, along with a sketch of the town itself and its location. He went ahead and placed the one hundred and sixty-five surviving akkoans in the units tab, which populated quite a bit of information automatically. It concealed their spiritual nature and history, calling them instead "Shapeshifted Demons." He was impressed to see that most of the akkoans were listed at level thirteen or above, compared to Omendine's level eight. For objectives, he described the problem without going into details about the Sanctuary.

"These are solid numbers," Omendine said once Ty was done. "Facing against an unknown army funded and outfitted by the God of Monsters is going to be a fun challenge. The funds you've allocated will barely be enough to get us started, you know?"

"I'll get more," he said. "I hope an uphill battle doesn't bother you?"

Omendine made a chuffing sound. "Lord Ty, my people are small. We are underestimated. Most of our battles are uphill, and against stronger opponents. I won't tell you I have a death wish, but I believe we can make a difference, especially if we can keep the individual battles small and decisive." His voice lowered, taking on a note of secrecy. "And, may I add, especially if my goods are delivered to me in a timely manner."

Ty shot the traesap a smile. "Good to have you on board, sir. Would you like to purchase any goods here before we go? When we come back to retrieve your belongings, I'm sure we'll also want to pick up anything you think we need right away."

"Yes. There's a standard list for this type of situation. A healer's installation would be good as well, though you do not have enough funds for that. We'll have to go with basic kits until we can afford to hire a person or get an intelligence to run a clinic." Omendine continued rattling off suggestions as Ty escorted him back to the Trade's Master.

Omendine's organization and fondness for lists eased his uncertainty. He understood organized people so much better than anyone else.

As they walked across the street, Theontsu stepped from a nearby building. "Ty, my men and I need to meditate for a few hours. I'm going to have Cleozun nearby to watch in case things happen, if that's acceptable?" The akkoan ranger's hands were trembling, and his eyes were red-ringed.

"Should be fine," Ty said. "Rent a room or go north. I don't want any ambushes or scouts stumbling on you when you're vulnerable."

"If you can spare twenty marks, I'll rent a room with soundproofing."

Ty, Theontsu, and a bemused Omendine detoured long enough to find an overnight apartment with sound dampening for his men. Leaving the akkoans behind, all save Cleozun who had not made an appearance in a while, Ty and Omendine continued their trek to the Trade Master's.

Omendine and Ty stayed until the shop was about to close, finalizing the goods and delivery plans just as midnight struck. With the late hour, they went to the apartment, and he rented them each a room.

Blessedly, the night passed uneventfully.

Chapter 32: Domain

Days Remaining in Cycle: 15

Progress to Next Level: 75%

Ty and his allies made their way back to the forest the next morning. A few hours away from the city, Cleozun removed their humanoid illusions. Omendine's Seneschal ability had already made note of the akkoans' true races, and he took the transformation in stride. Two days later, as they entered the forest, Boblin appeared to help the group move to the outskirts of the abandoned village.

Greeting Ty fondly, she enfolded him in a hug before explaining that her parents and Aquamarine were busy helping Ty's little army still. Boblin cooed her explanation as they traveled. "We can't go inside the black ring. According to one of your people, it will block teleportation, other than from someone aligned to the Monster God. It is nasty. Also, I do not like nasty things."

Upon arriving outside of the barrier, Cleozun made her way over to inspect it. Chanting and singing, the akkoan gestured at the ring. Grubs writhed at her gestures, the revolting creatures pulsing in place before a twenty-foot stretch of the things faded to a gray color and went still. Making a pleased sound, she announced, "I can remove the creatures and the barrier. It will take a few days, fewer with help." She looked over at Ty. "You do not mind if I rebuild my cabal, yes? A few of our people you've saved are quite adept spellcasters."

Ty said, "Seneschal, your thoughts?"

Omendine drew his Katana and moved to the circle, prodding one of the lifeless grubs. The traesap moved with energetic, graceful motions. "With so few resources, I would recommend small numbers of specialized magic users. A few who can summon. A few who can call the elements. If the mage can organize her cabal to include specialization, this sounds wise."

"I can do it, if Ty wishes," Cleozun said, giving Omendine a long stare.

Ty considered the two. Cleozun had made it expressly clear that she was loyal to her people first and foremost. Her devotion to him, although genuine, was primarily because of the souls within him. There was a chance that the mage would make decisions out of a sense of selfish preservation, rather than the goal of protecting the Sanctuary from the Monster God. Omendine had no interest other than survival. Part of Ty wanted to trust Cleozun more, but he felt obligated to give Omendine most of the authority.

Ty said, "Do it. Until Uneth is ready to make more decisions, I am trusting Omendine to handle the big picture. You'll handle anything magical, provided it doesn't keep Omendine from getting the overall camp ready."

Skewering one of the grubs, Omendine brought it up to his muzzle and inhaled. "I think these might be edible," he began, leaning in as if to take an experimental bite.

Cleozun snapped, "I wouldn't. Anything the Monster God touches, anything with flesh, is likely to have corrupting oil inside. A few drops in you and your organs will mutate. Without a Flesh Weaver or a Vat Master to guide the process, you'll develop cancers and die."

Omendine flicked the carcass off his blade. "I appreciate the warning."

"How do you know so much about the Monster God?" Ty asked, studying Cleozun's face.

She made an off-handed gesture. "This one is not the first Monster God. It will probably not be the last. Their powers are of a kind. Plus..." she reached into her robe and withdrew a book Ty recognized.

"Hey! That's mine!" Ty said, taking the book on monsters from the mage.

She gave him a flat, insectoid look. "You left it out one night. I borrowed it. Would you rather I pursue research that might help our cause?"

Ty looked down at the book, mouth tight. He didn't like being manipulated or stolen from. Stroking the rich leather of the cover, he wondered who wrote the book. It had been written on this world, not the one Cleozun and the other spirits he'd brought back were from. Did that mean that the ones who betrayed them collected the information?

"Next time, just ask. It bothers me when people mess with my belongings," he said, pocketing the book.

"Sure." Looking around Ty's shoulder at Omendine, she continued as though the exchange with him hadn't happened. "Let this be a lesson. You would be wise to consult me in all things magical or related to the Monster God."

Ty half expected Omendine to bite back at Cleozun's tone, but the Seneschal only nodded. He'd witnessed the akkoan "meditation" practices during their trek. He hadn't asked for details, even when the screams of anguish had echoed in the air. Omendine's prudence had reinforced Ty's choice to hire him.

Boblin's parents and Aquamarine met them when they arrived at the village.

Aquamarine made a graceful hand gesture of greeting. "Ty, we're done moving your people. Do you need anything else before we go scout for the Monster God's minions? There's nothing in my forest, so I expect it to take several days to find whatever the enemy is planning."

Ty shook his head. "You've done more than I could have asked for. Knowing what the god is up to and where her next attack will come from is huge. I appreciate you."

"We're protecting the forest, but I accept the sentiment."

Aquamarine moved away, leaving Boblin and her parents.

Boblin made a soft, heart-felt sound in Ty's direction and he grinned at her. "I'm not going to become a druid," he declared sternly at her. Still smiling, he walked over and gave her a hug. She felt comfortable, warm, and safe in a way that few things had in the magical world lately.

She held him back, close and tight, her great heartbeat resonating with his. Ty thought the spirits inside him responded to her presence, issuing their own sort of natural joy in the moment.

The sloths left and Ty's group returned to their journey. "There's nothing better than hugging a sloth," he announced a few minutes later.

None of the others spoke up to argue his point. He considered that a victory.

The akkoans in the village were already hard at work. Ty hadn't given Uneth any standing orders, other than to prepare for the expected attack by the Monster God. Uneth had taken the directives to heart. Several buildings had been deconstructed and merged to form a makeshift barracks. Stones from the well were stacked around the stairs at the center of the town, and water catchments had been set up all around the town with empty barrels.

Uneth met them shortly after they arrived. Ty introduced Omendine, who gave Uneth a small bow of respect, which the akkoan returned. "We have quite a few resources on the way to Sabontil, and a teleportation ring to set up," Ty said after they finished their greetings. "Cleozun says she can take down the teleportation block around the city in a few days, which means we should be able to get basic gear, along with Omendine's special goods within the week."

"My goods?" Omendine's eyes widened, and he licked his lips in clear pleasure. "I will need things to prepare! A special building!" He paused, realizing that Ty and the others were staring at him. Calming somewhat, he continued, "Lord Ty, may I designate a special abode and adjacent land for my needs? And requisition labor to help with construction?"

Ty said, "Sure. We have four or five days to prepare for the equipment, assuming Cleozun can get the barrier down as quickly as she says. I trust you and Uneth to handle the coordination of the rest, at least until we hear our scout report. Set me up a proper space in the tavern. I'm going to go into the forest and collect my convoy. I should be back in a couple of days."

"I'll have Theontsu accompany you," Uneth said.

"Nah. I'll be fine. Aquamarine has sprites everywhere in the forest. He'll know long before anything can attack me here. You all need time to get yourselves together without an outsider like me to worry about." Ty paused, weighing his next words carefully. "Uneth, you're all grieving and processing a lot of pain. Get your people in the right mental space if you can."

How did you tell a group of undead spirits possessing demon bodies about the benefits of group therapy? Ty wished he knew.

"We are trying, Ty. I do not know that we will ever overcome what they did to us, though."

Uneasy with Uneth's statement, he made a mental note to puzzle through the akkoan situation later. With proper planning and resources, anything was possible.

The tavern was as Ty had left it, albeit without the angel corpses. He assumed Uneth had seen to the deceased as part of the cleanup effort. He left the scion's enchanted armor and sword in the underground lab. If the village was going to become a base of operations, he might as well leave the non-combat stuff where it wouldn't get in the way.

Once he'd replenished his supply of Celestial blood and secured his gear, he made his way out of the village. After several days of traveling with his new companions on top of the attack in the city, Ty found himself eager for time alone. He'd missed the forest. Although he knew that spending days in transit, not training or overcoming obstacles, was time that might be better spent, he didn't begrudge himself the break.

"Take care of your mental" was tattooed on his thigh, after all.

Despite his decision to take in the world and enjoy its beauty, Ty added a little training into the travel. He experimented with using the Mind Fortress. At first, he searched for memories of akkoan culture, specifically their gestures. He found he could go into a trance-like state, reliving the moments of someone else's life while traveling. It wasn't efficient—he often stumbled or lost the thread of a memory—but he did learn.

With his self-imposed leisure and experiments with the Mind Fortress, it took Ty a day and a half to make it back to his convoy.

A display from Hagemi flared into view.

Warning: *You have entered an area of divine interference that is outside of the expected limitations.*

The sparse light allowed by the dense forest dimmed. Ty glanced up and around, seeing no source for the change. Other than the warning prompt, he didn't feel anything either. Drawing one of his guns, he crouched and crept forward until he came into view of the clearing.

"Oh no," Ty gasped, standing and sprinting into his camp.

Someone had ransacked his convoy. Crates were open, their contents spilling onto the grass, and cheap watches and food littered the area as if a bomb had detonated them. His tent was in tatters, the rifle case missing. Near the convoy, in a blackened circle, were the mangled corpses of half a dozen Opal Guardians. Their bodies had been torn apart, and worse; blackened growths protruded from their flesh, twisting them into nightmarish versions of their once-pristine beauty. In the middle of the corpses, spiked into the ground, was the stallion's head. Below it, drawn on the ground in blood, was a complex glowing, malicious rune.

If I mess up the rune, will it stop the magic? Ty thought to Hagemi.

Possibly. I cannot tell, and I might not be allowed to tell you if I knew. The Monster God may break the rules, but I still cannot.

Fighting back another curse, he grabbed a stick and made his way to the rune, intending to wipe it out. His gorge rose as he neared the massacre, the stench of the violated horses making his stomach quiver. Stepping over bloodied, mangled remains, he used the tip of the stick and drew a line through the rune.

Near the center of the violence, Ty's spirits began to quail and waver within his chest. Glancing from the disturbed circle and to the stallion's head, he felt the pull of the spirits grow even stronger. Even if they were unembodied, they sensed what had been done here and were outraged.

The barrier around the camp vanished, letting the light through. Blackened, spine-covered tentacles erupted from the bodies of the horses near Ty, wrapping around his limbs. His new barrier amulet flared, deflecting a few of the attackers. Others coiled around his legs, holding him in place. The spines weren't strong enough to punch through his robe, which allowed him a precious second to concentrate on his gauntlets. Spikes of metal sprouted over his hands and fore-arms as he began laying into the tentacles.

"Ooh?"

Ty looked up to see Boblin appear nearby, a glowing sprite on one of her shoulders. Her eyes were wide in horror. She stepped to him, reaching down to help lift him out of the killing circle.

Boblin's chest exploded. Ty heard the shot as gore showered his face. The little sloth's bloodied face was a mask of confusion as she fell forward, pushing him onto the ground. More shots peppered her body, making it twitch and jump. A bullet narrowly missed his head.

Two cries rang nearby. Trees began to thrash. Ty fumbled at the sloth's body, his gloved hands slick with blood, as he tried to tear himself free of both her weight and the tentacles that coiled around his limbs.

Crushing weight and heat pressed in. He felt more than saw motion all around, as writhing, alien things tried to kill him. Roars in the distance only added to the feral panting of his own breath. Twisting, turning, he leveraged every part of his strength to kick out from beneath the sloth, barely squeezing away from the thrashing tentacles.

Ty found his footing and stood. Tentacles still clutching at him, he scanned the edge of the clearing. Boblin's parents had a shadowy shape pinned between them and were ripping it apart. A hood flared and flapped back, revealing a human woman with strange, misshapen features. One of her eyes was decidedly larger than the other. Her skin was charred in places, bits of it replaced with leathery hide. She gibbered incomprehensibly, thrashing in the powerful grasp of the infuriated sloths. One of her legs abruptly crunched, twisted, then a sloth ripped it free with a sickening tearing sound. A third arm whipped out from beneath her cloak, stabbing into the paws of the sloths with a blackened, oily dagger. Made of writhing, purple muscle tissue, the new arm lashed about inhumanly fast.

Recoiling from the attack, both sloths dropped the woman to the ground. Between their mauling and the fall, the woman collapsed, falling atop Ty's stolen rifle. A shadowy globe sprang up around her, taking the injured woman with it.

The sloths, enraged, cast about with their paws, tearing into the underbrush.

Ty reached into one of his pockets and retrieved his revitalizing canteen, using a few drops of the celestial blood on the clinging tentacles. They still hadn't gotten through his robe, though he didn't think they'd needed to. He had fallen for the trap. The ambush had been a success.

With one look at Boblin to verify she was dead, Ty rushed to her parents. "Hold still!" he exclaimed, trying to get close enough to touch them.

They ignored him, instead rushing past into the clearing. More of the tentacle traps lashed out, ensnaring, and injecting the grief-stricken parents with their corruption. They almost absently reached down, peeling tentacles from their bodies as they attended their fallen child. New wails of pain and rage rose from the sloths.

Ty didn't know what to do. There was no plan for this, no contingency. Anguish and loss ripped through him. Boblin had died in his arms, her breath warm against his face. He'd heard her tortured voice, sensed her need to protect him even as she'd passed.

Biting back a wail of anguish, he focused on Boblin's grieving parents. They were still in the center of the clearing, cradling their child's lifeless body. He rushed over and touched one, activating Verdant Touch and transforming part of the energy to Celestial. He felt the purification rip through the sloth's body, heard its sudden cry of pain, and the sloth lashed out, swinging back at him. His shield flared into view as he went flying.

He landed, ignoring the pain in his legs and side as he rolled to his feet. Dodging through the remains of the Opal Guardians, he rushed to the other sloth. The first, seeing him approach again, rose to its feet and lurched toward him, too out of it to realize he was trying to help. Ty activated his healing touch on the second, just before both turned on him.

His shield crumpled as two sets of giant hands slammed into him, knocking him back. "I had to heal you! You were being killed!" he screamed, voice cracking. "Please don't do this, please! I am your friend!"

The sloths stalked toward Ty as he backpedaled. Their feet crushed tentacles and the remains of the horses indiscriminately as they came after him.

Several shapes burst into the clearing, drawing their attention. Leathery skinned humans armed with blackened polearms rushed toward him and the sloths. The newcomers were horribly twisted, covered in boils and growths, their faces misshapen around insane eyes. Their open mouths dripped blackened mucus as they howled in killing frenzy.

Ty drew his pistol and started shooting.

The sloths turned to face the newcomers.

There weren't many of the attackers. Ty counted seven as he poured bullets into them. Unlike nearly everyone else he'd encountered, his shots were effective. Four were down before the sloths came barreling into the rest, knocking their polearms contemptuously to the side and reaching for the attackers.

Tearing into the humans, the sloths didn't try to protect themselves. They were enraged, flailing about and ripping into anything that came within reach with abandon. One attacker, seeing an opening, adjusted his polearm and struck out. Ty shot the woman three times, twice in the chest and once in the neck. She went down before the sloths even acknowledged the threat.

Only after the sloths had finished ripping each of the attackers apart did they finally start to calm. Huge, tear-filled eyes took in the carnage and all they had done, took in Ty with the slow blinks of realization, and both whined.

Ty had never felt such guilt or grief in his life. Moving on impulse, he healed the sloths and himself. Then he sat down near a tree, folded into a ball, and cried with them.

Chapter 33: Grind

Days Remaining in Cycle: 13

Aquamarine arrived hours later. Several dozen lithe, green-skinned humanoids accompanied the dragon. Ty didn't register the people, who looked a bit like fantasy depictions of dryads, as they moved through the clearing. Magic poured from several of the newcomers, splashing over the corpses and causing the remaining oily ichor to hiss and steam. One of them, a woman draped in a mossy robe, approached the surviving sloths, making soothing sounds.

Are those dryads? Ty thought to Hagemi.

Functionally, yes. They occupy in our world the same niche as dryads and elves in your literature. They are savage, wild, and tied tightly to Nature.

The awe he should have felt at the encounter failed to kindle. His heart was a stone in his chest.

As the dryads began constructing a pyre near the center of what had been his camp, Aquamarine made his way to Ty's side. "Ty, I am sorry. My sprites in this area were unable to report. I had no idea what was happening until the barrier came down. When I told the sloths what my sprites saw, the little one rushed ahead to help you."

Fresh sobs wracked Ty, grief briefly overwhelming his ability to reply. He began pushing the worst of the memories into his Mind Fortress, forcing them away so he could function again. Deep in his grief, it hadn't occurred to him to do it until now.

I thought you were here to ease my emotions, he sent to Hagemi.

Hagemi responded with something like regret. *You know how to use the Fortress. I am here to help you acclimate. Once you no longer need my help, I may not provide the same service as I once did.*

Once Ty was functional enough to think past the pain, he told Aquamarine what had happened. "Where did they come from?" he asked, gesturing to the dryads. The woman he'd noted earlier looked at him as he gestured. From the distance, he thought she had bark-like skin that blended into refined, elegant features. She made a subtle gesture of covering her eyes with her hand and turning her face from him.

"Their god told them to come to me a day ago. Apparently, they have been instructed to help me for a period." The dragon looked at Ty, fingers flicking to point at his chest, then make a negating gesture in his direction.

"Ah, so they can't help me, just you?"

"It would seem so."

Green flames licked through the magically crafted pyre, consuming the Opal Guardians. Popping and hissing sounds rose from the corpses as ichor burned away from their bodies. Boblin's parents lifted her onto the pyre shortly after. Their faces were matted with dried blood and tears, conveying a loss so horrible that Ty felt his heart shattering anew.

"This ambush feels wrong," Ty said to Aquamarine as they watched the fire cleanse the bodies. "The girl who escaped was a scion, like me, but I can't believe her level of power. She went invisible, teleported, had a third arm, shot godly arrows, and who knows what else. Why would someone like that be coming after me?"

"The same reason the monster army is building a home base outside of my forest, Ty. They want what's in the quarry. They may have originally been placed there as an exploratory force, maybe even as a first test for you. That's changed now."

Ty exhaled, trying to think. "Wait, what base outside your forest? What have you discovered?"

"A small army of men, demons, and monsters, led by six Vat Masters are building a staging area just outside of the forest, beyond the range of my sprites.

We had to scout it in person to get the details, which is what we've been up to since you left. It's a full contingent from the Monster God. Complete with three of her breeding vats and a dozen Flesh Weavers."

"Vat Masters? What are those? Six of them?"

"Akkoans, ones born and bred by the Monster God. They specialize in creating custom monsters for their god."

"Akkoans?" Ty frowned, remembering the ones in the town. He described them.

"Yes, that's them."

"They must have been going for supplies, just like us." He remembered the expression Jessa had made when he returned. The shape of recent events coalesced in his mind. The "Vat Masters," or whatever they were, had indeed noticed when he'd entered town. They'd left early to avoid what had happened next in the alley.

Maybe.

Quest: Kill the Vat Masters. *The Vat Masters are high-ranking members of the Monster God's army. Each is invested with a significant portion of her power. Killing a Vat Master will not only reduce her military might, it will also slow her plans down.* **Reward:** *25% experience toward your next level per Vat Master defeated.*

Timed Quest: Help Defeat the Invading Army. *The first wave of the invading army has arrived, and it is far stronger than expected. If you and your allies can defeat this invading force before you return home, you will receive one free upgrade to any of your existing abilities.* **Reward:** *One free upgrade to an existing ability, up to a maximum equivalent of 2 merits.*

Custom Quest: Collect the Blood. *Your goal to enhance your race is partially within your grasp. To create her Mutation Vats, the Monster God must have supplied a small amount of divine blood to its Vat Masters. Collect the blood and you will be a third of the way toward your race enhancement goal.*

"One second," Ty said as the prompts came in, taking the time to read them twice before continuing, "Not that I needed it, but my god has offered me significant incentives to stop this army. Can you help me get back to Uneth and the rest? I doubt the sloths are in the sort of shape to move me around right now." He glanced across the clearing to the grieving parents. They held each other, bodies close, in a way that seemed very human.

"I can take you. It's not as easy for me as them, but I will."

Ty swallowed, hating what he had to say next. "We're going to need their help again, Aquamarine. We can't move our troops to assault those assholes without help."

"I know. They do, too, I am sure. This is their home, the home they raised their daughter in for the last eighty years. Give them time to grieve, Ty. Come. I will take you to your people. Give me a few days, and I will return to you with news of them."

* * *

The sloth's method of teleportation was almost instantaneous; it was like becoming one with nature. Aquamarine's ability, which the dragon explained consumed quite a bit of magical energy, was slower. Sitting atop the dragon's back, Ty watched the world bleed into elongated, slow-moving pastel colors. The saturated smears of color gradually wound around him and the dragon over the course of several minutes, before sliding away to reveal the village. Cleozun stood nearby, looking at them with an unreadable expression.

"Good timing. I just got the wall down," she said.

"We have news," Ty said, sliding off Aquamarine's narrow back. Opening his character menu and popping into the Units tab, he sent messages to Uneth and Omendine. *I was ambushed. Boblin is dead. Her parents are grieving and may not be available for a while. Aquamarine just returned with an update on the Monster God's army. They are just outside the forests and fortifying from Sabontil. We need to meet now. I'll see about bringing Aquamarine to the tavern.*

"Do you mind coming into town and going over the enemy army's disposition with us, Aquamarine?" Ty asked. He knew the dragon was loath to enter the settlement.

Aquamarine rose from the ground enough to nervously twitch the fingers of a few sets of its hands together. The dragon's head danced from side to side, anxiety in every motion. "We need to talk. Yes. I will come with you. Briefly. We will coordinate further from the village after this meeting. I dislike leaving my domain."

Ty led the dragon into the town and to the tavern. As they walked, he took the time to inspect his character sheet.

Name: Ty Monroe

Class: Merit Hunter

Race: Human

Level: 2

Progress to Next Level: 75%

Hit Points: 10

Health Shield (Lesser): 15

Mana: 12

Mana Shield: 6

Strength: 15 (with +2 Gauntlets; Peak Mortal)

Agility: 9 (Average)

Vitality: 8 (Average)

Intellect: 11 (Above Average)

Spirit: 6 (Wild-attuned)

Luck: 0

Applicable Skills and Abilities

Mixed Martial Arts (Sambo Focus): Proficient

Krav Maga: High-Adept

Edged Weapons: Skilled

Bows: Proficient

Guns: Adept

Survival: Adept

Meditation: Proficient

Unassigned Attribute Points: 0

Unspent Merits: 0

Achievements and Powers: *Wild Touched, Mana Prism (Celestial, Monstrous, Wild), Mana Siphon, Knight of the Wild Ability Package, Verdant Touch, Moderate Life Leach (Necromantic), Clone Surrogacy (Single Use).*

Quests: *Kill the Vat Masters, Help Defeat the Invading Army (Timed), Collect the Blood, Protect the Dungeon (Ongoing)*

Notable Equipment: *One handgun, Gambler's Monocle X5 (Unshielded), Ward Robe (Epic), Magic-Breaker Dagger (Epic), Shielding Amulet (Lesser), Alunite Gauntlets (Legendary), Mind Fortress (Divine)*

Unequipped Notable Equipment: *Armor of (Unknown, Sealed), Black Sword (Unknown, Sealed), Divine Anchor (Legendary), 2 Infernal Crystals, 1 Personal Locket, Nightmare Silk, Hellstone X 5, Forbidden Book of Necromancy, Monstrous Manual*

Spiritual Assets: *akkoan minds (29,598), akkoan souls (29,598)*

Ty noted that his sheet now showed additional details. His robe and dagger were named, along with there being an entry for unequipped notable equipment and spiritual assets.

Hagemi, what's with the new entries on my sheet?

New information is added as you process it or as you encounter suitable information in the wild. Mostly.

Mostly?

Mhm. Hagemi pulsed a sense of smugness. It reminded him a bit of the defiance the Arbiter had displayed when they'd spoken after the fight with the flying demon. Either Inspiration or his Arbiter was, in whatever way they could, doing their best to help him balance the odds.

They gathered in the tavern, with an open window for Aquamarine to slide his head through. Ty, Uneth, and Omendine pulled tables and chairs away, making room for Cleozun to take her place in the center of the room. She kneeled, using a piece of chalk to create a simple spell on the wooden floorboards. Once she was done, she stepped out and gestured at Aquamarine.

"Describe your observations," Cleozun said.

Aquamarine laid out the overall geography first. As he described the terrain, Cleozun's magic illuminated, projecting a shadowy sketch in the air that reflected his words.

"The camp is about thirty-five miles to the Southwest of this village, near the coastal cliffs. It's just a mile outside the forest, where neither my sprites nor the sloths can scout easily. We had to leave the woods to find them. The camp is spread out over a few acres, with some basic earthen walls surrounding it. Near the center of the camp are the vats. I think there are three. There is also a strange structure right against the cliffs over the ocean. It's enormous, with openings at the top. We counted six Vat Masters, a few hundred Warped, fifty or sixty demons, and a handful of mutated monsters. The demons are different than..." Aquamarine's fingers danced between Cleozun and Uneth.

Ty looked at the outline of the encampment floating in the air. "This doesn't sound too bad. We're nearly matched."

"Vat Masters make the situation more complicated," Omendine said. He looked from Ty to Uneth, Aquamarine, and Cleozun. "Are any of you familiar with them?"

"I've heard of them, but that's it," Aquamarine said.

Uneth shook his head, looking uneasy, and Cleozun said, "I know some theory. Elaborate."

Omendine pursed his lips. "We fought against the Monster God's forces for years, me and my people did. They thought we would be easy meat. I led many battles directly against her forces, and we learned much about them during that time."

Pointing to the map, at the sketched outline of the three vats, he continued, "Vat Masters are the captain-priests of the Monster God's military forces. They rank up there with generals. Whereas Flesh Weavers make dumb weapons, Vat Masters can inject a body with their god's divine essence. A Flesh Weaver might give a soldier a third arm that would be functional. A Vat Master could dunk a soldier in a vat and it would emerge with powers on top of the arm. Entire battalions of their armies have night vision and bleed acid, all thanks to the Vat Masters."

"There must be downsides to this?" Uneth said.

"Indeed. They call it Ascension, but the truth is there are costs for power. Their free will is reduced, and their thoughts are clouded. It makes them easier to trick. They also become more reckless and aggressive."

Ty said, "I guess it could be worse, maybe. How fast can they customize their troops? There has to be a limit, right? If the god is facilitating the process, there's no way they can just make infinite amounts of ultra-powerful mutants."

Omendine shrugged. "I can't say. Every time we tried to question their people, they just melted or laughed at us, no matter what we did to them. Everything I know is from observations." He hesitated, considering. "That said, we never captured a Vat Master. Their kind seem to keep most of their intellect. It might be possible to get answers."

"I'm fairly certain that the six Vat Masters they have are the akkoans we saw at Sabontil," Ty said.

Uneth and Cleozun exchanged meaningful looks. "We suspected as much as well."

"We have some resources we can leverage," he said, telling the gathering about the Celestial blood. "I don't know why it exploded on contact, but when I threw a cask inside the well, it created a huge blast. I bet if we can get more inside the vats, the detonation will be proportional."

Cleozun replied, "Celestial mana violently removes impurities. If the blood has the mana in it, that would explain the reaction. There's nothing more impure than what a Monster God does to their worshippers."

"On our world," Uneth added, "the Monster God eventually adapted to this sort of tactic. I suggest we use the blood while we can."

"If it's so dangerous, why would the god of Monsters have its agents collecting Celestial blood?" Omendine asked. "It does not strike me as intelligent to collect the means of your own destruction."

"I would guess for experimentation," Cleozun said. "It is best to understand your enemies. If the Monster God was preparing for some sort of maneuver, having information on its enemies would benefit it."

Thinking back on literature from his world, Ty said, "It is also the god of corruption, right? Where I come from, literally every kid who ever learns about angels and demons fantasizes about merging the two. Maybe it's trying to find a safe way to breed hybrids?"

Uneth looked in the direction of the well. "Or maybe it was trying to use it for the very purpose you did, Ty. Maybe it was willing to sacrifice its minions to open the Sanctuary? Sufficient explosives might do the trick."

"That makes sense," Aquamarine said.

"Regardless of her motivation, it will know we have them. I would assume that it has adjusted the layout of its camp to accommodate the blood," Omendine said.

"We will need more information," Uneth said. "What kind of monsters do they have? What are they equipped for? If they are waiting, what for? I would like to have Theontsu scout the camp. Mage, what about using magic?"

Cleozun made a negative gesture. "I would expect wards and retaliation were I to probe. I would not pit my will against god-backed magic even in my original form." She made a pointed look in Ty's direction.

"Let's get through this crisis first, alright?" he said to her.

"You all heard that. He said after this crisis!"

Ty cringed, wondering just what he'd unleashed on the future him. Focusing back on matters at hand, he said, "Give me a second to think. I may have an idea." Stepping away, he sat on the floor and got out one of his few clean notepads.

Exhaling meditatively, he tried to recall everything he'd learned playing real time strategy games. Reasoning that the simulations from his world could be valuable here, he began writing. He documented their known assets, and the key abilities he knew his allies had now, thanks to the Seneschal. Once he had that done, he started tracking variables such as time and distance.

Over the next few minutes, Ty remapped the scenario in terms he understood. He imagined playing through it as a computer game, and then again at his grandmother's table. The woman had been quite inventive, particularly when it came to complex war scenarios.

He saw the value in Uneth and Omendine's statements about gathering intelligence. Not knowing what the enemy was doing, or the cards they could bring to the table, could spell a quick end to every idea they had. One way or another, they had to find out what the enemy was capable of and what their plans were. They also had to do it all quickly, otherwise he would be sucked back to Earth while his allies dealt with a potentially overwhelming force.

Hagemi, I don't suppose you'd be willing to make a mental projection of that map and let me work through some ideas with you? You know, virtual style?

The Arbiter considered. *Technically, such an effect should cost a merit or require you to learn a psionic ability. In this instance, I am allowed some small wiggle room, provided you do not ask me to conjecture or extrapolate.*

That would be great.

I would recommend spending a few merits to upgrade my interface. That would make things like what you're asking less... gray.

Understood. Let's get some levels under my belt and we'll do that. Now, do me a favor and project a copy of Aquamarine's map in front of me. Show me the locations I've visited thus far.

The illusory map appeared far more detailed and colorful than Cleozun's projection.

Add the known troops and values, please.

Dots appeared on the map, color coded and labeled. When Ty thought about them, their meaning instantly became clear. He also found he could zoom in or out with a thought, affording him the "god" perspective of a real time strategy game, only with fine controls. Better yet, Hagemi had pulled in data from his enhanced interface from obtaining a Seneschal. He could see his troop names, their levels, and little icons showing their skill suites. Akkoans with military experience were labeled with little swords, while their spellcasters had scrolls, and so on.

Is there any way I can see the spell lists of the casters?

You'll need to ask them, either through your interface or directly. Fair warning, it's common knowledge that spellcasters are secretive about their spells on our world. Here, a spell represents the concrete manifestation of a holistic understanding of arcane concepts. Knowing a spell that someone can cast can give you insight into their background, training, and even how they think. It's far more intimate and dangerous than you might expect.

Ty didn't hesitate to send a note to each of his akkoan spellcasters, including Cleozun, asking them for any spells they thought would be useful in combat. He made a note that he didn't need ancillary details, just bare facts.

Hagemi populated the spell lists as they filtered into his interface, translating the terms into ones he'd understand. *Rolling Inferno of Soul's Fire* became *Enhanced Pure-Damage Fireball*, and so on.

"Okay, I think I can see a plan here," Ty said after a few minutes of studying the map and troops. He turned back to the group, who had continued talking in muted tones while he worked with his Arbiter.

"By all means," Uneth said.

Ty pointed to the floating spell-map. "First, we need to capture or kill the Vat Masters. We know they visited Sabontil once. I bet they will do it again, especially if they are outfitting an army. Hell, we need to do a run for our goods, too. We might as well kill two birds with one stone." He gestured to Uneth and Cleozun. "They are akkoan. You two will work on a plan for their capture. I must be there. My god has offered me a significant bounty to kill them, so factor me in."

"This makes sense," Cleozun said.

Buoyed by their support, Ty pointed to the area in the forest near the enemy army. "Aquamarine, I believe they will probably use scouts. If there's anything I know from my old gaming days, it's the danger of the fog of war. Can you and your allies make sure those scouts don't return? Or, at least, try to keep tabs on them?"

Aquamarine bobbed slightly in the window. "My sprites are already on it. Unless they come with the aid of powerful scions again, we will know their movements. I can see about allocating the forest's defenders to the area to stop any probes. The dryads might even be willing to help in some fashion."

Ty checked his resource assets with a glance. "We have thirty-two barrels of Celestial blood left. We don't want to just chuck those at the enemy. Omendine, can you work with Uneth to see which of our akkoans can retrofit arrows or other weapons to include a small amount of the blood in them or on them? In my world, someone speculated that a hollow arrowhead with a bit of liquid silver in it could be used against a werewolf. I wonder if something like that would work here?"

"I think we can work with that idea," Omendine said. "There are existing weapons that are similar here, particularly ones that deliver a special additive effect when used against magic protections. Perhaps we can replicate something similar. Or construct it into our weapons."

"We lack the facilities for broad production of such things though, Ty," Uneth added. "It might be simpler to just dip a blade or arrowhead in a diluted mixture of the blood, rather than undertaking a new engineering task."

Ty chuckled awkwardly. "Oh, yeah. That makes sense." Why hadn't he seen that as a solution?

Uneth continued, "Of course, the problem with that is we'll be delivering a reduced amount of the blood in each strike, assuming it doesn't simply evaporate during delivery."

"I may be able to help," Aquamarine said. "There is a material in the forest that I can extract from the plants. It may add a sticky property to the liquid."

"Do you mind working on that with Omendine?" Ty said.

"Of course."

"Good planning," he said. "Let's meet back here tomorrow morning and see what we've come up with, alright? I know it's a tight timetable, but I don't see any better options."

The group agreed and parted ways, Uneth and Cleozun partnering to deal with the problem of their wayward descendents, Aquamarine to gather allies and plant materials, and Omendine to discuss options with the other akkoans. One benefit of having ancient akkoan spirits on their side was the fact that there were literal generations of experience aiding each of them. Were it not for the insanity that afflicted them, Ty had no doubt his small force would prove overwhelming in most confrontations.

With his allies occupied, he didn't have much else to offer. He had provided vision and organization, for which he was pleasantly surprised, but he lacked the expertise to help in executing any of the tasks.

Walking outside of the tavern after Aquamarine left, he looked up at the sky. He had less than half a day ahead of him and nothing to do. Thoughts of what had brought him to this point rolled in. Images of horror, those he hadn't stored in his Mind Fortress, bubbled to the surface, threatening to steal his focus. He contemplated storing those, too. Who would he be without his memories, though? The Mind Fortress was an incredible tool, a magical device that might end PTSD for millions of people on his home world. Yet he sensed it could also be an addictive trap.

Painful memories taught important lessons. Without them, Ty wouldn't be who he was. Without his painful memories of his late father, would he have become the gamer he was? Would he have read the books that gave him the framework to interact with this world? Pain had, to some degree, motivated him to become who he was. He had to admit that it had probably also crippled him.

Ultimately, he figured using the Fortress was about finding balance. Store the memories that would cripple him, while keeping the ones that would give him the impetus he had to have to move forward. Remembering the Opal Guardians and Boblin was important. It helped him find his roots in this world, to feel genuine loss.

Deciding to follow in the footsteps of the akkoans, Ty searched for privacy. It was hard; with hundreds of bustling akkoans moving about, the village was practically full again. The sounds of construction followed him until he found a spare space to sit and be alone.

With his back to a stone building, Ty pulled his knees to his chest, wrapping his arms around them. Curled tightly, he let the feelings out. Slowly, deliberately, he pulled memories from his Mind Fortress. He remembered Boblin, her last moments. He remembered the Opal Guardians in all their glory. His sense of awe at their beauty, at their willingness to accept and trust him, returned to him.

In the pain of his memories and loss, he saw a deeper truth about the books Technology had shown him. He saw the wonder and beauty of a magical world; he also saw the reality of war. He saw what would come to his world.

The akkoan spirits he'd brought out of Sanctuary weren't from *this* world. They'd come from a *previous* world. The Resonance Bridge had been used before. He didn't know the full history of that first usage. What he knew was filled with horrors and death. If history repeated itself, his world would know a calamity that would put all wars to shame. The suffering he had experienced through the akkoan spirits and now, personally, could be visited on humanity. It could also be visited upon the denizens of this world.

I've never been a power gamer, Ty thought to Hagemi. *I always imagined myself living in the worlds I explored, you know? I wanted to thrive in them. To just... be. To be happy. Not helpless, but not a god. I had some friends who liked power. They min-maxed their way to the top of every combat. Some of them were so bloodthirsty, they'd just ransack entire villages for the chance to get a rare drop or some experience. I did my best not to be like that. I always thought about the books. You know, like the ones from the prophecy. I didn't want to become Thomas Covenant, even in my fantasy games.*

Maybe that's why the god included you in the lottery, Hagemi thought back.

Ty shrugged, the motion dislodging tears he hadn't felt himself shedding. *I can't think like that now. Not just like that, anyway. I can't die, Hagemi. Too many people count on me now. Fuck, do you have any idea what it's like to know twenty thousand souls live inside you, relying on you to give them their final rest or whatever?*

Hagemi manifested for the first time since Sanctuary, its magenta light shining warmly against Ty's face. "I am in you, Ty. I may not live in your skin or control your thoughts, but I feel what you feel. I know your burden."

Somehow, the Arbiter's confession only made him feel worse. "How can you know what I'm going through and not do more?"

"Ty, don't you realize? Me being with you, communicating with you, is significant. Our gods have come together and given you a legitimate chance to experience our world. You can save people here and on your planet. It's not a pleasant situation, but it is the only one we're given. I am doing everything I am allowed. You must make of it what you will."

Inhaling a shuddering breath, Ty began locking the worst of the memories back in the Mind Fortress. The pain slowly, mercifully, eased. As the source of his trauma receded, he felt determination replace the pain. Determination and anger.

"You know what I'm going to do?" Ty said, looking down at his hands. His Alunite gauntlets took on an emerald metallic sheen. Pulling his black dagger from its sheath, he held the handle flat against the back of one hand. Slowly, with careful guidance, he made the Alunite wrap around the material of the hilt, securing it in place. The knife didn't budge when he hit it against the stone building.

"What?" Hagemi answered his prompt, though the Arbiter no doubt sensed his intent, if not his exact thoughts.

"I'm going to grind some damn experience."

Chapter 34: Not So Fast

Days Remaining in Cycle: 13

Ty used the rest of his day in meditation. He'd begun looking for an akkoan with memories that could help train him in combat, particularly as it applied to his developing skill set. There were hundreds of potentially good choices, including quite a few who intimidated him too much to access completely. Avoiding minds too intense to deal with, he'd narrowed it down to half a dozen before he'd returned to the tavern and slept. To this world's credit, the mattresses were comfortable.

The next morning, he lamented leaving behind so many of his goods back at his forest camp. Whoever had ransacked the place hadn't precisely stolen or destroyed everything; he could have retrieved at least a change of clothes or rations. Time had been tight, and he hadn't been thinking practically.

After finishing one of his final meal replacement bars and checking his gear, Ty made his way out of the room he'd appropriated.

Uneth, Cleozun, and Omendine were waiting for him. They sat around a table, a parchment with a simple drawing of the surroundings weighted down with mugs. A plate of food sat in front of Omendine and another in front of an empty chair.

"Is that for me?" Ty gestured to the plate, taking the empty chair.

Cleozun buzzed affirmation. "We found food stores secured throughout the village. Omendine prepared the food. He assured us it would please you."

The plate had a mixture of greens, nuts, and thin slices of some sort of meat. Ty looked at his llama-shaped friend's plate. The traesap also had partaken of the meat. "I didn't think you were a meat eater."

"Why would you think that?" Omendine's lips peeled back. He had disturbingly human-looking teeth, complete with sharp incisors.

"Oh, no reason." There was no way Ty was going to tell him about llamas now.

Clearing his throat with a series of clicks, Uneth said, "Ty, we think we have a plan for dealing with the akkoans' leaders."

Cleozun somehow looked excited, despite lacking the facial features for it.

Ty attempted one of the akkoan hand-gestures meaning "please elaborate."

"Like this," Uneth corrected, showing him the proper motion, before continuing. "First, we believe that the Vat Masters have a contingent of troops stationed near the city. Kidnapping or killing the Masters outside of the city will require us to take that into consideration. To counter that, we will want to bring a sizable countering force. While we have the advantage of surprise, overwhelming force makes sense."

Cleozun added, "It is possible that they will have one or more spellcasters with them, and maybe a few assassins. We will want to bring myself, a few of the other spellcasters you resurrected, and all Theontsu's rangers."

"All of this sounds good to me," Ty said. "What else?"

"I have the teleportation ring in place. I do not recommend using it yet, though. As soon as we put it in the teleportation network, there's a chance that its magic will become visible to those who look for new rings." Cleozun made a wavering gesture with one hand. "We used a similar technology on Ako, though not quite the same. If this works the same, with resonances, it would be possible for one of our enemies to use its presence to track our city down. This means..."

"We'll have to do a lot of walking," Ty said with a grimace.

"Indeed," Uneth said, "This brings us to timing. Without the sloths, it'll take a hard day of travel through forest and swampy terrain. If we get there and the Vat Masters don't come back in a timely manner, we'll be in trouble. I'd suggest we bring our entire force, but that doesn't work. Our people still need time to adapt, on top of the gear we need them to get acquainted with."

"I also still need to work with Aquamarine around solutions for the weapons," Omendine said.

"What's your solution?" Ty asked.

Uneth pressed on. "We send a large force to Sabontil. As the mage suggested, we go expecting the worst. Once we gear up our strike force, we'll immediately send the rest, along with enough guards to protect the convoy, back to the town. That will probably be a four-day round trip, which will leave us with nine until you go. It'll give Omendine five days, if we're lucky, to get things secure here and help our people gear up. You've done a great job of putting experienced warriors and spellcasters in the demon bodies, but the psychological burden isn't going to go away. I would expect our people to need extra oversight and help to function as a combat unit in that short of a span."

Ty nodded, lamenting the fact that he couldn't give each of the akkoans a Mind Fortress. Such a device might give the spirits back a measure of their peace. "That also gives us seven days to take the Vat Masters before we pivot and go straight to the camp?"

"Indeed," Uneth said. "Either way, we coordinate with Aquamarine's sprites and meet in the forest within the next eleven days. That only gives us two days to observe and plan an on-site strike; however, with Aquamarine's scouting help, even without the sloths, we should be able to do better than going in sight unseen."

Omendine made a distinctly equine snort. "This is a good plan. Until we step in whatever shit the Monster God is sure to lay in our path. Good delivery, Uneth."

"Thank you, Seneschal," Uneth replied. He sounded genuinely pleased. "Most of the idea was yours, so I was glad to explain."

Ty said, "In my world, we have a saying. It goes something like, 'Everyone has a plan until they get punched in the mouth.'"

"Wise words," Omendine said.

"Do we have any word from Aquamarine?" Ty asked, spearing another mouthful of food. It was simple fare, lacking any sort of spices, but was tasty all the same. Especially compared to protein bars.

"The dragon checked in before you awoke," Omendine said. "No reports from the scouts yet. Neither of the sloths are ready to help again, and there's no way to know if or when they will be. On a positive note, it did provide me with a solid supply of material to experiment with on our weapons. I will be working with one of the akkoans who is familiar with alchemical mixtures to help in the process."

A pop-up flashed in the lower-right of Ty's vision, giving him a quick overview of the akkoan Omendine had identified as potentially useful. Her name was Meridian. She was labeled as having Alchemy at a "Peak" rating, along with several other science and dream-oriented skills. Her class and level were labeled 'Privacy Locked'. She also had the *Deeply Disturbed* status beneath her name.

What is "Privacy Locked?"

Hagemi sent, *People over level eight can conceal, obscure, or even manipulate information gleaned from passive abilities like these, depending on their abilities.*

Ah. Good to know.

Most of the akkoans had some sort of status showing their mental state during their nightly "meditation" Ty had noticed, but this was the first one he'd seen during the day. Curious, he checked Uneth's status. Sure enough, he had one too. His status was *Fractured, and* the word was red for some reason.

"We're going to need to do something about the mental afflictions crippling our people," Ty said. "Can we make Mind Fortresses and store some of the worst memories?"

Cleozun made a buzzing, approving sound. "Yes, yes. Absolutely. I plan to remake these demon bodies into something more familiar, which will help. It would be best to make the mind crystals after that remaking, since they need to be harmonized to the final biology. Unless this world has a manufacturing facility, we will also need quite a bit of resources for me to begin production. Which will also take time."

Omendine said, "Mind Fortress crystals are extremely rare. I've heard of them, of course, but I don't know of any easy way to acquire them. I wouldn't expect to find a cheap or easy source."

Ty said, "We can make that a long-term project. Once I get back from my world, we'll make it a top priority. Meridian looks good, Omendine. Her stats are exceptional, assuming her mental state allows you to work with her."

Omendine pursed his thin lips. The sheer responsibility of taking control of both the new settlement and the akkoans from Ty for the duration of his absence had not pleased the traesap. "I'll make it work. You're bringing my darlings back to me. I'll do whatever it takes to secure the village."

Ty bit back the reflexive question. He didn't have time to delve into whatever Omendine meant about his "darlings." "You all did a good job coming up with these plans. Our course of action is set. Let's get everyone coming organized and leave in the next hour, if possible?"

"Easily done," Uneth said. "The magic your Seneschal provides us makes communicating far simpler."

"Wait, does everyone have access to the interface?" He looked at Omendine.

"Interface?" Omendine said.

They do not, Hagemi sent him. *To them, the magic presents in a more organic, instinctive way.*

Ty said, "Sorry, not interface. I meant, uh, magic. I didn't realize you could give everyone access to the communications spells."

Omendine shook his head. "No, not everyone. As long as people are loyal to you and within the village, my power allows them to receive communications. You and I can designate up to eight others as leaders. Those can send communication as well. Only you and I get full details of the inhabitants. As of now, Uneth and Cleozun are the only ones on the leadership list."

"Good to know," Ty said. "Let's get ready and on the road. I'd rather not kill more time talking if possible." Standing, he asked Cleozun, "I don't suppose you have a spell to clean someone? I feel absolutely filthy."

Laughing, the mage replied, "Of course. Our people are quite fastidious, at least we are when we're not half insane and in demon bodies."

Her spell didn't just bathe Ty, it completely refreshed everything he was carrying, whisking away grime and blood in a moment. The spell did not, unfortunately, repair the hole in his robe.

Less than an hour later, he and his strike force left the village to begin their hard days' trek to Sabontil.

* * *

Days Remaining in Cycle: 12

Hit Points: 10

Health Shield (Lesser): 15

Mana: 12

Mana Shield: 6

"I'm going to go in and look around, maybe talk with that vendor we saw the akkoans talking with last time," Ty said the next day, as the large group gathered just within view of Sabontil's walls. They'd allowed themselves the leisure of sleeping in, as the Trade Master's didn't open until later in the morning. The day's moderate heat was pleasantly nearing its zenith, balancing the mild sea air wafting in from the south.

Uneth said, "You may be recognized. Those recent attacks were not coincidence."

Ty looked over at Cleozun expectantly. "Fine, but you will not go alone," she replied, casting the illusion spell.

He didn't feel any different, but when he looked down, he saw that the shape of his hands and the skin tone was different. She repeated the process with Uneth, Theontsu, herself, and several of Theontsu's rangers.

Once the spells were cast, he addressed the unconcealed akkoans, "We will go into the town, collect our supplies, and ask some questions. We'll return or signal if things go awry, alright?"

The crowd made gestures of agreement, and he led the disguised group to the city.

Sabontil was as Ty remembered it, with the same oddly dressed people moving atop their streets of light. He made his way to the Trade Master's and used his password with Jessa, who looked him up and down with an expression of vague suspicion. The other human was wearing a black outfit, with distracting lime-green stitching along the lapels.

"Yeah, we'll have them for you. As agreed. All on enchanted wagons. All tip-top shape. Even the animals are good. They gave a good ruckus the other day. Not a hair harmed, I promise. Where do you want the convoy to meet you, south road?"

"South sounds fine. Wait, did you say animals?"

Jessa chuckled. "Your master didn't tell ya? Yeah. Those are some real rare creatures ya have on your hands. I aughta charge your master an extra fee for all the trouble one of those cats caused when it got free. And those damn rabbits. Way too smart for their own good. Creepy, if you ask me."

"Rabbits *and* cats?" Ty blinked, flabbergasted. Just what was Omendine doing?

"Big ones, yah. Now, when did you say you wanted to do the handoff?"

"Can you give me two hours? My master wants me to do some shopping first."

"Sure, sure." Jessa frowned, looking around, then leaned over his desk and whispered to Ty. "Say, you don't know where your master is right now, do ya? There might be something in it for you if ya can give me his exact location."

Ty tried to roll with the question, dropping his voice and leaning in. "He wanders a lot, that one. If you tell me where you need him, I might be able to get him somewhere for you."

"Hard to say," Jessa said. "My, uh, friends come into town every other day. They're curious, you know, just wanna ask some polite questions. Actually, they aughta be back sometime soon. How's about I arrange a little meeting, and maybe you get paid double time?"

Grimacing, Ty held out a hand, rubbing his fingers together surreptitiously. If he didn't play the part of a grifter, someone who would turn his employer in for money, no doubt Jessa would get even more suspicious. At this point, he was working on instinct, channeling the rogue character he'd played during tabletop games all those years ago. Deep down, he was certain the act was transparent. "I, uh, I might be able to come back and have a little chat with them, but I'd need some convincing."

Jessa glanced at his hand, sneered, and passed him a chit from his pouch. It was worth five marks. "There ya go," the merchant said, "good money for a healthy conversation."

Ty pocketed the chit. "I'll be back in a couple of hours."

He left the store and set to rounding up the other akkoans. They were fortunate that Jessa had been so willing to give information away, although in retrospect, he wasn't surprised. It was a town for smugglers, after all.

Once the group was together and back in the field with the rest of their people, Ty laid his findings out. "I figure I'll meet with the traitors outside of the town after we secure our goods. If I can, I'll get them to go a ways from the city, so you all can just sweep in. We capture one or two for questioning and, boom, next steps just fall into place. That is, assuming we can get them to talk."

Cleozun shrugged. "Traitors. Easy to make traitors talk."

Uneth said, "Ty, I don't like you putting yourself in their grasp. It's possible this will end up being a double cross."

Ty looked at Theontsu. "We'll just make sure my bodyguard is nearby, won't we?"

Chapter 35: Ambush

Days **Remaining in Cycle:** 12

Ty and his bodyguards met the laborers with their goods before he headed back to the Trade Master. The merchants had been true to their word; each of the twenty open-air wagons was laden with Omendine's ordered goods. Barrels and boxes of armaments cluttered fully half of the wagons, while most of the rest had building equipment and trade tools on them. The last wagon was a bit of an oddity, however.

Cages decorated the front and back of the wagon, stacks of boxes separating them. Inside the front cages were a dozen big, long-haired cats. The cats had six limbs, and their bottom jaws hinged open to reveal an utterly terrifying cave of sharp teeth. No doubt any rodent on Earth would have had an immediate heart attack at the sight.

The back of the wagon held furry rabbits with pearl-sized forehead gems. When Ty stared at the rabbits in confusion, one of the handlers who had brought the wagons out spoke up. "Distributed hive-variant, very rare." The young man tapped his forehead, speaking in what Hagemi translated into something like English cockney.

"Distributed?" he asked.

"Yeah, the more of 'em there are, the smarter they become. Shared intelligence. Good thing these breed really slow, otherwise we'd have a damn army of the fuckers taking over the world."

"But why?" He looked between the crates, from horrific spider-cats to the adorable, but apparently intelligent, bunnies.

The handler shrugged. "It's not my job to ask questions, mate. I just kept 'em fed and from killing each other."

Several of his akkoans, wearing human disguises, stepped up to take the reins of one of the beasts at the front of the wagon train. With the magical endowments that Omendine had negotiated for the wagons, it only took four of the oxen-like creatures to pull all twenty at a decent clip down the road. The akkoans would escort it off-road at a point out of sight of the city in case someone was trying to track their comings and goings. Uneth and Omendine had been certain that their enemies would have some sort of plan to use the goods against them, either by magical tracking or visual, and they'd made plans accordingly.

Ty waved the handlers away after getting some basic feeding and care information from them, then headed after the wagons. He met Cleozun and Uneth a few miles south of the city, where Cleozun took a few minutes to cast several spells of detection on the whole train. She found six spells and ten enchanted items, each with an increasing level of nuance to their concealment.

"This is the last," she said, picking a bug out of the ear of one of the pack animals. "Next, I will cast some simple deception spells to make whoever is tracking them think they are still working. Perhaps they will follow the wagons into the ocean?"

"How do you know?" Ty asked, standing with Uneth and the others. Watching Cleozun work was a thing of disturbing beauty. She sang and danced in rhythm, making beautifully haunting song-spells, then at random intervals she'd jerk and spasm and seem to go into full-blown seizures. He guessed the fits were a result of her variety of madness. He wasn't about to ask her, though.

Cleozun stepped closer to Ty, dropping her voice. "Consider this a special secret yet? No sharing. The first spells I cast were simple overall detection and counting spells. As soon as I determined there were trackers, I used fate magic to determine the number of variables involved. Each time I removed one of the trackers, I cast the spell again until I could discern the total number. It's an mana intensive process, yet effective, even against lesser gods and their ilk. Fate itself hel ps."

"That's brilliant," he said.

"Thank you." She gave him one of her demonic grins. "Now, let me cast my deception spells. Plan on me taking four hours to recharge my mana after that. Give it at least half that before you go into the town, just to be on the safe side, yes?"

No one came from the town to investigate the wagon trail. Two hours later, Ty walked into the Trade Master's alone. At seeing him, Jessa exhaled a visible sigh of relief before coming from around the desk. Unlike the first time he'd visited, the shop was doing a brisk business and the other two staff members stared daggers at Jessa's back as he and Ty exited the building.

"They showed up an hour ago. I tole 'em about you. They are so excited, you're just gonna love em, wait and see. Love em!" Jessa spoke as he led him through a maze of buildings near the southern section of the city.

Ty affected an uncomfortable expression. "They don't mean to do anything bad to my master, do they? I mean, he's a little strange, but he pays well."

Jessa chuckled. "Nah, nothin', I'm sure. They just wanna have a word with 'em. Apparently, he might have hurt one of their friends real bad. Might cost a small fortune to get a new leg for her or something. They probably just want a little help with the money end of things, that's all."

Ty's stomach dropped. He figured the scion-assassin was still alive, but the confirmation just made matters worse. She'd nearly killed him twice, and he had no illusions about his powers being sufficient to face her for a rematch. Things with invisibility and movement powers were a nightmare to fight.

Rounding a building, Jessa and Ty emerged in a cul-de-sac facing a smooth section of the southernmost wall, next to the port. To his surprise, all six of the Monster God's akkoan Vat Masters stood in a relaxed half-circle near the wall, which rippled and slid open to reveal a concealed exit.

"Here ya go," Jessa said, pushing on his shoulder hard enough to make him stumble closer to the group. "Now pay up."

One of the akkoans, a nearly eight-foot-tall man with sleek blue plumage outlining chiseled features, sneered at Jessa and flicked a hand. A bag appeared, flying through the air and slamming into Jessa's chest hard enough to make the man stumble and drop the bag. Metal coins spilled out onto the street, the emblem of a woman visible on each. "Come in a week. We'll provide you with compensation for the Mother's coin."

Another of the akkoans, a woman with emerald feathers, moved in quick, liquid steps to wrap an arm around Ty's arm. Her grip was strong. Without Ty's strength-enhancing gauntlets, currently masquerading as simple workman's gloves, he knew that she'd have been his equal.

"Hey now," he said, continuing his masquerade as a simple laborer, though the hint of fear in his voice was real. He knew what akkoans were capable of, and these weren't half-mad from thousands of years of torture.

"Do not think doubtful thoughts," the woman said through tight lips, her voice a dry lisp. He thought he saw a stubby, forked tongue behind her teeth. "You will not be harmed so long as you come with us peacefully."

Stilling himself, Ty looked back to see Jessa scrambling for the spilled coins. *Is the Monster God female in the same way Inspiration is male? I've been thinking of her as "it."*

Hagemi sent affirmation through their bond, followed by a sense of caution. Ty figured the Arbiter wasn't going to take any action for the time being, lest some magic of the akkoans detect its presence.

After he'd collected his prize, Jessa swept the group a bow before walking away. He didn't even look at Ty as he left.

"That one fails to show proper respect. Always." The speaker was short for an akkoan, with orange-and-green plumage.

Blue Plumage chuckled. "Once he has Ascended, he shall." Jerking his head to the opening, he said, "Hurry. We want to implant him before the others realize he's gone."

Stub Tongue pulled Ty through the gate without a word, using her size and strength to manhandle him forward. "D.... did he say implant?" he said.

"Do not worry. You will enjoy it. Always." Orange Plumage flashed Ty what he thought was meant to be a reassuring smile. Orange had uneven eyes, like the human assassin who had killed Boblin. One was slightly bigger and a different color than the other. He wondered if that meant the akkoan had some ocular pow er.

Suppressing a shudder, he found himself walking in the center of the akkoans. Unlike those in his memories, this group moved with a sense of synchronous rhythm that had less in common with a bird and more with like a slither of serpents. They set a fast pace, taking them directly from the concealed entry to the road. Although a few travelers and merchant wagons moved up and down the road, none stopped to pay him or his captors any heed.

"So, um, what is it you want to know?" Ty tried. "I thought you wanted to know where my leader was?"

Blue Plumage made a short laughing sound. "Yes, we want to know that. But more, too. You will help us find him. And then you will help us deal with him."

"What, how? I thought this was just to ask me questions!" Ty made to pull away from the group, jerking his arm in Stub Tongue's grasp.

Stub Tongue backhanded him across the mouth. His protective shield flared briefly, softening the blow. At the flare of the shield, she hissed a word and hit him again, this time bypassing the shield and sending him to the ground, blood flecking his lips.

"The little traitor has a shield," one of the akkoans with violet-and-green plumage said. He sounded more intrigued than worried.

"Shall I take it?" Stub Tongue asked.

Blue Plumage made a negating gesture. "Leave it. It will not hinder the process, and it will be suspicious if the man returns to his former master without the trinket."

Ty let Stub Tongue pull him back into the center of the group. His mouth stung, but he'd learned something important. The akkoan Vat Masters could bypass his shield with a spell. He wasn't happy that his lesser shield wasn't effective against every source of damage, but he hadn't expected it to be. The upside was that he knew the shield *would* deflect their mundane attacks normally.

They traveled past the smooth metal circle of Sabontil's public transportation ring a few minutes later. The ground around the ring was dirt, hard packed into the ground, and the ring was framed by six silver pillars. Copper runes decorated the pillars, giving off a subtle presence that made Ty think of his Guide.

"I don't suppose you have anything to drink?" he said.

Stub Tongue squawked a laugh and reached down. Her uniform was tight-cut, in a style not too dissimilar to Earth military gear, but she had a hip-hugging skirt on over her pants. Inside a fold of the skirt, she reached into a small metal ring and withdrew a writhing leather pouch.

The bitch has vault storage, Ty thought bitterly as he shook his head at her. "Um, on second thought, maybe I'm not that thirsty."

His akkoan captor laughed, upending the bag of ichor-drenched worms directly into her mouth. Ooze rolled down her lips and cheeks, absorbing directly into her plumage. He saw the worms writhing down the column of her throat as she swallowed.

Orange Plumage leered at Ty. "You should be excited. The worms of change will know you soon. Make you anew. Powerful. You will embrace our true Goddess. Always."

"I don't see why we don't just fly him back to camp and put him in a Vat. A few hours with the Mother and he'd be far more useful a tool," Violet Plumage said.

"This has been discussed and the decision made," Blue Plumage said.

The trade road thinned out as they progressed southward. Bent grass in dirty ruts gave evidence to carts traveling down it, just fewer than in the northern direction. Ty wasn't enough of a woodsman to tell if the tracks were newer, though he'd guess they were. The Monster God's army couldn't have been setting up in their secondary location for long.

They crested a hill a bit later, and Ty got a deep whiff of unmasked sea air. He remembered that smell from his world, from a time when he and his parents had been a family. For a heartbeat, he genuinely missed Earth. Then he saw the waiting monsters.

There were thirty or forty dirty humans, each resembling the half-mad group that had attacked back at the clearing. Opposite the humans was a cluster of bear-like things covered in chitin, their torsos studded with gleaming gemstones. Finally, closer to the river, there were two massive demons that resembled winged hydras. With draconic bodies, each had six limbs and a pair of immense, leathery wings. The thick column of their trunk gave way to a dozen crocodilian heads atop long, prehensile necks that were in constant motion. At the apex of their torsos, just before their chests split into the necks, were basketball-size gems that flickered with sullen red magic.

As they neared, Ty noticed that the magic light in one gem echoed in the other, then back again. The hydras had mind gems.

He pulled up his character sheet and went to the tab with Cleozun on it. Working as fast as his mind would allow, he sent her a note. *Cleozun, I have an ability that lets me install akkoan souls into demons with mind gems. Do you believe this would count as demons?* He willed an image of the hydras to accompany the note and was pleased to see a little attachment icon appear with the sending.

Stumbling a bit, as much at the horrifying sight as his loss of concentration on walking, Ty was led down the hill and toward the congregation.

His interface flashed. He opened the prompt to see Cleozun's reply. *Those are mind gems, and those creatures classify as demonic. Yes. From what I've gathered, any creature with an organic mind gem here is labeled as a demon. Which is strange, and I wonder why? Silly new planet. How close do you have to get to take one over?*

I have to touch them.

Goody! He could practically hear the mad mage's cackling laughter over the text display.

Turning his attention from the exchange, Ty addressed the collection of souls in his chest. *Who wants to possess a demonic hydra? Raise your hand if you're feeling particularly angry.*

A dozen souls pushed at his Cage, their associated memories surfacing in answer. *Ready yourselves.*

"Why does he have that expression?" Orange Plumage said from a few feet away. He was peering into Ty's eyes, a look of suspicion on his fine features.

"Perhaps he is praying?" Stub Tongue said, jerking Ty's arm. "Are you praying, little man?"

Ty glanced around, seeing that the akkoans had stopped him near their backup. The humans were just to his left, looking at him with utter madness in their eyes. He wouldn't have been surprised to see them frothing or tearing at their own clothes, just from the way they gibbered and gestured wildly. The bears were furthest away, heads lolling about lazily. He suspected that as dangerous as the bears looked, they were probably the pack animals of the demons, so likely less overtly aggressive. The hydras were maybe thirty feet away. With so many heads atop each body, a few from each of the pair flicked in his direction at any given moment.

Are we ready? Ty sent Uneth through the interface.

"I said are you praying?" Stub Tongue shook him.

Orange Plumage laughed, reaching into his pants to retrieve a vial of ichor. "He will be praying soon. To the Mother. Always." His hand caressed the vial as he held it up to the light. The substance pulsed in the vial and the light around it warped inward, ripples appearing in the air.

"One drop this time," Blue Plumage said. "I won't have another captive melt because you were too enthusiastic."

"One drop," Violet Plumage echoed. "Mother's blood is too precious to waste. We have to maintain the vats until the next wave arrives. That means at least another month for your vial."

Orange Plumage scowled at his companions. "You treat me like I am damaged. Always. But my mind is clear. Am I not your equal? Was I not born and raised to be as all of us? Am I not capable? Always."

Ready, Uneth sent.

Ty slid one hand down to his side. The akkoans hadn't searched him, and he meant to make them pay for it. A focused thought allowed him to extend a tendril from his gauntlet into his pocket, just barely long enough to catch the hilt of the black dagger. Using a move he'd practiced on the trip, he rotated his hand and pressed the back to his thigh and the flat of the dagger's hilt.

"It sure sounds to me like they think you're a moron," Ty said to Orange Plumage. "Why do you follow his lead anyway? He's clearly thinking about having sex with your sister." He jerked his chin to Blue Plumage.

Orange's eyes widened in shock, alarm, and confusion.

Stub Tongue shook with rage. "You dare..." she began, only to freeze in mid-sentence as Ty whipped his free hand up and slammed the dagger into her throat. Her expression was one of pure shock as she fell.

Multiple arrows blossomed in the chests of the adjacent akkoans and in a dozen of the humans. The bears looked up and around, blinking in confusion, as the hydras roared in anger. Ty was already moving as the closest nest of hydra heads lashed around, looking for the source of the invisible attacks. One head exhaled mist into the air. The mist expanded with supernatural speed, flooding the area, and revealing several of his invisible allies as they raced to his aid.

Theontsu and his men were fast. Whether Cleozun had enhanced them, Ty couldn't tell, but the warriors moved with Olympic speed as they rushed among the humans, literally tearing them apart. Multiple hydra heads from both creatures extended toward the attacking akkoans, a volley of lightning bolts tracing paths straight into them.

Ty looked away from the fight and raced toward the nearest hydra. One head whipped down. The mouth shot lightning into him just before smashing him into the ground with one of its massive forelimbs.

The lightning zapped through Ty's body in a torrent of sharp discomfort, but the stomp felt like it nearly collapsed his chest.

Screaming in pain and rage, Ty made a fist and slammed the black dagger down into the hydra's leathery foot. Oily black blood spewed from the wound. Roaring, the foot withdrew long enough for him to roll toward the beast, popping to his feet at the last moment.

"Kill him!" Blue Plumage screamed behind him. He thought he caught a glimpse of Stub Tongue moving her hands in a spell gesture, but he ignored her. His allies would handle the akkoans. If not, well, he was dead either way.

New heads tried to reach Ty as he closed in. He'd gotten within their close range though and their necks, however flexible, could not easily target him any longer. Jumping to reach, Ty slapped his palm against the gem in the center of the hydra's chest.

Get this fucker, he thought, releasing the first soul he could reach into the gem. To his surprise, multiple souls pushed into the gem at the same time.

The hydra went berserk.

Rolling over onto its side, the creature just managed to get a head close enough to slam Ty away from the body. Moving on instinct, he rolled toward the second Hydra.

A crocodilian head snapped out, teeth puncturing Ty's robe and into the flesh beneath as it lifted him into the air. It shook him side to side like a dog worrying a rat, flesh tearing in bursts of agony.

His hit point display was flashing red. He didn't dare give it any attention.

"Little daughter, allow me to teach you something," Cleozun's roar somehow filtered in over the battlefield. Ty didn't see what happened, but he heard a bellow of horror from Stub Tongue. Bone fragments flew. What looked like multiple ribs directly impaled the hydra holding Ty in the face. One of its eyes burst and the head relaxed enough for him to apply a gauntlet-enhanced punch directly to its mouth. It finally released him.

Stumbling, Ty pushed past several of the heads, each impaled with dozens of bone fragments. Panting, he leaped and touched the second Hydra's mind gem.

Go! Ty thought, unleashing more of his soul reserve before he fell back to the ground and rushed away.

A stray leg kicked him again, this time pulping one of his knees. He rolled away, coming to a stop just outside the immediate melee area.

Darkness flooded the edges of his vision and he frantically funneled the worst of the pain into his Mind Fortress. Taking the edge off allowed him to think through the bone-crushing damage he'd suffered. Abstract concept or not, when he glanced down at his character overview and saw his hit points at one, he absolutely agreed. He activated Verdant Touch.

Just in time for Orange Plumage to throw a dagger at him.

It hit his robe with bruising force but deflected off the still-functioning protections. A small burst of energy from the dagger traveled through his body despite the deflection, making his teeth ache. Some of the burst entered his prism, where it renewed his mana. The rest just caused more damage.

"Fuck you," Ty growled through gritted teeth, trying to climb to his feet. The akkoan Vat Master had four arrows still sticking out of his body. Electric blue hues danced around the shafts, suggesting that they'd been enchanted prior to use in battle. Despite the damage, Orange Plumage still had the strength to rush toward him.

Chanting rose behind Orange Plumage. He continued, ignoring the threat, despite the surge of magic clear in the arrows impaling his chest. His head exploded, showering Ty with gore.

Cleozun, cackling, wiggled her claw-tipped fingers in Ty's direction. *I'm out of mana now*, she sent through the interface, not letting the fact show in her posturing.

Thanks for the save, Ty sent back.

He looked around, trying to get his bearings.

Both hydras continued to thrash around, the spirits he had unleashed upon them fighting for control. None of the humans were standing. Theontsu and his men had carved through the rabble like meat through a grinder. To his disgust and dismay, twisted coils of viscera twitched out of their host bodies and snaked away on the ground. The bears hadn't acted out, neither attacking nor defending their owners. A demon-possessed akkoan, one of Theontsu's rangers, he thought, stood near the group, hands outstretched. Little wisps of magic wafted from between her fingers and toward the bears.

Of the akkoan Vat Masters, four were dead. Violet Plumage was on the ground, still breathing but unconscious. Uneth stood over him, the bloody hilt of one of his new swords in one hand, confusion in his posture.

Blue Plumage was missing.

"Where did the leader go?" Ty called out to Uneth, searching for him frantically amidst the bodies. There wasn't much left of the akkoan Vat Masters' crew. Other than the thrashing hydras, the ambush had gone off near-perfectly.

"Teleportation spell, like the one you described the assassin using," Uneth replied. He bent down and pressed his hand to Violet's neck before standing and sheathing his sword. "Got this one, though."

"Well, that's going to bite us in the ass," Ty said sourly. He wondered how much Blue would be able to tell his god about the ambush. Certainly, the army wouldn't know Ty had triggered his possession ability on the hydras, would it?

"Not as much as that is going to bite *them* in the ass," Cleozun said from nearby, cackling and hooking a finger back toward the two hydras.

One had gone completely still, the possession a failure, and the souls lost along with the hydra's life. The other stood, its nest of heads weaving in a complex pattern. One of the heads opened its jaws and, with effort, spoke akkoan in a voice that sounded like a squealing avalanche.

"This feels weird."

Chapter 36: Questions

Days Remaining in Cycle: 12

Congratulations! *You have killed a level 5 Vat Master. Would you like to loot the corpse? If so, where would you like the loot deposited?*

Congratulations! *You have killed an Ascended, Demonic Hydra. Would you like to loot the corpse? If so, where would you like the loot deposited?*

"They didn't have Mind Fortresses," Cleozun said afterward. She, Ty, Uneth, and Theontsu stood together next to the road as the other akkoans piled the human corpses in a mound.

Oddly, Ty felt no remorse at killing the Vat Master. Seeing the corpses of humans didn't bother him either. *Are you doing that?* he sent to Hagemi.

A little. The rest is you.

Me? How?

There are consequences to being possessed. There are consequences to sharing the values of another species. You may not consciously realize just how changed you are, Ty, but you are. Working with akkoan memories will only accelerate those changes and magnify them.

That sounds bad.

Think of the books of prophecy Ty. Think about the men and women of your world who go to war. Does anyone in your type of situation, even in authors' dreams, remain unchanged?

Well, no. That doesn't mean I won't need therapy when I get home.

"What do you mean, they don't have Mind Fortresses?" Theontsu asked, pulling Ty from his reverie.

Cleozun bent over one of the akkoan bodies and held her hand out. "There is much magic, yes. More than you might expect. They look akkoan, but on the inside I suspect very little is. Even their minds have been bent sharply. But there is no Mind Fortress." She paused, hesitated a beat, then continued, "Also, these are children. Each has barely seen twenty years."

"Children who were warped and stuffed with power. It sounds like something a lesser god would do," Uneth said. One of his hands slid down to his hip, hovering over his sword.

"I have often wondered what happened to those who crossed the bridge," Theontsu said. "A few of the other races crossed, as must have many of our people. Did some of our cousins bring betrayal with them and help give birth to the Monster God, perhaps?"

Cleozun said, "An interesting theory. I like it. We murdered the old world's gods, but maybe a tainted few realized that they could create new ones here. A few hundred, with enough time, might have been able to shape a culture and give birth to a god tailored in their image."

"That might explain the books I found in Sanctuary," Ty said.

"Indeed," Cleozun responded approvingly.

"How does that lead to them having no Mind Fortresses, though?" Uneth added.

"Let's ask him," Ty said, indicating Violet. He walked over and rummaged through the unconscious Vat Master's belongings until he found one of the black vials. It was nearly empty.

Is that enough?

Yes, Hagemi replied.

Ty pocketed the vial and touched Violet's chest, triggering Verdant Touch and using Monstrous energy.

A sing-song chant came with the tainted mana. *Taint and warp. Twist and bind. Bring them all together. Make them mine. Worship me. Worship me. Be mine.* The voice teased the back of his mind, but he ignored it. There were enough things in his head for one more voice to matter little.

Violet's body shook and his eyes opened, rapidly focusing on Ty's face. His hand snapped up, clawed fingers wreathed in darkness as they slashed out.

Uneth's sword intercepted the hand, the flat of his blade clicking against Violet's nails. "I would not were I you," Uneth said.

Violet's eyes widened as he stared at Uneth. "How is it that you speak the language of your masters?"

With a gesture and a snarled command, Cleozun clenched her fist. The energy surrounding Violet's hand vanished, and she staggered in place, raising a hand to her head. It was the first time Ty had ever seen the mage react to a spell that way.

"His god is mighty within him," she said, hissing the words and taking a few steps away to sit on the ground. "That took all of my mana. It shouldn't have."

Violet sneered. "Little demon, do you not remember? Perhaps your kind are too simple. Our god *ate* yours. We are doubly blessed. It's impressive you managed even that cantrip against one such as I."

"Oh yeah?" Ty said. Bending down, he touched Violet's leg and activated Verdant Touch again. Prismatically Celestial energy ripped through the Vat Master's limb, making it jump. The flesh beneath his pants rippled as he screamed in agony.

"Stop! Stop! Please stop!" Violet sobbed, all bravado immediately vanishing from his demeanor.

"He really is a child. I've heard spoiled kids on my world use that whining tone," Ty said, standing and looking from Uneth to Cleozun.

Uneth gave him a level look. "That was Celestial energy you used, wasn't it?" When Ty nodded, he continued, "You just used the power of a rival god against him. Be reasonable with your expectations."

"No, he's right," Cleozun said, still sitting. Addressing Violet, she said, "Tells us what we want to know, or it'll be his power we use to wring the answers from you." She gestured to Ty.

It shocked Ty to be the focus of the mage's threat. He'd known that his prismatic ability was useful; he just hadn't realized *how* useful it might be in situations like this. What else could the power do if he invested merits in it? His gamer brain kicked on, spinning out a thousand possibilities. It also reminded him of the possibilities that his Mind Fortress offered him, should he pursue the route of a mind-based power set. He had more options than merits at this point.

"I'll tell you what I can," Violet said, sounding genuinely terrified. "I don't know much. I'm only a junior captain."

Ty, ask him about his god eating ours, Cleozun sent through their shared interface. *It will be better coming from you.*

Ty did as the mage asked.

Violet looked around, expression becoming guarded, until Ty extended a hand in the Vat Master's direction. "Fine, it's not like it changes anything. Millennia ago, when our god was the first born on this world, the Demon Queen and her daughter arrived. They gained quite the following in a short time, but Mother was strong. She overcame both, swallowing the Queen and enslaving the daughter. She gained the demon's powers and its followers."

Uneth and Cleozun exchanged unreadable glances.

"Why does it matter?" Violet pointed at the demon-bodied akkoans. "Your kind serve and destroy. You've never given a damn about your place in the hierarchy before."

Cleozun clicked her claw-tipped fingers together. "Why do you have no Mind Fortress? Do your kind no longer use them?"

An expression of profound confusion flickered across Violet's face. "Mind Fortress? Those are forbidden to akkoans by the decree of our Mother." His suspicious expression returned. "Who are you?"

"It is not your place to question us," Uneth said. "Tell us about the army, its disposition and resources, along with reinforcements. We want every detail."

Slowly, with some reluctance, the Vat Master revealed what Ty and his allies needed to know.

Hours later, after Uneth, Cleozun, and Theontsu finished questioning and cross-questioning Violet, the group stepped away from the prisoner to talk in private.

"Is he speaking the truth?" Uneth asked Cleozun.

"He has since the beginning," the mage replied. "I would have expected duplicity from one such as he, yet his mind is oddly simple."

Speaking in his soft, unassuming voice, Theontsu said, "It is as if he is a weapon, a tool forged for one thing."

"I think that is precisely it," Uneth said.

Ty said, "From what I understand of the Monster God, it makes sense that she would warp your people so completely. I still don't understand why she sent such a small force here, though. Forgive me, Uneth, but the numbers that Vat Master gave make this sound less like an army and more of a skirmishing party. A few hundred soldiers was obviously enough to overwhelm Aquamarine and the other defenders, but if she knew what the Sanctuary was, wouldn't she be leveraging more of her power?"

"I do not believe she knows it is Sanctuary. I would guess she thinks it is something else." The mage moved her clawed hands in time with her words, using akkoan gestures to punctuate and add meaning that he couldn't catch. "Sanctuary is a life raft, a vessel of immense power and protection, particularly against the gods. No vision, no divine power will penetrate it easily. That, in and of itself, may be sufficient to intrigue her."

Ty felt a spike of alarm as he realized what he might have done by freeing the akkoans. "Did freeing your people disarm the disguise? Did I unwittingly leave Sanctuary defenseless?"

Uneth made a negative gesture. "Not even close. The passive protections require relatively little to stay active. In addition, assuming the Sanctuary uses standard akkoan architecture, there will be more battery banks below. There might be tens of thousands of other minds and souls still trapped beneath."

"Fuck that. I will free our people," Ty said the words on reflex, not thinking about them until they left his mouth. Since when had the akkoans become *his* people? They weren't. He was a human man, not some bird-thing from another planet.

"An admirable goal," Cleozun said.

"This still doesn't answer the question of why she's here or the size of her forces," Theontsu said.

The group made their way back to Violet. Their captive had been tied up and placed in a complex diagram Cleozun called a "Ward Circle" to prevent interfering magic from getting in or out. He looked profoundly uncomfortable, yet as he watched the group draw near an expression of utter contempt crept across his face.

"What now?" Violet snarled. "After hearing about the Mother's awesome plans are you prepared to back down and beg for mercy?"

"Not precisely," Ty replied wryly. "You said the initial waves of your Mother's army included these demons," he pointed to Uneth and Cleozun, "followed by a reinforcement wave once they met resistance. You've also told us that an even larger wave is being sent in a month. Do you know why that timing?"

"I already answered this. I don't know anything other than my orders."

"Tell us your orders again," Uneth said.

"At first, it was just to come here, set up a camp, and make trouble. Whenever scions come to investigate, capture and turn or kill them. A few days ago, we received word to prepare for reinforcements. Apparently, there's some sort of ruin near the center of the wood that we're supposed to take and hold for one of the elites to come inspect."

"And you know nothing about the village near here? The one filled with monsters doing experiments on Celestial blood?" Ty asked disbelievingly.

"I don't know anything about a village." Violet practically spat the words. "Mother never has just one plan. And she never reveals all to one as lowly as myself."

Cleozun clacked her fingers for Violet's attention. "What of her other plans? I do not doubt that she has many times this number of troops. Why send so few here? What else is she doing?"

Violet laughed mockingly. "Many times this number? Idiot. She has millions, perhaps billions, of followers spanning *worlds*. Even now she visits the moon. If it were not for her need to..." The akkoan's eyes bugged out as his throat collapsed into a ruin of bone and tissue. Ichor-drenched tentacles exploded from his neck and mouth, lashing out and rebounding off Cleozun's barrier. A gold-and-violet dome, paper thin, flared around the remains, the light dimming with each impact of the tentacles.

Cursing, Uneth called, "Seseun, can you help?"

The hydra, now healed thanks to Ty's Verdant Touch, lumbered over. Tail trashing, it lashed multiple heads in the direction of the dome. "Drop the shield," Seseun growled with one of its mouths. It had told them that, technically, each head had a unique intellect and personality associated with it. The cluster had agreed to go by Seseun for simplicity's sake.

Cleozun complied, making a slight gesture that disrupted the rune. The tentacles dropped in place, bunching up as if snakes were about to strike. Seseun's heads shot bolts of lightning into the tentacles, cooking them along with Violet's remains.

Backpedaling from the noxious fumes, Ty groaned. "That smells like utter ass."

"Utter ass indeed," Uneth agreed.

Theontsu, who had moved silently beside Ty, murmured, "Unclean ass, perhaps. It would take many to match that."

Despite himself, Ty laughed. A round of clicks joined soon after. It took him a moment to realize that the sound was laughter from his akkoan friends.

Once they'd calmed down, he said, "It looks like he had a self-destruct mechanism. It also seems to me that you are all going to have your hands full while I'm gone."

"The Monster God did not learn anything from us during our questioning," Cleozun said with certainty. "We will have the advantage of knowledge, resources, and organization."

Uneth agreed. "Focus on the now. We will be fine, assuming the next few days go well."

Realizing that he'd been ignoring a growing itch in the back of his mind, Ty triggered the loot prompts, pointing to the ground nearby. Another vial of black material, this one full, fell to the ground atop a neatly folded stack of hydra leather. The leather was a matte gray color, unlike the blacks and browns of the living hydra. Several robes, wands, and other magic paraphernalia populated the inventory window. He made those appear as well.

Cleozun looked from the materializing goods to Ty and back. "What is that?"

"Oh, maybe you haven't seen this yet? I have a looting ability. When I kill something, my ability triggers and I get some sort of reward for it." Stepping over to the pile, he pocketed the vial. The folded leather stacked nearly five feet tall. There was no way he would carry that anywhere. "I don't suppose we have time to get this back to the village? I don't want to waste useful resources, but I don't see how we're going to carry this anywhere with us."

"A looting ability?" Cleozun asked, walking over and casually sorting through the Vat Master's gear. She pocketed several rings and a necklace.

"One of us will carry it for now," Seseun said. One of the hydra's heads reached down, disjointed its jaws, and lifted the stack of leather experimentally. It didn't so much as strain at the weight or size of the stack.

"Mhm," Ty said. He explained a few more details about the power, carefully skirting around his suspicions that Seeker had tampered with Hagemi to ensure he got both the black dagger and the Mind Fortress. As he did, Cleozun directed one of the other akkoans to collect the remaining gear.

"I'll need to check it for corruption before we go anywhere, but these will help," she explained at Ty's dubious expression.

When he finished, Uneth looked at Ty, mouthparts working. "Ty, why haven't you coordinated with us better? You could have been landing the final blow on a lot more of our enemies."

Ty flushed. "Oh. I hadn't thought of that, I guess."

Sunset's first hues burgeoned on the horizon. "We should prepare for the night. Our ceremonies will come due soon," Uneth announced.

They made a simple camp, around which Cleozun erected spells of sound dampening. She put an extra layer of wards around Ty's sleeping bag. As he lay beneath the stars, thinking about the day, Ty couldn't hear the tormented screams of his companions. If he looked, he could see them thrashing about, though. Every time he began to fall asleep, the hydra would stomp or shoot a stream of lightning into the sky.

Eventually, Ty knew, the insanity of his akkoan allies would become their downfall. Unless he could do something about it.

Interlude Five: Things to Come

Surviving Earth Participants: 17,041

    Average Level: 5.5

Days Remaining in Cycle: 11

"We all know what the Monster God is planning," Inspiration announced to the gathered gods.

At his statement, the divinities each looked around and shifted to make distance from one another. Tension filled the air, palpable and dangerous. Had the Great Arbiter not enforced the agreement, many of the gods would have left or taken direct action.

Balance spoke over the tortured silence. "We must accelerate the timetable if we are to retain anything of value in the coming years."

A few gods indicated agreement. Most showed uncertainty.

There was no talk of treaties or alliances. Each god thought they knew what would happen next, and none would speak new lies. With her disappearance and the revelation of traitors amongst them, it was only a matter of time before the war began.

Chapter 37:
Breather

Days Remaining in Cycle: 11

Ty woke at dawn with a sense of dread. The previous day had gone well. Other than the hydras nearly ripping him apart, things had gone better than he would have hoped. They knew the disposition of the enemy, which gave them a tremendous advantage.

Would that be enough, though?

He looked through his notes, face pressed close to the papers to make out his scribble in the gray morning light. His akkoan assets were on one list, the enemy on the other. Objectively, he thought the fight looked balanced. Oh, it wouldn't be balanced for *him*. He was still level three and had limited combat abilities.

Ty had known coming into this world that guns would be his biggest advantage. Distance was key when monsters could bite, claw, or just touch him to death. He'd gone from being a marksman to a brawler in a handful of days, and with a few achievements. His progression was a pinball. Marksman, druid, necromancer or whatever that class was Cleozun had mentioned, and now Monk-paladin. Yet he excelled at none of them.

In the fights ahead, Ty knew he was likely to be a liability.

Tucking the notes away, he slipped from his sleeping bag and looked around. Most of the akkoans had slept where they fell, after their nightly ceremony had exhausted their demon bodies. A few, mostly Theontsu's rangers, were up and greeted him perfunctorily when they saw him join them.

The sun slid over the horizon, rays of light striking through the air and reflecting a thousand rainbow-hued fractals through the blue-black sky. Two moons loomed, nearly aligned, as a distant flock of small, amethyst-colored flying creatures swept into complex formations. Nearby, several akkoans had come to their feet and begun a morning ritual. Using their new equipment, the warriors drew weapons and began to dance. Despite their unfamiliar, insectoid bodies with their strange joints and chitin, the akkoan spirits made the motions as haunting as a melody and as breathtaking as a poem.

His breath caught.

A few minutes into the rituals, Cleozun and three of her nascent cadre joined the dancers. Positioning their hands a few feet apart, they summoned colorful light into their limbs and moved in patterns that reminded Ty of Taekwondo.

As horrible as their nightly insanity was, this was the opposite.

Most akkoans lived lives dedicated to a simple pursuit of perfection, taking the time to master a single skill before passing the knowledge to the next generation. When they died, their Mind Fortresses became a living memory, a persistent voice to guide and inform whoever came next. Their spirits joined with nature, giving their children comfort and advice until they finally merged with the bodies of some fortunate newborn. Each generation of akkoan was wiser and more capable than the previous one. Seeing them in action, seeing the beauty in who they were, Ty felt hope blossom, pushing back the doubt.

Then something inside him, somewhere between the Mind Fortress and where Hagemi lived, stirred. A voice that was his, but was not, growled. *She took our children. She twisted them.*

Hope blossomed in Ty's chest that morning, and with it came renewed determination. Accompanying both was fire, a flame forged of unknown elements, yet clearly possessed of one defining characteristic: righteous rage.

"Shall I boil water for your coffee ceremony?" Cleozun said later, joining him by his tent.

"I'd appreciate that very much, Cleozun," Ty said, searching for the politeness that had been his go-to when he'd first come to this world. The morning's revelations had reminded him of this world's beauty. He wouldn't lose that, just because some parts of it made him angry.

He completed his morning ritual, drinking his coffee and securing his gear. The Ward Robe was in tatters but, miraculously, still worked. After sketching an outline of the tasks ahead of him, he joined the akkoan leadership near the center of their camp.

"We completed this mission faster than expected. It may be wise for us to return to the village before going to assault the enemy encampment," Uneth said. He sounded uncertain, looking at Ty to make the call.

"We need to think about the future, the one after this engagement," Ty said. "I'll be gone for three subjective years, which means we should shore up your numbers and resources as much as possible beforehand. All we need is a monster army to come at the wrong time, and half our numbers could be lost in a single raid."

"What are you thinking?" Cleozun asked.

"I think we go on now, ahead of schedule. We scout and," he nodded at the hydra, "if we can take advantage of our victory here, we push forward. The sooner we can be done with the encampment, the more time we'll know we can dedicate to preparing for the times ahead."

Uneth said, "I can send a messenger to Omendine to let him know. If we take our time and are cautious in our approach, our reinforcements will need two, maybe three, days to join us."

Ty said, "That way, if we decide to stay put, they can join us for a decisive push?"

"Just so," Uneth said.

"Delaying a day for on-site scouting seems wise to me," Theontsu added.

Ty looked at the mage. "Cleozun, unless you object, I say we execute on this plan immediately."

"I'll never object to determined action. Well, if it's stupid, I will."

Ty, you're level three now, Hagemi said later as they began their circuitous journey to the enemy fortification. They were moving through the high bush, keeping low and favoring caution over speed.

I'll assign the attribute points later. We're holding onto any merits I earned. Did I earn the full three, by the way? He hadn't checked yet. He wanted time to plan before he made any long-term commitments.

Of course. As far as I'm concerned, you've earned your full bonus merits for the next level or two. I'm not sure if Inspiration will allow me to do such a thing.

Check with him. It'll help me plan.

I will. He seems... occupied right now. Expect a delay.

* * *

They made good time to the enemy encampment, arriving a few hours before night. The scent of the ocean and the sounds of distant waves grew throughout the day, cresting to a near-constant hum by the time they arrived at their destination. When the first enemy scouts came into view, Theontsu and his men led the body of Ty's assault group away from the grasses and into the nearby forest.

A couple of sprites blinked, greeting their arrival, but there was no sign of Aquamarine or the dryads. Despite the relative thinness of the wood close to the ocean, they found a dense enough patch to cloak the nearly sixty-strong party. Seseun had a harder time navigating the forest while keeping as low a profile as the hulking hydra could, but when no one came to investigate, Theontsu decided they'd been cautious enough.

Once they were in concealment, Theontsu and the rangers under his command who could become invisible started climbing trees. Cleozun and three she'd recruited into her newly minted cabal set aside a space to cast spells and draw runes into the rocky dirt.

"I'm going to peek," Ty said.

"Hrm. Maybe not wise. Stay low and behind trees if you must," Uneth replied.

Wise or not, Ty wasn't about to stay idle while his allies did all the work. He wanted to see for himself. He made his way through the wood until it thinned, then crouched and eased forward until he could see the enemy camp.

The closest of the enemy fortifications was a little over two football fields, maybe six hundred feet, away from the forest. Framed by partially constructed earthen walls that would have been barely chest high to Ty, he could see into the camp with little trouble. Using his goggles and upping the magnification, he started making notes in the margins of his cleanest pad.

There were a lot of humans, many of which had been transformed into grotesque nightmares. Men and women with bone growths or extra limbs ambled through the area aimlessly. Sometimes the humans bumped into each other and fought, mindlessly ripping and tearing into each other.

A Flesh Weaver oozed into view, tentacles lashing out at a corpse, collecting the tissue to add it to another combatant. Over time, Ty guessed, the army would thin out, leaving the strongest alive to attack the forest.

Based on what Violet had told them, Ty knew that the back half of the camp was down a deceptively sharp slope, where it ended at the hydra cote. There were four more hydras in camp, along with several powerful demons and monsters, none of which were in view from his vantage. He did see the three vats, however. Each vat was about the circumference of a luxury hot tub, and boiling, tarry liquid bubbled from within the blackened metal confines. Ladders hooked over the rim of each vat, the handles smeared with grime and blood.

Without the Vat Masters there, no one was near the vats. They were a perfect target.

Frowning, confused at the lack of active protection measures, Ty kept low and made his way back to camp. He arrived just before dark, minutes before the nightly ritual. Cleozun, who had finished her magical scouting with her cabal, was already erecting barriers against sound when he arrived. He thought she looked relieved to see him, but he couldn't be sure. Insect faces were hard to read.

"They seem rather poorly organized. I didn't see any scouts or guards. There weren't any demons or monsters around, either," Ty told Uneth.

"We'll talk more in the morning, but I believe I know where the missing creatures are," Uneth replied. He pointed at the skyline, indicating that time was tight.

Ty nodded and moved to a private spot, allowing one of Cleozun's new assistants to cast the extra layer of soundproofing for him. Tonight, of all nights, he was not inclined to stay awake listening to the mad gibbering of his allies.

Once he bedded down, Ty checked his character sheet for changes.

Level: 3

Hit Points: 11

Health Shield (Lesser): 16

Mana: 18

Mana Shield: 9

Unspent Merits: 6

Unspent Physical Attribute Points: 2

Unspent Discretionary Attribute Points: 2

Hagemi, if I increase my Intelligence score, what will happen?

Hagemi stirred, waking for the first time in hours. *You'll think faster, remember things with greater detail. You'll also be able to process and learn more quickly. It'll make anything you do with your Mind Fortress easier. It will not improve your intuition or increase your mana.*

How much faster will I learn with another two points?

Instead of six subjective hours per real time hour, it'll increase to seven.

Let's say, in theory, I wanted some ability that let me do two things simultaneously. You know, like that spell in the old gaming days that allowed a spellcaster to do two mental actions at once? Is there an intelligence score I'd need to do that?

Hrm. Probably around twenty-five. Or you could spend three or four merits, depending on the details of your request.

Okay, new question. Is there any good reason to take my Spirit score higher, other than mana?

Not yet. Any future powers you get that are based on a connection to a deity will rely on it, though. If you go full-on Paladin in the traditional sense, smiting things and what-not, you'll want that score as high as possible. It may also help your Spirit Cage.

How would a higher Spirit score help that? You described it as an airlock, if I remember correctly.

Airlock. Filter. Shaping mechanism. It's an esoteric construct. The higher your Spirit score, the more attuned you will become to the Cage. Using abstract powers, including communicating with the spirits inside you, will become easier. There are other benefits, naturally. A higher Spirit score will make your Wild abilities increasingly potent and efficient. Not that you necessarily want that.

Why wouldn't I want that?

The Wild isn't a mortal power. It has no human minds to guide it, no mortal worshippers to give it boundaries. Empowering it is likely to pull you in unpredictable directions. It could even influence the souls in you.

Wait, you said it would change my Spirit Cage. Are you implying that the Cage and the akkoan spirits are interacting in some tangible way?

To some degree, they must be. I cannot detect how or why. The Wild is difficult to read or detect, even bonded to you as I am.

Could the Wild allow them to escape? Could one of the spirits possess me again, if it wanted to?

Remember, you have developed abilities to mitigate that. Without their minds to drive them, your Soul Cage probably feels like paradise compared to their previous habitation. I doubt any of them would do so, unless strongly triggered, or summoned. It would be possible, I imagine. Perhaps another scion could summon one, temporarily overriding your sense of self. It would not happen naturally, however. Oddly, I don't remember how this all came about. Do you?

Ah, no. I have no clue. Ty suspected it was the Seeker who had arranged much of what had happened with the spirits now, though he had no way to be certain. Even if the ancient god had interfered, he couldn't have known his choices or the outcome of his possession. Thinking of the deity rolling the dice with his fate made him shudder.

For all he respected, even felt a degree of worship, toward the god, Ty didn't trust him.

He was torn about his attribute points. Increasing his spiritual connection to Inspiration felt like a good idea, despite his Arbiter's warnings. His bursts of intuition, while infrequent, were overwhelmingly positive. Plus, the more mana he had, the more he could use later if he gained new abilities or spells. He felt confident that Cleozun had a pool of *hundreds* of mana, based on his glimpses at the spell-casting minds in his Mind Fortress. On the other hand, he was about to enter a period where adapting and learning new skills could be the difference between life and death. Being able to summon the memories of long dead akkoans and gain even a small measure of their abilities could be huge, especially if he could shorten the time it took to do so.

He put two points into his Vitality, bringing it to a ten. He instantly felt healthier and heartier and saw his hit points jump from eleven to fourteen. The attribute was still rated as "normal," but he now received a plus one bonus per level. His health shield likewise increased from sixteen to twenty-one.

Seeing the physical improvements made Ty breathe easier. He didn't doubt that every fight on Volar would be deadly, regardless of what his "hit points" said, but the increased vitality felt rejuvenating and powerful in a way that simply increasing his strength hadn't.

After more contemplation, he put his two discretionary points into his Intellect score. When the score slid to thirteen, the description labeled it as "Standard High IQ." Unlike Vitality, increasing his intelligence didn't make him feel radically different. Maybe his thoughts were clearer or a little faster, but he wasn't certain.

Ty didn't spend his merits. He planned to have more conversations with Hagemi before committing to further purchases. The sheer flexibility and limitations of his class kept him from charging in, particularly when he knew he was about to lock in his progression for a while.

Making plans around his merits kept him occupied late into the night. With both moons high in the sky, illuminating clouds and dimming the impressive clusters of colorful stars, he saw two flying shapes pass overhead. The twisting heads told him what they were. He held his breath, waiting to see one of them swoop down to inspect their camp. Neither did.

Seeing them scouting convinced Ty that he needed to act sooner than later. Had he possessed an invisibility power or some similar advantage, he might have sneaked off in the night and tried something reckless. Instead, he turned his phone back on. It was down to forty-three percent power, despite having been off for days. He made sure the phone was on airplane mode. The battery indicator said it had a day and a half of charge left at the current usage. Confident he wouldn't need it the next day, he set an early alarm and went to sleep.

If he had his way, they'd assault the encampment at first light.

* * *

Ty woke in darkness. Groggy and aching from sleeping on the ground, he activated his Verdant Touch. He was getting an intuitive grasp on the ability and didn't rely on Hagemi's help to gently "pulse" the power through his body. It refreshed him, consuming one point of mana to finish what sleep hadn't accomplished. Renewed and rejuvenated, he put his goggles on.

Alone in his tent, he let his fingertips trail across the insides of his forearm, then his thigh. He thought about the people he cared about, the virtual friends he'd met online and the new ones he'd only recently discovered. Describing the gently upraised outline of tattooed scar tissue, he remembered the phrases he'd placed on his body. Each was a promise.

Always find light. If there is none, become *the light. Embrace fear, and let it flow through you. Plan slowly, implement decisively. Save lives.*

Feeling the words, Ty went over his plan. His notes were full, every one of the little squares of paper completely inked in. This plan was only in his head. It made him uncomfortable. Centering himself on the bigger picture, on who he wanted to be, settled his heart.

A thought struck him, and he asked his Arbiter, *Hagemi, will the scars fade with healing?*

Yes. In time.

I guess I'll just have to get them reapplied when that happens.

Ty checked his gear, dressed, and left his tent.

Akkoan guards, standing outlined in green, waved at him as he made his way around the camp. He paused, recalling his plan, then mentally adjusted it. Making his way to each guard, he applied Verdant Touch to them, washing away their fatigue and the wounds from the past night's "meditation" ceremony.

"Wake everyone up," he whispered to the first of the guards, who went to work without questioning his orders.

Marveling at the oddity of beings of such age and experience listening to him, Ty continued on his rounds. Over the next half hour, he refilled his mana from his Celestial canteen multiple times as he rejuvenated everyone. Once Cleozun was up and moving, she helpfully cast a spell of night vision which she casually declared would, "last a couple weeks, as long as you're not stupid."

"Whatever that means," Ty retorted, then addressed the gathered akkoan leaders. "I want to attack them soon. Now, if possible, do you have any reason we shouldn't?"

Uneth looked in the direction of the enemy army. "If their demons are like us, they will be most restful now. I would assume the humans would be, too. Attacking at this time, if not today, makes sense to me."

Ty said, "I saw two hydras flying above late last night. I assume they were scouting or out for a hunt. If so, they will probably be exhausted by the time they get back."

"My scouts found the missing demons and monsters," Theontsu said. "They are near the rear of the encampment, on the other side of the vats, close enough to guard them. There aren't a lot of them, maybe a total of a hundred combined creatures, but they look formidable. At least a dozen of the monsters are branded with runes of power, and several of the demons have etched the same on their chitin. I expect spellcasters, too."

"We need to know if they are asleep or not," Ty said. He looked at Cleozun. "Can you tell?"

She made a negating gesture. "We found many layers of wards around the camp yesterday, piecemeal, and poorly constructed, but strong. Any scrying I do that far in will set off alarms."

"Shit," Ty said. "We need to know if they are asleep and if the hydras I saw are back, and we need to know now."

Theontsu looked at Cleozun. "I am in a demon's body. Perhaps the wards will not respond. Can you help guarantee that?"

"Not without a day or two to experiment. Speed is the best I can offer. Maybe make your invisibility slightly better. Not much more."

Theontsu looked from Ty to Uneth and back. "I am willing to risk it."

"What do you think?" Ty asked Uneth. "What does your military background tell you?"

Uneth's sigh whistled through his mandibles. "It tells me that attacking early, with surprise, can lead to the greatest victory. It also tells me that countering such an ambush can turn the tide of a war in the opponent's favor."

Ty read nuance in Uneth's body language and tone, an unspoken hesitation. Uneth's insanity haunted him, making it difficult for the akkoan to behave decisively. He remembered the man's red-colored status. It still displayed "Fractured" when he checked it. The general's projected calm concealed vast trauma.

A gentle bobbing light flared nearby, drawing his attention away from the conversation. There was a colorful flash near the sprite and Aquamarine appeared out of the shadows, Omendine on his back. The dragon was carrying half a dozen small casks in its arms.

"You're lucky I adore you," Aquamarine declared, luminous eyes focused on Ty.

Omendine snorted as he slid from the dragon to the ground. The llama-man landed lightly, knees flexing in a posture that looked like something out of a superhero movie. "He's lucky that I found someone in camp to help me build my fences, otherwise I wouldn't have offered to come with you."

"Why are you here?" Uneth asked.

"Because I know everything that happens in my forest," Aquamarine replied, still looking at Ty. "I know when one of my allies is planning something reckless and heroic."

Ty felt himself flush. "How are the sloths? Are there more soldiers coming?"

"Still not well," Omendine said. "And your soldiers were willing, but Aquamarine cannot bring them. His magic takes time to reset."

"At best I can bring another eight, which I will do if you are determined on this course of action," Aquamarine finished.

"To pair some good with the bad, we found a recipe that works with the Celestial blood." Omendine patted one of the casks Aquamarine set on the ground. Reaching into a pouch at his hip, he extracted a pinch of fine material that looked like hair. "On a whim, I tried mixing in some of the lynx fur with the mixture. Turns out, the fur acts as a stabilizing medium, soaking up more of the blood and adhering to the blades or whatever, even better than expected."

Those cats are definitely not called lynxes, Ty thought to Hagemi.

Would you prefer you hear them called hxyundondils instead? That is a much closer approximation to their true names.

Um, no, lynx is fine for now.

"You used the innate properties of lynx fur to act as a sponge for Celestial blood? That's brilliant!" Cleozun clucked, shuffling in place with glee.

Amused, Ty mentally labeled it her happy dance.

Omendine popped one of the casks open, saying, "It was honestly part my idea and part Meridian's. When she's able to focus, that woman is an absolute genius with this stuff. May I have an arrow please? I'll need to demonstrate."

Theontsu passed him an arrow, which Omendine dipped in the cask. When he pulled it out, the tip gleamed as a thin, mucus-like fluid leeched back into the container. "We mixed the adhesive in with the blood directly, rather than using water. As you can see, it does work, just not for long."

Sliding the arrowhead against the cask's rim to scrape the material from the blade, he dipped several of the hairs into the solution and pressed those against the metal. They stuck. After a few seconds, he dipped the arrowhead back into the solution. When he withdrew it the second time, the hairs seemed visibly thicker, as if they'd absorbed some of the material in the casks. Anywhere the hairs weren't stuck, the metal continued to drip the solution normally.

He handed the arrow to Theontsu, who began testing its new balance. "The hair and solution add a bit of weight, not much. On a standard sword or dagger, you'll probably need to reapply regularly, say once in every two or three hits. If your opponent is exploding from the strikes, I doubt anyone will mind."

Ty made a mental note to be careful if he used the solution in close combat. He didn't have chitin protecting his skin.

"I don't suppose you can tell us if the monsters and demons are asleep or not?" he asked Aquamarine hopefully. He didn't want to send Theontsu in there, especially if they didn't know if the wards would detect his akkoan spirit.

"I'm afraid not."

Ty nodded, figuring that would be the case. "I vote Theontsu scouts, with Cleozun's enhancements on him. That will give us time to coat arrowheads and distribute the mixture to our people. If he has good news, we strike now and do our best to cripple the enemy ahead of any reinforcements. If it's bad, we'll regroup." He looked toward the still-sleeping Seseun, the one ally he had not been brave enough to wake. "If they are asleep, I want to give them a rude awakening."

A few minutes later, an enchanted Theontsu moved as a blur into the enemy encampment, effortlessly bypassing the makeshift walls. They were lucky. None of the protective wards went off.

While the ranger was gone, Ty roused Seseun. Without a supply of food for the possessed demon's body, he had to use his Verdant Touch to energize the demon. He'd spent all his mana twice getting Seseun to a point of satiation, making him briefly consider rethinking their whole strategy of bombing the enemies with Celestial blood. While he was the main healer of the army, he'd need sources to recharge his mana far more frequently than he would have alone.

No doubt the remaining barrels of Celestial blood would be worth their weight in gold in the upcoming years.

Theontsu returned shortly after Ty had restored his mana. As they'd hoped, the camp was asleep. Better yet, all four hydras were accounted for.

It was time for him to tell them the rest of his plan.

Chapter 38: Early Assault

Days Remaining in Cycle: 9

Ty drew a rough map on the ground. He placed three rocks in the middle, a twig near the back, and then a few acorns to the left of the twig. "Okay, first, we're the berries."

"That's just outside the south wall?" Uneth asked.

"Yup," Ty said, grabbing an acorn and moving it to the twig. "This is Seseun carrying me." He dropped the acorn on top of the stick, then hovered his hand over the rocks. "This is Seseun throwing three casks into the vats."

He nudged the acorn pile forward in the direction of the twig, while rolling the Ty acorn back out to meet them. "See, you come in and save me after I convert the sleeping hydras," he explained, scooting the gathered acorns back away from the encampment. "This way, we deal with the hydras and get out before anything bad happens."

Omendine looked at Ty flatly. Uneth, Theontsu, and Cleozun didn't look much more amused.

"You want to risk your life to take out the hydras, is that what we're getting at?" Omendine said.

"Don't forget the vat explosions," Ty said.

Cleozun's mouth parts moved in an expression like a frown. "Actually, the plan could work. If the one who escaped alerts others, we could be hours from emergency reinforcements arriving. This might be our one chance to deal with the hydras."

Omendine sighed, looking imploringly at Uneth.

Uneth ignored the traesap's expression, gesturing instead at the makeshift map on the ground. "This is a bold plan. I've seen something similar before. I believe it has two major flaws."

"Please, go ahead."

"First, you put yourself in overwhelming danger. The hydras will wake when one thrashes, if not sooner. And there may be handlers nearby. Even a novice military leader would protect their greatest assets. Second, you're not using Theontsu or his rangers properly."

Ty gave Uneth a reassuring smile. "Awesome. I agree. Give me a solution."

"I uh, I am not sure," Uneth said, head jerking as if seeing too many possibilities to make any one decision.

"We don't have time for this," Ty said, stepping to Uneth. Reaching up, he put his hands on either side of the demonic head, turning Uneth to look at him. It was his first time out of combat making intimate contact with one of the demons. Their skin was smooth, almost waxy, and warm. "Uneth, I know it's hard. I know it hurts. I need you to take a deep breath and concentrate. Sometimes it's not about making the best choice; it's about making the one in front of you. I'm going to be gone for years. I need you to step up."

Uneth's shoulders shook, and he pulled away from Ty, his body language radiating shame. "I cannot."

Stepping between Ty and Uneth, Omendine held a furry hand out to each of them. "I will help with this, yes? Uneth, relax. This is what you hired me for."

Frustrated and heartbroken for his ally, Ty nodded to Omendine.

"We know that Theontsu can get past the wards," Omendine said, using a stick to point at the hydra cote. "We have twelve surviving rangers with invisibility powers, not including Theontsu. Five will go in first, killing any guard around the hydras. After we're relatively certain there is no ambush, they will retreat out of the theoretical blast radius." He tapped the space behind the hydra den, then made a rolling circle around the area of the vats. "While the first group is acting, the remaining seven, along with Theontsu, will locate the Flesh Weavers in the enemy encampment. Once the vats explode, the rangers will attack as one."

Omendine paused, looking to Theontsu, who made a gesture of agreement.

"The rest of the plan goes as Ty suggested. We will sweep in from the back, protecting Ty and any hydras he's possessed. If the enemy gets their footing, we exit the encampment and retreat to the forest where Aquamarine and any allies the dragon has brought to us will be waiting."

From where he hunched, Uneth said, "A brilliant plan. I could not have done better."

"You do see the flaw, though, don't you?" Omendine said.

"No true fallback. No support," Uneth whispered.

"Mhm. Ty, if we do this, it's all in. I'll stay back with Aquamarine and one or two others, just to keep our supply of Celestial blood safe, but this could go to shit fast. Are you sure you want to do this?"

Ty's earlier doubts threatened to surface. Memories of his past, his youth, where he'd made stupid mistakes out of confidence, stirred. Promising himself to restore them after the battle, he shoved the troublesome memories into his Mind Fortress. Clarity and confidence replaced his wavering will, leaving him to wonder why he hadn't excised more of his memories before now.

Allowing a hint of the rage he felt toward the Monster God to enter his voice, Ty said, "I am certain."

* * *

Hit Points: 14

Health Shield (Lesser): 21

Mana Shield: 9

Mana: 17

The group left the forest minutes before dawn. Omendine stayed behind to help coordinate and observe from afar. Keeping low and moving fast, the rest of them arrived at their target in seconds. Ty's mana ticked over to full again as Theontsu and his rangers vanished into the enemy camp. Considering what he knew about Theontsu and the akkoans like them, he wondered if the Earth parallel would have been Navy SEALS. *Probably*, he decided.

"You know, as soon as Seseun gets within the sphere of their wards, they will probably go off, right?" Cleozun whispered to Ty as they waited for the scouts to signal the all-clear.

"I think I have a solution for that," Ty said. "Not that it matters much."

"Oh? What solution?"

"I'm going to pulse my Verdant Touch and change the magical nature to monstrous. I bet the wards aren't set to detect scions of the Monster God. If I'm right, I can sustain a low-effort monstrous aura for maybe a minute before my mana starts to run out."

"Have you tried that yet?" Cleozun said, sounding skeptical. "It's quite possible that the monstrous nature of the energy will harm you."

"Eh, I've experimented a bit. I kind of already do something like it during combat when I heal myself. I think it'll work. Besides, if it fails, what have we lost? A few seconds, maybe?"

Uneth seemed about to speak, but stopped. Ty didn't bother asking him to voice his opinion, not this close to the start of the mission.

"If you're sure. I don't know your powers like you do," Cleozun acceded. "It is possible that saving a few seconds will mean all the difference between securing all four hydras and death."

A scout reappeared, holding a hand up with four fingers raised. He bent and extended the fingers twice, indicating that they'd discovered and dealt with eight guards around the hydras. Uneth waved in reply, and the scout vanished.

Ty's heart rate doubled. It was time for him to go. Looking at Uneth, he said, "Go with your heart. Know that I trust you." To the rest of them, he added, "Good luck. See you in a few minutes."

He turned and sprinted away from the group, directly to the rendezvous point with Seseun. To keep the hydra's presence secret, they'd had him stay back near the wood. He found the giant demon beast waiting for him expectantly, tail and heads thrashing with excitement.

"Good to go," Ty said, and three of the hydra's heads bent down to pick up the kegs resting nearby. With a few experimental flaps of its wings, the hydra leaped into the air. He felt magical pressure accompany the leap, just before one of the demon's clawed feet wrapped around his torso and lifted him into the air.

Fear and awe warred in him for a moment before he remembered what he had to do. Seseun moved quickly, practically bee-lining to the cote. They would pass through the barrier in seconds.

Mana, Ty had discovered, was a lot like hit points. It was an abstract concept. His Arbiter might translate a "mana point" into a discreet unit of energy, but that wasn't actually true. Over the past days, with careful observation, he realized that channeling his mana was less like moving a dial and more like controlling the flow of a river. Now, flying thirty feet in the air and moving at a blistering clip, he opened the dam of his mana just enough to activate his Verdant Touch ability without fully empowering it. He turned the ability on, just didn't give it enough juice to do anything.

When he felt his Touch tingling through his skin, Ty triggered his Prism, tainting the ability with monstrous mana the instant before they crossed into the encampment.

Warning: *You have entered a Salient Barrier. This zone has been consecrated and become an extension of the Monster God's personal Domain. Some of abilities may not function normally within this area.*

A wall of power passed through his monstrously aligned body. Pain lanced through his head and seized his muscle, freezing him in place. He lost all ability to think or reason. His Touch remained, now acting without his control.

Twisted, turning against its master, his Verdant Touch became a conduit for the Monster God.

Chapter 39: Mistakes

Days Remaining in Cycle: 9

An icy voice ripped through Ty's pain. Whispering into his ear, it crackled like breaking glass. "**You, a scion of another god, extend your hand to me in my temporary Domain**?" The presence paused, tone softening in an instant to something decidedly feminine, with a hint of alluring huskiness to it. "**Well, then, I absolutely accept. Here, let me help you**."

Time slowed to a crawl. He saw the wings of the hydra flapping as it aligned with the opening of the cote. He saw the outline of the four slumbering beasts, one stirring briefly to glance up before returning to sleep.

Horrendous force latched onto his body through the speaker, sending waves of corruption and darkness directly into his veins. His skin began to blacken and pock, his stomach clenching as *things* inside him changed.

For the first time, he thought he could feel his mana shield trying to react, like a strange muscle flexing in the back of his mind. The attack bypassed the reactive nature of the shield completely.

This was good. It was perfect. Ty had been angry, and anger was a tool of power. He would be a tool of power. What was it he'd been planning to do? Ah, yes. Touch the hydras and release his spirit army into them. There was nothing wrong with that. The Mother favored strength in her scions, even if that sometimes led to a little creative infighting.

Come forth, most wicked of my spirits! We shall possess this weak flesh and make the world anew! Ty's call to the akkoans in him was a raw demand. To his delight, several dozen of the spirits within responded immediately, eagerly even. They would be his true army, once he had purified those so-called allies who survived this little skirmish.

Hagemi stirred.

Silence, little Arbiter. He is mine now. The woman's voice came from within now, soft but steadily growing in strength.

Ty fell to the crudely constructed wooden floor of the cote, health shield absorbing the damage of the fall. Confident, uncaring of whether any of the hydras woke, he walked to the first and unleashed a barrage of spirits into the beast. He felt a small piece of the corruption pouring into him flow through that bond, easing the passage. This time, the hydra did not thrash and spasm. It seemed to accept the twisting of its mind, as if such a thing was natural.

Yes, I made the demons into my pawns ages ago. After I devoured their god, they tried to rebel. But it was like fighting against themselves. How could it not be? Changing them was simple. Now they accept my power and the power of my chosen readily. You are my chosen now, scion. You will be the master of many demons. You will lead armies for me, armies against my rivals.

Ty touched another hydra, possessing it, then another. As he walked, he felt parts of his body being replaced with the Mother's blessing. His flesh was marbled black, his eyes swelling in their sockets. Pain grew continuously, yet the god's presence in him allowed him to ignore the discomfort.

I will replace this little Arbiter with my own. They foolishly gave me quite a few of them, you know? Mine are better. You will see. I am unfettered, and they do my will. Even death is no bar to my will. My scions are virtually immortal. So shall you be.

Darkness wound around Hagemi. In Ty's mental landscape, he saw the magenta and silver light growing dim as Mother pulled it away. It didn't bother him. She had shown him the truth. With a new Arbiter, as her scion, he would surpass all limits, all arbitrary and senseless rules. He wouldn't worry about hit points or mana or anything else. He'd be free.

His hand came to rest on the final hydra. As the souls spilled into the beast, one of them froze, trapped between him and the demon. Inexplicably, the soul *pulsed* in place, and Ty felt that the little entity was somehow other than what it seemed. It hadn't belonged to a deceased akkoan at all. In fact, it belonged to...

*This fucking bitch corrupted my children. I will **not** allow this!*

Seeker's voice lashed free, shattering the Monster God's hold on him. Light blazed as Hagemi snapped back into place.

Hagemi's voice crackled with overwhelming authority, loud enough Ty was certain that everyone nearby should have heard it. "This is against the pact!" The Arbiter's presence reasserted itself, pushing out the invading darkness and destroying the connection between him and the invading god.

No longer out of control, but still in overwhelming agony, Ty adjusted his Verdant Touch, removing the monstrous mana. Healing poured into his shaking, blackened body. His vitality improved, but the darkness remained until he deliberately pulsed Celestial attunement into the touch.

Fresh pain replaced the old, the pain of cleansing fire. The Celestial Touch didn't heal the damage caused by the corruption; it just left him without the taint. He'd have to heal the rest later if he had time.

From outside, there came a roar, followed by a series of deafening explosions. Ty hadn't even been that close to the vats when they'd gone up, and still a wave of heat and pressure shot *through* the cote, knocking him into the body of one of the stirring hydras.

Twelve crocodilian heads grinned down at Ty.

Only then did it occur to him that the demons, possessed by the wildest and most insane of the akkoan spirits, might not care who he was.

Figures rushed through the double doors and into the building. Showing no signs of damage from the blast, the monsters were bloated abominations, their bodies sporting pulsating tumors. Eldritch, neon-glowing runes were imbedded in their flesh like cracks in magma, spilling horrific magic into the air. Misshapen and malformed eyes stared hate at Ty as they rushed to meet him.

The nearest hydra to the entrance made a dozen sounds of wicked glee as it attacked the monsters.

It seemed, Ty thought wryly, that there was at least one benefit to almost being taken over by the Monster God.

"Does that count as her trying to possess me?" he wondered aloud, backing away from the macabre scene. The front wave of monsters had not survived the surprise hydra attack, and all four of the possessed demons growled as they rushed out to vent their rage. Sounds of carnage rocked the ground outside of the building a moment later.

Hagemi surprised Ty by appearing nearby. "Not possession, invasion. You'd have still been somewhat you when she was done."

Ty shuddered at the thought. "Thanks for the save, by the way."

"I enforced the rules, Ty. You saved you with your well-timed use of Verdant Touch and your Prism."

Ty didn't mention Seeker. Knowing that it had taken yet *another* god's influence to wake Hagemi up bothered him more than he could express. The Monster God had suppressed Hagemi entirely during their encounter. If Seeker hadn't woken the Arbiter up, Ty wouldn't be Ty anymore. As much as he knew better than to trust the ancient akkoan god, he couldn't help but feel a sense of debt to him.

Ty, are you all right? Omendine's note popped through Ty's interface.

Yes, he replied. *Is it safe to come out?*

Marginally. The four hydras have gone berserk and aren't listening to anything we say. One appears mortally wounded. They have cleared a space for you, though. The demon spellcasters were far more skilled than expected. Cleozun is totally occupied. Be careful.

Ty took a swallow from the divine-blood mana potion, giving himself the time to heal his wounds. Renewed, he drew his dagger and affixed it to his gauntlet. He made his way out slowly, aware that an ambush could strike at any moment.

The scene outside was apocalyptic. One hydra had died thirty feet from the building, several of its heads missing. Another had taken to the air and was strafing the mutated humans with breath attacks. The final two were prowling through a solid chunk of chitin-covered insectoid demons. These demons, although built with the same basic shape as the ones the akkoans possessed, looked a bit more typically evil. They were bat-winged humanoids, their bodies covered head to toe in red-glowing script. Amber gems glimmered at their throats and junctures of their wings, rather than their foreheads.

Guess I'm not possessing those, Ty thought somewhat sourly.

I believe those are Demon Hearts. Possessed of the Monster God herself. Her will is in those demons. It would take something on par to disrupt them.

Good to know.

Two hydra heads veered apart, each biting into a different demon. Both demons jerked and twisted as the hydra heads lifted them from the ground and began shaking them from side to side, prehistoric teeth grinding through chitin. Ty winced despite himself, knowing how that felt. Unlike Ty, however, the demons simply shook off the attacks. They proceeded to claw and beat at the hydras holding them.

Uneth and a dozen akkoans shot into view, charging at the demons scouring the hydras. Ty felt a moment of awe as the akkoan general *became* the epitome of death. The man's sword, dipped in Celestial blood, cut an explosive swatch through the enemy as efficiently as anything he had ever imagined.

Turning his attention from the carnage, he made his way to where Cleozun and his other allies were waiting. Stepping over several corpses, a couple of which had arrows in them, Ty spotted the distant remains of a couple of Flesh Weavers. Theontsu's men had done their jobs.

A notification flashed, and Ty accepted an incoming update from Cleozun. *Ty, we have a problem. Uneth took a group of our men into the encampment to help the hydras. They left me and the cabal with only a couple of guards. We're being battered by enemy magic and a group of demons is coming this way. We need help.*

Looking around, Ty saw three of the winged demons skirting behind the hydra cote and the back wall of the encampment, heading directly for Cleozun. He saw Uneth and the other akkoans with him far away now, dancing in a circle of demons, utterly oblivious to the mages they'd left undefended.

Chapter 40: Savage

Days Remaining in Cycle: 9

Ty waited until the demons were just ahead of him. They walked by without looking around, their blazing eyes focused entirely on the figures of Cleozun and her cabal. A dome of yellow-orange energy surrounded the akkoans, making the mages visible even as it protected them.

Once the trio had passed far enough ahead, he sprang into motion. Grabbing his remaining Celestial blood, he followed them. Keeping pace, he poured a few drops of the glowing fluid into one hand. Concentrating, he drew the liquid into the substance of the gauntlet, creating five separate beads in the material. Once the beads were in place, he mentally guided the metal to migrate the drops to the tips of each finger, which he elongated into needle-like claws. He switched hands, repeating the process with the other. When he was done, he took a mouth full of the blood, trying not to swallow.

By the time Ty had finished his preparations, the demons were nearly to Cleozun and her three fellow spellcasters. Magic warped the air around the cabal. A spear of magic shot from the distance, slamming into the golden shield surrounding the trio and sending sparks flying in every direction.

The two akkoan guards Uneth left behind had their swords drawn and moved to intercept the demons. One demon's hand flashed up, clawing a burning sigil into the air. Liquid fire melted through reality, wrapping around one of the guards' heads.

Ty sprinted at the back of the rearmost demon. He hit, black dagger ripping into the thing's back, knocking it forward and pulling the dagger free. Reaching out, he clawed at the wound, injecting Celestial blood directly into the demon. A shaped charge of charred meat and bone exploded from its back. The force of it shoved him away from the roaring demon, the sound barely audible over the ringing in his ears.

The demon, still alive, tried to backhand him away.

Another demon gestured at the second of the guards, hand raised to summon a sigil. He hesitated at the sound of Ty's attack.

The last demon glanced over his shoulder at Ty, teeth bared in a grin as he moved to pounce on the new threat.

Timed Quest: Defeat the Demon Assault Team. *You have discovered a squad of assault demons, hand-crafted and imbued by the Monster God itself. Help defeat all three.* **Reward:** *Defeating these demons will allow me to purify your mind and spiritual essence from the Monster God's lingering taint. I'll also give you some nice loot.*

The backhand connected, sending Ty flying, his health shield flaring as it absorbed most of the blow. He landed hard, swallowing some of the Celestial blood. Pain seared his veins, though he reflexively used a portion of the energy to fuel Verdant Touch.

Mind clear, body energized, he drew his gun and rushed the grinning demon, who hesitated just a moment before drawing one of the sigil-spells in the air. At ten feet, his shot didn't even require much aim. His bullet nudged the demon's hand askew, forcing one finger to claw the sigil incorrectly.

Fire erupted in the air ten feet to his left, tendrils of it lashing out. One tendril hit the demon he had knocked down with his initial attack.

Ty sprinted, closing the last few feet. The demon smirked, shrugging slightly, and extended muscular arms for him. He spit a mouth full of Celestial blood into the demon's face, jerking his armored arm up protectively as he did.

The explosion blew half the demon's face off, skin shredded to the bone. Heat lanced through Ty's forehead, cheeks, and unprotected chest. He rolled with the impact, doing his best to keep in motion.

The second demon was waiting for him. It punched both hands out, claws digging into his sides. His robe and health shield reduced the impact, transforming what would have been an evisceration into a grapple. He grunted as he felt his ribs crack. The overpowering demon chuckled as it pulled him close.

Bypassing Ty's defenses, the demon's claws dug into his dwindling health. Writhing, growling like an animal, he raked a clawed hand against the demon's neck, adding Celestial blood to the strike.

The connection between the demon's neck and head vanished in a geyser of blood. It dropped him, falling to the ground with a thud.

That's one dead, Hagemi said.

Ty recognized the warning for what it was and spun. Too late, he saw the face-melted demon drawing a new sigil in the air. Fire oozed from the sky and reached for his throat.

A sword chopped into the spellcaster's shoulder, producing a familiar bout of gore as the material coating it exploded. The demon flew one way as the sword, propelled by the explosion, tore itself from the akkoan's grasp.

That's another one.

The first demon, the one Ty had stabbed in the back, moved quietly nearby. Ty hadn't even noticed it casting the spell until it was too late. A solid bar of fire twelve feet long and three inches wide, appeared in the air at chest-height and shot into him and the akkoan soldier, knocking both over and crisping the front of his already shredded robe.

Ty was about to activate his Verdant Touch but didn't have time. A new figure appeared nearby, appearing when its invisibility dropped. Like some sort of sci-fi cloaking device lowering before attack, the air pulsed around the person as gloved hands drew foul shapes into the air. Compared to the elite demon's crude sigils, these looked elegant and precise.

A hook of midnight and purple light shot from the robed caster and imbedded itself into the akkoan warrior who'd rescued Ty. At the impact, a duplicate version appeared within Cleozun's protective shell, winding around one of the three other spellcasters. The cloaked mage made a gentle yanking gesture, like reeling in a fish. The akkoan's demon body turned inside out, melting and exploding simultaneously. So did the mage in the circle.

Ty felt the backblast of magic from the robed figure's casting, recognized the taint of monstrous magic, and knew he was facing another scion of the Monster God.

Mentally cursing, he scrambled to his feet, only to find the final demon coming for him. It had closed the distance in an instant and lunged, its fingertips glowing magma red. He screamed as he tried to dodge into the clawed strike. He managed, mostly. Part of the demon's armored forearm clipped his shoulder, further reducing his shield. But now he was inside the demon's reach.

Ty slammed his black dagger into the demon's throat gem. The gem resisted, briefly, before cracking and allowing the tip of the weapon past. Mouth wide in surprise, the demon tore at Ty's back, hands still enhanced with a portion of its summoned power.

Fire raked down the sides of Ty's spine as he pushed the dagger deeper. Hot orange blood fountained between the cracks of the gem, leaking across his hands and forearms.

The demon stumbled under his relentless pressure, falling to the ground, mouth working feebly. Ty fell with the demon, allowing his body to collapse as if dead weight. It wasn't far from the truth.

From atop the chest of the dying demon, he saw the spellcaster's hooded visage move from him back to a beleaguered Cleozun. The newcomer was not the only one assaulting Cleozun and her allies; spears of magic continuously bombarded their position. With each impact, the yellow shield dimmed.

Cleozun, one hand raised to maintain the shield, extended another toward the hooded scion, gesturing frantically. Her body shook with the strain of holding the shield and casting a second spell. Air warped, pulsing out from behind the shield and toward the enemy mage.

A contemptuous gesture deflected Cleozun's attack.

Ty activated his Verdant Touch, desperately soaking in as much healing as he could. The scion raised both hands, fingers jerking like the legs of a spider.

Rolling off the demon, he rushed the enemy spellcaster.

The ground exploded around Cleozun and her cabal, knocking them off their feet. Another of the blasts rebounded off the yellow shield before the next struck through, landing just off-center from the surviving trio. A swirling, toxic mist blossomed where it hit. Black tendrils shot through the demonic bodies of Ty's allies, sending them into spasms of agony.

Ty made it to the scion just as they were raising their hands for another spell. So close, he could feel the powerful enchantment on the spellcaster's robe. He had no doubt it would protect the wearer from something as mundane as an attack from his dagger. At the last moment, he dove, throwing his elbow into the crease of the scion's knee.

The knee bent and the scion fell back, grunting more from surprise than pain.

Ty reached up, yanked the hood of the cowl back and shoved his hand into the robe. He felt flesh but didn't look at the face as he poured Celestial magic directly into the Monster God's scion.

Shadows exploded from the ground, threatening to cover Ty's jerking opponent and teleport it away. "Not this fucking time," he said, his voice tortured with rage so potent that he didn't recognize it. He expanded his Celestially aligned Verdant Touch from his hand to his entire body, accepting the pain it caused.

The shadow teleportation shuddered, expanding and contracting wildly as it tried to avoid coming into contact with his power. Beneath his hand, the scion started screaming. He felt flesh run like wax and bone crumble as the unfettered Celestial energy chewed through the Monster God's scion.

Memories of Boblin and the Opal Guardians flashed through Ty's mind, shoved to the forefront by his growing hatred of the Monster God.

Shaking with rage, he growled, "Die," and poured more of his mana and life into his defiance. He shoved down, pushing his gauntlet-covered hand into the skull of his enemy.

The scion's skull collapsed, and the shadow teleportation flickered into nothing.

Seseun, accompanied by Uneth and most of the other akkoans, came into view. One of the other hydras followed them. Behind the group was a burning encampment, literally hundreds of corpses piled on the ground. None of the Flesh Weavers survived. Two hydra corpses were visible as giant hillocks in the mess. There was no sign of the final hydra. Cleozun and two of her surviving mages stirred, albeit weakly.

Theontsu and four of his rangers appeared in the distance, two more robed figures, demonic chitin showing on their forearms, strung between them. The gleam of mind gems in their foreheads told Ty why they'd been captured instead of killed.

Hagemi pulsed in the back of Ty's mind as he extracted his fist. The rage he'd felt, the unstoppable and unceasing hate, diminished as the lingering influence of the Monster God washed away.

Ty looked at the person he'd just killed. He still didn't know if it was a human from his world or not, and he didn't want to know, either. Before he let guilt rise, he slammed the worst of what he'd just done into his Mind Fortress, promising again to deal with the memory another day.

Stumbling to his feet, Ty glared at Uneth. "What did you do?"

"What do you mean? We cut their heart out. We swept in while the hydras you unleashed had them distracted and..." Uneth stopped, looking at the corpse near Ty's feet, then at the devastation nearby.

"You left our fucking mages unprotected," Ty growled, stepping closer to his general, who went from looking confident to crestfallen in an instant. Uneth's shoulders folded forward, hunching as he backed away from Ty's anger.

"Ty, stop," Theontsu said, resting a hand on his shoulder. The hand shook. He looked over and saw that Theontsu's side was drenched in orange blood, his face blackened from the effects of fire magic. Practically whispering, he continued, "Now is not the time. Uneth made a decision. One that gave us a decisive victory. Things worked out. Do not berate the man for doing what you told him to do mere hours ago."

Ty froze, seeing the effect his words had on Uneth, really seeing the general's slump into dejection. "Oh Uneth," he said, heart aching. He moved to the akkoan, wrapping his arms around the flinching man's demonic body. "I'm so sorry. Theontsu is right. You did your best. We won. Please, let's just get out of here. We'll talk about it later."

Uneth's shaking grew worse. His body jerked as spasms of grief tore through the man. "Ty, I cannot take it. Please. Please take this pain from me. Take me back into you before I do something stupid." His hands clawed at his sides, fumbling for his sword.

"I refuse," Ty said, about to say more when Uneth's sword whipped out of its sheath. The experienced warrior flipped the blade around, plunging it into the vulnerable crease in the chitin on his chest. A soft hiss rose from the remaining Celestial blood on the weapon, caustic steam pouring from the wound.

"Hurry!" Cleozun called, her voice a dry rasp. "Take him back before it's too late!"

Closing his eyes in disgust, feeling like a total idiot and failure, Ty did as the mage demanded. He took Uneth, one of his staunchest allies, back into his body. For a moment, he felt Uneth's grief, his self-loathing, and his belief in his failure. He pushed Uneth into his Mind Fortress and led his soul back among the others of his kind.

Rest, friend, he sent the troubled general.

The demon's body went still, its mind gem flickering out.

Congratulations! *You have defeated a lot of bad guys. Would you like to loot the corpses? If so, where would you like the loot deposited?*

An inventory window popped up, showing him a collection of magical goods and weapons.

Feeling defeated despite their victory, Ty left the loot windows alone as he replenished his mana and healed the worst of their wounded. They'd lost six of Theontsu's rangers and fifteen other akkoans, not including Uneth and Cleozun's mage. It was a relatively low price to pay, considering what they'd gained.

Ty found it somewhat ironic that the hydras he'd possessed during the Monster God's invasion had made such a significant difference. How would things have gone had he not made the rash decision to attempt a monstrous aura, though? Perhaps Uneth would still be alive. Perhaps the hydras would have been willing to communicate and coordinate, instead of giving into their rage and insanity?

There were no survivors of the enemy army to stop them from looting the camp, which Ty had them do despite his eagerness to leave. As his allies went through the rubble, methodically checking for things of value or clues to the Monster God's next move, he wandered to the edge of the shoreline. A rocky cliff stretched a hundred feet over a foreign ocean, distant sea life spraying and playing off dawn-lit waves.

Looking out at the ocean, Ty spoke to Hagemi, "When I'm finished securing these memories, I want you to tell me what happened. Just the details. All right?"

Hagemi manifested nearby, the rising sunshine reflecting through its crystalline matrix in a beautiful splash of prismatic light. "Are you sure, Ty? It could be said that your memories make you human. You keep doing this..."

"I'm sure," Ty said firmly, focusing on the horizon. "Just tell me what I'm about to forget. Remind me. Let me know of my mistakes and why I made them. That way, I'll be able to learn from them and not feel this pain."

"Pain is part of learning for your kind, Ty."

Tears spilled down his cheeks as barely withheld emotion surged. He knew he was about to lose it, to give in to the terror, grief, and torment that he'd unleashed upon himself. "We'll deal with it later when we have time. Just do this for me, alright?"

"As you wish," Hagemi said softly.

Ty locked the worst of his recent memories away, leaving his conversation with the Monster God, along with the feelings of her presence, and most of the battle. He tucked away what had happened with Uneth, burying it deep in the Fortress. The artifact would store both Ty's pain and the echo of Uneth's death, saving them both from the emotional consequences of their choices.

When he was done, he nodded to Hagemi, who recounted the things Ty had made himself forget. He still felt bad in the end, a little guilt, but with the distance from not remembering, he saw it as it should be seen, from a distance. He understood his choice to confront Uneth, just as he understood Uneth's reaction.

There was no need for guilt or pain. Clinging to painful, restrictive memories was certainly not a way to accomplish anything.

Chapter 41: Last Days

Days Remaining in Cycle: 6

The little army hadn't brought much in the way of goods, although they discovered several heavy chests, each laden with money. Ty's force had earned close to half a million marks with their victory. There was also a small pouch of the gold coins minted with the Monster God's icon on them. They'd also taken a new hydra body, even if that hydra was erratic and prone to fits of violence if left untended. With Cleozun's help and Ty's careful selection of souls, they embodied two new mages.

Ty finally looted the corpses, much to Hagemi's relief. He gave the assortment of things to Cleozun and Theontsu to figure out. After all that had happened, he didn't have the stomach for inventory management.

The spellcasting demons were from a different species than the hive-minded ones. Once disrobed, they were revealed to have elongated torsos that concealed a second set of arms. Their vaguely grasshopper-shaped faces also had four eyes, just beneath walnut-size mind gems.

Cleozun said they were innately powerful and demanded to have her body swapped with one of theirs as soon as they were back at the village and had time. Ty agreed without hesitation.

It took them two days to heal up and deal with the dead, during which no surprise reinforcements or ambushes materialized. Cleozun and Omendine both thought the Monster God would probably have a good idea of what

happened and had delayed any immediate reinforcements for a bigger push in
the coming weeks.

The mage and her surviving cabal cast several subtle spells in the area, burying
bone-carved talismans to act as curses and early warning systems should the
enemy return to the encampment. Omendine thought it was unlikely but had
agreed that caution was wise.

Over the intervening days, more of the akkoan-demons came from the village
to help. Omendine oversaw it all, giving Ty the break he needed to process
what he'd felt and learned. After some consideration, he'd taken back a few
of the memories he'd suppressed. Cleozun and Theontsu had recognized the
symptoms of his use of the Mind Fortress to deal with guilt and had taken him
aside to warn him of the dangerous and addictive properties of the powerful
magic item.

He still wasn't about to unleash all his memories, not when the little grief and
doubt he allowed left him feeling like a husk.

He camped near the ocean, where he could sleep with the sounds of the waves
and admire the world's beauty. He kept the reality of what had happened, of
the corpses that took days to burn, at his back. His hand hurt sometimes. He'd
healed it and had kept the gauntlet in place for the whole last battle, but that
didn't remove the phantom pain. Deep down, he knew that he'd killed someone
with that fist. He couldn't consciously remember the details any more than the
spirits in his Cage could. Like those spirits, a part of him remembered, though.
That part made him ache.

"We're done," Omendine said early on the third day, approaching Ty with an
aura of reserved respect.

Ty looked back from where he sat, hands wrapped around his knees. His
forearm was bare. As Hagemi warned, the tattoos were gone. He didn't remember when at this point, probably sometime during the last battle, when he'd had
to heal himself repeatedly to stay alive. "Yeah? Time to go into final planning
mode?"

Omendine nodded. He'd adopted Ty's method of agreement as easily as he'd
learned the akkoan sign language. The little samurai llama truly was amazing.

Coming to his feet, Ty accompanied Omendine to where he'd left his things. Collecting his sleeping bag and backpack, he and Omendine walked into the forest.

They had six days left to prepare. Six days to give his people some sort of plan to survive the next three, potentially war-torn, years. It didn't feel like enough time. It felt like too much time.

Ty, Omendine, Aquamarine and the akkoans planned over the day and a half of easy travel. They discussed how to use their captured money. All agreed to bury and seal the Monster God's coins away from the village. Cleozun had cleansed the coin of several nasty enchantments, but still they preferred to be safe.

Most of their planning involved contingencies. What if the Monster God attacked with a proper army? What if she repossessed one of the demon bodies somehow? What if the insanity plaguing their people became worse? They talked and conjectured, spinning out problems and potential solutions for hours, each knowing that with Ty gone it would be their responsibility to act as leaders.

Ty felt Uneth's absence acutely. Although the general had been quiet and hesitant, the man had been like a mentor, always nearby to discuss ideas or oversee his decisions.

When they made it back to the village, it surprised Ty to find that a lot of work had already been done. Magic had transformed the adjacent marsh, making it into the outline of what might eventually become a water garden. To the south, where the ground was rockier, a series of enclosures were under construction. Two, each with several of the lynxes, were already functional. A third, half-built without a top, housed the bunnies. There were a lot of them, and none seemed eager to escape, even though the fence wall was barely hip height.

"I told them if they tried to get out again, I'd release the lynxes," Omendine whispered to Ty, following his gaze. He snickered. "They reached a population dense enough to understand my threats just before they were taken from me. Thank you again for getting them."

"Uh, sure," Ty said, still not quite certain about the knitting, samurai lla-ma-man. As a war adviser and leader, Omendine was top notch, no doubt. It was just everything else that was a bit odd.

Ty, I'd like to point something out if I may, Hagemi sent. The Arbiter had been mostly silent the past few days, letting him come to terms with everything that had happened.

Hrm?

At the end of that last battle, you went full Terry Brooks on that scion. Tech-nology totally failed to predict that. It's amusing, is it not? None of the Shannara books were in the prophecy.

It took Ty several minutes to process what Hagemi was getting at. He chuck-led when he finally did. *The face was the only obviously vulnerable target, in my defense. Eyes, mouths, and necks tend to be reliable targets on most humanoids.*

It's good to hear you laugh again, Ty.

Ty let the moment of humor carry him through the rest of the day. Most of what he had to do was maintenance.

He took a big room in the tavern, then sent Omendine and Cleozun a request for a special lock for it. His vision was to magically seal the room to him, or something he carried, so he'd have a safe space to return to. After arranging for that, he went to the basement and verified the remaining Divine blood barrels were intact. They were - all eighteen that were left. He made certain to hide one in his room, just in case things went sideways while he was gone.

When Cleozun arrived to install the lock, she had Ty make good on his promise to put her in the four-armed demon's body. He used the opportunity to shift one of the drone-dog spirits into the newly-emptied demonic form Cleozun had occupied. He made a note to prioritize getting the rest of the spirits inside dogs re-homed upon his return.

Later that evening, he went with a group of akkoans down the stairs and to the entry to the Sanctuary. Demon blood worked to open the doors, but they couldn't get out once they were locked inside. In the event of an overwhelming attack, someone would have to stay outside. None of the akkoans liked the idea of being in the Sanctuary again, much less locked in. Whatever its original intentions, Sanctuary had become their tomb and a place of torment. The fear of being locked inside again led several in the group to proclaim that they'd *never* go into that place again without a way out.

"Maybe we just get one of us to learn some necromancy. Necromantic mana should be all we need to get in and out," Meridian announced. He'd finally met the brilliant woman the night before. She'd been waiting for their return to the town, insect eyes fixed on Theontsu the whole time. She'd volunteered to lead the exploratory group into Sanctuary with Ty.

Another akkoan spoke dryly, "You realize you said that idea out loud, right? We're akkoans. We don't mess with souls, and we certainly want neither a necromancer *or* a warlock around."

"Maybe just a *little* warlock would be okay," Meridian muttered.

"Hey, I think it could be a great idea," Ty said, reaching out to squeeze her armored shoulder. "I am a firm believer in diversity. Maybe just not for today, though."

Perking up, Meridian moved her mouth parts in the demonic equivalent of a smile. It took every shred of Ty's focus not to shiver.

He announced, "All right folks, we've got an emergency retreat. We should head back up to the surface and finish the rest."

Don't you want to say goodbye? The voice came from behind him, through the closed doors. No one around showed signs of hearing it. Ty hesitated. "Actually, I want to go in and look around for a bit by myself. Would you let me out in about an hour?"

"An hour?" Meridian asked uncertainly, looking at the doors. "Are you sure you want to go back in there? It is not a place meant for humans."

Ty tapped his chest. "I have a few thousand of you in me, Meridian."

She didn't need further elaboration.

Slicing his thumb on the black dagger, Ty went into the Sanctuary and found Seeker waiting for him on the throne.

"You exceeded my expectations," Seeker said in his voice booming once the doors had closed behind him. The god was slightly more transparent than he'd been the last time he had seen him.

Ty ignored the welcome, focusing on Hagemi instead. The infusion was small and so subtle that he wouldn't have noticed it had he not been focused inward. It was Seeker's touch, once again applying his subtle will to the Arbiter.

"How do you do that?" he asked. "Make Hagemi into your tool."

"My secrets for you to discover, once you go below." Seeker's robed hand pointed at Ty's arms. "I see you purchased a key to help. It should get you to the second level, maybe even the third. Would you care to try now?"

"I don't have the time. I just came in here to visit. Do you mind if I talk to you a bit? Tell you about what I've gone through?" He realized in that moment that a part of him, a big part, respected the god. His akkoan memories venerated the deity, and the god had helped him in his moment of need. He knew better than to see Seeker as a friend, not with his suspicions of what had come before. Something had turned the gods of Seeker's first world against him. He *did* see the god as an ally, however.

Seeker leaned forward, arms on his knees. "I would love that."

Ty told Seeker about what he'd been through, mostly about the last half of his visit to the world. He told him about the Mind Fortress and his anguish. He also told the god about his growing anger.

"Your people are *my* people now," Ty said. "I can't get over that feeling. I can't get over how angry I am when I think about what's been done. And I can't get over how hurt I am over what happened to Uneth."

"Oh, poor mortal," Seeker murmured, sonorous voice conveying both curiosity and empathy. "I wonder if, in the future, you might allow me to peer more deeply into you? I would enjoy tasting the flavor of your mind."

Ty arched a brow at the divine shade. "My secrets are for you to earn, once you prove yourself to me."

Seeker laughed. For just a moment, Ty thought the god's semi-transparent body became completely solid, before fading back to its ephemeral state.

The doors behind clicked. It was time to go.

He waved to the god. "I'll be back. Next time, I mean to surprise you."

"I hope so," Seeker replied, fading out of view.

Meridian peered into the vault, multifaceted eyes gleaming with honey hues as she looked around. "Who were you talking to?"

Ty shrugged. "No one important. Just a friend. Maybe."

Later, he debated whether it was wise to let the old god imprint back on Hagemi. He kept telling himself that Seeker was not on his side, that the god had an agenda all his own, and he was using him. The response to that warning was a dry, "But isn't Inspiration using you just the same?"

The last day went by in a blur. Ty teleported with Aquamarine to collect the remains of his belongings from the assassin's attack. They found the sloths near the encampment, still grieving. He offered his apologies and bade them farewell. The meeting lingered far too long, leaving him in tears. Still, he felt better having spent time with them.

To Ty's surprise and delight, one of his notepads and a few pens had survived the attack on his convoy. Once he was away from the traumatizing location, he set about writing things down. He didn't start with a list of things he wanted to do next or contingencies about the Monster God. Instead, he wrote all the things he'd found on this magical world that had filled him with awe. He wrote about the stallion and Aquamarine, and finally he wrote about Boblin. Somehow, despite the tears he felt while he wrote, remembering the hope and joy he'd found here helped.

Later, he diagrammed all new plans. Plans for what to do when he got to earth and plans for what to do when he returned.

Finally, when the countdown showed that he had less than an hour to go, Ty opened one of the few intact containers from his convoy. He changed into a surviving set of civilian clothes. The gauntlets, along with most of his magical equipment, would stay behind, stored in his sealed room. Of his equipment, only the monocles would work in his world. Those and his Mind Fortress.

The magic is low there still. That will change rapidly. Within a year, perhaps less, your devices will function on Earth. At this time, nothing labeled Epic or Legendary will.

Stepping out of the tavern, Ty saw Omendine, Cleozun in her new four-armed body, Theontsu, Aquamarine, and even Meridian waiting for him.

Omendine had one of his bunnies with him on a leash. The pearl in the bunny's forehead gleamed as it looked at him, conveying a muted sense of amusement. He wasn't certain at all that the bunnies were as slow-witted as Omendine seemed to think. He wasn't about to tell the traesap that, though.

"I think I'll miss this place," he announced.

"You will," Cleozun said. "The more you heal, the more you will realize this place is wonderful compared to your capitalistic hellscape."

Ty chuckled, not surprised the mage remembered that random conversation.

Theontsu stepped up, placing a hand on his shoulder. "We will prepare, Ty. We know the stakes."

"The forest will be here, waiting for your return," Aquamarine said, dexterous fingers twitching in time with his words.

Omendine met Ty's gaze and nodded. The two had already said their words. Over the past days, they'd spent many hours together. He knew the odd little llama man would fulfill his duty.

Ty, it's time.

The glowing portal split the air. Taking one last, deep breath of magical air, Ty stepped through.

Chapter 42: Final Scores

The prompt appeared as Ty stepped into the portal. Between one world and the next, he had just enough time to digest the information.

Name: Ty Monroe

Class: Merit Hunter

Race: Human

Level: 3

Status: Mentally Unstable

Progress to Next Level: 25%

Hit Points: 14

Health Shield (Lesser): 21

Mana: 18

Mana Shield: 9 (Racial Maximum: 30)

Strength: 13 (Above Average)

Agility: 9 (Average)

Vitality: 10 (Average, +1 hit point per level)

Intellect: 13 (Standard High IQ)

Spirit: 6 (Wild-attuned)

Luck: 0

Applicable Skills and Abilities

Mixed Martial Arts (Sambo Focus): Proficient

Krav Maga: High-Adept

Edged Weapons: Skilled

Bows: Proficient

Guns: Adept

Survival: Adept

Meditation: Proficient

Unassigned Attribute Points: 0

Unspent Merits: 6

Achievements and Powers: *Wild Touched, Looting Ability, Organized Mind, Mana Prism (Divine, Monstrous, Wild), Mana Siphon, Knight of the Wild Ability Package, Verdant Touch, Moderate Life Leach (Death-Attuned), Single Use Clone Surrogacy, Necromantic Demon Bond–Temporary, Collect The Blood (1 of 3 collected), Defeat the Invading Army–you have one free upgrade to an existing ability, up to an equivalent enhancement of two merits.*

Quests: *Protect the Dungeon (Ongoing)*

Notable Equipment: *One handgun, Gambler's Monocle X 5 (unshielded), Shielding Amulet (Lesser), Mind Fortress (Divine), 1 Personal Locket, Nightmare Silk, Forbidden Book of Necromancy, Monstrous Manual*

Unequipped Notable Equipment: *Armor of (Unknown, Sealed), Black Sword (Unknown, Sealed), Ward Robe (Epic; 20% integrity), Magic-Breaker Dagger (Epic; 45% integrity), Shielding Amulet (Lesser), Alunite Gauntlets (Legendary), Divine Anchor (Legendary), 2 Infernal Crystals, Hellstone X 5*

Spiritual Assets: *akkoan minds (29,534), akkoan souls (29,534)*

Final Character Level: 3. *This puts you in the bottom fortieth percentile.*

Achievement Value: 4. *Based on your overall achievements and merits, we have awarded you effectively two additional levels. You are in the seventieth percentile for achievements and merits. This is to be expected, as you have a merit-based class.*

Maximum Designated Allies: 60. *Based on your final score, you may select up to sixty allies. These allies will be placed under the protection of your god. You may designate these people to join you on Earth or prevent them from being removed from Earth during Resonance.*

Domain: 1 Square Acre. *Based on your final score, you may select a domain. This domain will be counted as belonging to your deity, with you as the administrator. As an administrator of a domain, you may move to prevent identified areas within your Earthly domain from being removed during Resonance. In addition, you may exchange objects and features of your domain to and from Earth during each portal opening. You must have designated a domain on both sides of the Resonance Bridge to do this.*

Epilogue - Interlude Six: Precipice

Surviving Earth Participants: 16,041

    Average Level: 6

Days Remaining in Cycle: 0

"She's exerting direct control," Inspiration announced as the Great Arbiter's display reconfigured to show the destination planet.

"So is Divinity," a god pointed out, tone sardonic.

"Many of you are," Balance said. "You believe you are subtle in your machinations. You are not. A second round of recruits is required."

"With what power?" Inspiration asked. "We're spent." He glanced at a cluster of gods, detecting the outline of schemes within schemes. "Most of us, anyway," he added.

Balance said, "We will need to find new power. Direct your scions accordingly. Uncover the ancient secrets, plumb the depths. New anchors must join, or our plans will fail."

Red nodes appeared on the Great Arbiter's display of Earth. The Arbiter's voice filled the room with an echoing condemnation. "It would appear that her primary aim in this round is not to grow her power. She is sending assassins after your scions."

The End

Bonus Scenes

Author's Note: Unless otherwise stated, bonus scenes are canon. In most cases, I removed these for pacing purposes.

Bonus Scene 1: Efficiency

This scene takes place between the attack at Sabontil and Ty's arrival back on Earth.

Ty lay awake in his tent, the sounds of nature all around him, unable to stop thinking of what had happened in Sabontil and after. He'd become used to fighting from a position of relative weakness since arriving on this side of the portal. Having other humans overpower him and his allies so completely, and with apparent ease, had him rethinking his approach.

"Hagemi, can I theorize with you about how I should spend my merits at level three?"

"Absolutely," Hagemi replied, manifesting in the air above Ty's face. In the dark, the crystalline substance of the Arbiter flickered and glowed with haunting allure.

"How is the value of a merit calculated? How do the gods come up with three merits equaling one sub-par class power?"

Hagemi's lights flowed, one into the other, mesmerizing and oddly beautiful as the Arbiter considered its answer. "It's a combination of things. First, there's a consideration of how much any given ability would take a native to earn and obtain. The most obvious value of any merit is to say that each one is equal to about a year of dedicated, proper training. Second, there's a consideration of how much divine magic must be placed in you to activate a power. Giving you more strength is relatively easy. Artificially enhancing your connection to the gods is not. Third, it depends on the god. The God of Shadows can far more easily grant its followers invisibility than Inspiration, although Inspiration is more overall flexible in what he can bestow."

"Sounds like predicting the innate value of any power I want will be difficult, at best."

"I would not disagree with that statement were I in your position."

"How about I give you some specifics and you tell me what they might cost or maybe what the ramifications of obtaining them would be?"

"Absolutely."

"What if I wanted a teleportation ability?"

"Personal or can you bring others with you? How often can you use it? At what range? And, quite importantly, at what mana cost?"

Ty considered, trying to figure out what would have been the most useful configuration to have recently. "Personal, let's say thirty feet. And I'd want to use it a few times a day, with five or six mana per use."

"That's a relatively on-par power for most of our level-five specialists, if slightly more efficient. That one would cost four points."

"And if I tied the ability to my level? Say, make it so I can use it twice a day per my level and extend the range to five feet per two levels?"

"That level of scalability would increase the cost to seven. It would represent a major enhancement."

"Okay. New line of thought. What about adding five more hit points?"

"One point."

"Eight more?"

"More than one point. We'd round to two."

"Would adding mana cost the same?"

"Mana would cost more, since it's literally attaching divine magic to you permanently."

"So raising my Spirit attribute is the most effective way to increase my mana pool."

"Correct."

"What if I wanted to create a mana shield around me, basically extending the natural protection leveling gives? Say, adding half my mana pool as a damage-soak?"

Magenta tides flashed in his Arbiter, and Ty felt a pulse of subtle pleasure. "Enhancing existing mechanisms is far less expensive. That would cost you three points, even with scaling built in. It would have weaknesses, however. Double the cost if it's going to work against divine-backed effects, like the arrow."

"Perfect. New line, can I have powers that influence or communicate with Arbiters other than you?"

Hagemi's swirling colors froze. "Yes, but it wouldn't be useful. We are self-contained drops of raw intellect and magic, with a god aspect. You could not influence or alter one of us directly or sway our behavior in essentially any way. We can have our consciousnesses muted, but there is no power that can prevent our overall function."

"But I *can* enhance you, like with the looting power?"

"Yes. In that case, I behave less like an Arbiter and more like a Mind Fortress inhabited by a spirit of Artifice."

"How much to set up automatic filtering? Say, when I would be overcome with pain, have you shunt the memories *as they are written* into my Mind Fortress? Or maybe remove distracting observations and help me notice things that are important, kind of making me immediately forget useless information and retain only potentially useful things?"

"I could set up a series of filters like that for one point. It would, essentially, simply require you to purchase a decrease in my innate limitations, so there's almost no cost. The second part of your request would require rather specific targets, though. I cannot think for you. As for the first, why not just request immunity or resilience to pain?"

"How much would pain immunity cost?"

"One point."

Ty tried to hide his grin. "Hagemi, how much would it cost to have you filter *out* memories into someone else? Make them live what I want."

Hagemi flashed silver. "Oh, I see now. A psychic attack. That's.... interesting. Hrm, well. Setting up a psychic link of any sort with a willing recipient would be one point. Two points and you could do it with up to three willing recipients simultaneously. They have to be within view. Forcing a connection? Double the cost. Automatically filtering specific sensations or memories on top of that? Add seven points. And there will be severe limitations. People with Mind Fortresses properly set up may filter the attack out. People with mental resistances will likely suffer less than you anticipate. Gods will be immune. There will be others."

"Reasonable," Ty said, not too dissuaded. He was just spit balling possibilities, having not settled on precisely what he wanted. "And how much to detect thoughts nearby, but not read them? Kind of like psychic radar?"

"One point to detect the general presence. Two to detect their attitude toward you or your allies. Five to make it work against active psychic concealment. Seven to work against active psychic divine concealment variations. I should warn you that it would not work against other scions, though, not until you reach level ten. No powers that directly target or work against another scion are allowed until then. You could detect general thoughts, but not identify specifically those of another scion."

"Well, that's shitty. Moving on, let's say I want to acquire a Spirit Master package. The ability to possess and take on the knowledge and abilities of a willing spirit, the ability to communicate with them and learn from them more effectively. How much would that be?"

"In your case? Fifteen points."

"In my case?"

Hagemi bobbed in the air. "Ty, you have over twenty thousand spirits living inside you. The amount of time and training it would take a native to acquire the facility you're requesting is substantial. Your situation changes the cost."

Ty finally began to frown. The numbers Hagemi was throwing at him would take multiple levels to save up for. At the end of the Resonance process, he had no doubt that allocating significant merits in this way would be easy. The problem was he was *living* the leveling process. He had to make purchases now, or very soon, that would help him survive. Waiting multiple levels to get a new power could be detrimental.

Playing back some of Hagemi's earlier discussions, Ty struck on inspiration. "Hagemi, you told me that when another scion attacks a scion, there's some sort of overt benefit to the winner's god, right? What if I wanted to enhance my looting ability, specifically when I take power from another scion? Something that unlocks more merits when I level?"

"There is, but I cannot tell you that yet. And yes, such an ability would be easy. A small enhancement of your looting ability. The gods left provisions for things like this in the binding, if player versus player became inevitable. One point. You'll get one extra merit per scion you defeat, with a bonus if the scion is significantly higher level or has been heavily invested by their god."

Ty's wolfish grin shone in the dark. He didn't *want* to kill other people. If the gods were going to play dirty, though, he would, too.

Bonus Scene 2:
A Discussion with
Cleozun

Author's Note: *This scene takes place on the trip from Ty's town to Sabontil, toward the end of the book. This scene is canon but was cut for pacing.*

"Cleozun, what was your life like?" Ty asked the akkoan a few hours later, once he'd acclimated to the demands of the travel. Uneth set a demanding pace, one that the akkoans' demonic bodies handled with ease, and left him missing his ATV. Between his past several months of training and his Verdant Touch, however, he found the pace manageable.

Glancing over at Ty, Cleozun's mouth parts flexed. "What do you mean?"

"I have a general idea of what some of life on Ako was like, but most of the memories I've lived aren't of people like you or Uneth. I'm curious what it was like. Did you sing and dance and celebrate nature?"

"You put me in an interesting position when it comes to that question, Ty."

"How so?"

"There are secrets. Deep secrets. And yet you could, should you put the effort in, know any of them with no difficulty. My instincts tell me to share nothing with you. Yet inside you there they are many of my people, some of whom are, no doubt, trained spellcasters. This makes you one of the few people we *can* trust akkoan secrets with, despite your humanity."

He knew what she meant. He hadn't had time to go digging around inside his Mind Fortress, other than his recent attempts to locate tutors, but in those brief hours, he'd caught glimpses of cultural secrets. "How do your deep secrets work?"

"We were something of a caste-based society. Do you know that word, caste?"

"If my translation ability is working properly, it means that each of you had a role to play. Some might garden, or be artists, while others were warriors or mages. Is that right?"

"Yes. Indeed, quite similar. We were allowed to expand our caste through mating or the acquisition of Mind Fortresses that contained another caste's memories, so it was not inflexible. Still, you get the idea. Shortly after birth, we entered an apprenticeship with a mentor or a group. As we gained in knowledge and ability, mysteries would be revealed to us, until we earned a Mind Fortress inheritance. Essentially anything strictly related to our caste was considered 'caste-bonded,' a secret, if you will. Something we were not allowed to share except under specific circumstances."

"Sounds a bit like trade secrets and how they used to work on Earth, before the invention of the internet," Ty said, going briefly over the history of Earth's knowledge and how it was passed down, along with the nature of the internet.

Cleozun's replied, tone awed, "All of your knowledge as a species in one device, barely bigger than a Mind Fortress? Ty, that is...incredible. Your people must be incredibly powerful."

"Not really. We don't have magic. Plus, we have a capitalistic society. The majority work two-thirds of their lives, so time to innovate and make discoveries is basically limited to the few with the economic means and freedom to do so. Limitations slow humans down a lot. Plus, we fight a lot of wars."

"That sounds incredibly tragic. I am sorry." Cleozun tried to make a sound, but her mouth parts couldn't replicate it. He recognized it from one of his memories; it was a beautiful lament.

A slow-dawning revelation occurred to him, as he considered what Earth culture would look like to the akkoans. They were a tight-knit people, unified and able to pass their memories from one to another in a continuous line of virtue and values. To them, a world as disconnected and fractured as Earth must be horrifying. Thinking about it, he realized that with all the akkoan memories he retained, even *he* felt disturbed thinking about his home planet.

Maybe the Resonance Bridge would be the key to changing the future of his people.

"So, from basically the time you were born, you learned magic?" he asked, trying to change the uncomfortable subject.

"Indeed. Magic was taught to me during my early schooling, side-by-side with song, dance, and religious ceremony. You must know that religious practices were the heart of most of our lives. Glory to the Unknowing Hunger was a core tenant that continues to motivate me to this day. Magic became my way to become closer to god."

"Seeker, yes. I remember the god, at least pieces about him. And I saw some of his history in the Sanctuary."

Cleozun made a pleased sound, turning the discussion to her god and the nature of her devotion to him. Ty found out that she had achieved the magical pinnacle before going to war against the lesser gods. During the last battle, she had led her cabal to strike one down, only to suffer a killing injury in the process. Her last act had been to willingly commit herself to a Soul Battery in the hopes of furthering her god's glory. Only in the end had she realized that the priests performing the entombment had been misleading her and her people.

Her life sounded beautiful and bitter to him. From the start, it had been a spiritual revelation, a walking devotion to the living concept of Seeking. And then the betrayal at the end. No wonder Cleozun's insanity seemed so raw.

"Are you upset with Seeker?" he asked later. "For abandoning you in the end?"

"I do not think our god abandoned us, Ty," Cleozun said, wistfully glancing to the sky. "Do not misunderstand me. The Unthinking Thirst was not a deity of compassion, not most of the time. My sense at the end wasn't of absence, though. I think that our Lord was busy or distracted."

I was. The voice came from Hagemi, deep in Ty's mind, but was not the Arbiter's. Ty felt an echo of regret and wistfulness in the voice, a sense of eternal sorrow. It nearly broke his heart.

How are you here? he shot back to the voice.

Echoes. I am an echo of an echo of a memory. A touch of power laid upon this little betrayer. I am not here, mortal. But I am *a god, and this device is of me. My flavor resonates with a tiny piece of it.*

Ty felt the...presence, if he could call it that, of the Seeker vanish and Hagemi return.

Appendix 1: Power Summaries

1. **Mana Prism (Legendary/Wild):** Ty can convert one type of mana/magic into another. The types he can convert include Monstrous, Divine, and Wild. This ability can draw the attention of the associated god and may cause unexpected side-effects.

2. **Mana Siphon (Epic):** Regain mana by consuming divine-aligned substances. This ability does not prevent damage or negative side-effects.

3. **Organized Mind (Wild):** Ty's mind is stronger than others. He can resist mental attacks and outside influences far more than most others. He cannot be possessed except by Divine-tier entities.

4. **Knight of the Wild Ability Package:** Ty is considered Wild-aligned; abilities that would work on those creatures also work on him. He can talk to intelligent animals. This package is the source of his Verdant Touch.

5. **Verdant Touch:** You may deliver Wild-aligned healing energy with physical contact.

6. **Moderate Life Leach:** Use death-attuned magic to siphon vitality over time.

7. **Looting Power:** When Ty defeats a challenging enemy, his Arbiter will reward him. He may designate where the loot is deposited. For a short time, provided he remains within range, he may treat bodies as extensions of his inventory.

8. **Single Use Clone Surrogacy:** This one-time power allows Ty to create a clone of himself, limitations.

9. **Divine Mind Fortress:** Ty has a magical hard drive in his head. It has infinite space and can store memories for him.

Glossary

Arbiters: A proper Arbiter is a highly advanced device that, when paired with divine power, can act as a personal 'Game Master' of a scion. They can influence small portions of local reality.

The Greater Arbiter: The Greater Arbiter is a fusion of multiple Arbiters. It oversees the Resonance Pact.

Mind or Mind-space: This is the psychic space where Ty's Arbiter and Mind Fortress reside.

Mana: This is raw magical power. It is what gives rise to the gods. In areas where mana saturation is high, conscious beings create gods with their beliefs and faith.

Divine Mana: Divine Mana comes *from* a god and is 'super charged' with additional potency. Because Divine Mana is tightly affiliated with a divine being, the mana takes on special properties innate to that god. Divine Mana can also be restrictive; some spells or abilities simply will not function with the wrong type of Divine Mana.

Note: Using Divine Mana creates a link to its source.

Soul Cage: The Soul Cage is the airlock connecting a person's soul with the rest of reality. In most cases, abilities that target the "soul" interact with the Cage. Because it is conceptual in nature, it can house an infinite number of souls and an infinite amount of spiritual power.

Area Map

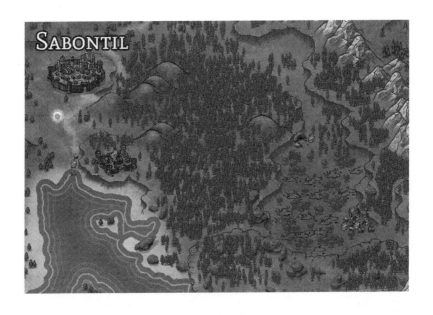

Author's Note

I hope you've enjoyed reading Divine Invasion, the first book in the Resonance Cycle. If you have, please consider checking out the Resonance Author on social media. I'm on Twitter, Reddit, Discord, and pretty much all other social media. My website is *litaaron.com*. You can find art and access early chapters on patreonand can join the Discord discussion at https://discord.gg/GXn8csy2gg.

Theater of War, the second book in the series, is due out next month. You can pre-order it here: https://www.amazon.com/dp/B0C73312YV

Appreciations

The author would like to thank the Alpha and Beta readers on Discord. In no particular order:

John C, Jonny, Myth, Poppisita, Rekinu, Rhexas, TJ

And, first among many, the amazing Ash for copy editing this series.

Additional Thanks

Thanks to the following Facebook groups for allowing me to promote on their page:

- Thanks to the LitRpg Books group

- The litrpgs group

LitRPGGroup Shout

We appreciate the LitRPGGame Group on Facebook for allowing us to promote our first book, and the audio version, to their amazing members.

LitRPG Society Shout

G o Visit LitRPG Society for more LitRPG books, recommendations, and discussions. You can find them at: https://www.facebook.com/groups/LitRPGsociety

GameLit Society Shout

B ig shout to the GameLit Society on Facebook for allowing us to advertise our work to their amazing members!

AI Disclaimer

No part of this text was authored by AI. Because AI is trained on content (voices, images, and text) using information scraped from the internet, it means vast quantities of content are being used and remixed without creatives' permission. Until laws are put into place to protect people like me, the artists who created my cover, and the narrator you are listening to, I believe profiting from AI is morally dubious.

Made in United States
Troutdale, OR
12/15/2024

26547008R10215